Hayner Public Library District

P9-CDZ-772

RECEIVED

MAR 1 2 2019

By

No Longer the Property of
Hayner Public Library District

HAYNER PUBLIC LIBRARY DISTRICT
ALTON ILLINOIS

OVERDUES 10 PER DAY, MAXIMUM FINE
COST OF ITEM
ADDITIONAL $5.00 SERVICE CHARGE
APPLIED TO
LOST OR DAMAGED ITEMS

HAYNER PLD/ALTON SQUARE

For the
KILLING
of
KINGS

ALSO BY HOWARD ANDREW JONES

The Bones of the Old Ones

The Desert of Souls

For the
KILLING
of
KINGS

HOWARD ANDREW JONES

St. Martin's Press
New York

This is a work of fiction. All of the characters, organizations, and events portrayed in
this novel are either products of the author's imagination or are used fictitiously.

FOR THE KILLING OF KINGS. Copyright © 2019 by Howard Andrew Jones. All rights reserved.
Printed in the United States of America. For information, address St. Martin's Press,
175 Fifth Avenue, New York, N.Y. 10010.

www.stmartins.com

Library of Congress Cataloging-in-Publication Data is available on request.

ISBN 978-1-250-00681-3 (hardcover)
ISBN 978-1-250-02292-9 (ebook)

Our books may be purchased in bulk for promotional, educational, or business use.
Please contact your local bookseller or the Macmillan Corporate and Premium
Sales Department at 1-800-221-7945, extension 5442, or by email at
MacmillanSpecialMarkets@macmillan.com.

First Edition: February 2019

10 9 8 7 6 5 4 3 2 1

F
JON

3674393

For my muse, Shannon

PLEDGE OF THE ALTENERAI

When comes my numbered day, I will meet it smiling. For I'll have kept this oath.

I shall use my arms to shield the weak.

I shall use my lips to speak the truth, and my eyes to seek it.

I shall use my hand to mete justice to high and to low, and I will weigh all things with heart and mind.

Where I walk the laws will follow, for I am the sword of my people and the shepherd of their lands.

When I fall, I will rise through my brothers and my sisters, for I am eternal.

For the
KILLING
of
KINGS

Prologue

He left his horse cropping long, seed-topped grass by the bent willow and advanced through the uneven ranks of tombs.

To his right the squat, low buildings of the old section marched in bare, orderly rows to the remote distance of the windy plateau. The cemetery's more recent additions sprouted in terrain-less level; owing to outcrops and rises, the paths weren't nearly as straight as those from ancient days. At least the modern builders had learned not to erect the tombs so close to the edge, where a few hallowed sanctuaries had tumbled to artful ruin at the foot of the eroded ridge.

By ancient tradition, dead heroes and rulers were placed here so their spirits might look down upon the great city they had served. And according to popular notion, they would rise to aid Darassus should calamity overtake her. The visitor had no faith in such tales. If the deceased had such power, N'lahr would long since have drifted from his tomb.

He stepped around some vines clawing at the side of a governor's grave, ignoring finely wrought moments from the woman's life half-obscured by leafy growth, and arrived finally at the front rank of buildings. Ten feet on lay the rocky edge and a hundred-foot drop to the plain. The visitor barely glanced at the domes of Darassus a few miles east, dulled beneath the gray skies.

He looked instead at the dead man's face.

The life-sized relief in three-quarter profile showed N'lahr turning toward the world of the living or reluctantly entering the world of the dead—the visitor was never quite sure what the artist intended. Under heavy clouds with the moan of the wind foremost on the ear, it was easier to believe the latter.

"I'm late again," he said. "And I drank my last bottle when I got held up by a storm in the shifts. Sorry about that."

He considered his friend's image, frowning. Not for the first time it seemed incongruous that there was no sword on N'lahr's belt. Tradition dictated those carved upon the tombs were shown only at peace. While older tombs usually displayed those interred as if they slept, the contemporary fashion showed the departed in daily activities, and that might be problematic when it came to portraying any one of the famed Altenerai, protectors of the realm, but most especially their former commander and general. His life was the corps. His sword's name was nearly as famous as his own, and before his death it had never left his side since the day of its forging. N'lahr looked somehow incomplete without it.

Otherwise he looked as he had most days. Long, angular face with high cheekbones, thin blade of a nose, deep-set eyes. His straight hair was parted on the left and hanging loose to his shoulders rather than tied off behind, as he usually wore it to facilitate donning a helmet. The tops of his leather cavalry boots were hidden by the edge of the long armored robe of office that clothed him from mid-calf to neck. Belted at the waist and loose about the legs for ease of movement, the khalat was fashioned with hooks along the right breast, so it could be closed all the way up to its high, stiff collar, but N'lahr's was open, like most Altenerai at rest, and like his visitor's.

"I can't find her," he said. He didn't bother saying who; N'lahr would know. Nor did he elaborate how dangerous and time-consuming it had been traipsing through the wilds of five Allied Realms and the horrors that lay between. "I've searched everywhere, even the deep shifts. And this year I tried some kobalin lands. If one of the kobalin had killed Kalandra they'd be bragging about it. So would the Naor. But there's nothing. I'm just about out of options."

N'lahr, unsurprisingly, didn't offer any.

"Damnit, N'lahr. You're the one with all the ideas. You should have . . ." The visitor paused for a breath to head off a pointless rant, then proceeded resignedly. "I'm going to talk to Sharn again. Near as I can tell, he was the last person to see her apart from us. Maybe something new will shake out. And maybe I can get a look at Denaven's records. He says he doesn't know where Kalandra went, but the stupid hastig couldn't empty his boot if the instructions were written on the heel, so who knows. . . ."

Denaven has his uses as well as his faults, he imagined N'lahr might say.

"You're way too forgiving." He sighed. "I don't really want to head into that city. It's a perversion of what it was, what it should be. But that's where Sharn is . . . and I guess I'll have to buy a few bottles there if we're going to drink to your birthday."

He figured N'lahr would comment on his terrible taste in wine.

"Maybe I have, but you won't be drinking it, so why complain?"

He suspected N'lahr would find that a good point. "I bet this is great spot to view your parade. I'm so late this year I'm finally going to catch it. I hear it's even longer than the ones for the spring games." He shook his head in disgust. "Did you ever think the queen would hold an annual parade for you?"

It was easy to imagine N'lahr's wry smile as his sole response. The queen had argued with almost every one of his choices during the Naor war, even when he had the clans on the run. She'd never trusted his judgment. And when the great victory N'lahr engineered against the invaders' superior numbers had killed him, the queen immediately sued for peace rather than pressing on to secure their advantage as so many of her senior warriors advised.

The Naor warlord Mazakan had snatched the offer eagerly, and his embattled clans had slunk back to their desolate realms to nurse grudges and bide their time. The visitor knew the queen had sacrificed true victory for a lull that would allow the barbarians to prepare a greater assault, one the realms would be hard-pressed to endure without N'lahr

"The roads are thick with pilgrims coming for the celebration," N'lahr's visitor observed. "Everyone loves you now, so she has to pretend she did, too. I hear she'll personally lay a wreath right here tomorrow morning."

He couldn't imagine what N'lahr would say to that, not really, so he turned fully to contemplate the city his friend's image seemed wistfully to study.

Darassus. Even under the stormy skies, golden towers rose gleaming from the city's center. Against his wishes, the visitor's heart swelled at sight of the venerable capital. Tree-canopied avenues stretched long and level, and walkways and bridges arched over the sparkling, twisted ribbon of the river Idris and its tributaries, captured in walled embankments. There was the famous east gate, two stories high and gilt with polished copper on tiered eaves. Just beyond, along the grand boulevard that led to the city's center, towered the immense statue of Darassa herself—only the top of her head was visible from here, but the visitor could well picture the Goddess, sword low, hand pressed to her huge bronze head as if in sorrow. Suburbs to the north crowded the immense, multiflag-crowned stadium, where each spring the greatest athletes of the Allied Realms competed for the right to join the storied ranks of the Altenerai squire corps. That was where he had first met N'lahr, on a searing, cloudless morning clearer in his memory than many more recent.

That day, too, he had first glimpsed Kalandra, little older than he or N'lahr but so talented she was already one of the vaunted officers of the corps. He had thought her stern and plain, for he'd not yet seen her smile nor heard her recite the poetry of Selana, whom he'd once been too ignorant to appreciate.

So much was different now.

He glanced down at the metal band adorning one of his dusky fingers, the large sapphire in the setting circled by the first lines of the sacred oath.

His hand tightened into a fist.

The power of the corps had faded. The old guard was halved, and those few who'd risen to replace them were pale shadows. The new commander had weakened the Altenerai by siphoning the best of their mages into a separate corps oathsworn only to the queen. And Queen Leonara herself was a recluse, lost in contemplation of the hearthstones that some whispered she worshiped rather than the true Gods.

Whatever the queen did, it had little to do with governance of Darassus or the realms. She was unaware or uncaring that the borders were being eaten by storms that grew in intensity and duration every year. Traveling the Shifting Lands between the realms had never been safe, but even short journeys had grown downright hazardous. Worse, the Naor were restive, numerous, and bolder; it could not be too long before Mazakan dared the realms again. The Naor hordes needed room they simply didn't have. They had nowhere else to go.

"Kind of like me," he said, to no one in particular now. He frowned to himself as he faced the tomb. "I guess I'd best be on my way. Maybe I'll stop by and see your sword while I'm in town, make sure the squires are keeping the edge keen. I've a feeling we'll need it soon." He didn't add that he wished N'lahr was around to tend it himself. He'd told him that too many times already.

Wind broke a gap in the cloud cover so that sunlight streamed down, and the illusion of his friend's presence was broken—he was just a lonely man in a lonely place by an image in stone. The company he craved had died with N'lahr.

He told himself he should stop riding here to talk to the air even as he stepped away and cleared his throat. "I'll come back with some bottles tomorrow," he said. "Not that you give a damn."

Unconsciously, his open hand went to his breast in salute. He caught himself before he hailed his friend and told him to fare well, then retraced the path to his dun mare, gathered his reins, and climbed into the saddle. Soon he was working his way along one of the cemetery lanes to the switchback that led down to the city.

The stone eyes of N'lahr's carven doppelgänger were aligned perfectly to watch his visitor's slow progress down the dusty road, the hood of his cloak pulled high lest fellow travelers glimpse him or his blue khalat.

The image had no remaining companions apart from the whispering trees and grasses, the monuments of brooding stone, and the mournful wind.

1

The Numbered Day

Asrahn halted before the tall glass case with the long straight sword, withdrew a key from his pocket, and set it to the lock. As Squire Elenai shifted uncomfortably in the cavernous display hall behind him the stocky Master of Squires wondered again if he should have undertaken the matter alone.

No. He wouldn't be furtive. He'd act before a witness, then tell the commander what he'd done.

He studied the sword as he turned the key. Even under dim light from high windows, obscured by a shameful coat of dust, N'lahr's blade had a distinctive blue sheen. Irion's only true ornament was an azure sapphire set in its hilt, and Asrahn well remembered that its former wielder had to be coaxed to permit that "useless ostentation." N'lahr would have objected to the gaudy red velvet behind the weapon, let alone the gilt pegs supporting each guard arm, assuming he'd ever have consented to allowing the great sword decommissioned for display.

Even if he had, he'd never have allowed Irion neglected. Asrahn had repeatedly pressed that point with his commanding officer, but Denaven had insisted no one touch the blade until a worthy successor emerged from the ranks. As N'lahr had been a military genius, that was likely to be a very long time.

Thus, in the seven years since N'lahr's death, the sword had grown more and more dingy. A ragged filament of spider silk languidly waved from the pommel to the cabinet's lock as Asrahn removed the key. He'd resigned himself to the situation mostly by avoiding the oak-framed case, visiting it only under special circumstances. Because the annual celebration of N'lahr's greatest victory would once again bring crushes of admiring citizens to the Hall of Heroes, today had been one of those times.

The veteran felt his blood rise as he looked again at the little teeth marks he'd noticed earlier this morning marring the old leather grip. Altenerai squires were forbidden to touch the weapon, but mice could nibble it with impunity? He'd served as Master of Squires under four commanders, a position demanding not only a thorough familiarity with the rules and traditions of the Altenerai Corps, but a commitment to instill those values in his charges by living them. He hadn't disobeyed an order since his squire days. Yet this wanton neglect of a heroic icon was a stain upon the corps, and a blot upon the memory of N'lahr, his friend and finest pupil. It could no longer be endured.

He opened the door and reached for the hilt. The faint scent of old leather and a stale musty odor emanating from the velvet attended his intrusion.

Asrahn fully meant to lift the sword from its display pegs and immediately place it within the sheath Elenai had brought from storage. But as his fingers wrapped those weathered leathers he paused.

There would never be another opportunity like this. Maybe advancing age was making him incautious, but . . . Could there be any harm in hefting Irion for a few moments, before it was returned to those same pegs, probably forever?

The dusty steel caught in a slanting sunbeam as he raised it level in the lonely marble hall.

His voice, roughened through years of calling commands across drill fields, betrayed neither hesitation nor expectancy. "Give me space."

Elenai backed off, eyes wide. Probably she wondered if he'd grown mad, or senile.

Perhaps he had. He grinned fiercely as he advanced into the opening stance of his favorite sword form.

As Master of Squires for thirty years, weapon forms were as natural to Asrahn as breathing. The click of his bootheels on the inlaid granite floor echoed from walls hung with storied weapons and tapestries of famous battles, and his own high-necked armored robe—the famed blue knee-length khalat of the Altenerai Corps—swayed with his steps. Hard-used knees creaked on his advance and shoulders strained to perform smoothly, but he was used to feeling that. What he didn't feel was the joy.

He grew more and more curious as he stepped through the form. The blade was balanced, true, and light. Yet something was wrong.

A twinge of pain passed through his calf, and he drew to a stop after the final flourish, setting his hand against the cool blue-marbled wall.

Elenai stepped forward. "Are you all right, Alten?"

"I'm fine, Squire." His voice was sharper than he intended. Again he lifted the blade and considered its length. Its heft. Its edge. It looked right, yes. Absolutely right. Every nick and stain that he remembered was visible in its metal.

Yet it wasn't right. This wasn't N'lahr's sword.

His heart raced on, not with exertion but panic. What if the Naor had stolen the real one years ago and replaced it with a fake? No . . . putting aside the unlikelihood of enemies penetrating the heart of Darassus and the halls of the Altenerai, if they had the sword they'd have marched across the border. It was the one object their superstitious king feared—a prophet had foretold Mazakan would die only on that blade's edge. Besides, Asrahn was fairly certain the Naor lacked the skill to produce such a duplicate.

Maybe this sword was an authorized copy, with the real one in protective storage.

Except that made no sense. Asrahn's eyes swept upward to Alvor's blackened axe. All of the other old weapons on display here were authentic. His gaze raked the bows, halberds, and blades meticulously placed around the hall between banners, paintings, and other illustrations of the realms' defense. Why house Irion anywhere else? Why deceive not only the squires who tended this display, but the Altenerai themselves? Surely Commander Denaven had to have tired of Asrahn complaining about the sword's condition. He could have confided the truth and avoided a half-dozen confrontations.

Unless Denaven didn't know.

Asrahn swallowed, for his throat was suddenly dry. Suppose the Naor clans were to learn the weapon was missing? It might be all the inspiration they needed to swarm from their dismal outer lands and try again for the realms, weakened after seven years of neglect and misrule.

"Sir?" Elenai prompted.

He'd almost forgotten she was there.

Elenai was garbed in a calf-length hauberk, similar in shape to his own khalat but constructed of heavy interlocking plates beneath a gray surcoat.

He almost confided in her. A squire of the fifth rank, she was ready to test for the sixth, the final level before joining the champions of the Allied Realms, equals without peer. She had talent and drive and discipline. And compassion as well, evident in the concern visible in her wide gray eyes.

But he'd broken enough strictures today. He straightened, still favoring his right leg. He wouldn't alarm her any more.

"The sheath, if you please." He forced a respectable calm.

She passed it to him, watching as he slid the sword home. It was a fair fit, if a little wide. She blinked in surprise as he handed the weapon to her.

He'd planned to care for Irion himself, with her assisting. But it wasn't Irion. He couldn't very well return the sword just now, after the big show he'd put on; that would leave her with even more questions. There could be no harm in her repairing the wrong sword though. He exerted effort to sound steady.

"See that the weapon's properly cared for," he instructed. "Replace the leathers." He bent to retrieve a slim brown cloth sack with handpicked materials he'd set down earlier. "You can use the table in the records room, but keep the work to yourself."

"Yes, sir."

Elenai took the sack but paid it no heed, for she fairly goggled at the weapon in her right hand, holding it out from her as though it were a fragile glass construct she feared to drop; then she sought his eyes once more.

"I'll meet you back here before nine bells."

"Yes, sir." She looked once more down at the sword, then back at him. She seemed to want reassurance.

So did everyone. But at the moment he had none to give. "I've other duties to attend to. Farewell, Squire." He turned and strode back to the case. As he closed and locked it, he heard her footsteps recede into the south corridor. He looked once to the massive cedar doors leading to the Hall of Remembrance, then turned into the west corridor, the polished gray and blue stone pillars sliding past regularly.

If Irion had been moved by someone in the court other than Denaven, there was one person who might know.

Sareel, the longtime Keeper of Keys, had given access to Irion's case the previous hour with a quirked eyebrow of surprise. Asrahn guessed she'd have pressed with impertinent curiosity if she weren't so busy. It took almost three-quarters of an hour to track her down this time. Like many in the palace complex, Sareel was harried and cross owing to the influx of visitors for the three-day celebration that began tomorrow. Her staff in particular was spread thin, for they were tasked with decorating rooms and passages normally kept empty or minimally adorned.

He found the woman in a rear parlor off the Grand Hall, bent over a book of inventories, holding it close to a large lamp while three of her assistants fussed with the top of a dusty wooden crate. It was strange to see her so gray and lined, a reminder of the long years they had held their posts. It seemed only yesterday that she had been a pretty, sharp-eyed thing that Tretton had courted.

She saw Asrahn as he approached, and straightened at her table, blinking. When he asked if Irion had a duplicate, she looked at him as though he were demented.

"No. Of course not. Why do you ask?" Her tone was more cutting than usual.

He would have to be careful how he proceeded. He didn't want to spread alarm unduly. "Has Irion ever been stored anywhere else?"

Her brow furrowed. "What's this about, Asrahn?"

He thought quickly and pulled himself a bit higher. "That sword's a national symbol, an inspiration. I simply want to ensure it's been handled correctly."

Sareel sighed and Asrahn realized she took his inquiry as a punctilious drill of some sort. "As you well know, the actual article's been hanging on the wall, properly labeled, ever since N'lahr got dropped into his marble box."

It was Asrahn's turn to furrow his brow at her callous words as she continued.

"And I'm the Keeper of Keys, so I should know. All those artifacts are in order, unlike these damnable staircase urns." She scowled down at her book to end the interaction, then looked up as Asrahn turned to go. "Do you have the key?"

"I'll need to hold onto it a little longer. I can have it back to you before the night is out."

"Well, I'll apparently still be here," she said testily, "I have a few dozen hallways left, and no one but gaping fools to aid me." The assistants buzzed more intently as her voice rose in conclusion.

He left her, deeply troubled.

Was he imagining things? Maybe it was he who'd changed, not the sword. N'lahr was dead seven years, but Asrahn himself hadn't held the blade for nearly nine. Maybe he'd forgotten what it felt like.

Asrahn wished he could sound out Melagar about the matter, but his husband was still making finishing touches to a frieze in the temple of Darassa. He wouldn't be available for hours. And Tretton was on long patrol, helping to see to the safety of the pilgrims as they passed through the Shifting Lands. He'd be unlikely to know the answer, but it would be a comfort to confide in an old friend.

More than anything, he wanted Kalandra's advice. Her nimble intellect had always pierced straight through to the heart of any matter. Yet he'd had to go without her input for as long as he'd gone without N'lahr's.

His mouth tightened at the thought of her. So many now were dead and gone.

Resigned to no other possible solution, he turned his steps to the south palace wing, marked with less expensive but still skillfully arranged ceramic tiles, and stopped at Denaven's office, only to find his commanding officer absent. The second ranker on duty suggested several likely locations, but Denaven wasn't in any of them, so Asrahn returned before long. When the squire assured him the commander would check in prior to retiring for the evening, Asrahn drafted a terse note explaining his concern and requesting a meeting at eight bells, which gave him just over an hour. He sealed the message with wax and instructed the squire to pass it solely to the Altenerai commander.

The Gods only knew how Denaven would react. He'd probably be livid but Asrahn had expected a dressing down from the start. Hopefully, the commander would focus less on the insubordination and more on the greater matter at hand—but how would he weigh the unsolicited suspicions of an aging veteran? The commander seemed somewhat impatient with tradition of late. Not to mention oblivious to the precarious state of the borders. Yet surely the disappearance of Irion would alarm even him.

Lost in reflection, Asrahn slowly retraced his steps, traversing the length of the southern hall to return to the empty display.

He looked away from the darker pattern in the velvet where the blade had hung and considered the other treasures from centuries of Altenerai service: the arrow Kerwyn had plunged through the burning heart of a kobalin lord; the spear of Jessaymyr, bent with age though its blade remained sharp. Asrahn knew precisely how sharp, for as a squire he'd tended many of these weapons—just like today's squires tended all but N'lahr's. The black ax of Alvor remained mirror bright, and he paused to consider the broadened, shortened image of himself in its reflection.

He was old. Weighted with time. Perhaps Irion felt different because his strength had faded. Asrahn little resembled the heroic figure woven into a nearby tapestry. There he was, depicted beside blue-tinted Varama as she sank to her knees on the battlefield. Tall, broad shouldered, his short brown hair windblown, although in life he'd worn a helm that day. He, like the rest of the Altenerai, was artfully rendered in a dark blue khalat, belted at the waist, with a tiny bit of azure silk on his left hand to indicate the ring denoting his rank. All about the tableau were shattered lances and bodies of the slain, but the tapestry worker had placed these aspects in shadow, as though the Second Battle of Kanesh had taken place under stormy skies.

The work was titled *The Fall of N'lahr,* and it was long enough to have draped the great hero's coffin twice over. On the tapestry N'lahr lay more handsome dead than he'd been in life. Kyrkenall cradled his friend's head in his hands, his black eyes leaking linen tears, while other Altenerai and squires sat on horses in the background, their faces pale in exaggerated grief. N'lahr's dead hands still clasped the great sword that had led him again and again to impossible victories.

His death hadn't happened like that at all, but it made for an arresting picture. The wound that slew him had seemed a tiny thing.

But the lie to the scene didn't trouble Asrahn so much as did the image of the sword.

He turned from the tapestry, bootheels echoing along the marble foyer, and pulled open the oversized and overembellished cedar doors in the north wall. There had to be a reasonable explanation about what had happened to Irion.

He just hadn't thought of one yet.

He paused, letting his eyes adjust to the gloom. He breathed deeply the stale incense that always lingered in that vast shrine. Light from the sinking sun starkly lit the narrow windows, burnishing metal shoulders on the regularly spaced statuary and striping the planks of the parquet floors.

In the lighter days of his youth, the bronze renderings of Altenerai heroes had intimidated him, seeming to look down in judgment from their cool stone pedestals to find him wanting. Even after he'd earned the sapphire ring, necessitating his own cast semblance join theirs, he never lingered. But as more and more of his colleagues left the living world he'd found himself drawn to the sterile exhibit more and more frequently. He craved the counsel of the people they represented. He missed their company.

His heels beat a hollow rhythm as he entered, scanning the faces. There was bold, cunning Renik, his hand raised in greeting, long since vanished on one of the queen's mad errands. To his right was sad-eyed Rialla, dead the day after winning her ring, forgotten now by all but the few who'd risen through the ranks with her. How many of those were left?

He held off counting. As usual, he avoided consideration of his own simulacrum as he passed.

He had almost reached Kalandra, halfway down. Of all those lost to him, it was she whom he missed the most. Wise, capable, hers had always been a grounded, calming presence.

A man's voice rang through the chamber. "'Who dares to walk these halls while I yet live?'"

Asrahn's heart sped and he pivoted, sun-wrinkled hands rising to a guard position, until he realized the words were quoted from the poet and playwright Selana, from her masterwork, *The Rise of Myralon*. And by that tone and timbre and certain exaggerated stage diction, the speaker could only be . . . A smile crept unbidden to Asrahn's lips. One of the missing had returned. He looked left. "Kyrkenall?"

"Wrong way," called the voice, a warm tenor.

"Kyrkenall the Eyeless," Asrahn called. He strode automatically toward the Alternerai's bronze likeness.

"Over here," the voice drawled. "You have me confused with the sot in bronzed breeches. I'm only Kyrkenall the drunk."

Asrahn willed his sapphire ring to light as he stepped past a solemn looking statue of a bearded ancient. A man in a familiar deep blue robe, mirror to his own, reclined against the wall.

Kyrkenall slouched beside the statue of a tall man with a long, angular face. N'lahr, of course. He raised a hand holding a bottle. "Asrahn! Join me."

Kyrkenall; mad, brilliant, impossible Kyrkenall. Sweet gods but it was fine to see a friend once more, even if he profaned the hallowed hall with inebriation. "Hail! What are you doing here?"

"I think that should be obvious."

"No, I mean why are you here, drinking?"

He hadn't changed a day, Asrahn realized as he moved closer. Kyrkenall was beautiful as a young god, smooth skinned and even featured. He might as well have stepped from the past twelve years ago when he was still a reckless squire. Radiance from Asrahn's ring stained the archer's necklength black hair and nut-brown skin shades of indigo. His "eyeless" orbs threw back an unearthly violet. Legend had granted him that sobriquet because the whole of those weird eyes, sclera and all, were midnight black, though, Asrahn knew, the lithe archer saw better than most men.

Asrahn waved away the offered bottle and crouched stiffly beside the smaller, scruffier warrior, noticing then the sword belt, the quiver, the curved end of the famed ebon bow poking out from behind Kyrkenall's pack. Kyrkenall hadn't even bothered to find a room after what had surely been a lengthy ride from some distant realm. He'd just taken up station here, with all his equipment and his wine bottles, two of which lay empty.

"You shouldn't drink here." Asrahn suppressed a wry grin, remembering his chiding never moved this former student.

"Pfft. I've been drunk with some of these. The people, I mean. Not the statues. Sit!" Kyrkenall patted the floor. "You were always so formal, even when you . . . even in the old days."

"The Gods have blessed you." Asrahn couldn't quite conceal a note of envy. "You look exactly the same as when I saw you last. Six years ago? Six and a half?"

Kyrkenall neither agreed nor disagreed. "The Grandmothers have smiled on me. You look fit still."

For an old man, perhaps. "I'm older, and rounder. Your blood holds true."

"May mine hold as true when I'm your age. How have you been? And how's . . ." Kyrkenall spun his fingers as if trying to unspool a memory.

"Melagar's fine," Asrahn said.

"Sorry. I forgot his name. Drunk."

Asrahn doubted Kyrkenall would remember the name of his espoused when sober, no matter that Melagar was one of the finest sculptors in the realm.

Kyrkenall took another pull from his bottle. "How's the court, and all the little squires? Are they an insufferable lot of yankers?"

"A few have shown real promise. Like you did, once. Before you crawled off to sulk." He couldn't keep the disappointment from his voice. Kyrkenall had abandoned the corps when he was needed most.

"Sulk?" Kyrkenall's eyebrows rose and Asrahn was reminded of the early days of their acquintance, when rage oft lurked in the shadows of his eyes. "The city of Darassus," Kyrkenall continued with the faintest of drunken slurs, "is a great, diseased canker that infects all who dwell within it—present company excepted—and tarnishes what it cannot rust. Pardon my mixed metaphor. As for what I've been doing, surely some word has reached the court. Righting wrongs, slaying monsters. Drinking. Fucking. A whole lot of fucking, actually. It never gets old, does it? Melagar good to you in bed?"

How like Kyrkenall to reduce the most complex and rewarding relationship of Asrahn's life to a matter of sex. "We're happy. And that's private."

Kyrkenall snorted. "You sound like N'lahr." At that, he raised his wine toward the statue profiled before him and drank once more.

"I've heard about your doings, Kyrkenall," Asrahn said seriously. "Some of the tales are a little troubling."

He laughed. "Like what?"

"That you whipped a Kaneshi stablemaster half to death."

"That guy? He had it coming. He was beating his horses. And his children."

That held the ring of truth. Altenerai were entrusted with meting justice wherever the local constabulary was overstretched, like in Kanesh. And it would be unlike Kyrkenall to consider how his handling of an issue might reflect on the prestige of the corps.

Kyrkenall was apparently still thinking of N'lahr. "He would never have accepted that peace treaty," he said, for the hundredth time. "We'd have been on the Naor doorstep in a few more months."

It was the natural lead-in for a discussion about the sword, yet Asrahn delayed. He wasn't certain why he hesitated. Kyrkenall was no Kalandra, true. Yet for all that he was an irresponsible egoist, the great bowman always spoke his mind. And it was a sharp mind whenever it occasionally turned from focus on self.

His own indecision was an irritant. It was mostly an unfamiliar sensation.

"Hey, who else is here?" Kyrkenall broke into the silence. "In Darassus. Altenerai, I mean."

Asrahn named the old guard first. "Tretton, though he's shepherding pilgrims. He'll be back tomorrow. Decrin and Varama. Denaven—"

Kyrkenall made a face.

"And the newer ranked."

Kyrkenall rolled his eyes. Perhaps rightly. To Asrahn's mind, most of them had been promoted too soon. But it had been hard to argue with Denaven's insistence that the upper ranks had grown thin.

"Kalandra?" Kyrkenall attempted to sound but mildly curious and didn't quite succeed.

"No one's heard from Kalandra. Still." And then it was as though the words were torn from him. "I need her advice."

His companion nodded very slowly. They sat there together in silence for a while, and Kyrkenall didn't even raise the bottle to his lips.

"Did you . . ." Asrahn paused. "Did you ever examine N'lahr's sword? After his death, I mean?"

"Sure."

"I mean really look at it."

The archer focused bleary eyes, and for a moment Asrahn sensed he had the full attention of that shrewd intellect. "What's your aim?"

"The notches are the same. The pommel's the same. But I swear it's a different blade." He shook his head, suddenly worried he was making a fool of himself. "The heft is wrong. Irion practically begged to be swung the moment you picked it up."

"I never held it," Kyrkenall admitted. "What were you doing with it? Isn't it retired, on display?" He nodded his head toward the immense double doors through which Asrahn had entered.

"Vermin were chewing the hilt wrappings." Asrahn couldn't keep the bitterness from his voice. "Someone needed to take care of it. Tomorrow's the anniversary of his greatest victory. We'll sell a hundred thousand mugs of mead but can't be bothered to tend his weapon?"

"Mice have been eating at the soul of this city for years."

Asrahn sighed. "I don't want politics, Kyrkenall." Even if he partly agreed with the sentiment, the last thing he needed was to encourage Kyrkenall, who had no compunctions about venting his vitriol on matters of state. "I just want an explanation. Where's the real sword, and who has it?"

"Maybe the one on display's an official copy."

"No. Not according to Sareel's records."

"Is it there now?" Kyrkenall looked as though he might rise and go see for himself.

"No—the blade I removed is with Squire Elenai. I asked her to repair it. I didn't want to draw attention to any irregularities. You know how rumors can start. "

"Rumors—you mean that the Naor have the sword and are coming for our heads?" Kyrkenall cursed colorfully. "Is that what you think's happened?"

"I didn't say that."

Kyrkenall was starting to sound more sober. "If word gets out we don't have the sword, it might be all the inspiration they need."

Asrahn had worried the Naor would return to invade ever since N'lahr's death, for the actual prophecy foretold Mazakan would be slain by the great general *with* the sword. Yet as the years had passed with only sporadic raids from "renegade Naor clans," common sentiment held that the sword itself might be enough of a deterrent.

He cleared his throat. "We need answers, not angst. I want to know if you've any ideas where the real sword could be."

"Have you asked Denaven? Pardon me. *Commander* Denaven?" Sarcasm dripped from Kyrkenall's words.

"Not yet. I left a message for him, though."

"He's probably busy preening in the mirror or kissing the queen's bony white ass."

"Kyrkenall!"

"It's true, isn't it?"

It was, from a coarse perspective, but Kyrkenall dishonored the corps by talking that way. "The queen rules us all, and Denaven's your commander so long as you wear that sapphire." Kyrkenall looked down at his own ring. "He's kept you on the rolls, despite your long absences. He didn't have to do that."

Kyrkenall snorted, then took another sip, his finger rising as he did so, and Asrahn braced himself for one of Kyrkenall's invectives against Denaven or the queen. But he returned instead to the topic of the sword. "Have you checked with Varama?"

It took a moment for Asrahn to unravel meaning from the question. "About the sword?"

"Yes."

"No. Why ask her?"

"She was always on about measurements and ratios and all that. I think she weighed Irion once, or calculated a density or whatever else she does. Trying to figure out why Irion was so much better, even than my sword. You could have her compare the old measurements with the sword on the wall. That was on the wall. You know."

"That's not a bad idea."

"You'll notice it's not a *great* idea."

Asrahn felt a lightness in his chest as he stood. "Thank you, Kyrkenall. You're wrong—it's a far better direction than I had before now."

"I'm occasionally useful."

He had been far more than that, once.

"You need any help?"

"No." The last thing he wanted was a half-drunken Kyrkenall indelicately agitating this evening. Especially when he spoke with Denaven. "I'll look into it, then tell you what I find. Will you be there tomorrow then? At the parade?"

"I've been thinking about it."

"You should go."

"I'll have to salute Denaven."

"He respects you."

"Sure he does."

"Why not join me and Melagar for dinner afterward?"

Kyrkenall's smile was refreshingly genuine. "That sounds nice, Asrahn. You still live in the suite over the Idris?"

Neither mentioned that it was near Kalandra's long-empty flat.

"Yes."

"All right then."

Asrahn nodded once, turned to go, then considered his old charge. "Kyrkenall."

"Yes?"

"You're better than this."

Kyrkenall shook his head. "The queen and the court never deserved you. Neither did I. Would that you lived in a better world."

Bemused, Asrahn replied, "Would that we had the strength to make one. I'll see you tomorrow. I hope you find a more comfortable place to sleep."

Kyrkenall laughed. "Hail, Alten."

"Hail and farewell."

Asrahn left Kyrkenall in the darkness and departed the palace through the heliotrope garden. As he passed under a wisteria trellis and into the vast open grounds of the complex, the sun stretched a dark finger of shadow after him as it sank below the high hills west of the city.

Asrahn smiled as he saw smoke curling from the chimneys of Varama's work buildings behind the Altenerai stables. His old comrade was working late, as usual. With her analysis, surely he'd be able to put his concerns to rest. But he'd have to hurry if he was to return to Denaven's office by eight bells.

He heard his name called.

Asrahn turned to find a broad-shouldered figure approaching, trailed by a tall woman in an unflatteringly high-necked dress. After a moment he recognized the first as Cargen, one of the newest Altenerai. With him was that mage sometimes used as supplementary instructor for Altenerai squires—what was her name?

Cargen halted before him and raised his hand, his blue ring flashing in the dying light of sunset. "Hail, Alten." His voice was low, clipped. His heavy, beard-fringed jaw was thrust forward truculently.

"Hail," Asrahn replied, eyeing them both. The woman, light of hair and eye, was lean, clean featured, and moved with grace and confidence. He wished he could recall her name.

"I've been looking for you this evening," Cargen said quietly. "Do you mind if we talk?"

"It's not a good time."

"We can walk with you if you're in a hurry. This shouldn't take long."

"Very well." Asrahn started forward.

Cargen fell in step and indicated the woman with a sweep of his hand. "This is M'lahna."

Ah, now he remembered, and felt foolish. This was Gyldara's sister; even if he'd only met her a few times M'lahna's resemblance to the alten should have sparked recognition. She had covered focusing spells with mid rankers last month. There was a time when all martial mages were trained in Altenerai schools, but this one had never served under his direction. "Well met." Asrahn tried not to sound brusque. "Come along then." He picked up his pace toward the bridge that would take him to the workshops. It arched over a walled tributary of the river Idris winding its way down to the heart of the city.

"I'll have M'lahna mask our conversation. I don't want anyone else to hear."

Asrahn halted in mid-stride and studied them both. The failing light caught Cargen's dark eyes.

"What's this about?" Asrahn asked.

Cargen answered softly. "The sword, Irion."

He almost breathed a sigh of relief. "Did Denaven send you?"

"Yes. It's all right, we can walk."

Asrahn stepped forward, Cargen at his side.

"Does he know where the real sword is?"

Cargen raised a finger. "One moment. Did you talk to anyone else about the sword being missing?"

"One or two," Asrahn answered. Cargen's manner was unusually tense. Perhaps he was worried that his more senior comrade had been indiscreet. Asrahn sighed inwardly, and not for the first time in dealing with Cargen.

They reached the midpoint of the bridge, and Asrahn glanced over to the woman, whose face had the glassy-vacant expression of someone in the midst of sorcery. She rubbed a charm dangling from her necklace between the thumb and forefinger of her left hand. Cargen stepped close enough that Asrahn could smell the mint he'd chewed, and the faint breath of a dry wine behind it. "It's important I know, Asrahn. Was it one, or two, and who were they?"

"Sareel." He paused, for some reason reticent. Owing to the oath that had been the lynchpin of his life, lies never made it past Asrahn's lips, and even one of omission was a difficult prospect.

"What did you say to her?"

"I asked if Irion had ever been kept anywhere else."

"And that's it?"

He held back from mentioning Kyrkenall's name, despite a strong compulsion to speak on.

"You didn't mention anything to, say, Melagar?"

"No. I haven't seen him since this morning."

Cargen nodded. "What about the squire, Elenai?"

How did Cargen know about her involvement? Asrahn sensed that he should have been more worried, but he found himself strangely untroubled. "Not really."

"So you said something to her? What was it?"

Why were his thoughts so muddled? There was something bothering him about this conversation, and he frowned as it came to him. "Cargen, you sound far more worried about who I spoke with than you are about the true sword. What if our enemies have it?"

"I'm worried about both. Believe me. We can't have people thinking their hero's sword has gone missing, can we? The day before his big celebration?"

Something was wrong. "It's getting dark," he said, and willed his ring to life.

Upon calling its power, the mazing M'lahna had woven around them loosened, though she still retained a sluggish hold upon his perceptions. Asrahn sensed her spell wrapped about his thoughts almost as though he'd blundered through a web in the deep woods. The strands stretched with the light of his ring, but still touched him.

He saw that he was not upon the bridge, but beneath it, beside the river itself in its stone channel. The bridge's shadow was a black stripe across the water.

"His will's strong," M'lahna whispered, which wasn't true. Asrahn had no mystical ability; likely the woman just wasn't used to fighting the power of one of the sacred rings.

Asrahn wore no sword this evening. But he was Master of Squires. He had trained the last five generations of Altenerai. Asrahn took Cargen's thick chin with a solid right that snapped the man's head back, then advanced with a left to his liver. Cargen threw up a block, but Asrahn's fist brushed past his arm and caught him with a blow to the cheek that staggered him.

"No marks on the body," the woman hissed.

So that's how it was. Did they think he'd go down easy?

He partly turned so he could see them, and M'lahna pressed at his will. His sapphire ring shone.

Cargen lowered his head and came in with his arms. Asrahn brought his knee into Cargen's gut and tried to pivot for a side kick to set his assailant off-balance.

Unfortunately, the leg that would have been solid under him even two years before betrayed him. The muscle seized up, and what should have been a graceful pivot was more of an awkward slump. Before he could compensate, a bloody-faced Cargen slammed into him and they stumbled.

No amateur, the woman threw her next sorcery while Asrahn fought for balance. Cargen suddenly disappeared. She'd blocked sight of him from Asrahn's view, an old trick. A good trick.

But a good spell couldn't last if its caster were injured. He rushed her.

She was fast and limber and sidestepped one blow, ducked another, then slid in to deliver a rabbit punch to his ear.

It wasn't a solid hit, but it was the one that decided his fate, for as he shrugged away Cargen grappled him from behind, pressing Asrahn's arms to his sides.

No longer restricted to keeping Cargen invisible, the woman hammered him with all her best magics. The world twisted and tilted as if Asrahn had just spun a hundred times in some childhood game.

A cool hand dug at one of his pinioned arms, pried at the ring that gleamed on his finger.

Not the ring. If she took the ring, he knew he was through. It was the final chance, and he bent his fingers tightly even as the man put a knee to his back. He struggled, cast back his head to catch Cargen in the forehead, missed . . .

And then all was still and he had no cares. The dizziness ebbed, and he seemed to float in a cool, dark place. The troubles of the moment before were but the lap of distant ocean waves.

He heard voices.

M'lahna panted. "For an old guy, he's pretty spry."

Cargen's response was sharp. "He's Altenerai. Ask him. This has taken too long already."

The woman's voice was soothing, like cool water on a dry throat. "Asrahn, did you tell Sareel you were afraid the sword was a fake?"

"No. I didn't want to alarm anyone."

M'lahna spoke softly to her companion. "We can easily manage this. Asrahn, what did you say to the squire Elenai about the sword?"

Graceful gray-eyed Elenai. So much potential. "Nothing."

Cargen sounded exasperated. "Nothing?"

"No."

Asrahn heard her speak but knew that she didn't address him. "I can see the memory—he speaks the truth. His manner might have confused the girl, but we should be able to manage it." And then she spoke to him. "Alten, I regret this. You were a loyal servant to the queen, and the realms. You shouldn't have asked questions."

"Someone smarter wouldn't have," Cargen added. "Someone dumber wouldn't have noticed."

"Shut up, Cargen." M'lahna's voice was still soothing. "What of your husband, Asrahn? Did you say anything to him?

"Melagar," Asrahn said tenderly. "I haven't seen him all day. He doesn't know."

Again he sensed that the woman wasn't talking to him. "I think Asrahn need be our only loss. I have one last question, Alten. Did you speak to anyone else about the missing sword?"

Asrahn had only a dim understanding about what he was experiencing, but something drew him up short before he could answer. A sense of lingering unease came to him.

"He's fighting me," M'lahna said.

"There's someone else, then," Cargen said. "Push it!"

M'lahna's voice rose in anger. "I'm already masking and silencing us. My magic's stretched—"

"Push!"

Asrahn gritted his teeth. He was *Altenerai,* one of the exalted champions of his people. He had served under bold Renik, and before him, brave, doomed, Anara, and he had trained some of the finest champions of the realms. He had sworn the oath and stood with his brothers and sisters before the enemies of Darassus. Confused as he was, his loyalty yet was a bulwark against the assault by a master sorceress.

"He's thinking of a hand, holding a bottle," M'lahna said. "It's someplace dark."

Asrahn snarled. They would know nothing more. There was one shield left him. "When comes my numbered day," he said slowly, as if he had to tear each word from the muck of his muddled consciousness, "I will meet it smiling. For I'll have kept this oath."

Cargen's voice rose in consternation. "Why's he reciting the Altenerai pledge?"

"He's using it to block me!"

"Make him stop. Push!"

But Asrahn would not stop. At the whispered words that formed the framework of his life, a spark flared within him and his speech grew easy. "I shall use my arms to shield the weak. I shall use my lips to speak the truth, and my eyes to seek it." That spark flared to flame and his voice strengthened. "I shall use my hand to mete justice to high and to low, and I will weigh all things with heart and mind. Where I walk, the laws will follow, for I am the sword of my people and the shepherd of their lands—"

He heard the woman's warning cry and suddenly he saw them, dark shapes against the stones beneath the bridge, Cargen grasping at him.

They were too strong. He had to get away, warn Renik. . . .

But as he spun, stumbling as fast as he could manage, he remembered Renik was gone. N'lahr was dead. Kalandra was missing. He had to warn the few who were left, for it was too much for him alone. Asrahn had always been a lesser light, and he knew it. He served the state as best he could, to lift those with potential to greater heights than his. Though he was Altenerai, he'd known, even when young, that he'd never join the ranks of the legendary.

Cargen's footsteps pounded behind him and M'lahna's weavings reached again for his senses, thrusting him into blackness even as he dove into the dark waters of the Idris.

The water was cooler than he'd anticipated. A surprise.

Mages loved surprises. Anything that gave the mind something new to wrestle dropped your guard. So had Kalandra always warned. If he'd yet worn the ring, awarded him in sacred trust, he might still have brushed M'lahna's spells aside.

She clamped down hard, and all went dim. His body fought, spasmodically, and then everything left him.

2

———— ≈ ————

A Changing World

E lenai had been an Altenerai squire long enough to know her superiors didn't have any special compulsion to keep her informed of their comings and goings. Still, as she woke the next morning in the predawn gloom her mind turned almost immediately to Alten Asrahn. He'd never come back to inspect her work or replace the sword.

Last night she'd wondered if his absence were some deliberate test of her character or initiative, and after waiting for more than an hour, had decided to rouse Sareel, the aged and surly Keeper of Keys, to restore Irion to its case.

Sareel had been astonished to learn Asrahn had given Elenai the blade, cross that she'd been wakened (apparently Elenai's intrusion was the capper to "an insufferably interminable day"), and frustrated because she felt duty bound to accompany Elenai rather than loan the only other key to Irion's case.

Elenai offered no explanation, as Alten Asrahn had provided none, so she just squirmed uncomfortably and tried to placate the angry woman with "yes ma'ams" or "no ma'ams" whenever appropriate. Afterward, she had sought her own bed in a swirl of uncertainty, hoping to consult with the Master of Squires in the morning both for reassurance and to confirm the repair was completed to his satisfaction.

She rose at the usual time, despite a long day of parade drills before her late-night activities, and sleep clung to her fitfully. She swung her legs out of the covers, then reached across a narrow distance to turn up the oil lamp to maximum burn. As a squire of the fifth rank, she had earned a room of her own, but not one of any real space—just a small rectangle, with nightstand, bed, and storage chest arranged along the wall leaving only a narrow aisle between the door and shuttered window. A proper stretch would have to wait until she left her quarters.

She lingered on the bed's edge, reviewing her options. A visit to Asrahn's quarters was as unthinkable this morning as last night. He maintained private lodgings somewhere in the city—she'd have to ask precisely where—and visiting his home seemed a presumptuous, and embarrassing, invasion of the old gentleman's privacy. Even inquiries about his whereabouts would invite questions she couldn't answer without disobeying him. No. He would take a dim view of her cravings for reassurance, and she didn't want to diminish the trust placed in her when, no doubt, he'd been called to a more urgent duty.

So, she'd carry on with the activities she planned for this morning. It wasn't likely she'd encounter Asrahn on the practice field, but she might be able to speak with him before the parade. He'd be there to inspect the squires' formal turnout before public presentation. Once everyone was in place at the lineup, he might have a spare moment to appraise her work. And he'd surely have stopped by Irion's case on his way to the assembly, if he hadn't already checked on it last night.

She got up to pour water from a brass pitcher into a porcelain bowl on the nightstand, washing her hands and face before peering into the tiny bronzed mirror that magnified the lamplight. She thought her eyes looked only a little tired. Her hair was a wild corona of chestnut, though. She stuck a tongue out at herself, rubbed more cold water on her face, and set to ordering her mane.

It didn't take long to dress and get ready for her dawn workout, shoulder-length hair in a utilitarian braid.

She stopped with her hand upon the door, ashamed that in her eager-ness she'd neglected an important portion of her daily regimen. She returned to the window, head bowed, and offered prayers, first giving thanks for an-other day to the Goddess Darassa, who'd founded the realm where she now lived. It was she who'd overseen the construction of Darassus and its great domes and bridges and who had once walked the streets of the city with her people.

Elenai then prayed to Vedessa, the creator of her homeland. She hoped the Goddess would watch over her father and sister, who might be starting their day, far away in the city of Vedessus, but were more likely still abed.

Finally, she thanked the God Elahn, after whom she was named, for the continued gift of health.

It was no bad thing, her father had told her, to be connected to three of the four great Gods.

Prayers complete, she left her room. The hall mirror showed nothing amiss, from calf-length black boots—slightly worn, for her best boots were reserved for special occasions—to the gray surcoat emblazoned with the sapphire star at its center. It draped her from collar to knee. She studied the familiar figure looking back at her, thinking that her eyes appeared guileless. How could she ever hope to be a full-fledged Altenerai if she looked so young?

She experimented with lowering her brows, as Asrahn seemed perpetu-ally to do, then laughed at herself and pushed out her lip to look even more ridiculous before moving on. Alten Enada had reached the sapphire when she was twenty-four, a year younger than Elenai was now. Earning the ring wasn't about looks, but performance.

The sun had just shaken off its own covers to set the sky aglow beyond the slanting stable rooftops and the golden domes of the city temples, vis-ible through the windows as she descended the central staircase. It was unusually quiet this morning, with even the songbirds silent and only an occasional rumble of thunder . . . as if the very air urged her to stillness. She had other plans, though. Elenai Dartaan wanted to make excellence a habit, just like the great N'lahr.

She reached the wider hall at the bottom, her footsteps ringing rebel-liously on the ancient marble. The quiet was not entirely unexpected. Fes-tivities were not to begin until the late morning. Normal routines were delayed or canceled. Squires could take their rest for an additional hour, an unheard-of luxury. She easily had time for a warm-up and several runs through the Falling Water sword form, including those tricky middle stances, before thoroughly grooming her horse and herself.

After that, and breakfast, would come several hours of rigid posture as the parade wound before thousands of eyes from all over the five realms. While the throngs began their celebration, the Altenerai and their squires would further escort the queen to a formal ceremony at N'lahr's tomb, but after that, three days of light duty were scheduled. The queen wanted her soldiers to revel with the rest of her people—a fine idea in theory, though it struck Elenai as ironic that the realms' finest fallen general, famed for his devotion to the corps, should be honored by a vacation from it.

Elenai hoped to follow her hero's example, so light duty didn't mean the lounging and feasts her friends planned, but the opportunity to work on her weapon forms without distraction.

As she emerged onto the worn granite steps and breathed deeply, she spied a figure striding across the yard. Whoever it was wore a knee-length azure robe with a stiff collar, crossed at the waist with a belt. Altenerai. Only a handful currently served in Darassus. Might it be Alten Asrahn after all?

As she started down she knew that the approaching officer was some-one else. The figure walked briskly rather than with Asrahn's measured mil-itary stride that subtly favored one leg. She realized it was Commander Denaven at about the same time he changed course to direct his steps to her. She halted, erect with hands behind her back.

The leader of the Altenerai Corps rested his hand on the old stone rail-ing at the bottom as if to signal this was a casual meeting. "Squire Elenai." Denaven's diction was precise as ever, but he seemed strangely affable, down to his crooked smile. "Good morning."

The commander had spoken with her before, but he'd never gone out of his way to do so. And she'd never seen him in the early morning hours. "Good morning, sir." She saluted, then descended to the ground level so she wouldn't tower over her superior officer.

Denaven's eyes roved over her. She imagined him searching for some unpolished button or frayed thread or even a hair out of place. She was fairly certain he'd find none, but she'd been in the corps long enough to know an alten could always find something wrong with a squire if he or she were in the mood.

Denaven himself was as impeccably dressed as always. His khalat, blue-black in the pale early light, was crisp and creaseless, and his boots shone like dusky glass. Not a single one of the rust-colored hairs swept back from his high forehead was out of line.

"What brings you out so early, Squire?" He strove for a relaxed air, as if these sorts of meetings were an everyday occurrence.

"I like to rise for stretches and informal practice on my own, sir."

"The dawn hunter on her rounds, eh?"

Denaven was a great one for maxims and proverbs. The dawn hunter, like the early bird, always caught fatter game, although in Elenai's experience a good hunter was out before the sun. "Yes, sir."

"And on a feast day! That's to be commended. I'm an early riser myself. Headed to the practice fields, then?" He didn't wait for an answer. "I'll walk with you."

Stranger and stranger. They'd already exceeded the amount of words exchanged in any single conversation she'd yet held with the corps commander. They paced together across the roadway and on along the edge of the gardens, passing a row of unbloomed bushes.

"I always forget how tall you are," he offered into the uncomfortable silence. "I didn't think Arappan girls grew so high."

"It helps my reach," Elenai said, unsure how else to answer. She might have mentioned that her younger sister was taller still, but this was the response she'd learned to dole out over the years when people said something foolish about her height. She didn't think her stature remarkable. She could measure up to most men in the corps, it was true, but she was shorter than some.

Denaven tried another line of conversation. "Asrahn has commented upon your sword use. And your overall talent."

"That's good to know, sir." An approving nod from Asrahn was more rewarding than precious gems, and she'd been receiving more of them the last few months. Compliments from his lips were rarer still, and she could count the sum total since entering the service on one hand. Still, she wished she could think of something more eloquent to say.

"He told me he'd picked you for a special duty. How did you like handling N'lahr's sword?"

"It was a tremendous honor," she asserted, trying to keep her relief and enthusiasm in check. Alten Asrahn must have reported to Commander

Denaven already this morning. Might the commander have noted her work as well? She'd certainly applied the leathers with meticulous devotion, taking care the risers were well skived like the originals. But . . . surely the simple soldier's grip, even well done, wouldn't garner a special visit from the commander? Had she somehow erred? Was this a prelude to reproach?

"What did you think of it?"

This wasn't the question she'd anticipated, but she didn't mind answering. "Irion's one of the most perfectly balanced blades I've ever held. And it was still incredibly sharp."

He nodded. "Indeed. Someday I'm sure you'll have a sword like it of your very own."

That was an astonishing sentiment, because so far as Elenai knew, no one had ever unraveled the secrets of the weapon's unusual qualities, try as they might to manufacture its equal.

He grinned in that lopsided manner. "I imagine Asrahn told you all sorts of stories about it."

"Not really, sir." Where was this going?

"No? I'm surprised."

She didn't know why he would be. Denaven had squired with Asrahn, and according to everything she'd ever heard, Asrahn trained all of his charges the same way. The older alten was never particularly garrulous. He kept a cultivated distance, careful not to appear overly familiar or to demonstrate favoritism among his pupils, on or off duty.

They turned a corner and strode by a dense stand of shrubbery from the Storm Coast. These were already heavy with yellow blossoms that reminded her of summer days of her childhood and the perfume of highborn ladies come to see the latest work at her father's playhouse.

"N'lahr was his star pupil, you know," Denaven went on. "Rather like you."

"Me, sir?" She felt her cheeks flush. So there wasn't anything amiss. Denaven was just familiarizing himself with those most likely to rise in rank. But the three sixth rankers were more polished with their sword forms, and two of her own rank managed some of them better. She hadn't heard of the commander seeking conversation with any of them. Was she truly the star?

He chuckled. "You're too modest. Surely you know it was a special honor to be chosen to care for N'lahr's sword. I just can't believe Asrahn didn't talk to you about it."

"Alten Asrahn asked me to clean it up and replace the leathers, but didn't say very much beyond that." Maybe Denaven was looking for some personal stories to accompany a speech he would give rededicating the sword. She probably should be saying something more meaningful, but couldn't think what.

"Hm. Well, I suppose Asrahn was terse as always."

They'd drawn close to the carefully tended field of brown sand behind the stables, across from the long barracks building for the third- and fourth-ranked squires. The dry pebbles surrounding it crunched under their boot-heels. She struggled to fill the awkward pause in their conversation with a stray thought. "Do you have any stories about the sword, sir?"

Something about that question unsettled the commander. His step faltered and his expression blanked. It was as though she'd thrown a log into a mill wheel. There was a delay before he spoke, as if that wheel strained to break the wood before it could reengage and turn once more at full strength. Denaven's bland smile returned, perhaps a bit more warmly. "I suppose I do. I was there for its forging, you know."

Eager to establish an easier avenue of communication, she urged him on without consideration. "You were?"

Denaven nodded. For a brief moment, her enthusiasm seemed to have struck a sympathetic cord. He opened his mouth to speak, then said nothing. His eyes took on a penetrating quizzical aspect as they searched her own.

She didn't understand that at all, so she strove to return a gaze of earnest sincerity. Her manner must have eased his suspicion, because the scrutiny dulled and Denaven cleared his throat.

"A story for another time." He smiled slightly. "Asrahn's remarks drew my attention to you." He stopped at the edge of the sand and clasped his hands behind his back. "I think I've neglected your education."

She answered this time with measured curiosity. "Neglected, sir?"

"I keep thinking I'll have time to personally instruct squires like you with magical talents, but my official duties continually interfere. So I'm bringing in an outside tutor, and I'd like her to meet with you this afternoon."

Elenai brightened. "That's kind of you, sir." Apart from Denaven and the reclusive Varama, who worked only with handpicked squires, none of the sorcerous Altenerai served in Darassus. Famous Altenerai mages like Kalandra and Belahn, she suspected, would have been far more skilled after six years of squire training; she'd had to make do mostly with self-instruction, using the library in her off-hours.

Denaven dismissed her thanks with a hand wave. "Long overdue. I'll have her meet with you after the parade, today. What say you to that?"

"That's wonderful, sir." She hoped this woman wouldn't prove to be another Mage Auxiliary officer trying to lure her from the Altenerai path. She'd long since grown tired of their recruitment attempts. "I'd intended on some extra training over the next few days, sir. This will be a perfect addition."

He looked at her in bemusement. "That sounds like something N'lahr would say. Of course, he wouldn't have been nearly as charming while saying it. No offense meant to N'lahr, of course," he added quickly. "It's just that he wasn't the warmest of men."

"I met him once," she said, then regretted it, both for blurting the information and because Denaven had clearly been winding up the exchange.

"Did you?" He sounded puzzled for a moment. "But he was dead the year before you joined the corps."

"Yes, sir. I met him in Vedessus when I was a girl. During the Naor invasion. You were there, too," she added.

"Terrible times."

The commander had the gift of understatement. The Naor had swept through the realm of Arappa on their long march toward Erymyr, a grim tide of blood and ashes. United for the first time behind a determined leader, their warring clans had left off murdering one another to systematically inflict their evils upon the nearest civilized realms. She felt her jaw tighten as unbidden memories washed against her.

"I should have realized," Denaven said in a lower voice. "You probably saw all sorts of horrible things, didn't you?"

"Yes, sir." She wished she hadn't opened this line of conversation. Pity wouldn't help her or impress her superior.

Denaven forced cheer back into his voice. "Did I speak to you as well?"

"No, sir," Elenai admitted awkwardly. "I don't think you saw me."

The shadows had been long the evening the Altenerai gathered after their great victory at the First Battle of Vedessus, eleven years before. The temple bells resounded through the central square. Vast crowds cheered and laughed and offered up wine. Denaven hadn't been the aloof and dignified man before her today; he'd snatched up a goblet and dumped its contents over a companion's head, the two of them laughing like idiots.

Elenai, all of fourteen, her mother missing, her father wounded, viewed the celebrations alone on the temple wall near the immense sandaled foot of the statue of Vedessa herself. She watched in awe as the dusty, dirt-and blood-flecked demigods jested roughly among themselves or danced with the most jubilant of the Vedessi people. A dozen of the great winged lizards known as ko'aye soared overhead, calling excitedly in high, shrill voices. As newcome allies to the cause, ko'aye had scouted out the Naor movements, and some had even dragged horsemen from their saddles. Yet only a few among the crowd cast nervous glances skyward.

She had climbed to her vantage point both in hope she might see her mother among the recovered prisoners and to escape the celebration because she felt certain she never would.

Amidst the carryings-on, a solitary figure rode up from an alley, reined in apart from the crowd, and climbed down from his horse. He looked over the noisy throng shouting and singing only paces away from the somber zone about the shaded temple. Satisfied, he carefully poured from a water-sac into a battered helm for his gray gelding, just as remote and indifferent to the raucous proceedings as his rider. Once finished, the man leaned against the wall beneath Elenai, a mere arm's length from her dangling feet. She stiffened, statue still.

The serious soldier, dressed in the famed khalat of the Altenerai, seemed oblivious to her as he uncapped a smaller wineskin and downed a drink, so she was startled when he turned to her and offered it up. She forgot to breathe as their eyes locked.

His face was too angular to be truly handsome, his nose a bit long, his eyes deeply set. Elenai had later studied N'lahr's image on his tomb enough times to confirm her impressions. Yet when he smiled encouragingly, she'd fallen a little in love with him.

She'd taken the offered wine and sipped, too nervous to note the flavor.

Denaven brought her back to the present. "And what did N'lahr say to you? Something encouraging, I hope?"

"He didn't really say anything," she confessed. To this day she wondered if he might have planned to speak before another alten, Kyrkenall she learned after, called him away. N'lahr left her with the winesac. It held a place of honor in her storage chest to this day.

"That sounds like him," Denaven said with an air of finality. "Well, I should let you get on with your day. I have duties of my own. I'm sure I'll see you in the line at the parade."

"Yes, sir." She wasn't sure he would.

He nodded once and walked back toward the Altenerai wing of the palace.

She ran the form a dozen times, then saw to her horse, ate with the upper-ranked squires, and readied herself for the parade. Despite the praise and prospects for enhanced training, a vague sense of unease haunted her. Astride her gelding, Aron, a black with striking points, she joined a long train of paired squires waiting behind the palace, feeling unaccountably smaller than she had at dawn.

Beyond, the Altenerai themselves waited in a disorderly mass, talking freely with one another. Elenai scanned them from afar, seeing both the faces of legends and the newly risen.

Asrahn wasn't there.

But then neither was Commander Denaven, nor one or two other Altenerai she felt certain were still in the city.

Her friend Elik, sitting saddle beside her, suddenly let out a low oath, his voice ringing with disbelief. "I think that's Kyrkenall."

Elenai turned in her saddle to follow his gaze as another horseman rode out of the stables on a beautiful bay dun mare with white blaze and feet.

So far as she knew, Alten Kyrkenall hadn't visited Darassus for seven years. Yet there was no mistaking him, even from a distance—she'd glimpsed him in Vedessus, and studied a half-dozen statues and paintings that featured him, or showed the archer in a supporting role.

Those artists had depicted him with incredible accuracy. If anything, they'd downplayed his appearance, for apart from those disturbing obsidian eyes Kyrkenall was the most beautiful man she'd ever seen, with flawlessly smooth almond skin and wavy neck-length hair so lustrous and dark it looked liquid. As he passed Elenai and Elik, he must have felt their scrutiny, for his gaze briefly brushed their own. It didn't linger, and Elenai sensed that he, too, was searching for someone.

As the Altenerai glimpsed him, they erupted in glad cries of surprise.

"That's something you don't see every day," Elik observed.

"I wonder how long he's planning to stay?"

"It'd be wonderful to meet him, wouldn't it?" Elik asked. His broad face was lit in a boyish grin.

Elenai nodded agreement. Kyrkenall had been N'lahr's greatest friend. According to popular gossip, the general's death had so shattered him he'd wandered into seclusion, popping up only occasionally to right some wrong in a remote land before vanishing once more. Some said he'd gone half-wild.

Elik must have been thinking along the same lines. "He doesn't look like a madman, does he?"

"No. Do you see Asrahn anywhere?"

Elik grunted and looked back down the line toward the lower ranked. "Now that you mention it, no. It's not like him to be late."

"Probably inspecting someone's horse back at the stable," Squire Sansyra offered behind them.

Elenai rose in her saddle, looking not to the low-slung stables behind, but up toward the imposing façade of the palace on their right. It dominated the surrounding buildings and gardens, a four-story expanse of white stone with casements and doors ringed by decorative carvings and a roofline ornamented with scrollwork. Could Asrahn be inside, in conversation with the queen? His devotion to the corps and long years of experience had long since made him the acknowledged expert on all matters of tradition and decorum related to the Altenerai. Was this delay connected to whatever duty kept him from checking on her last night?

"Looking for something, Squire?"

At the amused question, Elenai started and sank quickly back to her saddle as Alten Rylin came alongside upon his tall, coal-black horse. One of the newest ranked, he was dark haired and rakishly handsome. He casually returned Elenai's salute, smiled, met her eyes as if they shared some tender secret, then continued on for the rest of the officers. She discovered herself blushing, though she wasn't entirely certain why.

Sansyra muttered something about him. Elenai didn't quite catch it, but from the tone the words weren't complimentary.

"What's wrong with Alten Rylin?" Elik asked. He turned in the saddle to address their fellow fifth ranker. Elenai knew that the young alten was one of Elik's idols.

The square-chinned brunette behind them frowned. "He's never met a pair of breasts he didn't love."

That hardly seemed fair. Rylin was the most kind of the young Altenerai, always patient when teaching the lower ranks. "He's always been nice to me," Elenai said.

Sansyra scoffed. "That's because he wants to sleep with you."

Elenai was about to counter when Elik snapped a warning. "Look steady."

She sat back in her saddle just in time. Denaven trotted past on his horse, hand to chest in acknowledgment of the salutes given by the squires. On any other day he might have had a sharp word for someone craning a neck like a sightseer, but he said nothing to Elenai. His attention was clearly focused inward, his expression serious. As soon as he joined, the Altenerai left with him, presumably to take their position before the queen's carriage, parked by the grand front entrance around the corner of the palace.

Only a short while later the column advanced into the public streets, so the queen and Asrahn must have taken their positions out of sight. From her previous parade and their long rehearsal yesterday, Elenai knew the order of the participants. After heralds and banner bearers, the veteran foot soldiers of the Second Battle of Kanesh would precede the mounted Altenerai—most of whom had served in some capacity during the battle, some as squires. Then came the queen's carriage and attendant governors. Because the sixth rankers were all posted to border realms, the fine coaches were followed by Elenai and Elik and four other fifth rankers on horseback in uniform rows, then dozens from the fourth and third rank; the second ranked had been allotted sentry duty for all but the most important posts. After them came several score of the famed riders of Kanesh, the greatest cavalry unit in the realms, resplendent in their long gray coats, tasseled hats, and shining horse tack. Their nominal commander had long been Alten Enada, but she, like Kyrkenall, seldom traveled to Darassus. Certainly she didn't seem to be in attendance today.

A regiment of colorfully outfitted musicians brought up the rear. However, the noise of the crowds and clop of horse hooves masked almost every sound reaching Elenai beyond the rattle of drums and the occasional trumpet fanfare or shrill fife stab.

This was Elenai's third year riding in the parade, and it seemed the crowds had grown. Even if the directive to sit straight, eyes front, kept her from watching them, she could see that folk were piled four to eight deep along the boulevards, cheering and waving. Merchants moved among them hawking banners with the victorious Kaneshi regiment numbers, or Altenerai symbols, or artful drawings of N'lahr's face. All of these were held up and shaken by their purchasers, or draped from second- and third-floor balconies alongside homemade works.

The parade route passed first along the wide avenues of the central districts below the gilded domes of the marble temples to the four great Gods, then on across the old central bridge over the river Idris and into the city surround. If anything, the crowds here were larger, and Elenai's nostrils gathered in the scent of roasting meats and spiced nuts and ales. The drumbeats and hoof clatter echoed off the closer press of buildings. From the glazed look of numerous citizens it was clear some celebrations had begun even before the parade.

The veterans stood aside to salute the queen in ordered rows at the city outskirts. The musicians remained behind as well, so that the procession that rode into the hills to the western plateau was diminished by three-quarters. Climbing the packed earth switchback up Cemetery Ridge finally gave her a good view of the queen's carriage, decked out in crimson flowers, before the whole procession stopped along the outskirts of the vast city of the dead, the most honored of whom were entombed closest to the plateau's edge. Row upon row of small buildings fashioned of marble and stone stretched into the distance, many depicting their occupants in friezes as they had appeared in life, though by tradition no figures were shown carrying arms—they were at peace, now.

Elenai saw the queen emerge from her carriage as a space opened up between the Altenerai. She was a slim figure in gray, her face hidden by a plumed sunbonnet. Last year the queen had personally carried the tray of fruits to set before N'lahr's tomb; this time she merely looked on with a group of dignitaries, head bowed, while a servant performed the duty.

Elenai recalled with an uncomfortable jolt that last year Asrahn had stood to one side of the tomb, nearest the grim image carved in stone who had first been his pupil, then friend and commander. He hadn't said or done anything special, but Asrahn's absence today was not unnoticed. Though the squires around her maintained their disciplined posture, the horses beneath them shifted more restlessly, sensing their riders' unease. Aron actually tossed his head and snorted before Elenai could still him.

This year Asrahn's place was taken by Commander Denaven, who faced the assembled Altenerai. He was saying something in a low, sonorous voice. From the grand sweeping gestures it looked as though what he told them must be very important, although between the stiff wind rustling foliage and the snuffling of horses Elenai caught only an occasional word.

A knot of Altenerai was completely ignoring him, she realized, speaking in hushed conversation on horseback. Elenai watched intently, guessing their serious break in etiquette was kin to her own unease, and she couldn't shake the impression that lantern-jawed Alten Varama pointed specifically at her. Others turning with her gesture included hulking Decrin and Kyrkenall, who kept scanning her with his strange black eyes even after the others turned back.

He's not really looking at me, she convinced herself, and continued to think it even as Kyrkenall turned his mare away from his comrades and trotted through the scrubby grass toward her. Kyrkenall really *was* looking at her. What could he want? His expression was purposeful, almost menacing.

As he drew up, she saw the hilt of a slim sword hung at his waist and knew that this was Lothrun, as famous in song as the black horn bow, Arzhun, holstered at his side. He halted and raised one light brown hand. "Squire."

"Hail, Alten." She kept her voice low so as not to disrupt Denaven's speech.

Kyrkenall kept his voice soft as well. "Have you spoken with Asrahn this morning?"

"No, Alten." Did this mean that the Altenerai didn't know where he was, either?

"When did you last see him?"

"Yesterday evening, sir. About six bells."

"Where?"

"Just outside the Hall of Remembrance."

"What did he say to you?"

She hesitated only a moment. Asrahn had wanted discretion, but Kyrkenall was asking her a direct question. "He told me to care for Irion."

On the verge of her vision she saw Elik's eyes widen, but she didn't look away from Kyrkenall.

The archer studied her for a moment more. His eyes, like black cutouts, shifted to the squires nearest her. "Have any of the rest of you seen him since?"

There was a chorus of low, respectful noes.

Elik addressed him tentatively. "Alten, what's happened?"

"Nothing good," Kyrkenall said curtly. "Squire Elenai, ride with me."

Elenai was sufficiently surprised by the order that she didn't obey until Kyrkenall had ridden away from the group.

Her prior orders were clear—she was one of the squires assigned to the parade. Yet Kyrkenall was her superior, and he had told her to leave formation. And he seemed worried about Alten Asrahn. In the end, that's what set her after him rather than asking for clarification.

She glanced back at Elik, who looked as confused as she felt, then looked farther back to the knot of Altenerai. She found Rylin and Varama returning her gaze. Worse, the queen herself had turned her head. Elenai was too far from her to read her expression, but she saw bright green eyes before the woman returned her attention to Denaven.

Had the queen, too, been watching her? Or had she imagined that? She gulped, then self-consciously followed the legendary alten away from the parade route, hoping the sound of their exit didn't detract from the ceremony she could faintly hear continuing behind them. Once they started down the road to the city, Kyrkenall urged his horse into a gallop, and she was hard-pressed to keep pace.

Upon reaching Darassus, Kyrkenall's voice was like a savage whip. He shouted for festivalgoers to clear the street, and they scrambled aside, some alarmed and some outraged, while he and Elenai thundered past. More than once he came within a handspan of injuring someone.

Either Kyrkenall really was half mad, or he was sincerely worried about Alten Asrahn. Elenai wasn't sure how he expected her to help, but she felt beyond foolish for not considering the Squire Master might be in some sort of trouble. She knew he was old, but he always seemed so . . . eternal.

Kyrkenall sped past the startled second-ranked squires at the gate, who belatedly saluted, then led her around the stable and the training yards and on to the Altenerai wing of the palace. There he grabbed his bow, swung down from his mare, and trotted effortlessly up the dozen wide steps to the portico. Elenai was fairly certain Aron, damp and puffing, would stay if ordered, as Kyrkenall's mount had done, though she would have liked to tether him properly.

She ran to catch up to the archer. A single squire, his rank clear from his two shoulder brevets, stood sentry beside one of the fluted pillars holding up the portico. Elenai paused to exchange salutes with him before hurrying through the heavy wooden door through which Kyrkenall had already vanished.

He moved fast. The alten was already beyond the lobby and the stairwell. Elenai finally reached him and matched him stride for stride but a step behind, noting she was half a head taller.

Despite asking for her company, the archer seemed disinclined to speak, or even to acknowledge her presence. So she left off looking at the back of his head and considered instead the banners and paintings hung along the Great Hall between the closed doors to storage and meeting rooms. Kyrkenall ignored them, even a brilliant one of himself laughing and lifting his sword in a snowy forest clearing as he faced a trio of Naor in bronze helms and red capes. One of the famed ko'aye was lowering on leathery wings to plunge talons into a Naor. She supposed she could ask him, today, what she'd always wondered, and find out if that ko'aye was the one he'd ridden into battle.

The click of their bootheels was magnified on the venerable granite floor. Just when she thought he'd all but forgotten her presence, Kyrkenall suddenly spread his arms and turned dramatically. "Look at all these vaunted weapons of the dedicated dead! There's the broken spear of T'var. He was just as broken, after the battle. Maybe Lothrun and Arzhun will hang here someday soon, eh?"

Elenai had no idea what the alten intended. She simply returned his look.

Kyrkenall laughed mirthlessly, a chilling sound that echoed off the surrounding hard surfaces. "In fact, the only object that belongs to a living person on these walls is that shield there. It's not even the one Decrin had riven at Kanesh. Did you know that? The real one was so smashed it would have looked like crap on display, so he took an axe to a new one. Looks pretty good, don't you think?"

There was a mad, manic quality to Kyrkenall's delivery; Elenai could feel the rage swirling about him, as one feels a storm rising in the air. She didn't even look toward the splintered round metal shield the archer had indicated, wondering if she herself might be in danger.

He pivoted and walked to the glass display case where Irion hung vertically. N'lahr's sword was a magnificent weapon, four feet long and gleaming. The sapphire set into the pommel sparkled, the new leathers so well-oiled and crisp they practically glistened.

Kyrkenall halted before the case, and she wondered if he'd brought her here to ask about her work. No. That was preposterous. Shouldn't they be looking for Alten Asrahn?

"Now." Kyrkenall's voice was sharp. "Did Asrahn say anything more to you, yesterday, about Irion? Anything apart from care instructions?"

Why was there so much attention being paid to the sword? It no longer made any sense that it was her actions that had brought that scrutiny. Something had to have been wrong when Asrahn handled it. "He didn't say anything more about it, sir. But he looked troubled."

"What do you mean?"

An image came to her, unbidden, of Asrahn working through the stances, smooth, precise, and more flowing than when demonstrating on the practice field. She had carefully watched his transitions through the middle stances. "He opened the case and then tried out the seventh form with Irion. Falling Water."

"I know the name of the seventh form," he snapped.

"Yes, sir." Kyrkenall's tense manner had frayed her nerves. Normally she wouldn't have prattled.

"Did he say anything after?"

"No, sir. I could tell something was troubling him, though." Elenai remembered wondering if Asrahn's leg were giving him more difficulty than he wanted to let on.

"Did you ask him why?"

"No, sir. It didn't seem my place." A squire simply didn't question the actions or instructions of Alten Asrahn. Not out of fear, but respect, for the old warrior was the very soul of correctness.

Kyrkenall rubbed his face and considered the case again. Elenai hunted for the courage to ask him what he thought was wrong.

"I don't suppose you have the key?" he asked.

"No, Alten. Mistress Sareel has it. If you want, I can go get it."

"No. Hold this."

Without preamble she found herself gripping Arzhun. Despite her nervousness, despite her bewilderment, she had room yet to marvel. *Yesterday she, Elenai, had held the most famous sword in Altenerai annals, and today she held the most famous bow!* The weapon was different from Irion in every way. It wasn't just that it was dark and curved rather than shining and straight. Instead of the sword's striking simplicity, intricately detailed figures were incised into every visible inch of the black horn. They fought with sword and shield or hunted or rode mounts with streaming manes and proud tails. The lines were bold, sweeping: the weapon was an artistic masterpiece even more beautiful than described in song.

Her examination was interrupted by the sound of smashing glass.

She looked up to find Kyrkenall bashing Irion's case with his knife hilt a second and third time as sharp-toothed triangles rained down amid glittering smaller shards. They struck the blue granite on the floor, splintering further, the sound disproportionately loud, as if the case indignantly cried out for retribution.

Kyrkenall sheathed his knife and stuck his arm past one fang of glass still securely wedged to the frame. He grabbed Irion's hilt.

He must be deranged! Destroying the case was practically a desecration.

Kyrkenall pulled the sword free, then crunched through the broken remnants as he moved to the north wall and the double doors that led to the Hall of Remembrance. For a moment she thought he meant to enter there, but he stopped several feet shy and lifted the weapon into a slanting sunbeam. His ring of office glittered as he shifted the blade to left and right, studying it.

What was he seeing? Was there some obvious defect she'd missed while working on the weapon last night?

Kyrkenall lowered the sword precisely and advanced into the seventh sword form. The very form that still gave her trouble.

He moved with a careless speed that should have seemed sloppy. It wasn't. Asrahn had promised there was a point with weapons forms when you moved beyond conscious consideration of the movements. And then he had lapsed into a brief, rare moment of reverie to describe Renik and N'lahr in action.

But he hadn't mentioned Kyrkenall, one of the finest swordsmen she'd ever seen. He spun, parried, sidestepped, advanced, blocked, dropped, thrust, with astonishing precision. Even the awkward middle stances seemed somehow natural when Kyrkenall swept through them. It looked less the practiced individual movements she saw in the steps of the younger Altenerai and more a spontaneous and violent dance of deadly purpose.

Elenai had never seen sword work of the like. How was he doing it?

She doubted he'd say. And she had a strong sense that he wouldn't be around very long to ask, that he might depart Darassus again at any moment. She *had* to know how he managed it.

Hesitating only a moment more, Elenai centered herself, closed her eyes, and linked her will to the interconnected threads of the world around her. When she opened them she no longer saw the usual visual details of Kyrkenall and the hall, she saw their outlines and their internal energy matrices. The structures of old weapons upon the wall radiated fading glamours. Brighter by far was Kyrkenall's life force, shining even through his clothing, especially brilliant wherever there was exposed skin. He seemed a moving man-shape of intersecting lines fashioned of golden light.

His ring shone, too, though with a blue tint, and whenever he turned she glimpsed a luster even through his sword sheath, where Lothrun rested. Irion radiated a similar glow, though surprisingly it didn't seem as strong as that originating from the burning bow within her hands.

If she wanted to learn anything from him she'd have to move fast. He was nearing the end of the martial form. Elenai shaped desire into thought. In the real world her sorcery would have been invisible. Through magical sight the thread of her desire slung out like a spiderweb in the wind until it linked to the edge of the man-shaped frame that was Kyrkenall.

Temporarily linked, she reached for his mind. Reading surface thoughts required a deft touch. She didn't mean to pry, but observe, and congratulated herself on achieving a careful peek without alerting him.

As she considered the images floating at the height of his consciousness she expected to find some kind of mantra, or meditative exercise, or advanced state of focus. But he wasn't thinking about his actions at all. He was awash in memory, and she saw and felt what he experienced. She realized with a start that the broad-shouldered man in the muddy uniform walking in the mist beside her was Asrahn. He looked so much younger! She heard herself (or was it Kyrkenall?) cry out a warning and Asrahn ducked the blow of a monstrous armored Naor clansman, charging from the fog, then delivered a swift and deadly undercut between his protective plates.

Her weaving abruptly severed without her command. Startled, her attention returned to the real world, and to Kyrkenall, pointing that terrible sharp sword at her chest. His voice was disturbingly low and calm.

"Are you bewitching me, Squire?"

3

The Tower in the Snow

At her stunned silence, his lips twisted in a snarl that emphasized his large eyeteeth. "Are you trying to maze me?"

"No, sir!"

His voice was menacingly soft. "You were in my thoughts."

"I wasn't trying to attack you. I swear, Alten." She couldn't take her eyes from the sword point. "I, I just . . . wanted to see how you worked that sword form." Spoken aloud, her reasons sounded incredibly foolish. She almost didn't believe them herself.

Kyrkenall's rages were a matter of record. He'd never attacked one of his own, as far as she knew, but maybe none of them had ever done something so idiotic.

She met his eyes, determined to accept what she had brought upon herself.

At last, scowling, Kyrkenall lowered Irion. Elenai was too mortified to feel much relief. How could she have been so stupid?

Kyrkenall stared at her with those eerie, pupilless eyes. His voice was brittle with anger. "Asrahn singled you out, Squire. That meant he thought you had promise. That he felt you were honorable. Does an honorable person weave someone without their permission?" He spoke as if to a child.

Of course they didn't. "No. No, sir."

"I might have killed you," he said slowly. His eyes were black embers. "Only an enemy steals thoughts."

"I'm sorry." And she truly was. She fought the tears that threatened to further humiliate her.

He sighed in disgust. "It's a good thing you're so inept."

She winced a little at that, for she'd been proud of her spell work mere moments before.

"It makes me fairly sure you're telling the truth," he muttered. "No veteran weaver would get her identity muddled with her subject."

She felt a flush creep over her cheeks. Of course. He'd seen her thoughts while she focused on his.

Kyrkenall strode away and thrust the sword roughly into the cabinet. There was a solid thunk as he slammed it against the wall above the support pegs—hardly the sort of behavior one should evidence toward a weapon so revered. Desperate to change the topic, she dared to mouth a question. "Is there something wrong with Irion, Alten?"

His answer was sharp. "It's a fine blade." He extended a hand. "My bow, if you please."

"Oh. Right. Sorry." She hurried over to pass it on.

Kyrkenall took back the magnificent weapon, frowning. "I hope this was instructive to you. In more than one way. Pass on my apologies to Sareel about the glass. Tell her . . . oh, I don't care. She thinks I'm crazy anyway."

He turned halfway down the corridor. "If anyone wants to find me, tell them I'll be at N'lahr's."

"Sir?"

He paused, speaking more slowly. "His tomb, Squire. I'll be at his tomb. I didn't make it back to raise a goblet on his birthday."

As he started down the hall, Elenai suddenly knew she'd never see him again. He'd wandered into her life like a storm and would blow out and away into the wilds.

She remained beside the broken case, ashamed that she should conduct herself so poorly during the moment it mattered most. The tears that threatened earlier flowed freely now. She didn't know what she should do. Shame rooted her to inaction.

Probably parade participants were on their way back to the city by now. What would she tell the others about her wholly conspicuous departure from the ranks? What should she do about this mess?

It took her longer than she'd have liked to compose herself and track down an exasperated Sareel to report that Irion's case was broken. Judging by the caretaker's outrage at viewing the damage, Elenai dully assumed ill consequences would follow before day's end. She supposed she deserved whatever befell, as roundabout retribution. By the time she led Aron back to the stable and groomed him, she saw the rest of the Altenerai and squires returning with their mounts.

She wasn't in the mood to see any of them, not even Elik, so she quickly finished up, took the long way around the stables, and retreated up the back stairs to her quarters.

When she opened the door to her room, she was startled to find two visitors already within. The stranger at her window was a slim blond woman in a khalat with red piping—Mage Auxiliary. Alten Cargen sat in profile on her mattress rubbing the fringe of beard on his chin. He was another of the five newest Altenerai, promoted under Commander Denaven after the war. She didn't remember seeing him in the parade.

With all else that had happened, she had completely forgotten the commander was sending a magical tutor to speak with her. "Why now?" she groaned inwardly, but nonetheless saluted Cargen and the woman both, because she assumed a tutor worthy of such respect and she wasn't certain of protocol. She hoped her eyes weren't noticably red but resisted the urge to lower them.

"Forgive us, Squire," the woman said kindly. "We didn't wish to wait in the hallway." The woman had strong, even features, with a slim nose and bright blue eyes. Something about her was familiar. "I'm Exalt M'lahna," she said. "I believe you know my sister, Alten Gyldara."

"Oh, yes. Of course. It's an honor," she managed, struggling a little with this soft-spoken woman's resemblance to their blunt, open alten. The straight nose and full lips were somehow less striking upon M'lahna, as though the sculptor who'd shaped them both had stretched those features too far upon the mage. Elenai smiled to disguise her discomfort. "Would you like me to fetch you some water? I'm afraid mine isn't that fresh." She'd drawn it from the well yesterday evening.

"How thoughtful," Cargen said, though he didn't sound as if he meant it. He sat stiffly, partly turned away from her. "This isn't a social visit, though. We need to ask you some important questions. Please, close the door behind you."

"Forgive Cargen's manner." M'lahna's voice was soothing. "He's been in a foul mood since he looked the wrong way sparring yesterday evening."

He frowned. A fresh bruise discolored his right cheek.

Disconcerted, Elenai reached behind her to shut the door. The space was awkwardly close.

"I'm sorry to bother you on such short notice," M'lahna continued, "and to intrude upon your room. I've been looking forward to meeting you before I start your tutoring, and then this sad matter turned up. One of the other squires told us he thought you were already back, so we waited."

Sad matter? "It's fine." Elenai hoped she didn't sound as troubled as she felt. "Commander Denaven said you wished to speak with me. I'd thought it would be later this afternoon, or I'd be better prepared."

"We've had to accelerate our plans," Cargen said sardonically. His companion gave him a dark look, and he fell silent.

"We hope only to take a little of your time," the exalt said. "Please, make yourself comfortable."

There was no place to perch apart from the bunk and the chest at its foot, so she stood at the door. She tried to make a joke of it. "I'm afraid I don't have much furniture."

"Your commander speaks well of you," M'lahna said, ignoring the levity. "And he said that you were honored yesterday, by Asrahn."

"Yes." Elenai was pretty sure at the moment that she was unworthy of Asrahn's regard, or she wouldn't have bungled things so humiliatingly with Kyrkenall.

"He took you with him to see Irion," Cargen broke in blandly. For a panicked heartbeat, Elenai thought the Master of Squires must have heard of her conduct and conveyed his disappointment, but that didn't quite seem right. "Did he say anything to you yesterday that was particularly memorable?"

Again with the questioning about her interaction with Asrahn and the sword. There was something important here that she didn't really grasp. "No, not really. Alten Asrahn isn't very talkative."

"Wasn't," Cargen corrected.

Wait. Why was he speaking of Alten Asrahn in the past tense? "Your pardon?" Elenai asked.

The alten looked at her as though she were stupid. "He's dead."

"What?" The question leapt from her mouth, bereft of both decorum and wit.

"He was found in the river right after the parade got under way. How could you not hear?" Cargen sounded personally affronted by her ignorance.

Elenai felt the blood drain from her face. Kyrkenall's odd behavior, the questions, the memory of Asrahn . . . *Kyrkenall had known.* How?

"I'm sorry," M'lahna said. "We thought you knew. I thought word had been sent to the ridge."

Elenai steadied herself against the wall. She and Kyrkenall must have left before the messenger arrived. "He's dead? You mean he drowned?"

"That's what it looks like," Cargen answered readily.

The enormity of the news proved elusive, as though she were trying to clutch a fish in a dark stream. Alten Asrahn, dead! She'd worried about his absence, but realized she'd only imagined temporary troubles—secret state business, urgent personal burden, or at worst a temporary illness. Not gone forever. Asrahn was central to the primary purpose of her life, to the defense of the five realms. It was impossible to envision drills on the practice field without him there, in the sun, spear straight, calling instructions, setting them in motion, scrutinizing, correcting. Forming them into the finest warriors in all the realms, setting them well-prepared against kobalin and

Naor and monstrosities dredged up from the Shifting Lands since before she was born. In a very real way he had built the Altenerai Corps, at least in its present form. He *was* the corps. How could it endure without him? "When? And how did it happen?"

"We're not certain," M'lahna went on. "Right now we're trying to talk to the people who last saw him alive."

"And you're one of them," Alten Cargen finished.

"He was fine when I saw him." Elenai found herself hoping this was some dreadful mistake, and knowing it wasn't. "We weren't anywhere near the river." Her voice failed her. She reached up to brush her cheek, where she found new tears. "Forgive me." Damn.

"Your grief honors him," the woman said. "I hope you don't think it too obtrusive if I look at your memories about your last encounter with the alten?"

That was a troubling thought. "Why do you need to do that?"

"I want to see if there's something you might have missed in your last interaction."

"I suppose so." Elenai couldn't think of what that might be, but she was ready to assist the investigation in any way possible. Maybe they'd find something that would make sense of all this.

"I want you to relax, and I'll ask questions. You just close your eyes and picture what happened as I talk to you."

Elenai did as she was bade, pretending that she felt no discomfort, and as M'lahna spoke with her about Asrahn and what he'd said the day before, she relived the moments in her mind.

After a little while, as she was recalling Asrahn's inspections of the sword, M'lahna interrupted.

"Did I see a memory of someone else using Irion?"

"That was probably Alten Kyrkenall." Elenai opened her eyes. "He took out the sword himself today."

Cargen's head lifted.

M'lahna's gaze was suddenly intent, and her magical focus came across as a kind of spiritual pressure. "What did he say?"

Elenai hesitated, but at the exalt's sympathetic look she relented. "I upset him. He was trying out the sword, like Alten Asrahn had done, and I wanted to see how he performed the weapon form so well. I tried to observe his thoughts," she admitted, shamefaced. "And he noticed."

They didn't seem at all troubled about her humiliating breach. "Go on," M'lahna urged. "Close your eyes again and tell me what you saw."

"Mostly Kyrkenall fighting beside Asrahn, in the past." She imagined

M'lahna peering at the same images that rose to her as she spoke, but the sorceress was so skilled she didn't detect any sense of her. "I didn't learn anything at all about the sword form," she finished.

"What happened then?"

Was that a note of irritation in M'lahna's voice?

"He schooled me in manners. I wouldn't have weaved him without leave, normally; I was just curious." Elenai instantly regretted adding the unnecessary justification.

"But did he say anything else about the sword, or Asrahn?" Cargen sounded testy.

"I asked him if there was something wrong with the sword, and he said no."

M'lahna tried a final time. "You're sure Kyrkenall didn't say anything else, about Asrahn and the sword?"

"Well, he asked me what Alten Asrahn had said to me, yesterday. Like you." Elenai opened her eyes.

The exalt smiled encouragingly. "I think that's enough, Elenai. Thank you."

"I hope it was helpful. Did you learn anything?"

Neither answered that. "Do you know where Kyrkenall is, right now?" the man asked.

"He said he was going to pay his respects at N'lahr's tomb."

Cargen exchanged a swift look with M'lahna, who climbed to her feet. "Thank you. You've been very helpful. I'll look forward to starting our training. Tomorrow afternoon at about this time?"

"Yes," Elenai answered hollowly. How could they be making plans? As though this were some kind of normal day. "That will be fine."

Cargen was feeling his cheek as he stood. "We'd best get moving."

The weaver nodded quickly. "Thank you for your assistance, Elenai."

"Of course." She sidled out of the way as Cargen opened the door for M'lahna.

"Farewell, Squire." And with those words, Cargen departed. The door clicked shut behind them.

It had been such an innocuous phrase, but the words rang forcefully in her head, for it was the last thing the Master of Squires had said to her when he'd left the sword in her care. The last words she would ever hear him speak.

Her mind whirled. The tears kept flowing and she couldn't leave off thinking about the troubled expression on Asrahn's face when he studied the famous blade. His expression hadn't been that different from Kyrkenall's.

Why had both been so interested in it? For that matter, why were Cargen and M'lahna? The investigators charged with looking into the causes of Asrahn's death seemed more worried about his interaction with the blade than the circumstances of his demise.

Come to think of it, Commander Denaven had been very interested in Asrahn's encounter with Irion as well.

What was the connection?

Odd, wasn't it, that Cargen's face was heavily bruised? Why would an alten be sparring the night before the parade?

It might be that he was just blowing off steam, relieving some tension. And yet . . . he and M'lahna had been *so* curious about the sword, and then fascinated to learn of Kyrkenall's interest, and his location.

Surely not. As an unthinkable explanation clicked into place, she found herself opening her storage chest and grabbing the wineskin N'lahr had given her long years before. It was empty, but she wanted it anyway. She splashed stale water from her pitcher into the bowl then rubbed her face vigorously before leaving her room. She supposed she should change from her parade armor and best boots, but didn't turn back.

It might all be innocent coincidence. She found herself striding for the stables nonetheless. Even if there were nothing strange underway, it would do no harm to ride out and talk to Kyrkenall. She would simply go to N'lahr's tomb and tell him what had happened. She could apologize again and offer condolences for the loss. After all, Kyrkenall had squired with Asrahn, too. And, she recalled, they had fought together at both of the Battles of Kanesh. Clearly he had been upset by the sudden death. But how had Kyrkenall known for sure? And what if her fears were real . . . and she had told them right where to find him! She quickened her steps.

Her horse was reluctant to leave, as if he knew he'd already completed the assigned work that day. But no one challenged her exit from the stables or the palace complex; she was an upper-ranked squire, and she was off duty.

She rode too slowly, the streets packed with visitors despite grumbling gray clouds crowding one upon the other overhead. A few heavy heralding drops met exposed skin.

She thought she'd feel better when she left the north wall behind and pushed on into the country, but as the skies rumbled more insistently she worried she was already too late. She kicked the horse into a gallop.

Aron was one of the Penarda geldings, bred for endurance, but even he was winded after the tense ride and the push up the switchback path to the cemetery. Elenai left him on the track, puffing and lowering his head to a patch of clover near a willow. She hurried through the somber monuments. Thunder rolled on as she noted between looming tombs that clouds draped the distant city in blotted shadows.

"Alten? Alten Kyrkenall?" Her voice rose, but only the wind answered. A shifting noise surprised her on the left, but she discovered only a dun horse—another Penarda—staring at her with upturned ears. Kyrkenall's mount. The mare considered her with an almost human interest before she returned to cropping grass alongside Alten Kerwyn's tomb. The animal snorted at a distant flash of lightning but didn't leave off eating. Elenai guessed that meant all was well. The rain began a broken patter against the homes of the dead.

Elenai walked farther down the narrow path toward N'lahr's tomb and saw a light shining within. The stone door stood unlocked and open. Only someone with an Altenerai sapphire could access a military crypt, so Kyrkenall must be nearby.

She called again and leaned in, seeing a sarcophagus ringed by benches built into the surrounding three walls. But there was no one except the still stone form carved upon the marble casket lid. In the stark lamplight, under storm and doubt, the image of the dead general struck her as sinister and unworldly. The lantern in the corner rested near seven wine bottles, most of them quite dusty.

But there was no Kyrkenall. She stepped out and looked to the right. "Alten?"

"What are you doing here?"

The question came just behind her ear, and it wasn't Kyrkenall. She whirled, hand falling to her hilt . . . and then she found another voice within her mind, holding her hand in place, suggesting she move forward. This confused her, and while she wrestled with contrary impulses her body obeyed.

The questioner proved to be Cargen, and beside him stood an unfamiliar man, strikingly well-built and handsome save for two prominent front teeth. He was dressed in one of the Mage Auxiliary khalats with its red piping along cuff, sleeves, and shoulders. An exalt. His fingers were raised, and twitched almost as though he pulled at some unseen thread. He was practicing his magecraft on her.

Cargen nervously looked to left and right as the sorcerer marched her out to the little clear spot nearer the tomb of Kerwyn.

"What are you doing here?" he demanded again.

She hesitated, realizing she was once more in command of her own senses, though she felt the mage's presence hovering at the back of her thoughts like a light hand upon her shoulder. "Looking for Alten Kyrkenall."

Cargen's frown was lopsided on his scoffing face. "Obviously. Why?"

She wasn't sure how to answer, then gasped, feeling lightheaded as the sense of the other presence upon her thoughts pressed harder.

"She feels fear," the stranger said in a deep, even voice. "For herself. She thinks she's betrayed Kyrkenall. Thinks you might be involved in Asrahn's death." The sorcerer's tone changed, growing suddenly waspish. "I warned you to stay out of sight until you healed. M'lahna could have handled it on her own."

Cargen scowled at him, then at her. "You shouldn't have come, girl. Disappearing Kyrkenall is easy. Explaining *you* is another matter."

She saw what happened from the corner of her eye. An object sprouted suddenly from the exalt's mouth with an explosion of red and white she realized were teeth and blood. The mage's presence in her mind fell away as he dropped, choking, clawing at the black-feathered shaft that transfixed his face. Elenai was too shocked to understand exactly what she was seeing until Cargen drew his blade and shouted a warning: "Kyrkenall's here!"

Elenai stepped back and pulled her own sword. She meant only to defend herself, but as Cargen closed she realized he'd seen it as a challenge.

"You're no match for me," he promised.

"You might be wrong." She was surprised by the sound of her own bravado.

She parried his first strike without thinking, worried then about what Alten Tretton had once told them—it's usually the warrior who strikes first who wins. But where could she strike, when her opponent wore the vaunted Altenerai armor? He was open only at the calf and the wrist and the head. His neck was partly shielded by the high stiff collar.

"I'm stronger than you, Squire. My armor's better, my blade is finer, and I can outlast you."

She narrowed her eyes and tapped her fingers along the hilt, bringing to mind the little mask of a terror-stricken face hung from the necklace beneath her uniform. She hadn't learned to properly cast without a focusing agent, so wore several useful talismans at all times.

She sent him fear.

Cargen's sapphire ring lit, and he smirked. "You think to distract me with a feeble weaving?"

From close at hand came a scream of agony, and from almost behind the alten, in the darkness, a cackle of mad laughter. As Kyrkenall was said to laugh. But it didn't sound merry or gallant as the sagas had it, not in the least.

Elenai twisted to the side as Cargen thrust, and what would have been a killing blow to her throat hit her armored shoulder. She struck as he pulled away, driving the point of her sword into his hand.

Cargen dropped his blade, and she grinned, as much in relief as pride. The alten advanced anyway, kicking up with one foot to drive her sword arm back.

Used to sparring exercises, her instinct was to raise a hand to block a second kick before she realized she wasn't in the practice yards. They weren't switching into hand-to-hand exercises. She had a sword, and should use it.

This realization came the same moment Cargen hopped to his other foot and lashed out to clip her chin with his boot. She staggered back, blinking away darkness and stars. There was pain, too, but it was the dizziness she couldn't ignore. He pounced on his dropped sword and grabbed it with his off hand.

"Now . . ." Cargen said, then yelped and tripped over a long black stick.

Not a stick, she understood, but an arrow protruding through his right boot. The alten spun to confront a swift-moving figure behind him, but staggered awkwardly on his wounded leg.

His opponent was Kyrkenall, who parried a weak blade strike with a careless flick of his recurved ebon bow. The archer stepped in close and drove the palm of his hand into Cargen's bruised cheekbone. Cargen fell over his opponent's extended foot and sprawled face upward on the grave-yard soil even as water rushed in earnest from dark skies.

Kyrkenall tossed the beautiful bow aside and it landed only a foot or two to Elenai's left, close enough for her to glimpse the immaculately carved warriors struggling on its surface. He freed his sword, a long slim arc of blue steel, and suspended it over Cargen's throat.

The alten spoke in a strange, singsongy way. If this was one of the famed, spontaneous verses she'd heard so much about, Elenai decided it was more chilling than inspiring. "The battle's over, and the Gods retire. None fled, all dead, save you. The liar."

Though wincing in pain, a deadly weapon held to him, Cargen's face screwed up contentiously where he lay. "I'm no liar."

Kyrkenall's tone was taut with contempt. "You put the lie to all you pro-fess to serve."

Elenai thought herself unnoticed until Kyrkenall called to her, though he didn't look back. "Squire, are you wounded?"

She briefly thought of saying something jaunty, but she was still breathless, and a little stunned. "I'm all right," she managed. Her voice sounded tinny and far off, even to her. "Alten Asrahn is dead."

"Yes," he said darkly. "We spoke earlier of etiquette, Squire. Now's not the time. Put your skills to use as I put him to the question. You, liar, remove your ring."

"I'd die before doing so," Cargen asserted.

Kyrkenall's answer was startlingly venomous as he hissed, "So would Asrahn. I spoke with the guard who found him. He told me Asrahn had no ring." He cut the air inches from Cargen's ear. "He was a hero—you're nothing but a puffed-up bootlicker unfit to muck his stalls." His voice rose, fury barely checked. "Now, take off the ring or I'll cut off your rutting hand!" As Kyrkenall's volume pitched, Cargen fumbled with his ring and dropped it onto the wet soil.

"Now, Squire," Kyrkenall directed.

Elenai began to wonder if he actually knew her name. But she reached out with a thread of intent, bending her senses so that she might see the prone man's thoughts.

"Why'd you kill him?" Kyrkenall demanded.

Cargen didn't answer. The images swirled and she perceived him in argument with M'lahna. "They had to silence him," Elenai said, aghast. "He drowned when he tried to escape—"

Kyrkenall's tone was cutting. "You took his ring, mazed him, and threw him in the river, didn't you?"

The reply was shrill. "I answer only to the commander—"

Kyrkenall cut him off with a shout. "Where's the real sword?"

The sudden shift sent the visions swirling. A memory swam up before her.

"You getting anything, Squire?" Kyrkenall demanded over the din of rain.

"Images only—"

An electric surge of sorcerous energy coursed through her, the like of which she'd never felt before. And there was a voice. Elenai didn't hear it, exactly, but its command vibrated through to the very core of her being. She was told to drop, and she knew that she must, and so she slumped without question, and as the voice told her to lay still and sleep she started to do this, too. Except that her hand contacted something hard that sent a shock wave through the enveloping tide of weariness.

Her fingers had landed upon the great black bow, Arzhun, and at the touch clarity came to her. She clutched the warm and stiff arch, as a drowning woman clasps for timber in the water, and she lay listening while her senses settled. She was lying in damp earth, water pouring from the skies and into heretofore dry areas of her body.

Kyrkenall had frozen rigidly in place as the weaver M'lahna crept up beside Cargen, now awkwardly pawing the mud for his ring. She wore soft leather boots and a hooded rain cloak over her red-trimmed khalat. She carried no weapon but for a glittering shapeless stone held in one hand, a mix of moonlight and silver and diamonds and all shining beautiful things that had ever been.

"You're just as deadly as the tales say," she purred to Kyrkenall. Her face was contorted into a mockery of a smile.

Cargen sat up fully and fought with shaking fingers to slide his ring back into place.

"And as reckless," she continued.

"And as handsome," Kyrkenall offered through gritted teeth, straining. He didn't move. Elenai doubted he could.

"You're broken, Alten," the exalt continued. "I truly regretted having to kill Asrahn, but you . . . you're an arrogant, contemptuous rules breaker. If you weren't a war hero you'd already have been drummed out of the corps. While you're wandering around trading your fame for drinks and sex we're risking our lives, our very sanity, to restore the realms."

Kyrkenall's response dripped with sarcasm. "'Restoring the realms'?"

She answered with lofty irritation. "A glory seeker like you can't understand the quiet sacrifices of those brave enough to secure real peace, real order. When the Goddess is restored, there'll be no more Naor or kobalin or storms that eat our borders. We'll live in a true paradise. And they'll be no need to tolerate anyone like you."

Elenai sensed the pressure from the mage increase.

"But you heroes need," Kyrkenall managed, "a little murder or two, to help things along. Sounds righteous."

Elenai didn't know why the bow protected her from the full force of M'lahna's weaving, nor did she understand why she felt such an immense attraction to the shining thing in the mage's hand. Examining it with her magical sight, she discovered that M'lahna had projected all of her spell-threads through the object before they intersected with Kyrkenall. That transition strengthened each of them. Prior to encounter with the gleaming stone they were thin gold threads. After, and as they reached for the archer, they were transformed into blinding beams of energy.

If the stone enhanced the exalt's magic, it was reasonable to assume it would do the same with Elenai's. She cast a line of energy toward it. She was jolted to full clarity the moment her energies interacted with the thing, and exulted in the sense of capability and power that swept through her.

Magic was a complex and challenging endeavor, requiring vast expenditures from tiny reserves. Elenai had always likened throwing a spell to running laps. Weaving several in succession was like sprinting miles.

But touching this object gave access to a store of limitless magical energy with little endurance loss. Despite her fear, a smile touched her lips. She felt among the talismans hung from her necklace. Each was a small silver mask carved with an exaggerated emotion. Fear, fatigue, confusion, bravery, sorrow, joy. Elenai found the wide, downturned mouth of fear just as M'lahna somehow sensed her intrusion.

She saw the shock on the woman's face and sent her fear. The exalt twisted her head as if shaking it to stay awake, then countered with another command to sleep. A wave of somnolence rushed against Elenai and set her blinking.

Kyrkenall struck while the exalt's attention wavered.

M'lahna cried out when the sword was driven through her wrist but not when the same silvery blue weapon crossed her neck a heartbeat later. She dropped, a hideous mess that had been a beautiful living creature. The shining object tumbled to earth with her dead hand and her fingers twitched in the mud.

Elenai clambered to her feet, the black bow, Arzhun, clutched unnecessarily tight.

The archer advanced on Cargen, who'd been fumbling with a bandage. He struggled in alarm to fully rise on his good leg, trying to grasp the hilt of a knife at his belt. He fell back to the mud the moment Kyrkenall's sword came again to his throat.

"This seems familiar, doesn't it?" Kyrkenall followed the injured man down with the point of his blade. He might have meant to appear playful, but to Elenai's mind he sounded merciless. He raised his voice. "You all right back there, Squire?"

"I am," she answered with a shaking voice. She actually thought she was going to throw up.

"Did you pull anything out of his memory when I asked about Irion?"

"A tower on a cliff edge, in the snow," she answered. "Skies behind. There was a flag flying—"

"Red and white?" Kyrkenall suggested.

He was right. "Yes."

Cargen sneered. "That's not where the sword is."

"You forget I already know you're a liar."

"We'll hunt you down."

Kyrkenall laughed.

"You'll get nothing more from me."

"There's not much else I want. Except perhaps to carry a message. Tell your leaders I'll expose them. That whatever they build, I will tear down. That whomever they slay, I shall avenge. Tell them . . ." He smiled terrifyingly. "You know what? I'll just leave them a fucking note."

Kyrkenall drove the sword through Cargen's throat. As the alten fell back, there were two bright arcs of blood in swift succession, mingling with the downpour.

The sight of it set Elenai retching. She hadn't recalled eating quite so much rice as came up. Amid the changed, impossible world, she seized upon the peculiar detail that so many of the grains remained intact.

She found herself kneeling in the mud and vomited again, and she was still there, contemplating the mess, when Kyrkenall splashed up to her. His boots stopped just outside the disgusting rain-splattered pool.

"Elenai, isn't it?" he asked; then at her weak nod, continued conversationally, "That was you, wasn't it? Interfering with the woman's weaving?"

She nodded weakly.

"So you see the fundamental flaw with bringing those cursed hearthstones into a battle—no good when there's an opposing weaver nearby. Nice timing, though."

"What," she said, her voice a croaking parody of itself, "is a hearthstone?"

"You're better off not knowing."

She blinked up at him and discovered he was wiping his rain-bathed sword, carefully, on a scrap of cloth. He then sheathed the blade and bent down. She thought at first he meant to offer his hand and planned to say she was too weak to stand, but he instead lifted his bow and inspected it.

"Do you know," he continued, as if they were simply having an exchange over dinner and weren't surrounded by twisted bodies, "in the old days, N'lahr or Decrin or Kalandra were always there to pull me out of the fire. Or Asrahn," he added, his voice shaken for a brief moment. "That would have been it for me if you weren't here."

She eventually managed to climb to her feet and discovered Kyrkenall was watching her. There was pity in his voice. "You shouldn't have come."

"I wanted to warn you," she objected. "They came to question me. I told them where you were."

"Of course you did."

She wasn't sure she'd heard him clearly until he offered a thin smile and an explanation. "I made sure a few knew where I was going, and then it was just a matter of waiting. Although I hadn't expected them to bring a hearthstone." Kyrkenall studied the sapphire ring glowing on his finger until it winked out.

She could only stare at him. "You used me to draw them out?"

He smirked. "Why did you fear for me?"

"I just . . . How did you know Alten Asrahn was dead?"

"Nothing would keep him from his proper place. Nothing. Duty was everything to Asrahn." His hand tightened again into a fist. She saw it was shaking, and watched him stare at it until it stilled.

"How'd you know Cargen was behind it?"

"I didn't until he came to kill me."

She shook her head. It was all too much. Kyrkenall bent and began rummaging through the garments of the deceased.

"What are you going to do now?"

"First, I'm going to drag these four into N'lahr's tomb. That might slow things down for a day or two. If the rain comes hard it might even conceal the tracks."

She involuntarily gasped at the profane suggestion. "You're going to put them with N'lahr?"

"He would have thought it was funny."

"Wait—you said four. There're only three here."

"There's another alten I killed around back. Surely you heard the scream. K'narr shifted at the last moment." Kyrkenall sounded a little irked that the dead man had spoiled his shot.

Not Alten K'narr. He had always been so nice, so . . . well, gallant. If he had been involved, could that mean that other Altenerai were as well?

"Alten, what's going on?"

"I really can't say."

"Can't, or won't?"

"I'm not as mysterious as you might suppose—I don't know."

"Why would Alten Cargen and these people kill Alten Asrahn?"

Kyrkenall paused with his hand in Cargen's side pouch. "Apparently, it's about the sword. Asrahn didn't think it was the right one. He told me about it last night. And this lot killed him for it. And would have killed us as well."

"But why's the sword so important to them?"

He looked at her as though she were foolish. "It's *the* sword, isn't it? The one fashioned for the killing of kings. Rialla told N'lahr he'd kill Mazakan with it, and supposedly even Mazakan's been frightened of it ever since."

That added an extra piece of information to what Elenai had always been told about the sword's power to thwart the Naor leader. And she thought the name of Rialla sounded familiar, but she couldn't place it. He must have seen the confusion in her look.

"Everyone pretends the prophecy was really about the sword, not about the sword and N'lahr. They weren't there. I heard what was said." He shook his head. "It's no good without him to use it. Now why anyone would kill Asrahn for questioning its authenticity or what they're doing with the real sword, and how it links up with that nonsense about making a paradise I just can't guess. Yet."

"Is the sword on display a copy, then?"

"I think so. My bow and my sword were altered by the same weaver who helped forge Irion, and the sword in the hall feels different from both. I can only guess because I never wielded it. I'm deferring to Asrahn on that. Varama might be able to tell us more, but that would require a ride back in to Darassus, and I don't think I'll be returning anytime soon."

"Why?"

He laughed without humor. "You think it ends here?"

Stupid. With a moment's more reflection she realized that without knowing which of the remaining Altenerai were involved, Kyrkenall might step right into a trap if he returned to the palace. "Do you know who's behind it, Alten?"

Kyrkenall's lips twisted. "I'd say the queen. She was always a big one for secrets. And the Mage Auxiliary is pretty clearly involved. They're the queen's pets. I don't think it was just these two. I wouldn't be surprised if our dear commander's in on it, maybe all the new Altenerai. I hope none of the old guard," he muttered.

"I think Commander Denaven might know something about it, sir," she said slowly. "He was asking me about the sword today. I think he wanted to know if I'd been told anything by Asrahn."

"Right. So he *is* involved. Deciding if he needed to kill you."

He sounded so matter-of-fact. She tried to imitate the same manner. "I suppose so. I can't believe he'd agree to killing Asrahn, though. Asrahn was . . . Asrahn trained him. He was loyal to the queen and the realms." As her voice grew raw with emotion, she fell silent.

"Asrahn was loyal to the code, to the laws," Kyrkenall corrected. "And Denaven's always been an ass," he added.

She wasn't sure how to respond to that. Hadn't Denaven and Kyrkenall been friends? Could the commander of the Altenerai really be involved in murder? She was at a loss. "So . . . what do we do?"

"I'm afraid you can't return to Darassus."

She hadn't quite reasoned that yet, though she knew the truth of it as he said the words.

He explained, pointedly as if expecting protest, "They'll find the bodies, sooner or later. And then they'll look into all the doings connected with this group. And their successors will question all those that these questioned. They would come to you, and weave your thoughts, and learn what you'd seen, then kill you."

It wasn't easy to accept. So much had changed in but a single day.

She turned from him and considered the city even as a lightning bolt forked in the distance, lighting the gilded domes. The city, she thought, looked rather like the tombs that lay behind her. "What am I to do?"

"For now? Ride with me."

Despite the horror, and the confusion, she felt her heart lighten. To her knowledge, no one had ever squired with Kyrkenall, probably the most enigmatic champion in five realms. "Where are we going? To that tower?"

"Aye," Kyrkenall said darkly. "I'm going to rip that sword out of the Chasm Tower and carry it against them. I'll avenge Asrahn and stop their conspiracy if I have to carve open a thousand of them to do it."

4

Storm Ride

Dull white light suffused the whole of the landscape—the strange blue-stemmed bushes on her right, the gold sand, the black stones—but Elenai saw no sun. It was easy to doubt they traveled beyond the stable terrain of Erymyr for, apart from the odd scrub, the land features resembled country about its capital, Darassus. Even the wind-clawed clouds in the gray sky looked normal, but there really was no sun. It wasn't hidden behind clouds, or sinking, or rising, it simply wasn't there. And that meant, bright as things were, that there were no shadows. How, she wondered, did someone moving through the Shifting Lands gauge the passage of time?

Out in the wild areas between the five realms fashioned by the Gods, there was no knowing when a sun would rise, what characteristics it would have, or even if it would rise at all. The landscape might lie unchanged for a month, or a day, then transform entirely. She'd never traveled the Shifting Lands without a dedicated guide and had never glimpsed the horrors that were standard story fare on such journeys. Nothing moved out here besides herself, Kyrkenall, and their mounts, but Elenai kept constant watch for monsters, things born of madness that defied the rules of ordinary reality.

Kyrkenall rode ahead, seemingly untroubled, though his ring glittered at full strength.

At the thought of it, Elenai looked down to the band about her own finger, the back side of the ring that brightened her blue khalat where its light escaped her palm. Kyrkenall had taken both Cargen's and K'narr's, pocketing one and bestowing the other upon her. Too many had been lost through the years, he'd said, and he wasn't about to leave these in the hands of their enemies.

While Elenai could scarce remember a time when she hadn't craved the badges of Altenerai office, she'd expected to earn them, not to have them handed to her freshly looted from a murderer's corpse. She thought it inappropriate to wear a ring with the stone showing, so she'd turned its face. Regrettably there was no way to disguise the iconic khalat. Cargen's garment was broader and shorter than ideal, but still far lighter and more flexible than her squire's armor. Kyrkenall had insisted she wear it, bloodstains or no. She would, he had told her last night, need its protection when they were followed, just as she would need the magical shield of the ring.

Elenai had noted even then his assurance that they would be followed. He apparently had no doubt.

Kyrkenall had said the tower lay along Erymyr's lonely, mountainous northern edge, so she'd been puzzled when they rode more westerly.

"We've got to confuse them," he'd explained. "So long as we're in Erymyr they can send message birds ahead and requisition fresh mounts from staging posts. It's harder to track people through the shifts. We'll divert into them and ride just outside the border before we angle back in for the northern peninsula. With any luck that will slow the pursuit so we get to the tower first."

She supposed that made sense, though Kyrkenall seemed to take travel in the wilds a lot more casually than anyone else she'd ever met. They had to ride hard, well into the night, before they exited into the Shifting Lands, a shorter journey than during his youth, Kyrkenall had commented. They'd continued to trek into an unrelenting "day," with no breaks for rest, and weariness weighed on her. Elenai had no idea how used she was to regular meals and sleep until she was without them. She ached in unfamiliar parts of her back and legs, and her thoughts meandered sluggishly in fruitless circles of unanswered questions. Kyrkenall remained silent here, so Elenai imitated his example. She expected he was concentrating on unseen dangers, or calculating their next moves.

Some several hours on, or so it seemed, they halted. Kyrkenall led them to a high dry spot, poured water into an eelskin bowl, and offered it to his horse. While the animal drank greedily, the archer sipped from a worn looking wineskin.

Elenai slipped stiffly down from Aron, arranged water for him in the metal helm they'd pulled off Alten K'narr's body, and joined Kyrkenall in the consideration of the horizon. She resisted the urge to collapse to the invitingly verdant ground, hopeful that she'd rest easier knowing more of his plans.

"Do you feel that?" he asked.

He wasn't touching her or even looking at her, so she supposed he meant using her other senses. Was there some danger here? Wary, she exerted more effort than usual to reach out through the inner world. Everything in the Shifting Lands felt . . . tenuous. It *looked* real, like a carefully crafted stage backdrop, but she was worried that if she probed too hard she might accidentally puncture a hole through the simulated reality. Was that even possible? But she detected no imminent threat.

"Do you mean the Shifting Lands?" she asked him.

"Yes."

"I've felt their energies before, but I've never journeyed as deep. Not without a guide." Was he trying to introduce her to elementary sciences? Why weren't they discussing more urgent matters, like how close he thought the pursuers were and what conspiracy might really be under way and what they were going to do when they reached the tower?

"Try again." He stamped his right foot, twice, upon the ground. "We're on a splinter. A tiny one, no more than a half mile wide. It's real. Feel without weaving. You've got to be able to sense these things."

Elenai did as she was bade, and swiftly grew frustrated. It was difficult not to use her inborn connection to the inner world, and draining whenever she inadvertently did. She cleared her throat and ventured a thought. "Alten, maybe you're using sorcery and just don't know it."

He shot her a weary look. "Maybe you should take orders and not question them." Kyrkenall gestured back to the landscape and took another swig.

She was too exasperated to try again. "Are we going to make stop for the day? And how do you even know when a day is over?"

Infuriatingly, he ignored her query and inserted one of his own. "Why are you so angry all of a sudden?"

"Why am I . . ." She spluttered in disbelief. She hadn't meant to sound angry, but now that he mentioned it . . . "I pledged my life to the Altenerai and now I'm on the run and probably hunted by them, an enemy to the crown!" His derisive snort angered her even further. "But you're just talking to me about the Shifting Lands! *How are we going to clear our names?*"

Kyrkenall replaced the container at his side, frowning. "Things didn't quite work out the way you wanted. I do sympathize. Really. They didn't work out the way Asrahn wanted, either." His mocking tone stung her. "How nice it would be if you could simply close your eyes and live in that placid little bubble where you thought everything was perfectly fine. Here's the thing, Squire. It wasn't. It hasn't been 'fine' for a very, very long time. You just didn't know."

Kyrkenall barely paused for a breath, sounding angry himself.

"Shift storms raging all the damn time somewhere and belching out monsters to rampage the fringe. The Naor raiding with near impunity. And not only does our queen do nothing to protect the people of the outer realms, she actually weakens us futher by having her pet Denaven siphon off our best mages and equipment to that auxiliary of hers." He'd grown more agitated as he spoke, as if he lectured an invisible audience rather than her alone. "Why do you think so many of the old guard stay away? Only Tretton, Varama, and Asrahn, the 'duty first' diehards, station themselves in the center—and Tretton's off on patrol as much as he can be."

"But Commander Denaven—"

Kyrkenall cut her off. "Why do you think Decrin and Cerai and Enada are usually off on the frontier? Why do you think Belahn's in The Fragments, and Aradel resigned?"

Almost she retorted it was because Belahn was old and Enada was battle hungry. While Elenai was still struggling with an answer, he spoke on, sounding a little more conciliatory.

"You've been dealt some surprises. But then so have our opponents. And we're making good time. Now . . ." He raised his other hand and opened his palm to reveal a little gray rock.

"What's that?"

"What do *you* think it is?"

She was worn out and annoyed, but she forced calm and resisted the impulse to consider the rock through the inner world. He seemed to want her to study it with her eyes, so she did. It was rounded and plain save for a line of white through its center. "I don't know."

"They not teach you much about traveling the shifts?"

"No, sir." She resisted the impulse to vent her frustration again.

"It's a rock from Erymyr, pulled from the Idris itself, near the edge of the city of Darassus. As long as I'm holding this, I have a sense of where Erymyr lies in relation to me. You could probably sense it better, being a magic wielder and not having to rely on a ring."

"Oh," she said. Almost she added that she knew about focusing agents, but she guessed she sounded ignorant enough already. Her necklace talismans were focusing agents of a different sort.

Kyrkenall lowered his hand and patted a small black pouch on his belt. "We all carry a collection of rocks or other things to make travel easier."

"Isn't it hard to tell the focus agents apart?"

"That's why you pick distinctive items. N'lahr used to carve little letters on his." Kyrkenall snorted. "He was terrible at this. But Kalandra—she didn't need any objects for focusing agents." He looked off into the distance and fell silent.

"Do you really think someone's following us?"

"If not, they will, eventually. I'm hoping the rain will obscure our tracks and complicate things. But I'm not counting on it. If they've recruited Tretton to follow us, he won't be slowed in the slightest. And a talented mage might be able to follow the passage we carve through the shifts. We leave a tiny echo of order until those lands change over substantially."

"Oh." Elenai was starting to suspect there was a vast amount of information out there she wasn't aware of. She was just about to ask another question when he continued.

"And we've got another problem. The hearthstone I'm carting around is still active. A weaver who knows how to look for them can hone in on it with another hearthstone and follow us practically anywhere."

She'd had no idea about that particular problem, but then she'd never heard about hearthstones until yesterday. "How easy are they to make inactive?"

"Not easy at all," Kyrkenall said grimly. "It takes great skill."

That probably explained why he hadn't brought the matter up with her. She tried not to let her disappointment show. "Why don't we just drop it?"

"Tempting." She saw his lip curl, briefly. "But I'll be damned if I'm turning it back over to *them*. What I wouldn't give to have a pair of ko'aye. We could fly to the tower far ahead of anyone else without much trace. But that wagon lost its wheels when the queen broke the treaty."

At her raised eyebrows, he sighed. "I suppose they're teaching some crap in the academy about the 'primitive' ko'aye carrying on their blood feud with the Naor after we 'chose the path of peace.' They wouldn't bother to mention the queen broke a pact with our ko'aye allies when she declared her 'peace.' We promised we'd protect their lands if they helped us, and instead she left them to be burned from their homes and hunted like animals by any Naor mini-king wanting to make a name for himself."

Elenai had heard that the ko'aye had been incapable of understanding complex ideas and that they'd abandoned civilized lands when confused by the cessation of conflict, but she didn't interrupt to say as much.

"That was the end of our alliance. I think all the ko'aye hate us at this point, except for Lelanc. Can't say as I blame them."

Elenai knew the name Lelanc. She was the feathered serpent Alten Aradel had ridden in the war. Was he suggesting the current governor of The Fragments still held the loyalty of a winged ko'aye? That was news. But, then no squires had been posted to The Fragments since Aradel resigned her commission as alten. Elenai had been told Aradel refused contact with her former comrades but a different scenario now seemed more likely. "Have you seen Aradel since the war?"

"Sure. Just last year. Why wouldn't I?" Kyrkenall fixed her with a penetrating gaze from those weird black eyes.

"We were told that Governor Aradel wanted no reminder of her former service to the Altenerai, but I suppose Commander Denaven just wanted to keep us away from her."

Kyrkenall replied more warmly, as if pleased with her insight. "Aye. We've had a good laugh or two over that particular half-truth. Aradel certainly wants nothing to do with Denaven."

He lifted an arm and pointed off toward their left. "We'll be riding that way. I want to head out a little farther until we veer back toward the Chasm Tower. If they focus in on the hearthstone and see us heading that way, they'll assume we're riding on for Kanesh, if they haven't already decided that from our tracks."

"This tower—why is it out in the middle of nowhere?"

He considered her for a moment. "You ask a lot of questions."

She wondered if he meant she was being impertinent.

But Kyrkenall's answering tone was light. "It was built generations ago, back when the Shifting Lands were less chaotic, and dangerous stuff only crawled up out of a few spots around the realms. They erected the tower near one of those places. Nowadays the currents have changed and not much happens there. Maybe," he added, "because the storms are happening everywhere else."

She nodded.

"Here's the important thing. Until now we've been close to the realm of Erymyr. That's meant that the terrain in the shifts tends to resemble the secure land nearby. As we head farther out, things might get a little strange, especially with the way the shifts have been lately. Did anyone teach you how to anchor?"

"Anchor?" She recalled reading about the term, so she wished her voice hadn't sounded so naive.

"Don't they show you anything? Look. Your core is real." He paused to tap her diaphragm, completely oblivious to, or uncaring about, the sudden invasion of her private space. "Almost nothing else around here is."

She struggled to pay attention to his words and not the flush she felt at his proximity.

"When we go into the shifting deeps you've got to hold onto your own reality. And the ring. You may even need to use the hearthstone, if things get really bad. But don't get too close to the hearthstone when you drop into the inner world."

He'd already warned her about reaching for the hearthstone. He'd yet to explain. "Why not?"

"It might grab hold and never let you go."

She felt her eyes widen. "It's alive?"

He shrugged. "Not really. But when you lean too heavily on any tool, it's a crutch. And if you get used to having a crutch, you fall over when someone yanks it away. Don't get comfortable with a hearthstone, Squire. It's seductive."

"I'll be careful," she said without knowing exactly what she guarded against. Her skin still tingled where he'd pressed her khalat to her body, and that troubled her. This was the wrong time and place for an infatuation, no matter how handsome or capable the man was.

Kyrkenall didn't seem to have noticed her reaction. "See that you are.

You've also got to start trusting your other senses. Sure, employ your sorcery, but there're things out here that detect weaving. Things you don't want to meet."

Almost she asked him for details, but she decided against it.

"Now our rest time's over, so check your horse, check your gear, and answer any needs you have. Things might start getting real interesting."

This was a rest?

Kyrkenall walked a little way down slope. As Elenai turned away to inspect Aron's horseshoes, she heard Kyrkenall whistling faintly while relieving himself.

This was not what she'd expected when she'd dreamed of riding with Altenerai champions. Somehow the plays of Selana never depicted these details. She stretched her aching muscles quickly and splashed a little water on her face.

Once they were back in the saddle, Kyrkenall struck off in the direction he'd indicated, and she tried at first to "feel," as he'd said, finding nothing at all without using sorcery. The Alten rode on, seemingly tireless, back straight, content with silence.

Elenai chewed some jerky he'd passed her and tried imagining what would be happening in Darassus. Were the squires exercising in the yard, or were they enjoying the festival? Were there funeral preparations underway for Asrahn?

How simple and beautiful that boring, steady existence had been. And she hadn't seen it. She wondered if given the opportunity to unlearn what she now knew, she would.

Asrahn would still be dead. And Altenerai had killed him. Had it just been those few, or were there other traitors among them? How and why, precisely, had it happened, and who had ordered it?

On they rode, and Aron's steady gait grew monotonous, a hypnotic lure. She longed to lie down, and she had to fight against drifting into dreams. Two things had been stressed to her about travel through the Shifting Lands. Stay alert, and spend as little time there as possible. The alten was deliberately disregarding the latter admonition, and she was struggling with the former.

Kyrkenall halted his horse and turned, looking beyond her.

She stopped and followed his gaze. The hazy blue on the horizon to their rear had darkened to indigo.

"Tell me you felt that," he said.

"No," she was forced to admit.

He studied the horizon.

"Is that a storm?" she asked.

"Yes."

"Is it going to hit us?"

"Probably." His voice was tense. "We're at least three hours out. Come on."

With a light tap he urged his mare into a canter and Elenai followed.

Her own mount began to tire only a few miles later, and Kyrkenall realized it. He cursed, slid down from his saddle, and inspected Aron's hooves and fetlocks.

Elenai watched him from her saddle as he moved around. She was too tired to think of climbing back in the saddle if she left it. "Is there something wrong with him?"

Kyrkenall shook his dark locks as he stepped back. "He's just not as seasoned as Lyria." He glanced up, his eerie black eyes unreadable. "We'd better not press. We may have to tap their reserves if that's a bad storm. Are you a praying person, Elenai?"

"Yes."

"Then offer one up." He smiled faintly. "It can't hurt anything."

This was such a peculiar sentiment that she couldn't help blurting out a question. "Don't you believe in prayer?"

Kyrkenall paused in the act of lifting his boot to his stirrup. "What *just* god would be moved to aid you only because you ask for it? Isn't that a little egotistical? If I were on high and saw you were in dire straits, should I hold off helping until you told me how great I was?" He climbed into the saddle.

She was stunned by his tone even as his words invited some agreement. "Prayer shows your respect," she managed.

"Sure. Well, prayer's good for those who believe in it. Helps them get focused. Makes them feel better. And people fight better when they feel better."

She noted that in a few short words Kyrkenall had managed to be both casually blasphemous and condescending.

The character of the land grew more rugged. They had to detour around a deep canyon too wide to jump. Elenai was sure a more experienced mage could have shaped a land bridge for them. The Shifting Lands were supposed to be easy to manipulate, but she didn't feel comfortable attempting anything so complex, and Kyrkenall didn't ask her to try.

A short while later the sky behind them was dusky gray and the wind whipped little bits of grit at their backs.

Kyrkenall looked less and less happy. The glances over his shoulder had grown more frequent. At least the prospect of peril made it easier for her to stay awake.

Finally he halted and motioned her to ride up. They sat saddle side by side, staring at the wall of black sweeping behind them.

"There's no way we'll make it to solid land before it hits us. It'll be on us in about a half hour."

That storm front looked downright frightening. A maelstom in the Shifting Lands could remake the reality around it, destroying any solid bits of ordered matter it struck in the process. "That sounds bad."

"It is. On the brighter side, it'll completely obliterate signs of our passage." He let out a little breath and swung down without touching the stirrup, motioning for her to join him. Her dismount was far stiffer and clumsier than his. "I want you to start working with the hearthstone." He dug through his saddlebag and handed over the cloth-wrapped bundle.

She hadn't expected that, and wryly supposed she should be getting used to surprise by now. She felt a ripple of energy as her hands closed on the cloth, despite not being remotely connected to the inner world. If the magical energies had been water, her hands would have been thoroughly wetted the moment she touched the object.

Aron flicked his ears back, snorting uncomfortably as she pulled the cloth aside and confronted the glittering brilliance of the . . . strange rock. Is that what this great magical instrument was, really, an overgrown shining mineral? She felt her heart race, and her fatigue didn't so much fall away as diminish to insignificance. Nothing mattered but the mystery of the hearthstone.

"It's already drawing you, isn't it?" Kyrkenall asked. "I'm told the trick is to not completely submerge yourself, no matter how good it feels. Don't get lost. Stay rooted in your self. That's even more important right now, for us. You've got to make this landscape real."

He was asking a lot. She tried not to betray the alarm she felt in her expression.

"How?" she asked.

He frowned. His gaze shifted to the storm and back to her, then he spoke quickly. "With magical sight, you can see how the things around you are put together, right?"

"Through the inner world. Yes."

"And unless you're standing on a fragment or a splinter, the structure of everything is weaker out here in the shifts, right?" He went on without waiting for an answer. "So you just strengthen it. Bring in new supports to add to the existing ones."

But how? she wanted to scream.

"I'm not sure exactly how," he answered the unspoken query, "but you can use the hearthstone to increase the energy of spells. You can use that energy to enhance how inanimate things are held together, like adding more timbers to a house. Kalandra told me as much."

Elenai thought quickly. "So if I add similar looking energy lines to the ground around us, I can keep it from shifting when the storm hits?"

"Exactly. Can you do that?"

"I'll try." Elenai strove to sound confident.

"You'd damned well better try, Squire, or we're liable to end up breathing sand or swimming in a lake of lava. There aren't many mistakes allowed out here."

She sought to make a joke of it. "So no pressure, then."

He didn't laugh. "Just do whatever the mages have told you. Focus your energies, see into the—"

"I can do it," she said, surprised at the cutting sound in her voice. She swiftly added: "Alten."

"Prove it."

The key to looking deeply into the inner world without getting lost in it was to center one's self, and that was a little more challenging under the circumstances. But she closed her eyes, sucked in a deep breath, then counted down from ten as she imagined becoming light as a cloud.

Elenai had never been as interested in magery as martial training, despite her natural affinity, but had long since learned to find her center. Opening her eyes, she looked upon the inner world. Unlike the intricate, well-harmonized assemblies of energies she was accustomed to, objects viewed this way in the Shifting Lands appeared unfinished at a basic structural level, like homes built with far too few upright beams. Even the living matrices of the nearby plants looked slapdash, unsustainable, and she realized that just a casual adjustment might reorder them. She could never accomplish that with real creatures from one of the realms.

"What do you think?" Kyrkenall asked.

"I'm still getting used to it," she said shortly. His intrusion was an irritant. She turned her full attention to the hearthstone glowing gently, warmly, like a comfortable blaze in a country cottage. She saw that its own structure was too dense to study, the rich filaments that composed it so thickly twisted she grew confused trying to follow one of them even a little way to its source. They softly insinuated themselves into whatever lay nearby. She wasn't alarmed by that until she tentatively touched one with her life force and let out a gasp as they intertwined with the threads of her own existence, imbuing her with coruscating power. Her fatigue slipped away completely.

"You all right?"

She was glorious, but she only managed a nod. If he'd served so closely with mages, why was he constantly interrupting?

"We've only got a few minutes before the storm hits," Kyrkenall told her.

Either the storm had closed much faster, or it had taken longer to align her energies with the stone than had been apparent. She licked her lips. The hearthstone energy was now twisted about the surface of her own life force, as if she had pushed into a tangle of vines and withdrawn her hand to find some gently wrapped about her arm. By manipulating tendrils of her will through the hearthstone, she saw how easy it was to add energy to the surrounding material.

She swept her threads through the terrain around them in a circle ten foot in diameter. The fragile underlayment took on solidity before her eyes. It no longer magically felt as if they were standing upon thin roof shingles. This, she thought with a thrill, must be what it's like to be a goddess.

She released her hold on the inner world to better gauge what was happening in the distance and gaped at what she saw.

The sky all about them was howling black. How had she missed that? Kyrkenall, ring glowing bright, held tight to both animals as his garments whipped in the wind. The horses whinnied repeatedly in fright.

She sent a little pulse of energy through the hearthstone and with careless ease calmed both animals. Altering emotional energy had never been so simple.

The storm rolled into them and the substance of the land rolled with it. First everything but the tiny circle of dark soil she'd reinforced blew away, leaving only a landscape of undulating red rock. A searing eruption of white lightning filled the heavens.

Elenai had never struggled so fiercely with her weaving. A wave of water rolled over that red rock, tower high, and she threw out her hands to generate the magical energy to ward it with a gust of wind. Astonishingly, it worked. The torrent rolled past their pocket of safety.

And then the water receded and strange land features popped into view one after another before swirling away. One moment she looked upon black forested valleys, the next upon a dunescape with a tortuous blue sun that burned away the moisture in the soil beneath their feet and scorched their exposed skin. It vanished to be replaced by a cool, temperate night of looming purple stones. Kyrkenall's blue light set the nearest of them sparkling.

Still the wind blew, and with her inner sight she knew it for a physical manifestation of the magical currents.

Of a sudden, everything around them spun away to a gray blankness, like a canvas ready for painting. She gulped in panic for the sheer force of the energies striving to invade their little island of calm. There was no ground, and that around them was desperate to fall away into nothingness. Again and again she sent forth threads of her will to fortify the soil they stood upon. So great was her concentration that she temporarily lost hold of the horses, and Aron whinnied, wildly tossing his head as he backed away.

She couldn't have him distracting her while she weaved! She lashed out with her will to calm him, and the poor animal shuddered as he froze in place behind her. She noticed that in her exertions the Altenerai ring she wore had somehow twisted around with gem-side out. It glittered at full strength.

Lightning slashed the sky as the wind whistled up, and a strange creature large as a wagon undulated out of the darkness, borne on a thousand buzzing, glowing little wings, like a finned eel carried by hornets. Kyrkenall fitted arrow to bow as the monster moved closer and longingly extended a trio of proboscises toward them. In only a few more moments one of those things would be close enough to touch, and she could just about guarantee she didn't want that to happen.

She tried sending a gust of wind its way and saw the monster fighting to maintain course even as Kyrkenall launched an arrow. The shaft imbedded in the base of one waving proboscis, and its body contorted in fury just as the darkness was shattered by glowing rain that struck their skin without moistening them. The creature was lost to sight in the blinding deluge, and for a few tense moments Elenai braced for renewed attack from every direction.

But then the rain ceased and sun-blasted salt flats wavered into view. A pinkish orb hung low on the horizon and wind trailed little whirls of red dust in its wake. Nearer at hand lay the vast skeleton of a long-dead fish, its spines soaring like temple arches from the withered ground.

The storm had run its course, and she relaxed, only realizing as she sucked in breaths that she'd been winded from the exertions.

Kyrkenall nodded at her, a tight smile on his handsome features. "Not bad, Squire. Not bad at all."

"Not bad, sir?" She grinned at him, surprised by how weak she sounded. Small wonder—she'd wielded greater power in a single half hour than she would have been capable of in an entire month of spell casting. Maybe an entire year.

"You'd best pull away from the hearthstone."

"I think," she admitted, "it's the only thing keeping me upright."

"All the more reason to relinquish it. You risk losing yourself if you're still attached when you go under."

She had read about the inherent dangers of peering too long or too intently through the inner world. Death was one of the less nasty side effects. She didn't feel that much in danger. The hearthstone was a comforting presence. But she decided to humor him and withdraw.

It was the last thing she remembered for many hours.

5

A Dying Look

She woke within a small tent, so disoriented that for a moment she imagined everything had been a dream.

Light filtered through the canvas above, and she smelled cooked meat. She was ravenous, she realized, and pushed the blanket covering aside.

She found her borrowed khalat beside her. She felt her face redden as she imagined Kyrkenall removing it from her, then pushed that thought from her mind and paused for brief morning prayers. There was no room inside the tent to stand, so she dragged the robe outside with her and almost tripped over her weapons belt in front of the opening, next to her boots. She dressed awkwardly, trying not to think of his small, graceful hands unclasping the very hooks she now fastened.

A normal yellow sun hung beyond a distant stand of pine trees. Rocks striated with rust and brown littered the earth, and a small clear pool of water lay a few feet to her right, where Kyrkenall filled his waterskin. A snow-topped mountain ridge with blue-and-white craggy summits loomed on the horizon. Aron and Kyrkenall's mount, Lyria, nibbled grass near a stand of trees, a chill wind whipping at their manes.

Kyrkenall grinned at her. "Ah. You're up. How are you?"

In truth, her ribs were a little sore and her head ached. "Fine, I guess, sir. How long was I out?"

"A day or so. It's evening now."

She'd been sleeping that long? "And where are we?" This was a different landscape than last she remembered.

"Northern Erymyr." He indicated the ridge with a nod of his head. "Our tower's a few hours that way. Darassus is far to the south, across mountain passes."

"How did we get here?"

"How do you think? I had to lay you across your horse."

Stupid question. Why did he always leave her feeling so off-balance?

"What do you think we'll find at the tower, sir?"

"It's supposed to be empty. We did winter exercises there when I was a squire, and it was unstaffed the rest of the time. But I suppose if they're keeping something important there they might have set a guard."

"They couldn't have too many posted, could they?" she asked. "People would know if there were a lot of soldiers stationed there. Their families would wonder where they were, wouldn't they?"

"Depends upon who's assigned. Do you want something to eat?"

She answered with an enthusiastic yes and soon was hunched over a battered metal plate piled with food. Kyrkenall had browned some griddle cakes and warmed up some dried meat from his stores, then drizzled a little honey over the whole mess. She was delighted, declaring it one of the finest ways she'd ever broken a fast.

He laughed. "You must really be hungry. Good honey's a treat, though, isn't it?"

She nodded.

He sat down across from her, his strange dark eyes somehow warm. "You did well out there. Very well. That storm was worse than I feared."

She tried not to beam. "Thank you, Alten."

He sighed. "Look, I'm all for honoring your elders and like that, but can you trim it back?"

She looked at him questioningly. "Sir?"

"That's what I'm talking about, right there. It's 'sir' this and 'alten' that nearly every time you speak to me. Just be a little less formal, all right?"

She froze, wondering how best to implement the order.

"Relax," he insisted. "It's not been an easy time for you, I guess. A lot of changes too quickly. I doubt you wanted to be involved in a conspiracy any more than I did."

"A conspiracy?"

"Murders. Secrets. Lies. Sounds like a conspiracy to me." His expression darkened.

"A conspiracy about what, though?" She bit back from adding "sir" just in time, and swallowed another bite.

"Well, I've been trying to put that together. So. Item one." He lifted a pebble and sat it down on a rock in front of him for emphasis. "They've done something with the sword that they don't want anyone to find out about. They're worried enough about it that they're willing to kill a hero of the realm."

"What did they do with it?" Elenai asked.

"Seems like they put it away, far north in the Chasm Tower." Kyrkenall sat another pebble down beside the first.

"Is that actually a new point?" she asked.

"What?"

"If you're listing things our enemy did, isn't that just part of the first issue, about them doing something with the sword?"

He frowned and muttered, "Kalandra always made this teaching stuff look easy." Then he continued in a normal tone. "Anyway. They took the sword and put it in this tower for reasons unknown. They killed Asrahn." He set down another pebble, reached for a fourth and placed it in the line. "They were ready to kill us." He placed another. "It's so important that they brought a hearthstone to stop me."

"And do we entirely know who *they* are?"

"No. But we can be sure of the four dead ones, for starters. Probably the entire Mage Auxiliary. Probably Denaven. Probably the queen, since he's her hound and they're both in league with the Mage Auxiliary. The real question is, which Altenerai are involved? I'm wondering if all the new ones are part of it. You know them far better than me. What are they like?"

He was asking as he would an equal. She felt her face flush with pride and answered after swallowing another bite. "There are only three other new ones. Gyldara's been Asrahn's right hand for the last few years, and she's fiercely loyal to both him and the corps. I really can't imagine she'd be involved with anyone who'd want him dead. And if she were, she'd probably go for their throats the moment she learned they killed him. Oh."

"What is it?"

"M'lahna was her sister. She's the one who was carrying the hearthstone."

"Right. So you think that means Gyldara's in league with them?"

"No. I think it means she's going to be after both of us once they find her sister's body." Gyldara was efficient and capable and straightforward, and Elenai had always admired her. It saddened her to think the woman might now be after them. Moreover, she'd be a fearsome antagonist. That she was a deadly warrior was to be expected—all Altenerai were formidable. But she was also the most driven of the younger ring-sworn. "I don't think it will be good to have her as an enemy."

Kyrkenall snorted dismissively. "I'm sure I've had worse. What about the other two?"

"Lasren's kind of . . . " She hesitated, then from Kyrkenall's look decided to be bluntly honest. "He's in it for the prestige. Rylin's kind of the same, but there's a core of decency to him. I don't think either are the type for conspiracies. Both are more about going their own way and having fun."

"How sure are you about that?"

"Fairly sure. Lasren and K'narr were friends, which is the only thing that gives me doubt. But K'narr was usually following Denaven around, and Lasren is usually palling around with Rylin."

Kyrkenall looked unconvinced. "So there's a possibility they recruited Lasren, and maybe Rylin. And Gyldara is going to hate us regardless."

"Yes," she agreed reluctantly. "What about the older Altenerai?"

"I think we can rule out Aradel. She wouldn't have anything to do with Denaven or the queen."

The story behind Aradel's resignation was well known through the ranks, although Elenai now realized she'd heard a skewed version of it. An ingenious tactician, second only to N'lahr himself, Aradel had been expected to assume his place after the famous general's untimely death, but had been passed over in favor of Denaven at the insistence of the queen. The slight— or, Elenai realized, perhaps the peace treaty that followed—had so enraged Aradel that she'd publically excoriated both her new commander and the queen before storming off to The Fragments, where she was soon elected governor. The Fragments, like the other Allied Realms, went its own way most of the time, owing little but military allegiance in times of external threat, and it was even less deferential to the wishes of the crown under Aradel's leadership. It was impossible to imagine her linked to any scheme that required allying with Denaven.

Kyrkenall continued. "Belahn's been semiretired for about five years, focused mainly on protecting his home village, which lies not far from Naor lands, so I don't see how he'd be involved. And Cerai's always been kind of a lone wolf; I think she may actually despise Denaven more than I do." He shrugged. "So they're out. Enada almost never leaves Kanesh, and is too busy fighting kobalin and Naor there. Besides, she's about as subtle as I am. So she's out."

"That leaves Decrin, Varama, and Tretton. The ones in Darassus."

"And that's bad enough. Tretton can follow quarry across trackless stone desert. He's got skills I don't even pretend to understand. And you know all those stories you hear about how formidable Decrin is?"

There were an awful lot of them, usually about him carving his way through a mass of enemies.

"Every one of them's true. He's unstoppable. Even when he's covered in blood he just keeps coming. But he's too honest to be a conspirator."

Elenai agreed; she had a difficult time imagining the bluff, friendly war hero would be party to intrigue. She spoke before stuffing in the last bite of food. "How about Tretton? Would he league with the traitors?" She was fairly sure the answer would be no.

Kyrkenall made a sour face. "He's even more of a stickler than Asrahn. I could see him going along with something slightly rotten, if he was ordered to do so."

"But he and Asrahn are—were—friends. I've seen them off duty together."

"That doesn't mean much. He's the kind of soldier who doesn't question, who obeys authority because, to his way of thinking, rules and tradition keep us from falling into chaos." The archer sighed. "You've got to realize how sneaky Denaven is. He might convince Tretton and Decrin both. I love Decrin, but he's not that bright. And, it pains me to admit, Denaven's dangerous himself. He's wily and he fights dirty and he'll never, ever forget or give up until he has what he wants, even if he pretends to."

Elenai noticed he'd still left out one alten. "What about Varama?"

Kyrkenall didn't hesitate or equivocate. "If Varama's after us, we don't stand a chance."

His cold certainty surprised her, because she'd never heard that the blue-skinned alten was particularly well-known as either a blade or spell caster. But she didn't ask him to elaborate. "You think Denaven could trick her, too?"

He laughed. "No. She's usually thinking about five steps ahead of everybody else. I just can't be sure if she's paying attention, because she's usually thinking about something else even when she's looking at you. She did seem troubled when I asked if she'd seen Asrahn, but that might not mean anything."

Kyrkenall swept the pebbles off the rock, where they bounced out of sight into the tough grasses. "We're just going around in circles. Who might be with us, who might be against. What any of this is really about. We're not getting any further until we breach the tower and get to the sword."

Elenai took the opportunity to voice a nagging doubt. "The sword's not really going to have answers."

"Obviously. But someone guarding it will."

Hopefully. "What do we do if one of the Altenerai is guarding it? One of those who usually aren't in Darassus, like Enada, or Belahn, or Cerai? Their absences might just be a blind."

"We'll deal with whatever we find there." Kyrkenall's handsome features darkened with menace. "If they're involved with Asrahn's death . . ." He left the threat unspoken.

Elenai set aside her plate, along with her worries about direct confrontation with the most powerful warriors in the known world. "When you asked M'lahna what she was really doing, she said it was all about restoring the realms. She mentioned a goddess returning. What goddess, and how?"

"Damned if I know. Sounded a little crazy. Like she'd spent too long playing with hearthstones."

"What *are* the hearthstones, really?"

"Commander Renik thought they were arcane tools the Gods used to shape the world. Kalandra thought they might be naturally occurring reservoirs of energy swept out of the Shifting Lands. Nobody knows." He paused for a minute. "Well, maybe the queen and the mages have figured it out, because they've been collecting every one they can find. But they're not talking. All I know is that they're trouble."

"Where do they collect them from?"

"All the distant places. Apparently there was one kept in Darassus from early on, but it was inactive. And then about a generation ago an alten found a new one in The Fragments after a storm."

Elenai had never been there but knew The Fragments was one of the most fragile of realms because, rather than being completely solid like the other four great land masses, it was actually a series of closely linked splinters and islands through which tiny rivulets of the Shifting Lands were threaded, ranging in width from a handful of miles to only a few hundred feet. People and even animals freely roamed the gaps, which resembled the surrounding terrain except during the fiercest storms. Owing to those gaps, strange things, both terrible and wondrous, could spring up even deep in the middle of the realm.

"Queen Leonara was just the appointed heir then, in charge of whatever minor issues the old queen didn't care about. I'm told she'd always been curious about the hearthstone in the palace, and now another one had turned up. So she told the Altenerai to keep an eye out for them, and pretty soon they started noticing them scattered everywhere. They turned up in our realms. They turned up in the lonely realms where the Naor live, and the weird little fragments and splinters out in the shifts where the kobalin lair, and even drifting in the true deeps, where there are only the tiniest occasional pockets of reality."

"I could see why she'd be interested in them."

"They weren't active, though," Kyrkenall said. "A mage could sense the latent power, but no one even knew to open them until Rialla got ahold of one. She was just a squire. Kalandra's squire," he added.

In a flash she remembered seeing Rialla's service record upon Altenerai plaques in the Hall of Remembrance because she'd been struck by its brevity. "She was the one who was alten for only a day, wasn't she?"

"Yes," he said, his voice brittle. "She was brilliant. And she deserved a whole lot better. . . ." His voice trailed off, and she had to spur him to continue.

"What happened once Kalandra and Rialla got the hearthstones working?"

"Leonara was queen by then, and her interest had become obsession. She cared less about the Naor war than she did the damned stones. N'lahr was out there winning against impossible odds but she kept sending our best and brightest after the stupid hearthstones. That's what happened to Commander Renik." Kyrkenall's voice grew knife sharp. "She kept sending him to more and more remote places. Sometimes he'd be gone for months, and he'd come back bruised and bloody, but he'd always come back. Until one day, he didn't. The queen has a lot to answer for, starting with how she wasted his life. And how she wasted Kalandra's the same way."

He shook his head. "That's about all I know. You can see why the Altenerai don't carry hearthstones into battle. Other mages can use them as easily as the person holding one. So the queen gathers them up, and the auxiliary studies them." His manner brightened as he changed subjects. "Do you feel like you're getting used to the one we have?"

"It's wonderful," she admitted. "I've never weaved with such clarity."

"It'll be a lot harder for them to find us if the thing is off. Do you think you can deactivate it?"

"I thought you didn't think I could."

"That was before you showed me how clever you were."

That was nice. "Do you have any idea how it's done?"

"Kalandra told me about it. There's apparently a spot, a sort of weak point, or spigot, and there's a way of shifting energies around that opens or closes it."

Kalandra again. Well, she seemed to be Kyrkenall's greatest source of magical knowledge, and so far what he'd passed on from her had proven useful. "Let me try."

She wasn't worried about anything but failure. Despite all of Kyrkenall's warnings she'd felt no danger yesterday while using the hearthstone. And she certainly had never sensed that the hearthstone was alive and looking back at her. Maybe the alten was overcautious about things he couldn't understand.

Kyrkenall cleaned up the campsite as she sat down with the stone.

When she stared at its shining surface she was drawn to the inner world without any real struggle or need for concentration, and she was so awed by its beauty and power that she turned it over and over in her hands for a long while.

She found no weak areas in the flow of energy. Indeed, the entire thing was so solid, so . . . real, she couldn't perceive any threads to pluck apart for further investigation. In comparison to the hearthstone, even the workings of a real, living creature seemed elementary, like a windup toy.

She was interrupted in her contemplation by a hand on her shoulder, and dimly she perceived Kyrkenall's presence.

"You've been at it for more than an hour," she heard, though it took a moment for her to process the sounds into actual information. "Are you close?"

"No," she admitted.

"We need to travel."

Reluctantly she pulled free. The pine forest seemed pale and uninteresting in comparison to the glories of the hearthstone, even with the sun brilliantly dipping into it. Kyrkenall gently took the hearthstone from her and wrapped it back in the cloth.

She felt suddenly ashamed. "I'm sorry."

"Don't be. It took the best mages years to figure out how to open and close one."

Kyrkenall climbed into his saddle and looked back at her. "Come on. I want to get close to the tower before dark so I can look things over."

He sighed, as if to clear his thoughts, then led them forward, riding below the hill ridges so they wouldn't be spotted.

It was a rolling country. Spring might be fully bloomed near Darassus, but here in the highlands winter had but recently, reluctantly, loosened its hold. You could still feel its breath in the wind, and pockets of frost and snow lay in the shadows of the barren trees.

As they rounded the corner of the second hill, they spotted a square obelisk standing upright at the edge of a thick woodland. Kyrkenall called a halt a few horselengths out from it and stared, silent and still for a long while. When he advanced at last it was with arrow nocked.

Elenai wondered why he was so wary. The object didn't look especially threatening, just incongruous here in the wilderness. It stood as tall as she did in the saddle, and was fashioned of gray stone, completely featureless save for a swirling creamy pattern upon the onyx pyramidal capper.

"Do you know what it is?" Elenai asked.

"I've never seen it before. Take a look with your inner sight. Don't," he added quickly, "fix on it too hard." He didn't relax his aim, but Elenai wasn't sure what he expected to shoot.

"You think it's sorcery?"

"Yes."

She saw he was right as soon as she examined it. The problem was that she couldn't fathom the design choices its builder had made. There was power hidden in the pyramid on top, but it was latent, like a warm charcoal left at a campsite.

"There's magic," she said, "but it's inactive."

Kyrkenall tipped his head to the right. "Look over there."

It took Elenai a long while to spot what Kyrkenall meant, for there were a variety of land features beyond that vague gesture, including a hill line, a clump of trees, a rivulet, and a rocky outcrop.

But there was also another onyx-topped obelisk, probably a half mile to their east, planted at the base of a hill.

"What are they?" Elenai asked.

"Offhand," Kyrkenall said, "I'm guessing they're fence posts."

Elenai's eyebrows rose. "A magical fence? But it's not working."

"We haven't tried to cross it."

"You think it will come on if we do?"

Kyrkenall frowned, lowered his weapon, and looked off toward the middle distance at a copse of trees.

Another thought struck her. "If it flared on any time something crossed it, wouldn't there be a line of dead creatures on either side?"

Kyrkenall grinned. "I knew there was a reason I kept you around. Just for laughs, toss a rock past, will you?"

Elenai slid out of her saddle but found no rocks. She clawed up a clump of cold, dry dirt and pitched it underhand just past the obelisk.

It landed without incident a few feet beyond, under a pine bough.

Kyrkenall didn't move.

"Well?" Elenai asked.

"I'm thinking. Go ahead and look at it with your sight again. I'm going to try something."

Elenai did as he bade. If nothing else, this trip was giving her a lot of practice in sorcery.

The obelisk continually radiated a faint golden glimmer from the black stone at its height. Beyond it, the living trees presented a tight pattern of golden structures in the shape of boles and branches. "Ready," she said.

Kyrkenall nudged his mare forward and reached out to the obelisk with his bow. He touched it, deliberately, and held it there.

Elenai didn't see any change of energy within the black pyramid. "Nothing."

"I didn't feel anything, either." Kyrkenall replaced his bow. "All right. I'm going to ride past. Wait until I'm through. Actually, wait until I'm through and try to ride back again. If I get blasted to ashes, head to The Fragments and find Aradel."

"Right," Elenai said. She wasn't sure how to get to The Fragments from here, but she didn't want to admit that.

Kyrkenall, back turned, spoke in a falsetto voice. "Oh, don't worry, Alten, I'm sure you'll be fine. But your sacrifice is so noble, I'll cherish it always."

Elenai couldn't believe what she'd heard. "I don't sound like that!"

He chuckled at her and urged his horse forward, stopping just beyond the obelisk. He then backed his horse past, then forward again. She watched tensely.

"Looks like we won't die here," Kyrkenall said. "Come on, then."

Elenai half expected a magical beam to lance out, or to feel some intense emotion generated by the sorcery she knew smoldered there.

Soon, though, the strange contrivance lay behind them. The dark-haired archer kept to the right of the treeline, riding slowly, eyes constantly upon the horizon and bow at the ready. Another ridge lay to their north.

A hawk soared overhead and called out, and Elenai spied a doe watching from the woods.

"Are we close to the tower?" she asked. It looked like a tendril of smoke joined the thin clouds hovering above a distant rise of trees, but she couldn't be sure.

"It's on the—" Kyrkenall fell silent in midsentence. A gray-and-white furred thing loping on four legs mounted the rim of the nearest hill, at least two bow-shots ahead and to the left.

The distance confused Elenai's perception of its size until the creature moved past a spindly elm. She had never seen nor heard of any furred Ery-myran beast as large as her horse. Kanesh boasted huge animals, like the mighty grass-eaters known as eshlack and the axbeaks that preyed on them, but not Erymyr. This creature was generally catlike in its movements, but the jaw was shovel-heavy, the ears huge and winglike. She saw no eyes of any kind. It had to have been brought here from some distant realm, or maybe even the Shifting Lands. "What *is* that?"

Kyrkenall lifted an arrow to his bow and was already sighting. "No idea, but I'm pretty sure it's not going to be friendly."

Just then the peculiarity turned to snuffle at them with its long black snout. It let out something between a whine and a roar, and charged in their direction.

Kyrkenall fired. The shaft struck the beast's head, but the arrow seemed to slide through the furry ruff.

"You missed," Elenai blurted in surprise.

"No," Kyrkenall objected, "its head is narrower than I thought." He now had three arrows in hand as he nocked one.

The beast's roar this time was like a thunderclap. Kyrkenall's arrow launched, but Elenai knew even as it did that he'd missed again, for the thing leapt left, then right through rough terrain as it bounded toward them. "Gods, it's bigger than a bear!"

"Less talking, more killing!" Kyrkenall launched the next two arrows one after the other and then grabbed three more. The quiver, which had looked inexhaustible, was now half empty. One arrow took the beast some-where in the right temple, the other in the center chest. Neither slowed it a jot. Elenai heard it let out one annoyed huff, and it gained speed as it charged.

"Ready your sword!" Kyrkenall barked, even as he fired once more. Ele-nai muttered under her breath because she'd already drawn her weapon. She'd thought he'd come to expect competency from her.

Aron didn't like the smell of the thing and shifted beneath her, snorting in relief as she got him under way. He wanted to run.

The next three shots struck again in the head, deep in the shoulder, and through the thick foreleg, but the monster didn't slow. It let out another roar and Elenai wondered dully if it really could be stopped. As she circled for its right side, pulling against Aron, she supposed she might be charging to her death.

Kyrkenall let out a war whoop as he guided his mare to swing left.

Elenai had never grown especially proficient with off-hand blade work and cursed at herself for riding right. So much for competence. There was no good way to challenge the beast with her sword unless she got behind it.

There was magic, though.

As the shaggy hulk pivoted for Kyrkenall, she let Aron take the lead and undid the top hook of her robe so she could touch her necklace talismans. She wasn't sure she could get an angry monster to fear much of anything, so she found the twisted smile of confusion under her thumb and sent that emotion at the animal through a thread of her design. The spell struck the creature but was swept away by a surge of energy rising from the wide black neck strap decorating the thing's heavy throat.

Whoever had placed the strap on the beast had expected sorcerous attacks.

Kyrkenall and his mare swung wide away from the creature, which sprang sideways and clawed, just missing Lyria. He swiveled in his saddle and fired over his shoulder. An arrow went straight into what should have been the creature's brain case, but that, too, had no appreciable result. The beast snarled as it leapt.

Kyrkenall flung himself to roll across the ground to the creature's left, his horse bolting to the right. He reached his feet, bow in one hand, sword in the other, then leapt to a waist-high boulder farther on.

Elenai nudged Aron forward. "Go!"

Aron whinnied gamely and galloped for the beast's flank. She leaned down and slashed deeply into its left rear leg.

The creature spun with a growl, faster than she thought possible, and launched at her. Aron shuddered as the entire bulk slammed into him, and Elenai heard the sickening tearing of flesh and the scream of agony as Aron took a terrible wound. She threw herself from the saddle, landed on one foot, off-balance, rolled, and came up still holding her weapon.

A rain of blood and gore spattered from Aron's shoulder as the beast tore at the screaming horse, ripping open his chest like it was a paper package. Aron managed a frantic kick or two, then Kyrkenall suddenly appeared and plunged his sword deep through the monster's neck. He drew clear with a triumphant whoop, and the red-mouthed beast followed him, one clawed foot scoring the black earth where Kyrkenall had stood the second before.

Either that wound or the accumulated damage finally finished it. The shaggy horror collapsed, lying with its head buried in the grass, rear legs kicking. Yellowish life-blood from its wounds stained the thick fur and dribbled into the hillside. A half-dozen black-feathered shafts stuck out like random quills.

Elenai looked again at Aron, lying on his side as his breathing shuddered to a stop, and felt her eyes fill with tears. Her breath came raggedly. "Damn."

She'd trained with that beautiful horse for the better part of two years and hadn't considered she'd be losing him in the midst of everything else.

Kyrkenall came up beside her. He was breathing heavily and his sweaty dark hair clung to his neck. "I take it you tried magic?"

"Yes." Elenai bit her lower lip. "The neck strap has some kind of protective shielding. I couldn't affect it."

"I bet the collar's keyed to the fence posts. To keep it in." He didn't seem angry or even disappointed in her. But she was sure she could have done better. She should have been able to keep Aron from harm.

The beast growled. Its right front leg twitched spasmodically and a plume of dust billowed from beneath the huge paw. It slumped finally into the stillness of death, beside Aron's steaming remains.

Kyrkenall watched a moment more, then scanned the horizon. He went stock-still, and Elenai saw his ring light. "So much for a quiet look up close," he said.

She discovered a tingling around her finger meant the ring on her own hand blazed, and she understood suddenly what he'd meant.

The exact properties and abilities of an Altenerai ring had never been fully explained to her—she wasn't Altenerai—but she knew it provided a modicum of protection against magical assaults, and it heightened awareness, although you could also set it to remain inactive. She hadn't had much of a chance to explore how to operate hers, and Kyrkenall hadn't told her a thing about it. Somehow, though, she knew six figures crept into position around them even if she couldn't see them. Fear drove away regret faster than a fox scatters hens.

Kyrkenall grinned and addressed the air. "Show yourselves."

A man in ring mail and a black cloak appeared from behind a hillock eight paces out, and then, seconds later, five others came into view from each direction, all armored similarly. Erymyran soldiers. In place of a standard metal helm they wore thick, woolen hats. Every single one had a scabbard at their hip, although only two of them held swords. The others, including one fellow only a few feet from the nose of the dead monster, had arrows nocked to short bows aimed at Kyrkenall and Elenai.

Two of the soldiers were women, and the taller of these, holding a sword, was only a couple of feet from Elenai's back. "What do we do, sir?" she asked.

"We're to kill all interlopers." The man who'd first appeared tipped his sword at them.

"They're Altenerai," said the woman, understandably mistaking Elenai's rank from the khalat and ring she wore.

"Kyrkenall saved my cousin in Kanesh," said a short fellow on Elenai's left.

Elenai looked to Kyrkenall for some kind of sign. What should they do?

The archer smiled broadly and addressed their captors. "Let's not do anything drastic," he said easily. He sounded eminently reasonable. "I think there's been a misunderstanding. We're on a mission vital for the state."

"If it's official," their leader asked, "where's your sigil?"

"Ah!" Kyrkenall raised the hand holding his sword and all the bow-strings went taut in the hands around them. He chuckled as if he found the whole encounter quite droll.

Their leader seemed unamused. "Drop the sword."

"Perhaps I should say the same to you," Kyrkenall returned lightly. "I rank you, soldier."

"Yes, sir. But no one's allowed here, on pain of death, unless they have the sigil."

Ever so slowly, Kyrkenall slid the tip of his sword down and planted it upright in the earth. "Better?" He bowed slightly. "Now I'm just going to open my robe and show you my authorization. So don't be alarmed."

Elenai knew very well that there was no sigil under Kyrkenall's robe, though she briefly wondered if there was something he hadn't told her. Probably not. Which meant things were going to get very interesting very fast. She glanced at the nearest of the watchers in her line of sight. Most of their attention was directed to Kyrkenall, but they weren't completely ignoring her, either. And there were two behind her that she couldn't see.

"It's a funny thing." Kyrkenall reached delicately to undo the second hook of his khalat. He shifted his left arm a little, bringing Arzhun to hand as if to steady it. "About the sigil, I mean."

"Why didn't you activate it before the beast attacked?" the woman behind them asked.

Kyrkenall chuckled conspiratorially, as though he'd heard a tremendously amusing joke that was somehow offensive or inappropriate and he couldn't keep back from it. "That's a story. You see"—he reached into his robe and turned half sideways to face her—"I don't actually have a sigil."

At the same moment he uttered the final word he flicked the nearby archer in the face with Arzhun's black horn tip then spun as the man cried out. Kyrkenall took an arrow to the back, but it failed to pierce his armor and dropped away. Turning right, he dropped to a crouch and two more arrows sped over his shoulder and head. At the same time he launched an arrow stolen from the staggered bowman and snapped a shot that took the archer behind Elenai through the throat.

Kyrkenall snatched Lothrun out of the ground as he leapt to engage the swordswoman at Elenai's left, blocking her strike with Arzhun's end before negligently ruining her lovely throat with his sword tip. Before she'd even begun to drop, Kyrkenall cut an arrow from the air, his legendary blade spraying the swordwoman's blood. He laughed madly and sprinted to confront the leader.

Elenai finally woke to action, shocked. In a heartbeat Kyrkenall had killed two soldiers and injured a third.

She slashed at the nearest archer as the woman drew a bead on Kyrkenall.

The sword bit deep into the bow and she dropped it.

For an instant that was an eternity, Elenai saw the woman's amber-flecked brown eyes, saw the muscles around the lids tighten in anticipation of the coming blow.

And then Elenai thrust her sword past an arm lifted too late and drove it into the hollow of the woman's neck.

There was so much blood. Elenai stepped away in a crouch, all too conscious another archer remained, the one Kyrkenall had struck with Arzhun. The man might even now be aiming at the back of her head.

She needn't have worried. Kyrkenall dealt with him even as Elenai turned, driving his sword past the fellow's bow, raised in a pitiful parry. He plunged Lothrun through the archer's chest armor.

Elenai didn't quite manage to turn away before she saw the result.

No one was left alive. In the time she'd handled *one* warrior Kyrkenall had killed five.

The leader lay facedown, his dark cloak soaking up blood from a widening puddle. His posture concealed his injury, but there was no missing the gruesome wound on the man whose neck was half lopped, for his head sagged to one side, as if upon a ghastly hinge.

Kyrkenall's laugh was startling as a nearby lightning strike. At its sound she whirled to find him raising his bloody sword high in salute. He turned, taking in the scene, his peals of laughter giving way to shaking gasps of mad energy.

"You're certainly thorough." Elenai was astonished by how loud her voice sounded from her dry throat.

He seemed to see her for the first time. His shoulders heaved as he breathed in and out.

"Shouldn't we have saved one to question?" she asked.

"Why didn't you?"

"Um." Elenai thought again of those frightened brown eyes. She doubted she'd ever stop thinking of them. Could she have captured that woman? "I was worried about the last archer."

"I had him." Kyrkenall bent to wipe his blade on the leader's cloak, and chuckled again, an utterly mirthless sound. "Creep up to the hill's crest and scout, Squire." His voice was low and full of forced restraint. "Search with your ring and your sight."

"What are you going to do?"

Kyrkenall stared down at his hand gripping the bow. It shook. "Try to find my arrows. And my balance."

Elenai hesitated. More than anything she wanted reassurance. Was he okay? Had she acted rightly? Had she been useful? It didn't really seem that Kyrkenall had needed her at all, which was astonishing and humbling both.

As she started up the hill she heard the alten chuckling once more, a mad, desperate noise. She felt a chill spread up her back and stiffen her arm hairs.

The stories about Kyrkenall were true, but somehow failed to capture the stunning degree of his prowess and his madness. Had he always been like this, or was it the result of years of warfare? What would she be like after staring into as many faces as he had, dealing death and remembering their eyes? Did he recall them as easily as she could call up that woman's?

Was that why he was a little crazy?

She struggled to focus on the task at hand, as Asrahn would have told her, and reached the lip of the hill. There could be another one of those monsters just over the rise. Or maybe a reserve cadre of soldiers.

She looked down at the bloody sword in her hand. She hadn't remembered she was carrying it. Maybe she was going a little crazy herself. And then she looked at her other hand, and the sapphire shining in her palm. It looked so incongruous there against her skin.

She had to pull herself together. Focus.

Kyrkenall had told her to "use the ring." Very well. She wasn't sure entirely what he meant, but she had felt the presence of the concealed attackers through it. Maybe she could do the same now, feeling her way into the distance without poking her head above the summit of the hill.

She sent her thoughts toward the ring and tried to peer through the inner world at the same time.

Working with the ring wasn't quite like using her normal magical skills, and the sapphire certainly wasn't as powerful as the hearthstone, but touching it with her conscious energy allowed her to sense the strength of nearby life forces. She felt Kyrkenall's strong, swift heartbeat behind, and was momentarily worried about the other heavy heartbeat nearby until she realized that was his horse, Lyria. No life energy from the dead lingered, and she was glad for that. She'd rather not encounter battlefield remnants.

Lesser life forces, tiny flickering candles, bloomed across the landscape before her. None, though, was anywhere near the power of Kyrkenall or the horse, so she knew they were small animals and insects of the field.

Her senses through the ring didn't extend very far. Kyrkenall and his mount seemed to be at extreme range. She had no way to know what lay within the tower, or beyond. The important thing was that nothing waited for them close by.

She relinquished her focus on the ring and discovered there was not the slightest fatigue after, as there was when tapping into her own inner sight, nor was there the untangling and utter exhaustion when she used the hearthstone.

An amazing tool. Had Kyrkenall been using his ring when they'd scouted the terrain earlier? Why hadn't he said anything to her about it?

Because, she told herself, Kyrkenall had other things on his mind. He wasn't especially focused on teaching her.

Elenai glanced over her shoulder at him, found him dragging the soldiers' bodies together in a row. Why, she wasn't sure, but she saw him rooting through their belongings. Probably he searched for the sigils they'd mentioned, or for some other information.

At least he'd stopped laughing.

Elenai dug fingers into a patch of loose soil and liberally smeared cold dirt over her cheeks so there would be no reflection from her skin, then slowly poked her head above the rise.

The ground sloped gently down into a plain. Highlands rose steeply and suddenly to left and right, but flat grassland rolled on for the next half mile, up to a stone fort that filled a level region between the rocky uplands. From her vantage point she saw a few thatched roofs surrounded by a wooden stockade a quarter mile west of the wall, near the tree line. Wispy gray smoke rose from one rectangular chimney.

The long low buildings within the stone fort, though, looked neglected and abandoned. Climbing above all was a round, narrow tower, pale and stark, flying a ragged red flag with a white diagonal slash.

The tower she'd stolen from Cargen's memory. Irion had to be hidden somewhere inside.

6

The Emptied Tomb

At dawn, Rylin wakened in his bed in the Altenerai wing of the palace. Still sleep-fogged, he half expected some leggy beauty to be lying beside him, but a turn of his head showed him he was alone.

He'd anticipated nights of revelry and several days of languid comforts, but then the news came in: Asrahn had drowned in the Idris. The shock still reverberated dully in his mind. The whole of the city continued celebrating N'lahr's great victory, but the Altenerai Corps was in mourning, even without an official declaration.

Rylin rubbed his eyes to clear them. Back when he and Lasren were cocky second years—stupid, really—he used to mock Asrahn as a humorless has-been, drilling them endlessly from lack of imagination more than necessity. But he'd warmed to the master's method after Asrahn put him in the dirt three times in succession, despite all the energy and bravado Rylin could muster for the sparring exercise. He recalled Asrahn helping him to his feet, each time calmly but clearly explaining to the assembly what Rylin had done well and how it could be countered. Others received the exact same treatment.

And they got better, or they got out, all with little direct advice from the famously stoic Master of Squires. Asrahn had been an unassuming but inspired instructor who worked tirelessly to pull the best from each of his trainees for the corps he loved. He was the only master most of them, including Altenerai, had ever known. There'd be no replacing him anytime soon. In speaking with Lasren last night, they agreed that Gyldara would try, but Rylin took less pleasure in the thought than did his friend, who joked she'd be a lot nicer for the squires to look at.

He sat up in bed and the sheets slipped down his chest. Today didn't seem likely to be better than the one preceding. Meetings to divvy up newly vacant duties would be the least of his headaches. The expensive bottle of spirits he'd purchased for N'lahrin festivities remained unopened near the empty glasses he'd staged on his bedside table. He would have to remember to bring it to Asrahn's remembrance ceremony after the funeral. He frowned. If he'd known he'd never see the Master of Squires alive again, last week he would have given him something at least as nice. Asrahn had quietly handled so much around here that it took ten in his absence to do little more than keep the place from falling into chaos.

It didn't help that three additional Altenerai, a squire, and two members of the Mage Auxiliary had disappeared. Speculation was running rampant through the barracks. Kyrkenall, of course, hadn't been expected to hang around long, though no one had foreseen his graceless exit from the tombside ceremonies with Squire Elenai. Lasren asserted with undisguised jealousy that the mad archer had gathered the others for a grand adventure that would cover them all in glory. Heading out without so much as a by-your-leave or an explanatory note was entirely in keeping with Kyrkenall's character, as far as Rylin could ascertain, but it hadn't impressed most of his fellow officers, who'd led search parties in increasingly wide patrols to hunt for signs of him and the others. So far they'd found nothing. And Rylin couldn't shake the sense that this was no lark.

As he was considering how best to order the day, a bugle call rent the air. By the time the notes sounded a second time, Rylin was out of bed and pulling on his undergarments. He pushed the curtains apart, wincing at the stab of sunlight as he rooted quickly through the pile of clothes by the nightstand. In moments he was wearing his dark uniform pants.

An immediate summons. It might mean anything from a decision on the new Master of Squires to word of some new Naor invasion. It probably concerned the missing, though. Whatever the cause, all Altenerai would report to the hall without delay.

He grabbed his shirt, sniffed it quickly and discovered it decidedly unfresh, then dropped it to the floor and threw open his wardrobe. There wasn't a good shirt clean. Between the mourning, the disruptions, and the reveling, routine tasks went unaccomplished by the civilian help and squires alike. All that was left him was that blue bit with the ripped collar. He stepped back, frowning, then pushed into the outer chamber.

The Altenerai maintained a suite of rooms on the second floor of their palace wing. Like most, Rylin's apartment consisted of a bedroom, a lounge, and a small office, and featured lofty ceilings, black marble fireplaces, and heavy wooden furniture generations old. Rylin strode barefoot through the open balcony doors, stepped past the wrought-iron cooking stove and utensils stacked on a table beside it, and grabbed the white silk shirt he'd tossed out four days ago. There'd be no getting that immense wine stain out of the front, and he'd thought it might be useful as a rag. But its collar was clean, and it smelled fine owing to all the rinsing he'd done in a futile effort to save it. He hooked it closed as he headed back inside.

He peered at himself in the bronze mirror. Not too bad. His eyes looked a bit puffy. He could use a shave, but that would have to wait.

An immediate summons didn't leave him much time, but he dared not turn up looking like he'd just fallen out of bed, so he ran a brush through short dark hair, scrubbed teeth and face, then pulled on his khalat, socks, boots, sword belt, etc., and headed out. As he turned into the hall, Lasren was closing his own door, and he heard a woman call out from inside: "Strike as one!" The last word of the Altenerai battle cry was dulled as the door fell shut.

The full line, from an ancient play about the war with kobalin for the arid realm of Ekhem, was "when one of us has struck a blow, we have struck as one." It had worked its way into countless speeches and the most rousing of the corps songs. He'd even heard N'lahr himself shout it before leading a cavalry charge. Apparently the somber atmosphere hadn't fully dampened Lasren's ability to enjoy life's pleasures.

His friend grinned at him and pushed black hair back from his widow's peak.

"Who was that?" Rylin asked.

"I think her name's Lasren," his friend answered. "At least, that's the name she kept moaning last night." He fell in step beside Rylin as they headed down the shadowy hall, their boots beating a rhythm on the tile floors.

Rylin's eyes shifted to the doors on their left and right. Few Altenerai occupied their rooms regularly, as most were away from Darassus. "Are we the only ones in the suites this morning?"

"Yes, unless Cargen and K'narr have turned up."

"I figured that was what the summons was about."

"I hope it's something we can act on this time."

Rylin hoped the same. He might have earned the right to wear the ring, but he'd yet to accomplish anything heroic. By the time Kyrkenall and N'lahr had won their rings they'd already played a crucial role in a dozen engagements, and by the time they'd served for three years like him, the enemy could be panicked just by mentioning their names. He was fairly certain no Naor or kobalin had even heard of Rylin Corimel.

They reached the first floor and passed from the Altenerai wing into the main palace. The display of banners and paintings depicting famous moments from corps history continued on for several hundred paces, ending with the life-size bronze statue of a stern, sharp-nosed woman in interlinked scale armor. Her high brow was crowned with a circlet. One hand clasped the hilt of an unsheathed sword, the other was pressed to her chest in salute.

According to custom, Rylin and Lasren stopped to return the gesture, for this was the statue of Queen Altenera, founder of the corps. Thirteen hundred years before, she had led the strongest people of Darassus into battle against a kobalin horde, afterward establishing a permanent institution to train soldiers and hone the most gifted to serve and protect the realms.

Not for the first time, Rylin wondered what it would have been like to serve under so active a monarch, wistfully thinking he might have been better suited to live in earlier days. Back then there had been constant action and a lot less paperwork.

As one, he and Lasren finished their salute and pressed open the dark paneled doors that Altenera's tribute guarded.

The thrill on entering the venerable Altenerai council chamber remained, even after three years, and Rylin smiled a little as he breathed in the scent of dark paneled wood that adorned the six walls. His gaze swept to the lofty white vaulted ceiling, pierced with semicircular windows now aglow with morning light. Stained glass scenes below the dome depicted each of the five realms to either side of a white glazed pane adorned with the slim silver crown of Altenara suspended above a shining sapphire, opposite the door. To the right were the artistically rendered green fields of Erymyr punctuated by the domes of Darassus shining beneath cerulean skies. To its left were the forested mountains of The Fragments. The dunes and palm-lined central river of Ekhem shone brightly farther left. Behind him, he knew, other windows featured the mesas of Arappa and the plains of Kanesh.

In the center of the blue-and-gray chevron-patterned flooring stood the famed hexagonal table, four chairs to each side but that beneath the image of the crown, which only held three. Here the Altenerai had gathered for long centuries to conduct their most important meetings.

And he, Rylin, had earned a place in their number. If he'd yet to achieve greatness, he'd at least come farther than most.

Today the table was empty save for two veterans, Decrin and Tretton, sitting in close conversation.

Rylin stepped up to his chair and found the familiar worn spot in the polished wood where generations of Altenerai had grasped it in the same place. Like the table itself, the chair was scuffed and notched, and handsomely crafted with archaic flourishes and snarling beast faces.

Even Lasren wasn't entirely immune to the overwhelming press of history, for he'd fallen quiet, striding past Rylin without a word. Rylin would have preferred to sit directly beside his friend, but the chair between them had to remain empty until such a time as a trio of Altenerai voted Kalandra dead, and not simply missing. Rylin had known the gifted alten during his early squire days in the war, so he understood the reluctance—but seven years was too long.

There were twenty-two Altenerai posts in all. With Kalandra officially missing and eight vacancies that hadn't been filled, not to mention three who almost never turned up, the chamber was more than half-empty most of the time. The queen attended only rarely, and as usual her chair, directly beneath the symbol of the crown, was unoccupied. Rylin's eyes drifted to the seat left of the queen's, reserved for the Master of Squires. It was like staring up into the night sky and noticing the moon had vanished.

Rylin tightened his lips and nodded to Decrin and Tretton. They returned the gesture before resuming their talk.

Tretton held himself stiffly, radiating icy control. Areas of gray were prominent in his short, dark hair, and almost completely dominated his spade beard and mustache. His black skin was weathered by long days in the sun. For all that he appeared as fierce and implacable as ever, his gaze still seemed a little hollow. Tretton had come up through the ranks only a few years after the Master of Squires, and the two had been close. The loss would perhaps have been less jarring if it occurred in the line of duty.

Decrin was of a younger generation than Tretton, though a seasoned soldier with almost two decades of experience. He was also the largest alten in active service, a huge, fit man whose uniform was tight over his broad chest as he flourished his arms to make whatever point he now emphasized to Tretton. Olive skinned with curling brown hair, he, like Tretton, was native of Ekhem. Though most of the veteran Altenerai maintained a somewhat formal distance with the newer ranked—and Rylin had never decided if it was deliberately affected or the result of their combat experience—Decrin seemed never to have met a stranger and was always ready with a warm word or a friendly smile. But today he seemed as solemn as his companion.

As neither was inclined to invite him to join their conversation, Rylin looked away, his gaze drifting over the rest of the room.

There were four double doors into the chamber, and only the one Rylin and Lasren had entered by saw regular use. It opened wide again as Commander Denaven himself pushed through. Rylin rose with the others, open palm to his heart.

Denaven returned the salute crisply as he strode for his chair, to the right of the queen's. "At ease."

Morning rays from the upper windows caught the commander's immaculate copper hair. His narrow face seemed even more pinched than usual, as though he'd been sucking lemons. "Gyldara won't be joining us," he said as he took his seat. "She's had a family tragedy."

Lasren glanced at Rylin as if to gauge his reaction, so Rylin cocked an eyebrow at him.

Tretton's precise alto cut through the chamber. "Is it something serious, then?"

Denaven frowned. "Yes. Gyldara's bad news has some bearing upon our meeting, as I'll explain momentarily."

The primary door opened once more, and this time Varama walked in.

Perhaps the oddest of the Altenerai, Varama was almost never to be found in uniform anymore, although she wore one today. Her long face was large chinned, and she had dark brown, curling hair she wore pulled tightly back, an unflattering style that emphasized her high forehead and showed more of her strange blue-cast skin. Some with magical talent or phenomenal athletic prowess carried aberrations along with their gifts, and Varama's peculiar hue marked her as surely as Kyrkenall's strange eyes marked him.

"Thank you for waiting," Varama said. So far as Rylin knew, no one had been. Varama's seat was at least three chairs apart from everyone else. She looked in turn with unblinking blue eyes at each of them as she took it.

Denaven cleared his throat. "That's everyone."

"Everyone?" Decrin asked. His voice, from deep inside that powerful chest, would have carried even in a room without fine acoustics. "Cargen and K'narr still missing, then?"

"They won't be coming," Denaven said flatly. "Nor will Kyrkenall. Enada remains in Kanesh and I've no idea as to Cerai's whereabouts. We might as well consider Belahn resigned, at this point."

No one looked surprised by this last; it had been more than five years since Belahn had requested an indefinite leave of absence.

Denaven put his hands flat on the table. "We were dealt a terrible blow with Asrahn's death. And I have to bear witness to another. Kyrkenall's killed two more of us."

Rylin gaped. Tretton sat straighter. Decrin leaned forward, as though readying to throw himself into combat, and Lasren audibly sucked in a breath. Even Varama raised her head a little.

"He's slaughtered K'narr and Cargen and the missing mage exalts. One of them was Gyldara's sister. Gyldara found the four bodies this morning. They'd been dragged into N'lahr's tomb."

Lasren sat stock-still save for his huge hands, knotting into fists. He and K'narr had been close.

"What about Elenai?" Rylin asked, and then felt everyone staring at him. "The missing squire," he added, although everyone had to know who he meant. She'd vanished along with Kyrkenall and the others. She was clever and talented, and pretty enough to be distracting.

The commander's stare seemed to see right through him. "There's no sign of her."

Rylin was struck by a sudden sense of profound loss. Not only were the past and the present imperiled but the future was suddenly dimmer as well. He genuinely liked the determined squire, and simply assumed she'd one day be sitting near him at this very table.

Decrin's voice was very low. "How do you know Kyrkenall did this?"

"I sent Cargen and K'narr to ask him questions about Asrahn's death. Because it looks like he murdered him, too."

Gods. Everyone had always said Kyrkenall was a little crazy. But what could possibly have pushed him to murder his old mentor?

Tretton's voice was sharp, challenging. "Do you have proof, Commander?"

"I have more than I'm happy with. Cargen overheard Kyrkenall arguing with Asrahn near the east bridge the night before Asrahn's death. When he passed closer he saw only Kyrkenall, who was drunk and acting strange. When Cargen asked him what was wrong, he was cursed and threatened."

That wasn't at all hard to believe.

"Kyrkenall wouldn't have killed Asrahn," Decrin protested. "No matter how drunk he got."

"No? I can just about tell you what happened. Kyrkenall's indiscretions have become more and more outrageous, even if you ignore the fact he's flaunted orders to return to Darassus. I told Asrahn that the next time we saw him we'd have to have a word with him, but he hasn't been in Darassus for years. I think Asrahn took the opportunity of Kyrkenall's reappearance to try to set him straight, right on the banks of the Idris. And Kyrkenall snapped, as he's so often done before." Denaven's look was angry, almost challenging. "Maybe," he conceded, "he was too inebriated to realize what he'd done until later. You said he was asking you about Asrahn's whereabouts at the parade." Denaven met Decrin's eyes, then glanced at Varama, who looked inscrutable as always.

"But he must have remembered," the commander continued, "which is why he left the ceremony, and when I sent Cargen and the others to question him, he killed them, too."

Rylin let out a long, slow breath. To lose not just one alten, but three, killed by the hand of a fourth. And now they'd have to hunt him down like a rabid beast. The corps certainly wasn't the shining example of honor, loyalty, and unity it once had been.

"Why did he take the squire with him when he left the parade?" Decrin asked.

Denaven turned over a palm. "We can't know for certain, but she's one of the last people who saw Asrahn alive. Maybe he wanted to know if she'd seen him after he did. She's probably dead, too, and we just haven't found her."

Rylin sighed heavily. He'd really hoped his presentiments were wrong.

"How do we know for certain it's Kyrkenall who killed these people?" Tretton asked.

Denaven looked disappointed in him. "First, they were found dead, together. Two Altenerai and two talented weavers are a force to be reckoned with. For all his faults, Kyrkenall remains a deadly warrior. Second, they had been sent specifically to interview him before he vanished again." The commander paused before continuing, his voice more certain than ever. "Third, he left a note. Gyldara found it with the bodies."

The commander removed a small torn slip of paper from the inside of his khalat and set it in front of him. "It's in Kyrkenall's hand. 'Next time you come for me, you'd better send an army.' He signed it."

"Let me see that." Decrin extended a long arm.

Denaven passed it across the table to him, and Decrin took it, staring hard while Tretton leaned to get a closer look.

"By the Gods," Tretton muttered. He made the Sign of the Four across his chest, diagonally down from right to left, across, then left to right.

"I have two questions," Varama broke in, her voice clear and high.

Denaven turned to her. "Yes?"

"First, how many bottles were in the tomb?"

"Bottles?" Denaven asked, completely taken aback.

"There were bottles in the tomb. I'd like to know how many."

"What has that got to do with anything?" Lasren asked under his breath.

"There were some there," Denaven slowly confirmed.

Rylin wondered less how Varama had known about the bottles and more about why the strange woman fastened upon such an odd detail.

"I can't say as I counted them," Denaven continued. "I was too busy taking in the bloated bodies of our fallen."

Varama ignored the icy contempt in his voice. "I would like a count. Second—"

"Hold on, Varama," Decrin rumbled. Kyrkenall's letter shook in his scarred hand. "Denaven, I still can't believe he'd kill Asrahn. Maybe these four attacked him, and he fought back."

"They weren't under orders to arrest him, just question him," Denaven said. "And as I told you, I can't believe he killed Asrahn on purpose. Maybe he lost his temper and pushed him into the river and didn't notice Asrahn hit his head. But we have no way of knowing, because Kyrkenall fled. And he clearly killed the people he left rotting in N'lahr's tomb. Even if it were some misunderstanding, he's got a lot to answer for. I'm sorry," Denaven added. "We weren't close, but I wouldn't have wanted this for him any more than you would. He's stained the honor of the corps."

The only sound was the note crinkling in Decrin's hand.

"My second question," Varama interjected into the silence, "is whether the mages you sent after him carried a hearthstone."

Denaven froze for a moment, seemingly uncertain how to respond. Rylin wondered how Varama could sound so completely unfazed.

"They did," Denaven admitted reluctantly.

Rylin looked at Varama. How had she guessed that? So far as he knew, every hearthstone ever discovered had been put under close watch by the Mage Auxiliary. After some disastrous experiments in the war, they'd never been carried into the field. Hearthstones were so secret he'd only been made aware of them after his elevation to the sapphire, and he'd never actually seen one.

Varama didn't follow up her question, though, and no one else seemed interested in pursuing the tangent.

It was Lasren who broke the silence at last. "I volunteer to track him down."

"Thank you." Denaven nodded.

"Then I'm going," Decrin declared. "If my brother alten's to be brought in, I want to hear the explanation from his own lips."

"He may be too far gone for that," Tretton said. "But we'll try. I'll track for the expedition."

"Count me in," Rylin promised. Somewhat guiltily, he knew a surge of excitement. Perhaps this hunt, at last, would win him some renown.

"Very well," Denaven said grimly. "I'll lead. We leave in two hours' time.

Bring a squire and arrange for supplies. Gyldara rides with us. Varama, I leave the corps in your hands. Your first duty must be the funeral arrangements."

"I'll need Rylin." Her strange cold eyes sought his, though her expression was bland as ever.

Rylin stiffened. Fortunately, his commander came to his aid.

"You can get by with assistance from the squires."

"No," Varama said, "the sixth rankers are on the borders. I need Rylin."

He felt his jaw drop and quickly closed it. Objecting would be unseemly.

Denaven almost looked apologetic. "You heard her, Rylin. Stay here and assist."

"Yes, sir." Damn it!

"This is a dark business," Denaven said, rising. "I hope the corps never sees its like again."

Rylin stood with the others, still a little shocked. What could Varama possibly need him for? Bottle counting?

Tretton caught up to Denaven as the commander headed for the exit, and the two quickly fell into conversation as they left. Varama called for Decrin, who obligingly stepped over to one of the cold fireplaces to speak in hushed tones.

Lasren smirked at Rylin and patted his shoulder with one large hand. "Tough break. So I guess I'll be comforting Gyldara. And hunting down a menace to the realm. And you'll be answering any weird questions Varama can think of." Lasren pushed back his hair and glanced surreptitiously toward the blue-skinned woman. He rendered a fair impression of her high-pitched voice, affecting a glassy stare. "'Rylin, what color is the nearest fish? It's vitally important I know what the queen had for breakfast. Count the times I fart today.'"

"I thought you'd be more upset," Rylin said.

Lasren's smile faded on the instant. "You don't think I'm upset? I want to skewer that little brown hastig. What am I going to say to K'narr's mother?" Lasren smacked one fist into his palm.

Rylin nodded slowly and watched as Decrin and Varama, still deep in conversation, exited the room.

Lasren punched Rylin's shoulder. "I'll kill him extra for you."

"Sure. Keep your robe hooked up."

Lasren laughed as he put his hand to the door. "Who are you, my mother?"

That hadn't come out right. Lasren habitually left his collar open rather than closing it all the way, and Rylin didn't want Kyrkenall shooting an arrow through his throat.

Lasren looked back once as he pushed open the door. "Try not to get too bored."

7

Seven Bottles

Rylin's duties proved more aggravating than boring. After vague instructions, Varama absented herself, which meant Rylin spent the day making seemingly endless choices about coffin and tomb decorations, conferring with city functionaries about the funeral procession and dozens of other small but related matters.

The next morning, Varama made a brief appearance in the Altenerai offices to present Rylin with a thick tome written in crabbed handwriting. It detailed official memorial rituals. He'd never imagined the stunning array of important rules and customs that had to be observed. For instance, no squires were permitted to dismount before the coffin was interred, and no oration was allowed to continue for more than a quarter hour, not excepting the occasional instance of double funerals.

His second full day of administrative duties stretched late into the evening, for the sketches drawn by tomb artisans proved either ostentatious or overly morbid and he had to order corrections. None of their proposals approached the elegance of sculptures by the great Melagar, still hard at work on Asrahn's tomb design, and in mourning for his husband besides.

When Rylin had finally coaxed appropriately sober and coherent designs from the artists, he returned at last to his suite of rooms, ate a cold duck in red wine sauce that his cook had prepared hours before, and fell into an empty bed. Life had altered drastically in the last few days, and rather than contemplating some beauty as he drifted off, he was a little amused to realize he was instead thinking irritably about pale-eyed Varama.

She'd completely abandoned him to wrestle all the tedious matters Denaven had expected her to resolve. At the least she could have been supervising field training for the squires. Instead, she retreated to her workshops as usual, so Rylin, busy with everything else, had temporarily placed a fifth ranker, Elik, in charge of the squires. Contributing to the instruction of first and second ranks was a routine function of upper squires, but to Rylin's knowledge, no one below sixth had ever acted as Master of Squires, and he didn't like the idea of setting the precedent. For all he knew, he might be violating Altenerai tenets as obscure as those for memorials. He was a little frustrated by the thought that he would take the blame for that decision and countless other tiny choices he'd had to make, bereft of input from more experienced advisors.

He woke from a dreamless sleep, still disgruntled, when the cook pounded on his door. Sight of her cheery smile spread one across his own face, and he returned to his bedroom to shave while she hummed merrily on the tiny patio kitchen. She was a nice little tidbit, round in all the right places. When he'd hired her last year, he'd thought her appearance rather ordinary, but frequent proximity had made him more conscious of the woman's physical assets. She seemed constantly to be bending over to reach an ingredient or to stir something. Depending upon Rylin's angle, that presented an enticing view of either a curvaceous backside or generous cleavage.

Maybe it was time to revisit his promise to himself about not . . .

There came another knock. Rylin rinsed his razor and imagined the cook's swaying trot to the door as he heard the light pad of her feet. Then came the creek of hinges and a throaty "oh" of surprise.

The conversation that followed was pitched too low for him to hear. Probably a servant was delivering ingredients for the meal.

He jumped at the unexpected loud thump on his bedroom door. And it wasn't the contralto of the cook that came through the wood after the knock, but the high-pitched voice of Varama.

"Rylin, this is Varama. We must talk."

He frowned into the mirror, tapping hair off his razor. It was an abrupt shift from thinking of the cook, dripping with sensuality, to Varama, erotic as a plank of oak. He forced a pleasant tone. "Do you want to join me for breakfast?"

"No. I've sent your cook away."

Of course she had. "Give me a moment." If Varama planned to leave him with cryptic, minimal instructions prior to wandering off today, she was going to get an earful. Especially if his breakfast was ruined. Technically, Varama didn't even outrank him. There was no way he was going to go on taking care of all the menial work while Varama continued her . . . whatever.

Rylin finished his shave with three more swift passes. He put on a freshly laundered white shirt but didn't bother donning his uniform coat before opening the bedroom door.

Varama had helped herself to two of Rylin's goblets and set them on the table. She finished pouring liquid from an amber bottle into the first, then started on the second.

She wore full Altenerai regalia, but she looked a little odder than usual, for her hair was slicked back more severely and dark circles rimmed her eyes. Her khalat was rumpled and its collar was hooked all the way up to her chin, as if she thought someone might assault her at any time. It was a wonder she didn't have her helmet on, cheek pieces lowered.

"A little early for drinking, isn't it?" Rylin lifted a golden pear from a basket the cook must have brought in, and took a bite. He didn't join Varama in a seat, but propped himself against the wall opposite her.

"This is cherry juice. It's delicious." Varama tapped the stem of one goblet as she lifted the other to her lips.

"If this is about my orders for the day, we have to talk."

Varama lowered her drink. "Who do you suppose came to see me after I went to N'lahr's tomb?"

Rylin's annoyance made him flippant. "N'lahr's ghost?" He took another bite, which produced a satisfying crunch even if the pear itself was a little tasteless.

She either ignored or didn't understand his sarcastic tone. "Sareel. Why do you suppose she sought me out?"

"No idea."

"The glass door on Irion's display case had been shattered. Sareel's aware of my experimentation with glasswork and hoped I could manufacture something more sturdy to replace it."

So she'd come to talk to him about broken glass? Was Varama planning to tell him this had been more important than the funeral arrangements the commander had personally instructed her to oversee?

"You're supposed to ask me who broke the case," she said.

He swallowed and asked carelessly: "Who broke the case?"

"Kyrkenall."

"Kyrkenall?" He lowered the pear. Maybe Varama actually was heading toward something important, though she meandered there like a stumbling drunk. "You mean he's back?"

Varama immediately disappointed him by shaking her head no. "He damaged it before he left. But it was Elenai who reported to Sareel that Kyrkenall broke the case. He was examining the sword the day he left. And

I suppose you know that Asrahn had handpicked Elenai to repair Irion's hilt, don't you?"

"I'm sure this is all very interesting, but—"

"Listen, Rylin! Who do you suppose is the last person in Darassus to see Asrahn alive?"

"Kyrkenall, probably. Since he's the one who killed him."

"Unconfirmed. Sareel is the last person currently in the palace who interacted with him. Asrahn was asking questions about Irion. The night he died."

"Why would he do that?"

"That's it! Now you're asking the right question." Varama tapped the goblet with her index finger, a scarred stub beyond its final knuckle. "All three of them were involved with the sword."

"What three?"

"Asrahn, Elenai, and Kyrkenall. Aren't you listening? One dies, the others vanish. How do you suppose this is all connected to the other deaths?"

He sighed. "I had a late night."

"Not as late as mine."

He glanced again at her rumpled uniform sleeves and wondered if she'd even changed out of her khalat since yesterday. Maybe she'd slept in it. Maybe she hadn't slept at all.

She kept staring at him. The unblinking gaze out of that lightly blue tinted face made it hard to think. Suppose she'd been investigating the way these disparate pieces of information intersected? The veterans claimed she was brilliant, if admittedly peculiar. Maybe he should give her the benefit of the doubt.

"All right," he said, raising his hand with the pear in resignation. "You've got my attention. Are you saying Kyrkenall stole the sword? What's he planning to do with it?" Surely he'd have heard if Irion were missing.

"That's not it. The sword we've known as Irion is in its case now. Stop guessing."

"All right." She had an odd way of phrasing things. He set down the half-eaten pear and crossed his arms. "Tell me more."

"Alten Cargen and M'lahna the mage also came to consult with Sareel just before their deaths. Their central concern? What Asrahn had asked the Keeper of Keys about the sword. After they were done talking with Sareel, they paid a visit to Elenai. Who had been caring for the sword."

Rylin nodded, encouraging her to continue. "So the sword is important to all of this. I've got it."

"Do you? I can never tell if people really understand or not. The sword *is* at the center of 'all of this,' and Denaven didn't bother to say anything to us about it. Don't you think he should have?"

"Maybe he didn't know."

"Of course he knew! He's the one who sent Cargen after Kyrkenall, by his own admission. Remember?"

He'd said that. "Yes. But suppose it was a matter of security—"

"That he wouldn't reveal to Decrin and Tretton and the rest of us, but that Denaven would share with just Cargen and K'narr? Junior Altenerai? And Denaven saw the connection about the bottles, too."

What? Junior Altenerai? That was a new insult; he'd never heard the old guard put voice to the prejudice that clearly before, but . . . wait a moment. She'd said something else. "The bottles . . ." Rylin had forgotten them. "You mean in N'lahr's tomb?"

"Exactly! Only someone with an Altenerai ring can open the tomb door to pay respects directly. And every year around N'lahr's birthday I find an empty bottle inside, on the prayer bench."

Rylin wouldn't have pegged her as particularly reverent, which was mildly interesting all on its own. More germanely, though, he still didn't see what the bottles had to do with anything. "Meaning?"

She studied him, frowning slightly, as if in frustration. "Kyrkenall has returned to Darassus every year. Denaven had to have seen those bottles and known it. Asrahn certainly knew; he commented about being the third visitor that month when we happened to meet after the fourth year."

"Some other alten could have left those bottles."

"It's Murian wine," she said, as if that made the difference. "No other alten drinks that rot. And what other alten would drink wine with N'lahr? Anyone else would have been burning incense and offering prayers."

Rylin supposed that was true. "Maybe Denaven just didn't make the connection."

"Unlikely. There were seven bottles, one quite new." She continued with an air of overexplaining that two and two made four. "Kyrkenall's returned every single year, despite Denaven's accusations to the contrary."

He thought he understood, now. She was simply trying to exonerate a friend in some weird way. It was touching, really. "Even if Kyrkenall came to the tomb, he didn't actually come to the city. That's probably all Denaven meant."

"Don't be an idiot," she snapped. "This is further evidence that Denaven's deliberately misleading us."

It served him right for feeling momentarily sympathetic toward her. He cleared his throat and spoke slowly. "I'm not an idiot."

"Then start thinking. You're supposed to be the bright one."

That sounded like a backhanded compliment if he'd ever heard one. Rylin reached down, touched the stem of the extra goblet she'd brought, and then, because he needed something to do, lifted it to his lips. He was sorting through everything Varama had just said and finding it a little like rebuilding a rice pot from a dozen shards he'd thought came from a wine jug. He could see the shape of her argument, and, although pieces were missing, they fit as well or better than the previous explanation.

He drank the cherry juice, and was surprised to find a warm glow spreading down through his chest, as if he'd swallowed a ray of sunlight. "That's nice."

"Are you following, Rylin?" Varama's eyes were fever bright.

"I'm starting to. If you're right about all of this, what does it really mean?"

"It means things happened differently from what we were told. Asrahn found out something was wrong with the sword. He said something obscure to Elenai and then wandered off to be killed, and his death was made to look like an accident."

"How—"

She talked over him. "The next day, Kyrkenall talked with Elenai at the funeral and something she said alerted him. She didn't know what was happening, or she'd have been more worried, you see. And then—"

"She and Kyrkenall looked at the sword," Rylin said. Everything was growing clearer.

"Exactly. They went to see Irion. Kyrkenall broke open the case for want of a key. Sareel had one, and—I checked—the other was among Asrahn's wetted effects."

Varama might be on to something. "But Kyrkenall did kill four people."

"You're still fixated upon the wrong things. Think about the sword, Rylin. In N'lahr's hands we've seen it slice through armor and other blades like they were paper. Yet after N'lahr died, Denaven's never permitted another alten to carry it. Now that I'm experimenting with metallurgy, he won't allow me anywhere near it, either. You'd think he would want me to know how to make multiple swords with those properties, wouldn't you?"

Rylin felt compelled to remind her of a few other important facts. "But Kyrkenall killed Altenerai." He almost hoped she'd disagree.

"Almost certainly. Cargen and K'narr and two mages went to question him, or more likely to kill him, because they took superior numbers and a hearthstone. Now you should ask why."

"Oh, I am."

"Because Irion's a fake. I sneaked in to remove it late last night and examined it thoroughly at my workshop."

She'd broken in to steal Irion? Rylin's sense of outrage surprised him. "You stole a sacred weapon?"

"I borrowed a hunk of metal as sacred as my boot."

"Did you know that before you took it?"

"I suspected. The sword's well balanced and looks perfect, but its magic is a complex glamour. It radiates enchantment without conveying any benefit whatsoever. The one on display isn't N'lahr's sword. It's never been N'lahr's sword, which is why Denaven never let me examine it. You follow that, don't you?"

"Yes." He'd heard Irion was never to be touched because it was an honored artifact, but now that he thought of it, that seemed more like a specious excuse. None of the other weapons in the hall were untended. "If all this is true, why did Kyrkenall run instead of talking to you, or Decrin? Didn't he know that would make him look guilty?"

"He probably wasn't sure whom he could trust. That seems a little cautious for Kyrkenall, but it's the only conclusion I can reach based upon his actions."

Rylin reached for the chair beside him, pulled it out, all but oblivious to the loud scraping of chair legs against the stone floor. He sank into it as his mind raced. "How do we warn the search party that Kyrkenall's innocent? That Denaven's trying to kill him?"

"Kyrkenall has a head start. He's wily. He could well evade them."

"They say Tretton can track anything, anywhere." The old alten was supposed to be able to follow trails into the deepest regions of the Shifting Lands.

"He's very good," Varama agreed. "And Denaven knows some weaver's tricks. But I warned Decrin about my concerns. And Kyrkenall's always been absurdly lucky. We'll have to hope, for his sake and the squire's, that the Gods continue to smile upon him."

At least Elenai might be all right in this scenario. Rylin ran his hand back through his hair and studied the gawky, long-chinned woman standing before him. Why had she pulled him into all this? "Why not keep Decrin back to help you? Or Tretton?"

"Denaven wouldn't have permitted Tretton to stay back, and I need

Decrin with the search party because he's doggedly certain Kyrkenall's caught up in some tragic confusion. What you really mean is, why you."

He nodded slowly. "How did you even know you could trust me? I mean, it seems like there were three Altenerai involved in this conspiracy already. What if there're more?"

"I chose you because: one, you needed more to do."

What did she mean by that? She raised her mutilated finger and ticked off an invisible check mark in the air.

"Two, you had a vital connection."

This time he interrupted. "A connection?"

But she went on anyway. "And three, I'd rather keep to myself."

Then why had she even bothered mentioning it?

"I'll address your other questions in order. I can't be sure if other Altenerai are involved. I suspected you weren't because you were neither particularly favored by Denaven nor especially close with Cargen or K'narr."

"Lasren was tight with K'narr, but he's no traitor."

"Can you be sure of that?"

He started to answer in his friend's defense, then realized there couldn't be a statement of absolute surety. "I'd like to be."

"But you can't be. I'm reasonably confident Tretton's not involved. Likewise Cerai and Enada. But I can't be sure. I'm suspicious of Gyldara, given her sister's complicity, but even if she's innocent she wouldn't have been as useful."

"So I'm useful to you?" Was that a compliment?

"When you reached the fourth rank, you once turned down an invitation to join the Mage Auxiliary."

"Yes." They'd tried to convince him to switch to their service, just as they routinely did with anyone showing magical talent, especially Altenerai squires. Where was this going?

"You were intimate with a fellow squire now an exalt in the Mage Auxiliary."

How did she know about her? The name slipped from his lips as he thought of her warm, taut body. "Tesra. How is she important?"

"We don't have enough information to know why Denaven's lied about the sword. I've looked in vain through his office. That's a dead end. But we do know the Mage Auxiliary is part of all this. Denaven works closely with them, and they contributed two people to the attack on Kyrkenall."

"Wait—how much of this did you suspect two days ago, when you pulled me out?"

"Enough."

He was both disturbed and impressed. "All right then. But you can't think that Tesra's just going to spill any secrets she knows. I mean, I'm good, but—"

"You're to make overtures. Tell her you're thinking about switching to the Mage Auxiliary."

"You want me to lie to her? That's against my oath."

"Deceptions are permissible when you work against enemies."

Of course that was true, or ambushes and battlefield tactics would never be permitted. But to assume that their own sister units were morally equivalent with Naor barbarians was a leap. "The Mage Auxiliary is our enemy?"

"I believe so. You must seek the truth, Rylin. Use all your wiles to gain access to what they know. You must do so quickly, before Denaven returns or one of his agents catches on to us."

This was all moving quite fast. He shook his head and thought of Tesra. She'd been delightful, but he hadn't spent time with her in years, unless he counted a few casual conversations in palace corridors. Varama, who didn't seem to have any deep emotional attachments, let alone romantic ones, might not understand the difficulties. Wasn't there an easier way? "Why not just present what you've told me to the queen?"

"She's probably involved."

That startled him. He began to ask her why, then held back. He could tell by Varama's look that she expected he should already know. After a moment, the answer was obvious.

Denaven was known to be close to the queen, and some gossiped that they'd been lovers. In any case, their relationship was much more cooperative than those between the queen and the previous two commanders. Some grumbled openly that Denaven had granted her every wish, even permitting the newly created Mage Auxiliary to recruit from among Altenerai squires, which was widely seen as weakening the corps.

Yes, all and all, it was almost impossible to imagine Denaven acting so boldly without the queen's approval. And that meant Rylin wasn't just being asked to investigate a conspiracy involving his commanding officer, but that the queen herself might be a traitor to the realm.

Or that he himself might be accused of traitorous action if he opposed her. He envisioned himself in Kyrkenall's position, with a search party after him soon—assuming he could even get away from Darassus.

Rylin reached across the table and poured himself another goblet full of cherry juice. He quaffed it like it was hard liquor. "What do we do if she *is* involved?"

"Once we have enough evidence, we approach the Council of Governors.

And our brothers and sisters in the corps. But we still don't know the motive. We'll need a lot more to convince."

"Which is why you need me."

"Yes. I hope it goes without saying that you must be extremely circumspect. There are a lot of corpses connected with this already."

"Yes."

"If you're not careful, one of them might be yours."

"I got that."

"I hoped you would."

8

———≈———

Old Friends

As recently as Rylin's first squire years, the ground where the new palace wing stood had been flower gardens. Now it was, for all intents and purposes, a separate building, though it adjoined the palace and mimicked its four-story stone structure complete to green tiled roof. It always irked Rylin that second-rank Altenerai squires were posted before its wide entrance doors. Bad enough that the auxiliary siphoned equipment and mages away from the corps. Surely they could protect their own holdings.

He hid his feelings as he reached the height of the building's outside stairs and saluted the two spear-bearers on the flagged portico.

Both men returned the salute, and the one on his left stepped forward, a tall, dark-skinned man from the Storm Coast. "Hail, Alten. Do you have an appointment?"

Rylin lifted the wicker basket he carried, heavy with red and yellow fruits and honey-roasted almonds. "I'm visiting an old friend."

"Is your friend expecting you, sir?"

The youth knew his duty a little too well. "It's a surprise, Squire."

The guard nodded reluctantly, the horsehair crest on his parade helmet shaking as he did so. "I'm sorry, Alten. I'll have to get permission to allow you entry."

"I'm Altenerai, Squire. " He lifted his left hand and willed his ring to light. "And we wouldn't want to spoil the lady's surprise."

"I'm sorry, Alten. My orders are very clear. Who are you here to see?"

He shut down the ring and lowered his hand. "Tesra Gerenar."

"I'll convey your request immediately."

Not an auspicious start. Rylin stepped back, pretending to study architectural detailing around the cornices while the squire entered the building. He'd left his rooms two hours ago and set out in search of gifts appropriate for courting, although now that he considered the produce, he wondered if he hadn't delayed this visit so he had more time to let everything Varama had told him sink in.

He'd wasted time, and he was afraid he wasted it now, waiting on a second-rank squire to convey his message. He fretted his plan to get information was feeble. Why would Tesra tell him anything of import, even if he convinced her he'd leave the Altenerai? Maybe she didn't know anything anyway. He frowned at himself. He wanted a chance to prove himself, didn't he? A hero of legend wouldn't be so indecisive.

He started forward the moment the door swung wide. The squire returned with someone Rylin briefly mistook for a fellow alten. He wasn't, though. The tall, thin man with wheat-colored hair wore a well-fitted khalat, rendered blue by the lengthy curing process to interlock the fibers. But the decorations on the metallic shoulder guards were red, as was the piping along his pants, and a ruby shown on his finger. This, then, was one of the auxiliary's officers, supposedly of equivalent stature to Altenerai. They didn't often wear uniforms.

"Alten Rylin?" The fellow smiled without using his eyes. "I'm Exalt Verin. I'm afraid Tesra's indisposed at the moment, but I'll be happy to take a message."

Of course he was. "When will she be free?"

"I'm not really sure."

He returned that cold smile with a very warm one. "That's a shame. I've a personal matter I need to speak to her about. A rather urgent one. Here."

Verin blinked and took the basket as Rylin pushed it into his chest.

"Why don't you carry that in to her, and I'll come with you." He walked toward the door.

"I'm really not sure that's—"

"She won't mind. And if she's still too busy, I'm sure she'll let me know herself."

Rylin opened the door and walked through, holding it after for Verin, still carrying the basket and looking irresolute. Rylin took in the high stone walls, found them brighter than those in the Altenerai corridors, though he didn't see why immediately. There were many doors, and ahead were branching halls. Missing were the numerous plaques and cases of mementos to be found in Altenerai corridors. The auxiliary corps had no heroic moments to immortalize.

He knew that his command of the situation was tenuous. And there wasn't time to look around.

"Tesra will be glad I've come," he insisted. "This is more important than I've let on, believe me. Now which way is she?" Rylin started forward.

Verin hurried to match his stride. "It's really not a good time, Alten. And I'm not sure—"

"How long has the Mage Auxiliary been routinely wearing khalats? I've only seen you in them on special occasions."

"After Alten Kyrkenall killed M'lahna and Kerst it seemed like a good idea." His eyes held a challenge, as if he expected argument.

"It is," Rylin agreed. They were coming to an intersection. "Although Cargen's khalat didn't seem to do him much good. Which way?"

Verin looked a little off-balance still. Good. "She's in the Great Hall." Almost against his will Verin nodded toward a set of oak doors on the right. "But you really shouldn't interrupt, Alten. I've let you come too far already."

Rylin lifted the basket from his hand. "I'll take it from here. Thanks." He glanced briefly at the door as he pushed it, noting it was cut approximately like that on the Altenerai meeting room. Carved into its central panel was a slender feminine figure in a flowing gown, arms upraised, and what appeared to be a fiery sun suspended between her hands. A goddess, then, and from her long hair, perhaps Vedessa, though Rylin knew no story of her carrying the sun.

Inside was a vaster space than he would have guessed. This portion of the hall stretched all the way to the vaulted ceiling four stories above. High, wide windows along what would have been the third and fourth floors cast long rectangles of light down upon rows of tables where men and women crouched over glowing, beautiful crystalline things he guessed must be hearthstones while others beside them scribbled on parchment paper. Yet more watched the pendulums of small clocks set beside them.

Beyond the tables stretched row after row of high shelves, and Rylin realized with a start that hearthstones sat upon them all. How many, he could not tell. Certainly more than the dozens he had guessed in existence. There were hundreds, possibly approaching a thousand, each sitting a few feet from its neighbor, and organized on the shelves by color. He'd had no idea that there was a rainbow's variety of them, from pure white to ebony.

And he had no idea how dazzlingly attractive they were, especially the ones under active study.

"Stay here." This time Verin's voice held a warning note. He motioned Rylin to a brown flagstone to the left of the door before he walked forward.

At the sound of his footfalls some of the clock watchers and note takers looked up. One fixed him with a long, disapproving stare and he recognized her for the commander of the Mage Auxiliary, Synahla. Her eyes were some of the most striking Rylin had ever seen, their vibrant violet obvious from forty paces out.

Rylin nodded politely, even as he knew what all were thinking. Not only was he uninvited, he was about as welcome as a roach in a flour jar.

And so he fixed a smile on his face, as if he were simply happy to be here and only mildly curious, and watched Verin bend over to consult with one of the women jotting notes.

Tesra.

She had always been pretty. Her black hair, now grown past her shoulders, was pulled away from her forehead by a silver band set with a small ruby. It suited her. He considered that hollow in her neck where he'd liked to kiss her and his smile grew a little more wistful. She seemed softer now. Probably she didn't have to run drills every day here in the auxiliary.

Her eyes found his. She didn't return his smile, nor did she look especially pleased when the violet-eyed woman strode over to consult with her. They spoke briefly, and then Synahla took Tesra's place as Rylin's old lover walked toward him, motioning Verin to stay behind.

Yes, still fit but a bit curvier, obvious even in the dark gown with the red sash. Red was the Mage Auxiliary's answer to the sapphire. He wondered if their rings were endowed with the same powers, or if they were somehow different.

Tesra stopped before him, her reaction not the least bit warmed by his welcoming smile. Her voice was hushed. "Rylin, you're not supposed to be here."

He lifted the basket. "That's no way to greet an old friend bearing gifts. My apologies for staying away so long." He searched her eyes in vain for like feeling.

She took him by the arm and walked him to the door and out. Then she pulled the door shut with her free hand and looked up at him. "We're in the midst of some delicate studies."

"I can be delicate," Rylin quipped. "And studious."

She sighed, unable to suppress a slight smile. "It's always nice to see you, of course," she said, "but not here. And this isn't a good time."

He slowly put a hand to her shoulder and considered her with sad gravity. "This is important or I wouldn't have barged in."

For the first time, she seemed to be actually looking at him as her old friend. "Nothing's happened to your brother, has it?"

He remembered how much she'd taken to his brother when he'd visited. "He's fine. This is about me. I need your help."

The warmth was still there, but more guarded.

"I want . . . I need . . ." He looked away, as if he were embarrassed. He spoke softly. "I'm thinking about leaving the Altenerai."

She was very lovely indeed as she watched him with widened eyes. "But why?"

He shook his head, and spoke to her about all of his true misgivings. "It's just not what I expected. Half the officers don't even turn up for meetings. The veterans barely talk to us. And Kyrkenall . . . Well. It feels like the Altenerai are fading. I want to be part of something greater."

What did that look of hers mean? She was debating.

He spoke on. "Remember what you told me when you left? That the Mage Auxiliary would tremendously improve our understanding of sorcery. Has it? Have you gotten better?"

She nodded enthusiastically. "Oh, yes. Rylin, it's been amazing—" She fell silent, for the door to the Great Hall opened behind her and violet-eyed Synahla swept out. She had at least ten years on Tesra, but carried it well, and he admired the cut of dark pants against wide hips, and the white blouse tucked tight into the band to better accentuate her small waist. Those beautiful eyes appraised him with little warmth, but she presented her ruby-ringed hand as she stepped forward.

"Alten Rylin, isn't it? I don't believe I've had the pleasure."

He enjoyed the pressure of slim fingers against his wrist, and returned her greeting clasp.

"I hope Tesra has explained to you that we're on a schedule?"

"A schedule for what?" Rylin asked innocently.

"I was going to, Commander," Tesra said quickly, "but Rylin has come to see us about joining the auxiliary."

"You have?" The commander arched an eyebrow at him.

"I've been considering it for a long time. Ever since I got the ring, actually." As Rylin wasn't entirely convinced that the Mage Auxiliary was an enemy of Darassus, he was attempting to tread a narrow path and say few if any outright lies. There was, in fact, a fair bit of truth to his words, for he really had been disappointed by the lack of chances to do anything mean-

ingful. The promise of greater magical training if he'd transitioned to the
auxiliary had been a tempting lure during his squire days, and he'd often
wondered afterward about the path not taken. "The Altenerai Corps's not
what I expected."

Still she stared. He'd always thought he'd know if someone were reading or mazing him, and was unsettled by the sudden notion he might be
entirely wrong. The people within this building had spent years doing little
but honing their craft and working with the hearthstones, which were said
to enhance any magical gifts. Could the commander skim his surface
thoughts without detection? Would it matter that his ring would alert him
if the warning came after she learned the truth?

"I've grown more and more frustrated," he admitted, which was entirely
true. "And I've been thinking about the offer I was extended as a fourth
ranker. When Tesra herself stepped over."

Synahla's response was cool. "Coming over now is a different matter,
Alten. There would be . . . repercussions."

"I know."

"Have you spoken with Denaven?"

"I'd rather this be kept quiet for a time," he said. "I hadn't wished to
inform you yet, either, Commander." He gave her his best apologetic look,
but she wasn't having any of that.

Her tone grew biting. "Were you planning to tell me after you joined?"

"I assumed we'd talk eventually."

"Of course. You're aware that no one's permitted within the auxiliary's
Great Hall without express permission? That includes Altenerai."

"I had no idea. Verin should have mentioned it."

"Verin was ill-equipped for your forceful personality. I see you're a man
who's used to getting his way. Either through inclination or accumulated
arrogance you think you can simply charm your way past any challenge.
It's not that easy, Alten. You were a minor magical worker, at best, five years
ago."

Minor?

"My ranks are full with talented mages who never hesitated to join. Why
should I welcome you? The only reason you could be coming, now, is that
you're embarrassed by your own corps. As you should be. Its days are over,
and if you'd shown Tesra's wisdom when you were a squire you'd have
seen that circumstances like these were inevitable."

Tesra alternated looking between her commander and Rylin, clearly
troubled. He understood how she felt. Unless he changed the tenor of this

conversation, and quickly, his assignment was a failure. A wink and a smile might have worked with Tesra, but it wasn't going to get him past Commander Synahla.

"You must think very little of me, Commander." He passed his gift basket off to Tesra. "Maybe I *am* used to getting what I want. That doesn't mean I haven't worked hard to earn it. I admit I crave glory. Who doesn't? But if you think I became Altenerai solely because of misplaced loyalty to the corps, or some failure of foresight, you're wrong. I swore to my father I'd never give up until I had earned the sapphire. And I held to that oath. Tesra can confirm the truth of it."

Tesra finally rejoined the conversation. "It's true, Commander. Rylin was torn, but he felt honor-bound to keep his word."

"Your dead father, I suppose?" Synahla asked.

He was tempted to play up the dramatic potential of the situation, or to act affronted, but he merely held open, empty palms. "I'm a man of my word, Commander." He didn't mention that he had emphasized that oath when talking with Tesra all those years ago because he'd long since decided to remain with the Altenerai. The tragedy of lovers torn apart by circumstance had been immensely appealing to her at the time.

Synahla's voice wasn't quite as cold as she spoke on. "What of your Altenerai oath, Alten? Didn't you swear to hold to it until your death?"

"'If this be my numbered day, I will meet it smiling. For I'll have held this oath.' I've mulled it over quite carefully." Indeed he had, especially the portions about keeping the truth. "I'll still be working for the realms if I serve in the auxiliary. I can live up to every part of that oath."

"You may make enemies who were once your friends."

"Something that's held me back. Until now."

The commander brushed hair away from her forehead. "Tell me, then. If you hadn't run into me so quickly, what had you hoped to do?"

He glanced at Tesra. "Renew a friendship. Apologize for keeping too distant." He was pleased when his nod was greeted by a tentative smile from his old friend. "And then I hoped to see what I might be getting myself into before I switched horses. So to speak. The auxiliary's closemouthed. I'm not really sure how you serve the realms. I gather you sometimes head out on expeditions for hearthstones, but it seems like most of you just stay here."

"And you'd want the former more than the latter, I suppose." Synahla paused for a moment, but Rylin decided to say nothing that might imperil the conclusion she seemed likely to make. "Well, Rylin, if I do take you, that's exactly the sort of thing I'd have in mind. I imagine you have other uses as well, but, to be frank, our martial prowess is not as pronounced as that of the Altenerai. We do have a few skilled enough to train our division to defend themselves physically, and some of your colleagues occasionally drop by to assist. Pardon me. Your late colleagues used to come by."

Good. That seemed to suggest that only Cargen and K'narr had been directly involved.

Synahla continued. "To have someone more soldierly on staff full-time would be a tremendous asset."

"I would have access to the hearthstones, though?"

"Eventually." Her eyes held his. "Have you ever used one? Or have you simply read accounts?"

"Accounts only."

"I see." She looked mildly disappointed. "Some Altenerai may still hold shards or even full stones, though Denaven's never gotten any to admit it."

"I've never seen one until today," Rylin averred. "I would have liked to have viewed them through the inner world. But that seemed rude."

"Did it. Unlike your presumptuous entry into a restricted area?"

"I don't argue I was presumptuous. But no one told me I was in a place Altenerai were forbidden." So far as he knew, there was no such place in all Erymyr, including its capital, or any of the Allied Realms.

"Indeed." A smile quirked at the corner of her mouth. "Tesra, I'll have Verin finish your work today. Show the alten our training facilities. Let him see where he'd be working."

"Yes, Commander."

She started to turn away; then, as though it were only an afterthought, she paused. "And check out a shard for him so he can have his curiosity satisfied. If you like what you experience, Rylin, speak to me tomorrow and we'll work out what to say to Denaven."

"So I've a formal invite, then?"

"So long as you behave more tactfully from here on out." Synahla looked at him once more as she opened the door, then passed confidently through before closing it after.

Tesra seemed oblivious to her commanding officer's subtle flirtation. She all but beamed at Rylin. "You won her over! She's a tough one, too."

"She doesn't seem so bad."

"Then you weren't paying attention! I thought she was going to have you formally reprimanded before the queen."

Rylin had thought so, too, but he only smiled and shook his head.

"And this basket you brought is very sweet. I do love cherries: these look perfectly ripe."

"They are."

"I'm glad you came. We're working on so many exciting projects. You're going to love it here."

She turned the basket over to him, promising that she'd be right back. Before the door closed, Rylin looked past her swaying figure to the long desk she approached, just visible beyond the field of tables. And directly behind it sat a rack of leather-bound tomes. He imagined Varama would give a lot to know what they held. She might even be more curious about them than the shelves of hearthstones beyond. He hoped he wouldn't actually have to pretend to resign from the Altenerai to find out.

Tesra returned after a few moments, adjusting a lock of hair that escaped her silver band. She showed him the bright lavender shard she'd brought, but didn't hand it over, promising to orient him properly after a tour.

"Tell me about these projects that are so exciting."

She laughed. "You're always so keen. But I really shouldn't talk about them yet. Not until you're full-fledged auxiliary."

"Don't you trust me?"

"It's not that. I'm sworn to keep these matters secret from all the uninitiated. And," she admitted as they started up a side stair, "even some in my division aren't permitted to know what I do."

"So you're saying you're special."

"I thought you knew that."

She shifted the conversation to small talk about friends and family in between pointing out various functional aspects of the building. The living quarters were airier than those in the Altenerai wing, but the walls didn't seem as thick. There were quite a number more rooms than Rylin expected, but many appeared unoccupied. The recovery wards were well stocked—usually for magical injuries rather than physical ones, Tesra told him. The conference room doors were decorated with more of those female figures who weren't quite Vedessa or Darassa.

"What goddess is that, Tesra?"

"If you're good," she said with the hint of a wicked smile, "I'll tell you later."

Finally she led him to a courtyard where eight recruits worked through sword forms under the tutelage of a broad-shouldered swordsman dressed, like Verin, in a khalat with red decorative piping. He looked familiar, but with his back turned Rylin couldn't place him.

Their arrival almost immediately brought the training to a standstill.

Pair by sparring pair, the men and women on the flat, sandy surface lowered their dulled practice swords and stared at him.

After a moment, the instructor turned as well, and that was when Rylin
realized he should have recognized him from the start. Wavy auburn hair,
close cropped; flat brown eyes; a narrow nose with a proud hook.

"Thelar," Tesra said, "we're sorry to interrupt. The commander wanted
me to show Alten Rylin around."

Thelar barked at his pupils to return to work. He strode over sand
shaded by three and a half stories of building, his bootheels crunching the
soil with every step. The others saluted one another with their weapons
and returned to slicing, thrusting, and blocking, their swords clacking dully
as they met. Rylin didn't see the rank novices he'd partly expected.

Thelar didn't bother nodding and directed his question to Tesra. "What's
he doing here?"

She started to speak. "Rylin's considering—" And then she quieted, apparently remembering that Rylin sought discretion.

"I might start training work with your division," Rylin offered.

Thelar's expression was naturally inclined to frowns, and it went mid-
way on to sneer. "I think I have things well in hand. I thought we were
through with Altenerai around here."

"Maybe not," Rylin said. He had been surprised someone so tempera-
mentally unsuited had reached as high as the fourth rank of the Altenerai
and glad to see Thelar leave the corps when he did. And then he remembered, with striking clarity, that it was Denaven who'd argued for Thelar's
continued advancement back then. Just as it was Denaven who'd pressed
other Altenerai to back Cargen's promotion, and then K'narr after him. If
the Mage Auxiliary hadn't been created, might the man before him be wearing a sapphire rather than a ruby?

"Nice ring," Rylin said cooly. He regretted the comment immediately. It
drew attention to Thelar's failure to advance with the Altenerai, surely his
original goal. He could never quite resist needling the thin-skinned rustic
from Alantris. But he didn't expect the venom that followed.

"You arrogant ass." Thelar's voice was low, ugly. "You still think you're
better than me, don't you? I bet you could scarcely wait to volunteer your
services after Cargen and K'narr were murdered. But then you were always
ready to jump on any undeserved opportunity."

Oh. "Is this still about that blonde?" Rylin couldn't even remember her
name. Nira something.

"This is about you." Thelar stabbed a finger at him.

Rylin kept his eyes planted on Thelar's upper chest, just below his neck, the better to watch any peripheral movements. An attack might be imminent. And here everything had been going so well. Synahla had admonished him to be tactful. "I didn't come here to fight you, Thelar."

The sparrers continued poking at one another but kept glancing toward the more engaging conflict at the courtyard's edge. Tesra looked like she might intervene, but Rylin raised a hand to warn her off; he realized he'd have to set some precedent for interactions with Thelar if he were to mingle with the auxiliary regularly.

Thelar wasn't interested in conciliation. "You think you're such an excellent trainer? Here. You show us how it's done." He spun and clapped hands twice.

On the instant, the assembled students ceased their half-hearted sparring and pivoted so that each stood beside another, at parade rest.

Rylin caught the scent of perfumed hair as Tesra leaned close. "Maybe we should go," she said in a whisper.

"It's fine. I can play along."

Thelar was addressing his pupils. "We have a special guest today. Alten Rylin. One of the sapphire-bearing Altenerai. He's agreed to a small demonstration."

Rylin leaned toward Tesra. "I don't recall doing that."

"You don't have to join in," she said, then added, "you probably shouldn't."

He knew he shouldn't, just as he knew he'd never live it down with Thelar if he demurred.

"A practice bout to a count of three," Thelar said, his teeth flashing in a grin. "What do you say to that, Rylin? Against two of my finest pupils?"

Two? He'd have preferred one, or none, but he could hardly refuse, even knowing Thelar was planning something. "If you think it will be instructive. You're in charge here, Exalt, so I defer to you."

For some reason that set the man sneering. "Oh, it'll be instructive." He motioned for two tall, young redheaded women. They wore sleeveless leather-reinforced shirts, and their pale skin gleamed with a sheen of sweat.

Rylin unbuckled his sword belt, wondering what Varama would say about this. Probably she'd advise him not to tarry, to make excuses and get out with information. Yet, if he was supposed to infiltrate the corps, he had to obtain the respect of its members, and a martial instructor who didn't want to fight wasn't especially impressive.

Neither was a martial instructor who lost.

Rylin mulled over his motivations even as he strode to the practice rack and looked at the battered metal swords. Most had a fair balance. One proved almost as light as his own, though its reach was a thumbspan shorter.

He still wasn't entirely certain this was a wise course, or a necessary one, but he stepped up to the browned sparring circle in the courtyard's center. Its edge was marked with a scattered spray of black pebbles.

Thelar announced: "M'vai, Meria, the combat is to last three rounds. Each round concludes if one of you scores a point against Rylin, or if he scores against both of you. If he should score a point against one of you, the round has ended only for the person scored against; the round continues for the other combatants. All other rules are standard."

"Yes, Exalt." The squires answered as one, their voices blending smoothly. They moved at the same instant to take up equidistant points on the circle, forming a triangle with Rylin. Judging by their lack of hesitation, they'd fought together before.

Rylin raised his own sword in salute before he brought it sweeping down at the same time as his opponents.

M'vai, distinguished from her twin by a small brown mole above her lip, darted in with a thrust to Rylin's chest. He parried high, pivoted on his right foot, and kicked her sternum with his left. She stumbled toward Meria. While Meria danced clear he swatted M'vai's small round backside, temporarily visible when the tail of her leather tunic flew up. One point, and the impact sent her sprawling to the dirt.

Meria gritted pearly white teeth and charged. All he had to do was parry and wait for the opening—and then his leg slipped forward and he staggered. Meria pounced and just managed to touch his shoulder as he leaned away.

He stepped back and saluted. "Nicely done."

She nodded. As she turned to help her sister to her feet, Rylin glanced at the sand. It didn't appear any looser where he'd slipped. He surreptitiously inspected the sole of his right boot and found nothing amiss.

Thelar grinned at him. "They're better than you supposed, aren't they? Alten?"

He'd faced better. But he'd underestimated them, and possibly been too reckless.

And then it came to him as he saw Thelar's glee. Standard rules might not mean the same thing here as it meant in the Altenerai training rings. And even if it did, who was to say Thelar wouldn't cheat?

"Quite surprising," Rylin called back. He breathed out, focused a kernel of energy from deep within, and used it to keep his ring's lighting mechanism disabled. An important skill, lest the thing act as a beacon while moving at night. He pretended to brush something from his blunted sword's edge as he willed the sapphire to life without its glow. Instantly he grew conscious of the different sources of energy surrounding him. The pulsing life force of all those in the practice field. Thelar's ring, Tesra's hair band—interesting.

If a spell were being thrown, he would know its source.

Rylin resumed position across from his opponents and saluted them. This time he sensed the passage of energy between Meria and M'vai and understood they worked together through a mental link.

Rylin exploded forward, rolling away from M'vai's strike and parrying Meria's as his momentum carried him past both. As M'vai recovered and swung to follow, his blunt sword struck her twin under the left arm.

In the stumble that followed, Rylin tapped M'vai in the kidney then stepped back. He'd felt no other magic at play, but then he'd moved so fast, perhaps there hadn't been time.

The sisters' eyes held a predatory gleam as they raised their swords for another pass.

This time Meria went in first and M'vai followed on Rylin's right flank. He swept Meria's blade aside. As he pivoted he sensed the pressure against his heel this time, as well as the surge of energy that rose from Thelar. Sensing and acting were two different movements, though, and even as he recovered his footing two swords swung toward him at the same moment, one toward his shoulder, the other toward his chest. He slipped away from one and felt a magical push that thrust him straight into line with the second strike even as he raised his sword to block Meria's. Too late.

He stepped apart.

"Two points on you now, Rylin," Thelar said.

The shoves from Thelar had been well-timed, and unlikely to be registered by the ring's defenses, because they weren't direct physical or mental assaults. They were also ill-mannered in a training bout, which should be between contestants only.

But then this wasn't really about the sparring on the sand.

Rylin nodded. "Indeed." He glanced over the rest of the assembled mages, saw them fingering their blades, felt them watching with their own power.

So they knew their master cheated. He might ask if magics were allowed, or permitted from outside the circle, but then he could be mocked for having to ask, or for not being up to the challenge. He also was certain Thelar knew he'd assume the rules were the same here as in Altenerai training where this use of magic would be declared and only from combatants.

Better to act than to ask.

As Rylin dropped his sword in salute he sent a superb wave of nausea toward Thelar while stepping in toward Meria. She thrust at him on the instant.

Even as he felt his spell rebuffed by Thelar, he dodged Meria's point, which passed near his throat, and he slammed his pommel into her knuckles. Just then Thelar pushed at the back of his knee, but Rylin was prepared with a spell block. Meria, with a cry of pain, released her hold on the blade and Rylin grabbed it from her with his off hand. He swatted her shoulder even as he swung his other up to block a savage head blow from M'vai. She was wide open for his new second sword, but Rylin backstepped instead and coaxed a fluff of air toward Thelar.

Meria, disarmed, scrambled clear of the circle as Rylin maneuvered himself closer to Thelar, to his right but a little behind, and while the latter wove a defense for an assault that was nothing more than wind, he sent a more powerful gust into the small of the man's back.

That broke Thelar's guard and tripped him a step forward just as Rylin extended the weapon in his right hand and took Thelar in the temple with the flat of his blade. He felt the satisfying thud, heard a moan and the sound of a body slumping to the sand.

Rylin easily parried M'vai's second and third thrust. As she withdrew to circle him, he whipped Meria's sword at her.

Practiced she might be, but she gasped a little to find a spinning length of metal flying at her head, even if she knew its edges were dull. She managed to block it, only to find Rylin's other sword touching her shoulder.

"Point," he said.

He stepped back to look down at Thelar, crumpled and groaning feebly. "And seeing as our referee's been injured in the bout, I think that's match. If any of you have healing talents you might want to look him over." Rylin drove his sword into the practice field sand. "But I doubt there's any lasting damage. His skull's fairly thick."

Tesra handed over his sword belt, and he walked for the exit as he fastened it. He heard her following, but he didn't speak to her until they'd left the courtyard for an empty corridor.

"Well, that was interesting," he said.

"I'm so sorry. I had no idea he was going to do that."

"He's always hated me. Didn't you remember?"

A flush had spread over her cheeks. "Not until we walked in. And then it was too late." Her embarrassment looked genuine. "He's not usually like that anymore."

"Hard to believe. But if he was like that all the time, I suppose someone would have killed him."

"It's not a total loss. Everyone's going to be talking about that training exercise. But couldn't you have dealt with Thelar without embarrassing him so badly? Now you're going to have an enemy waiting when you join."

"I always did and just didn't know. Besides, I couldn't very well ignore the challenge." He cleared his throat. He should get back to business. "What about this hearthstone shard you were going to show me?"

She gave him a half smile and took his hand. "All right."

He felt a stab of jealousy when he saw Tesra's suite was larger and more sumptuous than his own, with colorful wall decorations and elegant modern furniture with plush cushions. All the bright scarves and hangings paled to insignificance, though, against the shining object she brought forth from the pouch tucked up one sleeve, like a diamond afire from within.

Was this the shard he'd seen earlier? It looked entirely different now and far more fascinating.

She stared at it hard for a long moment, and then the glow brightened enough to throw long shadows. Yet it wasn't the sort of light to ward your eyes against, but one that soothed and welcomed.

His voice was a whisper. "So this is a hearthstone?"

"Part of one. We've classified them into different sizes. This is a size three shard." She touched his hand and guided it toward the stone. "Go ahead. Reach into the inner world and feel it."

He resisted the pull, but didn't release her fingers. Why was the touch of her hand so enticing? He hadn't been this aroused by such light contact since his first real kiss, long years ago. It was a struggle to maintain concentration. "What were all of you doing in the Great Hall? Studying their effects?"

"Well, yes. Each hearthstone has different energy flows. We have to see how they fit together. What their powers are."

"And the people with the clocks?"

"The hearthstones are alluring. We have to have someone monitoring so none of us get lost in their glories." She tugged once more. "Now stop. I can't tell you any more until later. Don't worry. I'm not going to hurt you."

"I didn't think you would."

"But you're nervous." Her eyes sought his. "If you're serious about this, Rylin, you have to trust me."

He definitely was nervous, though he hadn't meant to show it. Would she be able to see into his mind with that thing? "Oh, I'm serious."

She seemed to like that, and nodded slowly.

"What will happen when I touch it?"

"Wonderful things."

There was promise in her eyes. Rylin readied himself and opened his view to the inner world.

The words rose, unbidden, to his lips. "It's lovely." There was nothing so lovely as a lovely woman, but that astonishing, vibrant, coruscating energy had something of the feminine in it. Certainly it was beguiling and mysterious and beautiful all at once.

He needed no urging to touch his own fingers to the surface, but he felt Tesra's against his own, and it was powerfully erotic.

"Careful," Tesra said. "Reach for it."

He touched the sorcerous power with his, and his ring lit even against his wishes, so great was the surge of energy washing through him.

"Fill yourself with the power! Drink it in."

Aches and pains he hadn't heeded and even lingering wariness washed away from him until he found himself laughing in pure, unbridled joy. He hadn't been so carefree in ages.

And he found her eyes looking into his, reflecting that joy, saw her back arch in ecstasy as that energy swept through her as well.

"Goddess!" she cried.

He felt the energy spiraling away, felt her own spirit pushing him out, and then they cleared and the hearthstone was dim and she stared at him, panting, with smoldering eyes.

He wasn't sure who threw themselves at whom.

"Did you feel her, Rylin?" she gasped between kisses. "Did you feel her heartbeat?"

"Whose heartbeat?"

She fumbled with the hooks to his khalat, and he stood, lifting her bodily from her couch. She wrapped her legs tightly against him, her pelvis pressed to his. "The Goddess," she whispered, even as he bore her toward the doorway to her bedroom.

He was too busy with the goddess in his arms to ask her anything about another.

9

Semblance of Truth

He made his excuses after noon and found his way to Varama's workshops, striving his best not to grin stupidly, like a virgin after his first roll. That was a challenge in itself. Sex with the hearthstone enhancement had been astonishing. He could get used to that.

But that was part of the danger, wasn't it? That the damned things were so seductive mages had to safeguard against being completely absorbed. Still, he looked forward to further experiments.

Varama's buildings were long and low and crammed full of artisans. Near the entrance to the largest, a trio of people were working with long, lightweight wooden poles. He wasn't sure what that had to do with the defense of the realm, but he did hear the distinct sound of a hammer on a forge close by, so at least there was some metalworking underway.

As no one seemed inclined to stop him, Rylin walked through the next doorway and found a fourth-rank squire and a cluster of craftsmen studying a large construction of stitched fabric, shaped like an inverted jar, hung from the ceiling. Light from high windows fell brightly upon its panels but left the floor in shadows. Rylin paused to consider it himself, wondering what the group was hoping to see.

"Hail, Alten."

Varama's high voice addressed him from his right.

She looked exactly the same as when he'd left her. High collar, strangely bunched hair, rumpled khalat, tired eyes. Her odd coloring was less obvious in the dim room.

Rylin saluted. "Hail."

The squire and the others turned from their contemplation, but Varama motioned them back to work and bade Rylin come with her as she turned away. "How did your meeting go?"

"I found it revealing." He smiled at his own small joke as he fell in step beside her.

"Have you eaten?"

When he shook his head no, she called over her shoulder for a squire to fetch them food, then led him back to a rectangular room cluttered with wooden models of breastplates and saddles and other objects he couldn't identify draped by long sheets of paper. Drawings of complex gear systems were tacked along one cluttered wall. All other walls, apart from the one with the window, were concealed by shelves overflowing with books and various objects. There was barely space for a desk, its chair, and two visitors' seats, and one of those was piled high with upright scrolls of tightly rolled yellow paper.

Varama waved him toward a chair as she shut the door, and he dropped onto its faded red cushion. She lifted a bottle from a desk drawer. "Apple juice?"

"Sure."

She set the bottle down and then wandered around the room, fiddling with stacks of documents. At first he assumed she was looking for goblets, but he glimpsed her touching what looked to be a white crystal.

"What are you up to, Varama?"

"Keeping the spies away." She glanced over one shoulder at him. "They used to pry around here all the time, trying to see what I was doing. Stealing my ideas." She bent down to make a final adjustment then joined him. "You're looking at me like you think I'm crazy."

A little, yes. "Who's spying on you?"

"The auxiliary."

He froze. "Then won't they have seen me come here?"

"Of course. But we're supposed to be arranging funerals of state, aren't we?"

"I suppose so." He relaxed only a little, still worried about spoiling his introduction to the auxiliary. "But what exactly were you doing?"

"Blocking any chances of remote listening or viewing through magical means by using a series of resonance disrupters to generate a magical screen." Varama returned to her chair.

Rylin had no idea what a "resonance disrupter" might be, but he decided against going off track. "How long have they been trying to listen in on your office?"

"At least four years." She lifted two glazed goblets from her desk and sat them on its surface. Each had a stunningly bright blue band cradling its stem. "I often have magical experiments running, and they want to know what they are." She fixed him with a hard stare. "You think I'm paranoid."

"No, I don't," Rylin objected. He'd been thinking that Varama was probably suspected of retaining hearthstones and was wondering if he should ask.

"Oh, all Altenerai are mad. Kyrkenall says we're just cultured killers, and there's some truth to that. At least our generation. I haven't decided about yours yet."

"We haven't had to do much killing."

"There is that." Varama touched her hand to the bottle, then poured out the brown-colored juice. Rylin reached forward for the goblet and found it cold. Peculiar. The liquid itself was chill when he brought it to his lips. Surely she didn't store a block of ice in her desk. "How did you do that?"

There was a hint of pride in her response. "I've been experimenting with the hearthstones myself."

"To chill juices? Is this what you're afraid the auxiliary will steal?"

"That wasn't the intended result of the experiment." She sat the goblet down. "But I think you can agree that, for a failure, it's not a bad one. I've managed to generate a drink that helps restore magical strength, and that's cold besides. Now, what did you learn?"

He seemed fated to hear something interesting from Varama whenever they met. He paused in consideration of the juice, deciding that he did feel a little better after consuming it, quite apart from the pleasant cold. He pulled himself back to her question. "Nothing about Irion. A little about the layout of the wing, and the hearthstones."

"Good. And the people?"

"I met a number of them."

"Did they talk to you about the Goddess?"

He started. "Yes, they did, but they didn't mean to. She's not Darassa or Vedessa, is she?"

"No."

"Who is she, then? And why do they try to be so closemouthed about her?"

"I don't think she's one of The Four, Rylin."

"There are no Gods but The Four," he intoned reflexively.

"There were six, once," she reminded him. Varama peered over her goblet to watch him closely.

Yes, there'd been Syrah, Goddess of what became The Fragments, until slain by Sartain the betrayer, who'd been killed in turn by The Four. Images of Sartain were extremely rare and inevitably male. Rylin had seen only occasional depictions of the lost Goddess, and she had always looked sad and small, not joyous and powerful.

Varama continued speaking as if reading his thoughts. "But this goddess isn't Syrah. As near as I've been able to determine, the people involved closely with the hearthstones worship a new goddess, and they're silent about it. Presumably to avoid ridicule or accusations of heresy."

"A new goddess? Of what realm?" There was simply no room for any other gods or goddesses. Everyone knew the creation story. The Gods had individually designed each realm, and Sartain, playing with little pieces of less savory lands, had grown jealous when he saw what the others had wrought and fought to take a better place for himself. It left Syrah's realm shattered, and when the battle was over Vedessa mended and adopted The Fragments, neighbor to her own Arappa.

"I believe her to be a goddess of the hearthstones rather than of any realm."

"They're worshiping hearthstones?"

"Not in the sense that you mean. If I understand the hints rightly, they worship a goddess they connect to the hearthstones and think her superior to The Four."

He snorted at the idea.

Varama took on a patient air as if explaining the elementary. "If the Gods truly walked among us, I think them unlikely to do so again. So the only facts relevant today about a god are those that reveal the core tenets of their believers' faith. Understanding motivation helps predict the actions that follow a given set of circumstance, do you see?"

He must have shown a puzzled look related to the fact that he couldn't "see" at all where Varama was going with this.

She went on: "For example, the Naor hold that their god needs blood to hold back the storms and secure their borders. Some among them use that blood to work magics in his name."

"The Naor are homicidal maniacs."

"To us," she emphasized. "Yet their faith must seem eminently reasonable to them, as they expend a lot of effort shedding blood. The same may hold true here."

Rylin nodded slowly. "We need to learn what beliefs the followers of this new goddess hold so we can better figure out what they're going to do. Right?"

"Yes." Varama relaxed a little. "I've managed to learn almost nothing beyond what I've told you." She called out for the person knocking on the door to enter, and Sansyra, an aloof fifth ranker, walked in to set a platter of cheeses and fruits and bread on the desk, oblivious to the piles of paper there. As usual, she avoided eye contact with Rylin, though he had no idea why she was so unfriendly.

Varama dismissed her, then waited for the door to close before facing

Rylin again. "Rather than ask you a tedious series of questions about what you saw, why don't we simply link?"

Rylin hadn't linked with another caster in a long while, and he hadn't enjoyed it much. He took a long gulp of the juice. It might be interesting to see her thoughts about his trip while he reviewed them. And, though there were any number of possible problems with a sorcerous link, he didn't expect either he or Varama would lose themselves in the other's thoughts, or that she was given to prying overmuch.

At least he hoped not. "All right."

"Set your thoughts about the visit foremost, if you will."

"Of course."

"And try not to be distracted."

Why did she keep assuming he was an idiot? Because, he thought as he closed his eyes and focused on breathing, she's smarter than you are.

He felt his ring light, and willed its defenses off. He sensed her close, as if they both read from a book he was holding. He raised the events of the last few hours up for her, working hard to place them in order, which he'd learned early on was far more difficult than he'd supposed. While he was thinking of Tesra in the hallway, the sensation of thumbing her nipple rose boldly to the surface of his memory. He wasn't embarrassed that Varama knew of his amorous activities, but that he wasn't disciplined enough to keep his memories in line. Unfortunately, he was too distracted by his efforts to pay much attention to Varama's own thoughts.

After a while her presence eased away, and he opened his eyes to find her standing, hands braced on the table. She tapped her goblet and took another drink. "You spend an inordinate amount of time thinking about sex."

"Doesn't everyone?"

"No. The approximate number of hearthstones is higher than my expectations. We'll have to get our hands on their records."

He expected as much, but it wouldn't be easy. "You think that they'll tell us something about Irion?"

"They'll tell us something about the hearthstones. And if the Mage Auxiliary is involved with this sword business, then hearthstones are involved as well."

"That's why you asked Denaven if they had one, isn't it? At the meeting."

"In part." Varama fell silent and stared into the middle distance.

After several minutes in which Rylin had begun to wonder if she remembered his presence, he cleared his throat. "I don't think I'll have easy access to that hearthstone room anytime soon. And I'm certain I won't be able to bring you."

"That's why we'll sneak in. Tonight."

His voice rose in alarm. "If you were planning to sneak in, why did I spend all that time getting into their good graces?"

"My planning involved many different contingencies, Rylin," she said, once again with the tone of someone speaking to a simpleton. "I've altered my plans based upon the information you learned."

She didn't seem to understand. This could ruin all he'd accomplished in gaining their trust. "Are you going to want me to continue my deception about joining the auxiliary?"

Varama frowned irritably. "That will depend upon what we find." She consulted the distance once more, then drank. "I'm glad we have an accurate layout of the place, and its people. It will be easier to blend in."

He scoffed. "There's no way that either of us is going to blend in."

Her gaze was piercing. "I'm growing tired of this, Rylin. Either trust me or not. Either follow my directives or not. Decide if I'm brilliant, or a fool, and then move along. I don't have time to convince you about every stupid prejudice you carry."

Her rebuke stung him. "I wasn't saying—"

She cut him off. "I know. You didn't think it through, did you? You must always think things through. You've got a rather lazy intellect."

She was impossible. "Will you quit insulting me? I'm sorry! I'll stop commenting. But you're going too fast. How are we getting to those records and why tonight?"

"Rylin, you must recognize that while we hold the same rank, I am your superior in this. You must defer to me. If you feel compelled to question me for clarity, do so politely."

"Yes, ma'am."

Varama looked at the table a moment, then back to him. "As to the timing, we must act before they can, although we have another errand to complete beforehand. About our blending in: you're handsome and I'm distinctive. There are ways, though." Once again she stared. Suddenly she was gone, and in her place was Tesra, her hair held back with a silver coronet, her trim waist crossed with a red sash.

"Gods!" Rylin stood on the instant.

Tesra turned her head to look at him, and it was only the strange blank gaze that alerted him to the figure not quite looking like Tesra.

"I took her image from your mind, Rylin," Varama said in a voice that

was reminiscent of his lover, but not quite right. "The method has its limi-
tations, but—"

"I'm impressed. How can you concentrate on all the aspects for so long?
Or maintain them?" He'd heard that some weavers could render themselves
"invisible" by wiping themselves from the sight of those who looked at
them, but this grew more challenging the more people who watched. It just
took too much concentration to control all the variables. A detailed illusion like this should be impossible under close scrutiny.

"I've created a tool to help me. I store the desired image there." Varama
flashed back into existence. Gone was the smaller, shapelier woman. By contrast, Varama seemed even more awkward and odd, her hair unkempt and
faintly ridiculous.

"What tool?" he asked

"I call it a semblance." Once more Varama reached into her desk; now
she pushed across an obsidian stone small enough to hold in his palm. "This
one's for you."

Rylin reached out through the inner world even as he stretched his fingers
toward it; he felt a power pulsing within, not as enticing but still interesting. "A hearthstone?"

"No. Its power has been shaped with one, though. Now I want you to
try. Call someone to mind, then put the image forefront as you're linked to
the gem. It may help you to touch it."

He didn't put fingers to the stone. Only amateur spell casters needed
direct contact to further their sorcery.

Rylin's first thought was to consider Velin, the ineffectual man who'd
tried to bar his entry. But his mind turned to smug, arrogant, angry Thelar.
He knew that face and those manners far better. When at last he had the
image fully in his mind he willed the black stone to power.

"Ah." Varama said, and a smile twitched at the corner of her mouth.

Rylin felt a tingle rippling across the surface of his skin and looked down
at his hands.

They weren't his. He flipped them over, saw that the ring on his hand
was ruby.

"You've done it, Rylin. I wasn't sure you could on your first attempt."
She pulled a nail from one of the schematics on the wall and revealed a
bronzed mirror underneath as the paper fluttered to the floor. Seeing her
reflection in it, she let out a little grunt of displeasure and fussed with her
hair.

That was the first indication Rylin ever had that Varama cared about her appearance. Perhaps she simply got too busy thinking about other things so that she forgot. Perhaps a kinder person than himself might have said something to her about her disheveled state. He felt a jab of shame that it hadn't occurred to him he should. Maybe he did need to reexamine his "prejudices."

"See what you've wrought." She gestured him to the glass, and Rylin examined the reflection of the wrong man. Thelar was a little shorter and far more scowling.

"Say something."

"This is pretty amazing." He was fascinated with moving the mouth that wasn't his. "Damn! That's not my voice!" It was lower, harsher.

"It's probably not entirely his, either. I think most of us are far more visual than aural. But then if we do this properly we'll be seen by very few and have to talk to fewer. The idea's to blend, not to mix."

"How long does this spell last?"

"An hour or so. The stones can't store unlimited energy. Speaking of which, you should will yours off. They're difficult to charge."

This he did just as he willed off his Altenerai ring. The semblance deactivated on the instant, and he confronted the square face he knew so well: short, unruly brown hair; thick eyebrows; easy grin. "This fellow's better looking."

"Yes," she agreed absently.

He turned to her, still grinning. "That's quite something, Varama. What else have you been working on?"

"All sorts of things. Denaven and Leonara think I just experiment with shields and swords and the like."

"You affect a stranger persona than you have."

"Oh, I'm mad, remember? But I let them think I'm foolish, too."

"I'm sorry I thought so."

"Some of the fault's mine. I suppose I've gotten good at the part. Or maybe it's easy because I *am* eccentric."

"Are you worried that we'll be detected when we go in to look at their records? The place is literally filled with mages. Won't they feel a magical aura around us?"

"The nice thing about walking around a place filled with mages is that every one of them is liable to have some kind of bauble with a glamour or enchantment. The semblances really don't radiate much of one."

"How come you haven't tried this yourself yet?"

"I've only just perfected it."

So in the time he'd taken to talk to a few people, she'd invented a whole new magical device? Presumably she'd been working on it a little longer than that. He chose not to ask. "And what will we do if we get caught?"

"That depends. If we find nothing at all and we get caught, we'll have to make apologies."

Rylin grunted. That was an understatement. "And if we find something else?"

"If we find something incriminating, then we owe no one an apology, and we fight to our last breath to get out and spread the truth. I'm rather thinking it will be the latter, but I'm hoping not."

"Right."

"But before we risk our lives in daring deeds, we should eat. I'm famished." And with that, she took her seat and delicately lifted a slice of brown bread.

Rylin was struck by her ability to quickly shift focus. He stood and massaged his forehead. "You mentioned another errand?"

She spoke while chewing. "We'll make a short trip to N'lahr's tomb."

"Should I ask why?"

"No. Eat first. You'll feel better."

He doubted it. The corps and the Mage Auxiliary could be filled with traitors. Or—"Are we traitors now?"

Varama swallowed. "Someone replaced Irion, then killed Asrahn and framed Kyrkenall for it when discovered. Denaven and the queen are up to something with the mages and that collection of hearthstones, something that they're apparently willing to kill for. You're not honestly suggesting that the liars and murderers are in the right, are you?"

"No."

She spoke as she chewed. "We're going to take this thread and pull on it until the carpet unravels."

"And if we're standing on the carpet?"

Varama swallowed and stared at him. "You're wearing the Altenerai ring. I thought you signed on for action, and that you swore to defend the realms."

"I did."

"There you go. Now have a seat. It's harder to defend the realms on an empty stomach."

Sighing only a little, Rylin took his chair across from her and reached for a hunk of white cheese.

10

With Sword in Hand

There doesn't seem to be any activity in the tower's compound," Elenai called back softly. "But there's a cabin near the line of trees with smoke rising from the chimney." She turned to see Kyrkenall daubing his face with dirt just below the rise of the hill. Their shadows were stretched about as long as they would get, as the crimson sliver of sun sank to its bed beyond the tree-lined, white-capped mountains. In its wake the vast blanket of blue overhead was darkening to purple.

Kyrkenall replied quietly, "Either someone's left the kettle on, or there are more guards stationed there. Come take a look at this while I spy up top. I think this is the sigil they were talking about."

She slowly crawled back. Kyrkenall tapped the grass beside an object he'd apparently pulled from the dead. To regular scrutiny it was a twisted brass spiral the length of her hand, set with green gemstones. Through her inner sight it glowed with a complex magical aura, one linked by slim gold strands of mystical energy to the leather collar around the distant dead beast, still lying five good strides from the line of corpses at the base of the hill.

It was hard not to think about them even as she focused on the sigil. After she'd studied it for a time, Kyrkenall slid down beside her. "You figure it out?"

"It has a connection with the collar. I'm thinking that the beast couldn't approach anyone with a sigil without the collar activating in some fashion."

"Probably it would have given a jolt of pain. I bet that's what the fence posts do, too."

"I guess this will make it easier to deal with the next beast."

"We probably won't need to," Kyrkenall replied. "They couldn't keep many of those. It would take a lot of game to feed even one."

"But, how do you know how large the fenced-in area was?" she pressed. "Maybe it had a hundred acres to forage."

"You wouldn't want to make it too large, or the thing would be miles away when unwanted company turned up. What I don't understand is why there's a station outside the fort. There's plenty of space inside. The barracks there are large enough to accommodate fifty. There's a solid stable near the south wall, so there's surely no need to build that flimsy horse shelter I spotted beyond the cabin. They'd have to hobble the horses under guard to graze them with that 'gralk' wandering around. The tower compound even has a bathhouse, which is about the nicest thing out here in the winter, so you'd think they'd want to live inside." By the end he was clearly talking to himself.

"Maybe they have so many people they needed extra room," Elenai suggested.

Kyrkenall shook his head. "I did some training out here, remember? Even if they crammed the existing barracks, there's plenty of room within the stone wall to add buildings. Besides, I can't see any sign the base has hosted anyone recently, let alone a full regiment. That flag is in rags."

"We could visit the cabin to learn more. If we take some people alive." She had labored to sound circumspect, but Kyrkenall picked up on her tone.

"Is that a criticism, Squire? I don't recall you offering any terms."

She blurted out the question that had been tearing at her. "Why didn't you? Couldn't you have captured the last two? Or one?" If they had more information now they wouldn't be huddled in the cold deciding how to best fling themselves into uncertain disaster.

For a long moment he offered nothing but an unblinking stare. "What do you think this is?" he asked finally. Apparently he didn't expect an answer, for he went on. "We were surrounded, and they were going to kill us."

"Not all of them wanted to."

"The one in charge did. Look, maybe they would have, and maybe not. And maybe they would have taken us prisoner and done who knows what with us. I had one chance, and I took it. Do you understand?"

"I guess so." She frowned, unsatisfied.

"I don't think you do." He raised his voice for emphasis. "This isn't the training field. If someone scores on us it's not with a blunt instrument. Whoever put these people out here murdered Asrahn, so you can bet they won't think twice about the two of us. Maybe some of the guards were hesitating, but they weren't in charge. Don't count on kindness. Especially when your life's at stake. Now do you understand?"

She nodded slowly, struggling to halt the flood of emotion as she realized what was really upsetting her. Need she have killed that woman? In the heat of combat it hadn't occurred to try to wound her or ask her to yield. She realized with a sinking certainty that she was childishly blaming

Kyrkenall not because he killed the soldiers, but because he failed to keep her from her own actions. She took a slow trembling breath. She was a soldier. Her choices were consequential and she was responsible for them.

If anything, he appeared more exasperated than ever. "What's wrong now?"

She felt her throat constrict but managed to sound fairly normal when she spoke. "Nothing." She held off admitting that this had been the first time she'd killed someone.

He gave her a searching look, but said only, "Good. Let's see that cabin."

Kyrkenall had already recovered some of his own arrows, and apparently searched through the equipment of the dead, found the most suitable shafts, and fitted them into his newly full quiver. He led the way into the dark landscape.

Elenai set aside her sentiments and focused through her ring, watching for life forces that might creep up on them through the waist-high grass. Kyrkenall's horse, Lyria, quietly brought up the rear, obedient as a well-trained hound, stopping when he stopped, moving forward when he signaled. It put her in mind of poor Aron. Someday, he too might have responded so well.

They saw nothing more dangerous than a few small bats flying out for nighttime feeding, and before too long they arrived at the wooden stockade that surrounded the cabin and its companion buildings. She'd had little doubt the longer structure was a stable, and she had even less once the horses within whinnied at the scent of Lyria, who snorted her own response.

Kyrkenall cursed softly, and with a running jump set hands to the head-high stockade wall and vaulted over.

"Kyrkenall?" Elenai called quietly. He didn't answer. Grumbling a little to herself, she followed him. By the time she had climbed over he was already at the closed door on the narrow cabin porch. Before she reached it, he'd burst inside with naked blade.

After a short moment, he leaned out to wave her in and they searched together, finding a half dozen beds and chests and a few personal belongings, a dining table and cooking area. There had been six dead guards and there were six beds here, so it looked as though they'd met up with everyone. In back was an outhouse, and a long, slant-roof shed where they found eight curious horses and a pair of goats.

While Elenai let Lyria into the stockade, Kyrkenall lit a sturdy lantern he'd found inside the barracks and studied a large wooden wheeled structure behind the cabin. It was a catapult just over eight feet high. Leads in front suggested it was to be hauled by horses.

"Why do you think they needed a siege engine?" she asked.

"I'm still figuring that out." He had remained oddly quiet throughout their investigation, communicating almost entirely by hand signals except when he'd ordered her to bring in Lyria and when he'd told her not to put his horse with the others.

He stretched up to examine the bucket. The arm was stored in the up position, standard practice so that there wasn't constant tension on the throwing support.

"So," she guessed, "there's something in the tower compound, behind the walls. Maybe it's another gralk. The guards were its keepers. They hunted for game, then launched a carcass in to feed the thing from time to time. Whatever it is." Though her voice was level, the thought of some unknown beast lurking inside that enclosure was far more alarming than the prospect the place was stuffed with soldiers.

His look to her was sharp, and he cursed, then smiled. "Damn. You're right. Why else would they erect these lousy buildings instead of using the good ones next to the tower? Why else would they have a bloodstained catapult?"

She was glad he agreed.

"How are you at sensing things through the hearthstone?"

"What do you mean?"

"Kalandra could stretch out her senses with a hearthstone and sort of feel ahead a bit."

"Like what we do with the Altenerai rings?"

"Exactly. Rialla was really good at it, too."

Of course she was.

He continued enthusiastically. "Try to reach into the fortress. If you sense anything really strange, pull back."

"Strange?"

"Any kind of strange. But I guess we've been seeing a lot of that, haven't we?"

She nodded, already thinking of the possible dangers. One of the first lessons taught all those with magical gifts was to be careful looking around too long in the inner world, for there were entities out there that hungered for unprotected souls.

Though she thought herself prepared to touch the hearthstone once more, it was as much of a shock as the first time, and so pleasurable that she couldn't suppress a smile. Once she had the hearthstone's threads wrapped about her life force, she extended filaments of will toward the fortress wall. It rushed closer, faster than anticipated, while she worked to keep part of herself rooted to her body. Too late she remembered that when you projected you were supposed to sit, or even lie down, lest you injure yourself while your attention was elsewhere.

When her awareness reached the wall, she could have spent hours studying the pitted stones in detail, for the moonlit contrasts of shape and shade presented beautifully to her hearthstone-enhanced sight. But she pressed through them, sensing the outlines of the long roofed stables Kyrkenall had described against the south of the fortress, and the row of dark, wooden buildings to the tower's west. Mostly, though, her mind was drawn to the whirling energies beyond the north wall, the sudden drop to chaotic void that apparently justified placing all the adjacent fortifications to address it. Kyrkenall had not mentioned how spectacular was the multihued view!

As if on cue, she heard his voice. He sounded very far away. "Do you feel anything?"

"Wait a moment," she said. Her speech sent shock waves along the tendrils of intent she used to explore her surroundings. She'd have to watch that. She knew she'd made her presence more noticeable in the magical spectrum, even if she'd produced no audible sound there.

Try as she might, she felt no life-forms of any interest anywhere near the tower or its outbuildings. There were rodents and insects in abundance.

She tried whispering to Kyrkenall. "There's nothing—"

And she fell silent, because something was racing from the west end of the compound, a large undulating form shot through with matrices that were both intact, as you'd find in an ordinary animal, and changeable, as with something from the Shifting Lands. It seemed to know exactly where her threads of intent were, for it closed upon one; she had the fleeting impression of a longish reptilian thing with too many legs and a many-toothed maw lunging for her.

She recoiled, blinded by pain, and before she was entirely sure what had happened she found herself blinking rapidly and being supported by Kyrkenall. She appeared to have slumped, for he tightly gripped her upper arms.

"—ser me," he was saying, his voice agitated. "Are you all right?"

She relaxed her mental hold upon the hearthstone, adjusted her footing so she stood upright, and felt herself redden as he let go of her shoulders.

"What did you see?"

The pain was clearing but lingered between her eyes. "Something strange," she croaked dryly.

"Funny. How about some details?"

"It's a monster all right. Probably from the Shifting Lands." She blinked a few times. "It's about the length of a horse, maybe a little longer, with a tail like a lizard, except it has too many legs. And," she added, "it knew I was there. It deliberately attacked." She pressed her temple as everything settled.

He appraised her with concern, but said only, "It must not be able to climb, or the walls wouldn't keep it in."

That seemed a fairly safe assessment. She discovered her hand quavered a little as she put it to the top of her waterskin, and hoped Kyrkenall didn't notice. She held tight to the stopper until she had calmed herself, then uncorked the cap and drank long and deep.

"There's a walkway that runs all along the fortress battlement," Kyrkenall mused. "At least there used to be. They probably took out the stairs to keep the beast in. We could get fairly close to the tower that way, but we'll still be a good fifty feet off. And you can bet that the tower door's locked."

"Why don't we heave a carcass over, to keep it distracted?" she asked.

He seemed to consider that for a moment before shaking his head. "Better to just climb to the walkway and shoot it to death. Also easier. You don't want to have to cut up the gralk or your horse, then drag the pieces back here and load them in the catapult basket, do you?"

Now that he mentioned it, no.

"The complicated way's usually not the best." He grinned. "I guess Denaven and his lot never counted on someone figuring it out ahead of time and killing whatever they've locked in there at a distance. Shows a lack of foresight." He started back for the cabin. "I'm going to need some rope."

By the time they'd walked to the fortress wall, the stars wheeled in the heavens and the moon was a high golden crescent. Kyrkenall tied a rope to a wicked looking metal hook he'd found in the stables near some hay bales. He grinned mirthlessly at her as he worked the knot. "'Had I such wings, to you I'd fly each night.'"

Elenai recognized the words. They were from the courtship scene of doomed Iratahn to his lover Donahlia, after he had climbed her garden wall and pointed to an owl. She answered as Donahlia had done. "'Had we them both, the moon should light our way as we soared forth to seek the shining stars.'"

His grin broadened into a real smile. "Ho ho! So my squire's seen a play or two?"

"'They are numbers beyond knowing, my queen.'" This time she quoted not Selana, but Pendrahn. "My father runs a playhouse," Elenai explained. "I grew up around the theater."

"And here you struck me as such a fine upstanding person." He finished the knot. "You like Selana?"

"Yes, but I prefer Pendrahn."

"He's not without his charm. I prefer the beauty of her language, though."

Selana was old fashioned, but she didn't tell him that.

Kyrkenall hefted the hook and line around three or four times, presumably gauging its weight. "They sure went to a lot of trouble to keep Irion hidden, didn't they? Makes you wonder if there're some other secrets within."

"Like what?"

"Well, if this was a play, we'd find a manifesto of their plans and the map to their secret installation, wouldn't we?"

"Or magic armor."

"I wouldn't mind some magic armor," Kyrkenall said. "Let's be on with it. If we stay low, we should be hidden between the stable roof and the walkway as we get up there."

"How are we going to get through the tower door?" she asked.

"You'll have to blast it with magics. You can do that, can't you?"

"I've never done it before."

"It's been a whole week of firsts for you then, hasn't it? I've faith in you."

"You must think this magic stuff is easy," she said.

"On the contrary. I just think you're good."

The unexpected compliment surprised a smile out of her, one that left a warm glow. It didn't keep her from thinking ahead, though. "Are you sure you'll be able to kill it from the walkway?"

His answer was supremely confident. "I don't see why not. You think this thing is going to be harder to hit than the gralk?"

"I just think it might be more dangerous. It's on the inside, even closer to the tower they want to protect."

"Excellent point, but I'll be closer to it than I was the gralk, and shooting from a vantage point. I should be able to pick out a vital area." He handed her the lantern. "Here. You should hold onto the hearthstone, too."

She was astonished at how casual he was about it. While she stowed it in her pack, he threw the hook.

His cast was true, and lodged solidly over the fifteen-foot wall with a minimal *clank* as it caught. With the chill night breeze ruffling his hair and clothes, he was up the rope in no time, and disappeared over the battlement. She hurried after him ably enough, though less quickly. The dimmed lantern tied to her belt banged against her thigh. She was oddly grateful for all the terrible exercises Asrahn had inflicted upon them over the years. As a first ranker, nothing had bedeviled her more than the climbing wall.

She felt another pang of loss for the old Master of Squires as she reached the merlon and clambered after her companion.

Soon she was hurrying at a crouch along the wall's walkway, a lane between the battlement and the stable roof. The air was full with the smell of rotten hay and fouler alien odors, intermittently freshened with gusts from without. She could perceive no sounds other than the minimal reverberations of their footfalls on the creaky wooden walkway. Dark buildings dotted the inside space off her left hand, and the main tower loomed alone over all, gray against the black. Ahead, much smaller twin turrets flanking the fort's gate were just visible over the archer's shoulders and head.

Kyrkenall paused beside the barbican with arrow nocked. She crouched with him near the steep stone stair, which was barred with reinforced stone debris at the ground end. She searched in vain for the fell creature, then spotted it unexpectedly emerging from under the walkway beneath their feet; a bluish bulk, its conical head pointed unmistakably in their direction. Had it silently stalked them along their whole course?

The exotic being regarded them hungrily but with absolute silence. Elenai could perceive no eyes along its smooth surface, and there was no indication of the toothed mouth she thought she had seen earlier through inner sight. The thing's long reptilian body suddenly lit with running lines of bright energy, like molten iron pouring into a bladesmith's mold. It was eerily beautiful. In the darkness, she only partially sensed its shape and wasn't able to count its legs, but it looked larger than she'd believed. There appeared to be some kind of fringe around its head. Its lights went on and off intermittently, though she could perceive no pattern.

"Kind of pretty, really," Kyrkenall whispered, then launched the arrow, readying a second the moment the first soared out. When Kyrkenall's arrow embedded itself just behind the frilled area at the base of its skull, the flashes of light along its back converged at the point of impact.

Beside her, Kyrkenall stiffened in the act of loosing his next arrow. He collapsed upon the battlement, then let out a string of colorful curses.

She sank beside him as he blinked, his mouth contorting in pain. "What happened?" she asked frantically. She searched in vain for sign of injury—a stone or arrow sent by some unseen assailant. She found nothing, though through the inner world his energies flared around a point at the back of his head.

The creature whipped around and clawed vigorously at the debris barrier on the stairs below. Its jaws opened vertically, and impossibly wide; previously unseen fleshy antennae waved at the end of its snout. It still seemed to have no eyes. Most disconcerting of all, Kyrkenall's arrow was sinking slowly into its now-iridescent surface, as it would if dropped into the mud. Defying all of her understanding, the creature was somehow absorbing the shaft.

Kyrkenall cursed again while propping himself up, and gingerly touched the back of his head. He considered the monster as it ceased its scuffling to point its maw at them and clacked its jaws open and shut. Something dripping from the sharp teeth sizzled as it struck the ground.

Kyrkenall spoke with quiet effort. "When I hit the damned thing, I felt it. Fully, I'd guess. Otherwise I'd be tempted to fire a volley right down its nasty gullet."

The beast paced back and forth beneath them, its long tail dragging. Elenai was able to count what looked like eight stubby legs on one side and seven on the other. It was hard to keep track, especially since the limbs shifted so quickly and, like the rest of the body, were randomly illuminated with bright lines of light. Sporadic sizzling sounds continued and an acrid odor drifted up.

"How did it just absorb the arrow?" Elenai asked. She didn't actually expect an answer.

"No idea. It looks like if we touch it in any way, we're the ones who get hurt. That doesn't leave us with a lot of options."

They'd have to get it away from the tower. "Do you think it would follow you if you shot arrows right in front of it? And led it away?"

"We can find out. You planning to run down and open the door while I'm doing that?"

"Exactly."

He grinned at her. "That's downright reckless. I like it. How long do you need me to keep it away?"

"I've no idea," she had to confess. "I've never tried to magically unlock a door before."

He clapped her shoulder. "Most of life is just making it up as you go. What are you going to do if you're trapped outside the tower while the thing is coming for you?"

"Run."

He let out a short bark of a laugh, then ran his hand over his face and stepped around in a tight circle, frowning. He came to rest after a deep sigh. "All right. I'll give you plenty of notice if it starts to head back. You ready?"

"When you are."

He handed her the lantern she'd set down, then stepped west upon the battlement, raised his hands, and waved his arms. "Hey, you ugly spit-dripper! Look at me!"

It stopped its pacing; then, as he shouted and stamped, it followed after him under the walkway. When Kyrkenall reached the stable roofs he began hopping in the air and shouting even more loudly.

She waited until the monster was on the other side of the compound beneath Kyrkenall. Just to be a little safer, she connected again with the hearthstone, thinking it might alert her if the creature drew close.

She carefully and quietly picked her way over the barrier, then sprinted for the tower door. In only a few heartbeats the tower spread menacingly overhead; night seemed to have lengthened it. She twisted the lantern back on and opened its shutters, yellowing the white stones around the weathered wooden door. She focused on the tarnished metal lock, feeling every hair on her neck rise as she exposed her back. Little noises she'd paid no heed to, like the wind against the roof shingles of the barracks behind, or the flutter of the flag above, were like claws across her heart.

Elenai wasn't a locksmith, nor had she spent much time contemplating how they worked, although she gathered there was some kind of mechanism that allowed a bolt to be extended from the door and into the wall. And that's exactly what her energy probes found, for a touch of the magic enabled her to detect that a particularly solid substance extended from the door to a housing inside.

Could she shift the mechanism that moved the bolt, somehow shape energy to fit the keyhole and twist it? Might she instead alter the consistency of the lock? Normally such a task would be beyond all but the most accomplished of mages. But then most mages didn't have access to a hearthstone. How long would it take? How long could Kyrkenall keep the creature at bay?

She shook herself and sent threads of will into the lock bar. Rudimentary magical theory taught that it was always simpler to alter rather than to create or even destroy. Her first thought was to try to rust the lock, but she wasn't sure how to go about that. Instead, she decided to manipulate its shape. Something so powerful should have been far beyond her, but with the hearthstone's aid she brought enormous forces to bear, shifting the metal that composed the bar into the spaces around the mechanisms until little was left but a slender core.

She paused, gathering a metaphorical breath, then whirled at a noise to her rear and saw Kyrkenall sprinting toward her, his black recurved bow in hand. Panting quietly, glancing over his shoulder, he arrived and asked in a whisper: "Are we in yet?"

She wiped sweat from her brow. The image of the inner world overlaid across the outer, so he seemed both himself and a hazy mix of golden threads pulsating with energies that likewise burned in his ring and upon his weapons. "I've weakened it," she said.

"Good. We'd better get inside."

"Where's the thing?"

"I fired some arrows at the far wall, and it dashed off to investigate. I don't think we have much time to waste, though."

"I'll give it a try, then."

"Let me." Kyrkenall set his hand to the handle and pulled. She saw him strain slightly, and then there was a clanking noise, as of metal on metal, and the door swung open in his hand.

The sensory threads about her vibrated madly and, without intention, her vision narrowed. All she saw was the door and Kyrkenall's action and dozens upon dozens of strands stretching off to a dark future. Only one was golden, and she laid her hand to it. . . .

. . . Was that her voice screaming for him to get down? Without thinking, she was tackling him.

A storm of events crashed at the same moment. Something hard slammed into the front of Elenai's shoulder. She heard the footfalls of a large thing racing out of the night to their rear, and the air whirred as it only did when arrows pass close. There was the distinctive sound of shafts striking flesh behind her. Then Elenai slammed into the dirt with Kyrkenall, driving her breath away.

At some point she'd relinquished the hearthstone. She hadn't remembered doing that consciously, but the magical overlay was gone. Elenai looked down at Kyrkenall, found his dark eyes fixed upon her. In the bright light of the lantern she'd dropped, Elenai noted it was just possible to see the outline of Kyrkenall's pupils against the black sclera. He smelled of his horse, and his sweat, and road dust, and he was so very splendid.

Then he rolled, grabbed her wrist, and yanked her to her feet.

The lantern had fallen but somehow landed upright, uncracked, and it shone on the weird sparkling horror only six feet off, and the jagged teeth within its clacking jaws. The feelers were waving at the end of its snout. It had been pincushioned with a dozen bright red darts, illuminated by the gathered bright points in its skin as they were drawn inside the porous, glistening hide.

"Go!" Kyrkenall roared.

She snatched up the lantern and threw herself through the tower entryway. She was moving too fast to avoid collision with a sturdy metal shelf set a few paces back. As the construction wobbled it pulled the slim chain linking it to the door itself. Kyrkenall cursed, for the tightening chain slammed the door against him as he was halfway through.

Elenai whirled, the wildly shaking light in her hand passing over dozens of holes set into the odd shelf unit at head and chest level. Kyrkenall slid through.

And then the door was smashed open by the terrible scaly head of the eyeless horror. This time the chain attached to the shelf was simply ripped away, and the creature lunged in to snap at Kyrkenall, who kicked it squarely in the jaw. She lashed out with all the pain and fear she'd felt the first time she encountered the creature. She'd never tried such an attack without focus on a talisman, but she didn't have the time to feel for it and she didn't think she needed it. Not after experiencing it so intently herself.

As her thread touched the monster, that imagined pain struck her, too, and she staggered backward into the chamber. The creature, though, writhed in agony with her, and Kyrkenall crawled to safety.

Reeling, Elenai sank to cold stone, in too much pain to worry about what she couldn't see behind her. Agony washed not just through her limbs, but her gut as well, so that she doubled up on the floor, eyes squeezed tight. She felt as though she'd swallowed fire.

Vaguely she was aware of Kyrkenall calling to her, squeezing her shoulder.

And then suddenly the sensation ebbed, and she was able to sit up. Kyrkenall smiled at her, then stepped back to peer out the door. "Hey, look at this!"

It was about all she could do just then to stare at the tower's stone floor. "What is it?"

"The thing's dying!"

Surely she hadn't done that much damage to it.

"I bet those darts were poisoned," he said with a laugh. "Hah! The hastigs who rigged that dart-throwing thing to go off when the door opened couldn't imagine they'd be saving our asses by killing their own monster! Take that, Denaven!"

Maybe that's why she felt such excruciating discomfort inside her, over and above the blast of her magical attack. She'd magically touched the thing while it died of poison. Finally she sat up completely, and a cheerful Kyrkenall was looking down at her.

"You're sure it's dead?" she asked.

"Either that or it has a weird sleep cycle. Hey, how did you know to pull me out of the way? You couldn't see the trap, could you?"

She shook her head. "I'm not sure how I did it," she said, and her ignorance embarrassed her. "I guess I saw ahead a little."

"Well, you saved us both. Nicely done. You going to live?"

"It feels like it." She took his offered hand and climbed unsteadily to her feet. She stepped around and looked over the dart launcher, now fallen through the threshold of the door. The creature lay absolutely still, the light lines fading along its skin. The terrible jaws had shut forever, and the stubby legs ceased their shifting. Sending such a unique creature to its end made her feel somehow shabby.

Kyrkenall was talking calmly beside her. "You note that the darts were designed to launch at head level. Do you know why?"

Elenai shook her head.

"To take out Altenerai. Those darts couldn't drive through Altenerai armor. But a lot of us don't bother with helmets or the first few hooks of our robe unless we're riding into battle."

She thought back to the impact she'd felt against her shoulder, thankful for the protective fabric. If not for her borrowed khalat a dart might have poisoned her as well. "Do you think the tower has more traps?"

"Almost surely. You ready to find them?"

"I suppose I have to be."

"That's the right answer."

She followed him in as he lifted the lantern and played it over the room. To their left, an open timber staircase wound up along the inner wall. To their right, and beyond the dart launcher, a dark and dusty room took up the remainder of the tower's lower floor.

The room itself was fairly spare. There was a cold hearth, a stone floor with an ancient rug, and a cupboard with a serving shelf waiting with dusty mugs. A door stood in the far wall. But drawing the eye more than anything else was a huge upright hunk of irregular crystal near the fireplace. Chairs were pushed to the periphery near a dried-out old table. Elenai, opening herself once more to the inner world, was nearly overwhelmed by the energies she perceived within the weird rock.

She felt pulled to it as if dragged on puppet strings.

"Watch out for that thing," Kyrkenall warned.

"It has hearthstone magics," she said without looking at him.

"Then it's probably a trap."

"Maybe this is what everyone was guarding," she said.

The object was so dense she couldn't see individual threads the way she did when she looked at any ordinary living objects. Just like a hearthstone. It was brighter but somehow different than her hearthstone. And it was vastly larger.

"You think they were hiding this instead of Irion? You said Cargen was thinking about the sword when he pictured this tower."

"He said he wasn't," Elenai reminded him. "Maybe it's inside."

"It's like an overgrown hearthstone, isn't it? Can you hide things inside of a hearthstone?"

"Your guess is as good as mine."

"Well, let's steer clear of it for now. It's a big tower. Maybe the sword's hidden somewhere else."

Unfortunately, it wasn't. They searched the empty quarters and storage rooms above, abandoned save for some old mattressless bunks. They even went up to the tower's height, where Elenai got her first non-magical look at the chasm. She took in the endless sky, complete with swirling stars above and below, for long moments. According to Kyrkenall, no explorer had ever arrived at the tip of this mountainous peninsula from outside the realm, nor had anyone ever returned from a downward climb into the bottomless shift. Though horrible miscreations had crawled out of or flown up from that void in times past, now the area was a testament to emptiness. Much like the tower.

In the end, Kyrkenall reluctantly returned to contemplate the giant hearthstone, and she joined him.

He shook his head. "I don't understand why it's here. The way the queen collects hearthstones, she'd want it in Darassus, wouldn't she? Unless there's something wrong with it."

"They certainly went to an awful lot of trouble to protect it."

"All of this seems like too much trouble. If you were going to hide Irion, you could keep it under your bed, couldn't you? I mean if you were Denaven or the queen. Surely you wouldn't have to haul it way out here and dispatch guards who might occasionally let things slip about their secret duty."

"I'm going to take a closer look at it."

He frowned. "Be very, very careful."

With hand to the hearthstone in her satchel, Elenai walked forward, her power rooted to it as she sent sensory threads toward the huge crystalline column. Strange, that it was less potent than the smaller stone for all its bright glamour.

As she slowly stepped ever closer she realized there was an interplay of energies between the stones, small to large. It seemed as though they might blend. Her mother had once tried to explain why melody worked, saying that some notes called more strongly to others, so that the tune wanted to keep moving until that tension resolved. She sensed that tension from the hearthstone, and she felt it easing as she walked near.

Kyrkenall's voice was a grating interruption. "Do you have to get so close?"

"I think I should bring them together."

"Is that a hunch, or is that the hearthstone talking?"

She halted. She'd never had a conversation with the hearthstone, and never brushed against what she thought was a personality, either. Why was Kyrkenall always speaking as if the hearthstone was a hungry entity ready to devour? "I think it's what's needed." She lifted the stone from her pack.

"You don't sound sure. It may be some kind of magical trick."

Elenai ignored the firm hand suddenly gripping her arm and pressed her hearthstone to the man-high crystal.

The resulting magical light blinded her. She gasped and staggered, dropping her link with the stone immediately lest the flaring energies sweep her up.

Kyrkenall pulled her back and pushed her into the space below the stair. She blinked repeatedly to clear her eyes, and could just glimpse her hearthstone, shining but no longer blinding. It had affixed itself to the surface of the crystal block, also glowing from within. The satchel she'd carried it in lay on the floor.

Kyrkenall cursed ferociously and unsheathed his sword.

Golden light flashed over the block's crystalline surface. And then, in an eye blink, the block's energies shrank and intensified into two stones smaller than her own. All three dropped away and struck the rug.

A tall, russet-haired swordsman was left where the crystal had stood, his Altenerai robe half undone, his hair tousled. He turned their direction, the long, straight length of Irion shining in his hand and glittering under the light of his sapphire ring.

Elenai's hand was already on her sword hilt, but she paused with the weapon half drawn.

For facing them was none other than the man who'd once given her his winesac. The warrior who'd led the armies of Darassus to a dozen victories and staved off the Naor invasions. The legendary commander and hero, N'lahr the Grim.

Record of Truths

Varama led him from the city at dusk, out through the suburbs and up the lonely way to the great dark bluff where the dead were housed. With stars glittering above and city lights shining below, she found her way to N'lahr's tomb and reined in outside it.

Rylin wasn't sure what was in the shoulder pack she asked him to take from her horse, though it felt heavy. She set her sapphire ring into the indentation beside the stone door engraved with N'lahr's solemn life-size image. The door swung outward with the mildest of grating noises, and her ring bathed the crypt's recesses in eerie blue light.

Rylin willed his own into brilliance and followed her, playing the light through the chamber. The lack of dust and cobwebs inside surprised him until he recalled the chamber had been cleaned after the bodies were removed. He didn't see any of the bottles Varama had mentioned, and he supposed they'd been discarded.

A stone bench was built into three sides of the small, windowless structure, and a stone sarcophagus lay along the building's axis. The life-size image of N'lahr at rest was carved into the sarcophagus lid, eyes closed, hands crossed over his chest. There was no missing the stone ring crafted to resemble the Altenerai badge of office, complete even to the tiny first lines of the oath inscribed in the setting. It was a stunningly detailed and artful creation.

Varama stopped and looked down at her friend's image, then made the Sign of the Four over her chest. Her voice, though soft, was high and curiously bright in the grim place. "I'm sorry, old friend. This is for the good of the realm." She motioned Rylin forward, then dug through the pack until she produced a mallet and chisel. She glanced at Rylin. "I wish we had time to take more care."

She struck the chisel deftly and with surprising force even as Rylin opened his mouth to object. The sound of metal-on-metal reverberated off the hard, close surfaces and the brittle lid cracked, sending pebble-sized fragments flying. Varama slammed the hammer a second time and the crack widened to split the image of N'lahr's head.

Rylin was aghast at the careless destruction of a priceless artwork. "Couldn't we just lift the top off?"

"Sealed," Varama answered, and smashed a third time. A wedge of stone slid off part of the carving's chin and dropped onto something within, for there was no clattering sound.

There was no stench. Rylin supposed that there might not be from a body lying here seven years.

Varama set the mallet aside and tugged on a wedge-shaped section beside the image's neck loosened by her destruction. Rylin shook off his misgivings and helped her pull it free. In the stone receptacle below he saw fabric, the shoulder of a blue Altenerai khalat.

They tugged broken pieces away from the upper third of the left side of the sarcophagus.

Varama shone her light down, and they looked at a pale, drawn face. N'lahr's eyes were closed, but otherwise he might have been sleeping.

Rylin drew an involuntary breath. "Gods. He hasn't decayed at all."

Varama leaned into the sarcophagus, apparently feeling for the sword, for she reached deep inside.

"No sword." Her voice echoed hollowly at him. "I didn't think there would be."

Finally she withdrew, her hair mussed and dusty, and Rylin groaned in dismay as she touched the dead man's face. Hadn't this gone far enough? Whatever they'd hoped to prove wasn't here.

"There's definitely something odd here."

At such a bland remark, Rylin struggled to fight down a scoffing noise. This whole exercise was beyond bizarre.

"The skin is fresh. Here. Feel." She encouraged him to touch the corpse's face.

Repulsed, Rylin nonetheless echoed the gesture. She was right. Cold flesh. But then flesh sitting there so long should be decayed or devoured. "It's got to be some kind of magical spell to preserve him, doesn't it?"

"Do think before you speak, Rylin. Look again."

He frowned as he withdrew his hand, wondering why he hadn't used his inner sight first.

In one swift motion, Varama pulled a knife from her belt, leaned in, and sliced off a chunk of flesh pinched between her fingers.

Rylin swore in amazement.

"It's not real." Varama stood up and lifted a hunk of dead hero. Rylin grimaced, then forced himself to stare harder.

"It's all the same color," Varama announced. "There's no muscle fiber. No bone."

Rylin mouthed another oath and stared down at what should have been a gory mess. But as he shone his light at the wound in N'lahr's cheek he found Varama's summation completely accurate. N'lahr's body was the same color inside as out.

Rylin looked up. "What is this thing? And where's Commander N'lahr's body, really?"

"I wish I could say. It seems we have another mystery."

"Like how they created such a perfect imitation. And why."

"Now you're thinking."

She unceremoniously tossed the scrap of fake flesh past him into the sepulcher. Even knowing it was artificial, Rylin cringed.

"It's time to take a look at the hall of the auxiliary. Just as we planned."

As they rode back toward the city, Rylin tried not to dwell on how much his perception of it had changed over the last few days. Those lights had once represented ease and comfort. Now they seemed only to provide sources for the shadows eating away at all remaining security. He hadn't thought the sword would be hidden in N'lahr's tomb, but he'd never imagined N'lahr himself would be replaced with a horrific duplicate. Any lingering doubts as to the truth about a conspiracy had completely vanished.

They paused at Varama's workshops to leave their horses and don their semblances, then openly approached the portico to the Mage Auxiliary. The squires on guard stepped aside without a word.

Rylin had wondered if he'd have to imitate Thelar's gait, but it came naturally to him; shoulders taut, hands clenched. Perhaps the semblance stone transferred that information along with the man's image.

He expected the central corridor might be filled with men and women who were off duty, like the squire halls sometimes were at night, so he breathed a sigh of relief to find it empty, dark save for the flickering lanterns that threw indistinct luminous circles on the inlaid marble floor. He tried not to hold his breath as they strode past the stairs that led to the living quarters. Those, too, were empty.

They both had anticipated some challenge accessing the Great Hall, and Varama carried specifically chosen tools for that eventuality, yet the elaborately fashioned door opened to her hand. Rylin wondered only briefly why the auxiliary would leave the entrance unwarded at night, then his eyes tracked to the pool of light at a nearby oaken table. Verin sat beside a large, opalescent sphere nearly the size of an adult's head, resting upon a lump of dark fabric. He looked up from his study of a collection of papers and stared hard at Rylin.

Had Rylin made some error? Was the semblance fading?

"I heard you had your own run-in with that smug alten," Verin greeted him.

"So." Rylin answered flatly, unsure of Verin's intention. He didn't have to strive to imitate Thelar's growl; it occurred without effort.

"He tricked me into letting him in," Verin continued, now tapping papers in order. "So, the commander's had me running errands and organizing back paperwork ever since." He turned to Varama. "You might have warned us your old boyfriend was set to invade."

Rylin's companion arched an eyebrow and tightened her lips. Was that a slight smile? "Errors are often more instructive than triumphs, Verin. What are you working on?"

"That strange new hearthstone they found last week. The queen's been making notes about it and I'm supposed to index and file them."

Now *that* was interesting. Rylin desperately wanted to ask more, but didn't want to betray his own ignorance. Instead he moved closer to the referenced hearthstone, which looked little like any of the others he'd glimpsed. Its surface was far more regular than the typically jagged crystal lumps he'd noted before. He resisted the urge to study it through his inner sight, though. Verin might be able to sense the magical energies were different from Thelar's. "Is she coming back tonight?" Rylin asked.

"Who can say?" Verin said. "She keeps odd hours these days."

"You look tired," Varama offered. "Do you want us to file those for you?"

Verin considered her quizzically. "Is there something wrong with your voice?"

Varama put a hand to her throat and coughed delicately. "I think it's Spring."

"Do you want help or not?" Rylin inserted quickly.

Verin brightened. Probably Thelar wasn't in the habit of being nice to people, and his surprise at the generosity was reflected in the sound of Verin's voice. "That's awfully kind of you. I was afraid I'd miss the whole game, but if I get over to The Lion quick, I might be able to join a few hands."

Rylin shrugged as though the matter were inconsequential, but Verin looked as if the sun had come out.

"Can you lock up?" Verin hesitantly offered a key, almost as if he expected to be ridiculed for suggesting it.

Rylin sighed, so as not to be too eager. "Fine."

"Thanks, Thelar. I really appreciate it."

Rylin grunted.

Verin, with a last look over his shoulder, left the room.

Rylin watched the great door swing shut and listened to the sound of receding footsteps.

"Good enough," Varama asserted quietly, then bent to examine the strange stone. Rylin considered the papers, overflowing with Queen Leonara's script. He'd seen her signature at the bottom of various proclamations over the years but never studied any actual documents from her hand. He was surprised at how looping and undisciplined her letters were. The actual words were a little challenging to read. "How much time do you want me to spend with this?" he asked.

"You be the judge. This is very strange. It's like no hearthstone I've seen before." She folded it up in its cloth and then tucked it into the pack she unslung from her shoulders.

Rylin blinked at that. "So we're not worried about being caught?"

"Caught, yes. Come."

She walked—swayed, rather, given her semblance—on toward the counter in front of the long rack of books that stood perpendicular to the rows of shelves holding hearthstones behind it.

She moved behind the counter as if she owned it and immediately searched the titles.

Rylin followed with the notes and struck a match to a lamp he retrieved from a nearby counter, then turned it low as Varama bent to examine lower bookspines. Rylin couldn't keep from admiring her backside as she did so. Illusory or not, Tesra was a striking woman.

She handed him a book.

He strove for a normal tone, though he kept his voice low. "What's this?"

"Find out."

Had she chosen the book at random? The title on the spine read only Volume 6.

Varama selected a text of her own and set it on the counter, flipping it open. Rylin did the same with his, abandoning the tedious papers. He didn't know if merely anyone was allowed access to these records, but in case someone were to enter, he cultivated the attitude that he belonged.

He tried not to wonder just how much time they had left. They'd already been under their disguises for a quarter hour. Should he suggest they drop the semblances and only wear them if someone came in? Varama didn't seem inclined to do so.

He turned to the task at hand. At first, he had trouble making sense of the long lists at the front of the book. Pages and pages consisted of nothing but signatures and dates and rows of numbers. After a little while he understood that these were records of who had examined which hearthstone, when, and then a notation identifying the pages where each examiner had recorded their own impressions.

As he leafed through descriptions of the hearthstones, he discovered that the mages had created a power scale of sorts that rated every one. Additionally, they'd analyzed them for which emotions they were mostly likely to arouse in their users, a peculiar side effect largely identifiable by the shade of hearthstone. He didn't have to guess what the purple ones elicited, but smiled at Tesra's apparently deliberate choice.

As interesting as all of this information was, though, none of it had anything to do with Irion, so he slid the book back into place and studied the other volumes' spines.

Every single one of them was labeled the same way, and he found each similar to Volume 6: columns with notations and observations.

Varama/Tesra was engrossed in her book.

"Are you finding anything?"

Her answer was short, quiet, and a little sharp. "Yes." She flipped forward a page, then rifled ahead.

He hefted Volume 1, idly wondering as he did so what book Varama was reading, since the others were in sequence. Maybe hers was more relevant to their search.

His book, at first glance, seemed identical to Volume 6. On closer examination, though, he discovered that the experiences with the hearthstones described in this book were very different. Several hearthstones recorded in it were far more difficult to engage, or left the users with disquieting and unpleasant effects. At the bottom of one page was a grim note: *Experiment terminated. Mage convulsed during immersion in stone. Unable to be revived.*

So merely using that hearthstone had killed someone?

He glanced at Varama, who was staring contemplatively into the middle distance. "What is it?"

"This book solely catalogs all the hearthstones that have been found. By whom, and when. The queen lists the first one, long in storage."

Rylin nodded.

"Commander Renik's name is all over the first few pages, then others, including Kalandra, but his name features prominently for years. Belahn turns up as finding some, and sometimes Kalandra in tandem with Asrahn—"

"Your pardon, but how is that important?"

"It's a record of who and when, and there are some curious patterns. One in particular gives me pause."

She turned to replace the book.

"What is it?"

"After Commander Renik's time, the large discoveries of hearthstones die off. Today, the mages, Denaven, or Cerai are the only ones bringing them in, and only one or two at a time. But just seven years ago Denaven had a huge find. He brought in fifty-six. No one immediately before or after came in with more than fourteen."

"Maybe that's why he got promoted."

"No. Think. The date coincides with the signing of the Naor peace treaty. Denaven was newly appointed commander, and there at Kanesh to witness the signing. How could he have found one hearthstone, let alone fifty-six of them?"

"So what does it mean?"

"It's idiocy. I can't believe that they'd just record it right here in the book like that. You think they'd break something so obvious up into different entries. Obscure it."

"I'm not following you." With Thelar's voice, the statement came out like a growl.

She might have been looking at him with Tesra's face, but the blank, disappointed expression was solely Varama's. "Denaven got them from the Naor. That's the real reason the queen signed the treaty rather than pressing on. N'lahr had won decisively, and we could have advanced right into the heart of Naor lands and defeated Mazakan once and for all, ensuring security for at least two generations, if not longer."

Rylin breathed out slowly. He tried to compose himself. "So this means the peace treaty was engineered to obtain more hearthstones."

"Yes."

"So the Naor gave us the hearthstones, and we gave them breathing room to rebuild their offenses?"

She nodded once, sharply. "And maybe we gave them N'lahr's sword. And maybe his head, since he would never have agreed."

Rylin went cold. "Surely not."

"They murdered Asrahn. Wouldn't they murder N'lahr or give him to our enemies? He's certainly not in his tomb."

"But Commander N'lahr had just saved us from annihilation." Rylin had only been a second-rank squire in those days, but he remembered the chill dread that preceded the astonishing victory. "We were outnumbered by Naor at least three to one and he still beat them—"

"By that point in the war, the Naor feared N'lahr more than anyone else alive. It's reasonable to conclude that any negotiation would have included some reference to him. And he died immediately before we were told the deal was struck."

"*You're saying the queen handed our greatest general* and *his sword to the Naor?*" Rylin's voice, he realized too late, was rising to imprudent levels. "For hearthstones?"

Varama replied coolly. "I'm saying that the stones were obtained from the Naor at some price and that, barring an incredible coincidence, that price appears to have included cessation of hostilities and, possibly, N'lahr and his sword. The sword that's reputed to be the only thing that can kill Mazakan."

Even with the evidence before him, Rylin had a hard time accepting Varama's accusation. The depth of betrayal that would have to be involved was almost physically revolting to him, and then if he factored in the threat to the security of the realms the queen purported to rule, her actions were almost suicidal. "What now?"

"I think we must give up on the sword. And I think we must give up on Darassus. If Kyrkenall had learned any of this, his most likely destination was to Alantris, to seek counsel and sanctuary with Aradel. He might not know where any of us stood, but he surely knew her feelings. We'll link up with them in Alantris and assemble a quorum of governors and present the information we've learned. We may already have enough grounds for them to replace the queen."

"You make it sound simple."

"Do I? It won't be. Let's go pick out some hearthstones."

"You mean we're going to steal some?"

"That's an ugly thought. We're requisitioning state property for lawful purposes." She lifted the lamp and walked around the bookcase to the stacks. "We'll select mostly lighter-colored ones. The blue and clear seem simplest to work with. Did you note that curious notation when they found a 'match'?"

He hadn't noticed anything of the kind. "There were a lot of curious notations."

She gave him an empty satchel she pulled from the one she carried. "It was under the heading 'Fittings.' Some hearthstones, apparently, have affinities for others and their energies grow more powerful when those stones are deployed together. When the mages find any that are closely attuned with others, they move them out of this library. Where, I'm not sure. But I'd like to know."

Rylin noticed that Varama was selecting hearthstones—not at random, as he would have, but by remembering the descriptions she'd read. Fortunately, the shelf where each one sat had been labeled. While she made her choices, Rylin debated looking around for one of those lavender shards. Just as he'd resolved to do so, Varama handed over a light blue and pinkish stone, which he placed gently in his canvas pack. She deposited two more, along with some shards.

"Won't we look suspicious as we leave?" Rylin said. "With the satchels?"

"Perhaps. But it's essential to have comparable weapons of our own and deprive them of key tools they may wish to use against us."

They shouldered the satchels, left the stacks, and started for the door. They were only eight paces away when it was thrust widely open.

Thelar, frowning, with drawn sword lowered, came to an abrupt halt, with the twin women Meria and M'vai banging into him from behind. Verin backlit all three with a lantern. Though clearly expecting something amiss, Thelar apparently found facing himself more alarming than he'd imagined. His eyes widened in surprise.

Rylin touched his enemies with a wave of confusion at the same moment his hand closed on his sword hilt. Then he charged them.

But Varama moved more swiftly. Her disguise carried no weapon, so she swept up a nearby chair and swung it sideways in one smooth motion, trapping Thelar's sword arm between leg and support spindle. There was a terrible cracking sound as she twisted, then he shrieked in pain and his weapon clattered to the floor. For a brief moment it looked as though Varama had lost balance. She went half down following the motion of the chair, dragging Thelar's trapped arm to the floor, but she planted the simple furnishing solidly on all four legs, using it as a pivot point to kick out and take Meria in the head and shoulder.

The twin slammed into her sister as Rylin drove his sword point into the back of her wrist; M'vai, screeching, dropped her blade. As both weapons rang against the stone floor, Varama landed a handspan from Thelar's writhing shoulder, and freed the chair for a broad overhead strike that smashed the signal horn Verin was raising, and broke the lantern in his other hand for good measure when he crumpled. The lantern's fire greedily ate the oil spilled across the stone floor.

Varama and Rylin bolted from the room.

While he'd been fully aware that anyone bearing the ring had passed innumerable martial trials, Rylin had never imagined Varama in the field. Her reaction time had been phenomenal, but so had her precision and economy. Not a single one of her movements had been wasted. She'd been twice as effective as him without using sorcery or even a sword.

Now she sprinted down the corridor, her disguise melting away as she ran, but it wasn't her own appearance she assumed. Rylin didn't recognize the back of that head, although he realized as they neared the exterior doors that she wore an exalt's khalat.

Varama pushed through the portal even as shouts to halt rang through the air behind them. A horn call signaling alert echoed in the halls.

The two squires who waited in the nighttime air just beyond the portico were so nervous that both spun on the instant, hands to sword hilts.

It was then Rylin saw who Varama imitated. Synahla, commander of the Mage Auxiliary.

Varama drew herself up to Synahla's full height. "Intruders are headed into the east courtyard! Run, fools! Head them off!"

The squires saluted, replied in the affirmative, and hurried away to the east. Neither seemed to have noticed that Synahla's voice wasn't really hers. The moment their feet left the stairs, Varama started down to the west. Rylin followed.

There was another shout of "Halt, intruders!" as they veered around the side of the building and raced into the darkness.

"Lose your semblance," Varama called through gritted teeth. Her true appearance met his gaze. "Call on your personal energy. No hearthstones. Run for the workrooms."

He'd known from a young age that every mage had a core of power to tap into for enhancing performance. Many believed that the souls of mages were blessed, or cursed, with a connection to the chaotic energies that swirled in the Shifting Lands. He'd never much cared where the power came from, only that he had a limited quantity. Improving magical endurance wasn't like strengthening yourself by doing push-ups. No matter how much he'd practiced, he'd only managed to increase his built-in sorcerous stamina by a little.

He called upon it now with spells he'd honed in long years as a squire, first under the tutelage of Alten Kalandra, then on his own. He lent strength that was more than human to his legs and sharpened his awareness to a fever pitch so that he tore ahead through the darkness even as Varama vanished from view. He had no idea of the spells at her command—all mages, even Altenerai, were a little protective of magical secrets.

She'd seemed to suggest they separate, and he didn't know where she was, so he tore on alone over the flagstones, racing along the darkened length of one palace wing, his steps all but silent. He veered north toward the tributary of the Idris that crossed through the palace grounds, and he decided against the bridge where he saw a figure crossing, backlit against the workshop's glow.

As he sprinted along the sward he felt his energy reserves ebbing and cursed himself a little. Was he really so weak that he couldn't hold out any longer than this?

He willed the shadows to embrace him and raced toward the walled river, a line of darkness with glistening ripples of silvered moonlight at least ten feet across. He boosted his speed, thrust all his strength into his legs, and leapt with a running start.

The hostile spell touched him as he was airborne. He felt the distant regard of some powerful sorcerer, searching from afar, sensed an almost rapturous glee as that someone understood it had found a magic worker. He hit the far side with inches to spare, stumbling as he lost focus. The cloaking shadows drained away from him like inky water leaving a tub as the presence pressed on.

And his ring lit. With that he knew a brief sense of shock from the person searching for him, and in that moment of surprise he glimpsed a facet of his watcher's personality. He realized with sick dread that the queen herself had discovered him. Her connection with him fell away as he picked himself up and ran flat out across the darkness that lay between him and Varama's central workbuilding

He thought he could guess what had happened. When his ring kicked on, it had marked him as Altenerai. And there were currently only two Altenerai stationed in Darassus, just as there had been two interlopers within the Mage Auxiliary wing. They were found out. The queen would be marshaling all necessary forces to stop them at this very minute. She was said to be a powerful caster, and he feared whatever spells she might bring to bear after years of working with hearthstones.

As he came panting to a stop, he found Varama before a line of her craftsmen and squires in the open space. With them were a handful of saddled animals. She'd warned him that if everything went badly they might have to flee, but he hadn't realized she'd been so careful about contingency plans.

A horn sounded from the barracks or stables. An action call. The queen must be preparing to set the squires on them. He hoped this wouldn't come to a fight against unwitting lower rankers.

When he came up, Varama was speaking quickly to her workers, telling them to throw their papers into the forges. "Retreat and blend."

Gods. They were going to destroy their work? "They know it's us," he reported to her between breaths. "They felt my ring come on."

"Then there's no more time." Varama flung herself into her saddle. "Mount up."

One of the burly craftsmen, grim faced, handed a pack to her. Rylin wasn't sure whether to be unnerved or impressed that his favorite horse, a black named Rurudan, was waiting for him with apparently full saddlebags. Two of Varama's squires climbed onto the remaining horses as he climbed into the stirrups himself. Varama urged her horse into a canter even as those remaining called farewells.

So now, Rylin thought, I'm a fugitive. He wondered what his sisters and brother would say to that, and what lie would be concocted to explain his disappearance. How would he be framed? Would they kill someone and lay the blame at his feet, like they'd done with Kyrkenall?

Varama led the way straight for the north palace gate. Rylin realized the fifth ranker on his left was haughty Sansyra, one of his least favorite squires in the corps.

From out of the night came the thunder of hooves and Rylin tensed.

"Easy," Varama called. "They're expected."

A half-dozen third rankers were in the lead of what looked to be more than two-thirds of the squire corps posted to Darassus, probably close to seventy-five individuals.

"How—" he said.

"I ordered all but a few to drill all evening," Varama replied.

Another horn call rent the night, high and clear. Rylin imagined a squire racing to the balcony overlooking the main courtyard and setting the horn to her lips. Like the most important alerts, it was short and to the point, so there was no mistaking intent. The palace was being locked down. No one was to exit or leave.

The gilt, iron-topped stone palace wall loomed ahead. Currently the heavy and well-polished wooden gates hung open, but as they galloped toward them Rylin spied a trio of squires racing from the little gatehouse.

The second-rank squires had just set hands to push on the gates as Varama shouted to close it after them and watch for intruders.

The squires looked up in confusion as they all passed, lantern light from the gatehouse showing in the whites of their eyes. They gave no challenge. Varama had simply planned too well against the worst possible outcome. Who would see fit to stop two Altenerai leading a vast swathe of forces off to some battle? Surely they looked as if they were out to confront whatever had caused the signal.

And now they were mounted and speeding through the dark city streets with a small army of squires in tow. They made quite a racket, and brought a few bleary-eyed stares in their wake, but the streets they chose were wide open at this time of evening. Most of the city's nightlife lay south, along the Idris. Here shops and homes were sealed up as folks were already in their beds. Far behind, Rylin spied quite a few lit shutters thrust open to investigate horn calls and the clatter of horseshoes, but no one lagged to offer explanation to the citizens.

After a few minutes, the bugle calls changed, alerting distant outposts of the city's guard to fugitives on the road. But the dilapidated post they neared hadn't been manned in a generation, despite some repeated appeals for funding, and the old west wall was low enough for a man to leap, much less a horse. They pushed past it and diverted around the Cemetery Ridge, skirting southeast until they could angle toward the eastern road, and The Fragments.

Rylin found himself laughing. "Who do they have to send after us?" he shouted to Varama. "Damn, you're good!"

"I am," she said. "But don't get too cocky, Rylin. They have the Mage Auxiliary. And they have the hearthstones. There may be much that they can do to harm us. We're in grave danger until we cross the border to The Fragments."

Rylin's eye swept back to the troops obediantly following. "Even against all of us?"

"Even so. We've declared ourselves now. The queen need hold nothing back."

12

Dueling with the Truth

The impossible vision before her was a perfect duplication of the man Elenai had seen years before. The straight brown hair that hung to the nape of his neck. The sharp nose and deep-set eyes. The spare, angular frame draped in blue Altenerai khalat, the dark pants and knee-high boots.

The twin of N'lahr addressed them in a low, tense tone. "Kyrkenall? What are you doing here?"

The archer stared, his sword leveled. "Elenai, is someone weaving us?"

Her sapphire glowed. A warning that magic was being employed, or a leftover effect from her hearthstone use? She still didn't know enough about the rings to be certain. The most recent exercise of power had already left her short of breath, but she acted without hesitation.

With her eyes open, the inner world lay across the outer. There was no missing the brilliance of the hearthstone now lying on the moth-eaten rug or the diminished glow of its shattered look-alike in two halves nearby, or the shifting golden corona around Irion. More importantly, N'lahr's duplicate was formed from the same complex mix of threads as she and Kyrkenall. He was no more an illusion than either of them. But was he the real N'lahr?

"Squire?" Kyrkenall demanded without looking away.

She stammered her answer. "He's real."

"No he's not," Kyrkenall said savagely. "This is some hearthstone shit. Another trap."

"Kyrkenall?" N'lahr asked. "What's going on? Where's Denaven?"

"You're not real!" Kyrkenall charged him.

N'lahr neatly batted the swing aside and back-stepped to the fireplace, brow drawn.

"Stop!" Elenai shouted, but the archer bore in.

"You're not him!" he screamed.

N'lahr parried each of the attacks. His eyes slitted as he parried a deft slice.

"The real N'lahr would fight back!" Kyrkenall said.

"I *am* N'lahr!"

"He's dead!" Kyrkenall beat his opponent's blade to thrust home.

"No!" Elenai cried.

She needn't have worried. N'lahr wrenched himself to the right—his only movement, she realized, that hadn't looked effortless—and locked his opponent's blade at the hilt with his own. "I'm not dead!"

They stared, face-to-face. Kyrkenall bared his teeth. "I saw you interred!" He strove to push the blade away by sheer force of strength.

Though his voice was strained, N'lahr still somehow sounded calm. "I swear I'm as real as you are. Put down your sword."

"Tell me something only N'lahr would know."

"Like what?"

"Prove you're him! What did you say to me before the battle at Broken Ridge?"

The taller man's brow furrowed. "I don't remember. You were galloping ahead of me anyway."

"No, you idiot, before! When you and Rialla and I rode out after Asrahn!"

N'lahr looked blankly back.

Gods. Elenai licked her lips. Was Kyrkenall right after all? Was this some kind of elaborate trick?

"You mean when I laid out the ambush," N'lahr asked, "or how I asked Rialla to link us?"

"Not the tactics! You don't remember the speech?"

"Something about standing together? I don't know."

Kyrkenall cursed under his breath and backed away. He spoke softly, almost resentfully. "It *is* you."

"I've been telling you that."

He slowly lowered Lothrun. Still staring, he slid his blade home into its sheath.

"Now would you tell me what's going on?" N'lahr looked to sheath his own weapon and found no sword belt at his side. "And where are we? This looks like the Chasm Tower."

"We *are* in the Chasm Tower," Kyrkenall answered dully. "You've been dead seven years." To N'lahr's stolid look, Kyrkenall replied: "I used to come to your tomb on your birthday and raise a drink."

"I was dead?" N'lahr asked.

"I saw your body."

"It must have been faked."

"I guess so! But it was a good fake. It fooled all of us."

N'lahr frowned. "You still haven't answered me. What am I doing here, and what's going on? And why is a squire wearing a khalat and ring?"

Kyrkenall tensed a bit, but indicated her with a wave of his hand. "This is Elenai Dartaan."

N'lahr considered her formally and offered a courteous nod while Kyrkenall looked to the floor. It took a moment for him to muster an answer, and when he did so, Kyrkenall was uncharacteristically terse. "A few days ago, Asrahn took your sword down to polish it for a big festival they hold in your honor each year. He could tell it was a fake, and when he talked about it, he was murdered."

"Asrahn? Murdered?" N'lahr looked disconcerted for the first time. He glanced at the sword in his hand but didn't challenge anything else in his friend's narrative. His voice dropped. "Who killed him?"

"Do you remember Squire Cargen and Squire K'narr? They were made Altenerai. They did it, along with some weavers. I killed them. Elenai helped."

She felt N'lahr scrutinize her. The lanky general sank onto one of the battered backless chairs near the crude camp table opposite the door. His lips were pressed in a thin line and his hands were clenched, but his tone continued an enforced calm. "Go on."

"We don't know much more," Kyrkenall confessed. He pointed a finger at her. "Elenai pulled an image out of Cargen's head right before I drove a sword through him. It was of this tower. We were asking him where Irion was. As for the khalat and the ring, well, we've been chased ever since, and I figured she could use the protection because she was riding with me. Cargen sure didn't need it. Now maybe you can explain to me what you're doing here. Alive."

"What about the war? Have we won?"

Kyrkenall held up a hand. "You've got a hundred questions, I'm sure. I don't blame you, but I really need to know what you're doing here."

N'lahr stared for a moment, then set his famed sword across the table. "The war, Kyrkenall. And where's Kalandra?"

"I'm asking the questions, remember?"

N'lahr's gaze was fixed.

Kyrkenall threw up his hands. "She's missing, N'lahr. Like Commander Renik."

Elenai had never before heard anyone refer to Renik as "missing," although she supposed that was technically correct. Missing and long since assumed dead.

N'lahr's expression darkened further. "For how long?"

"Since right before you . . . died. Or whatever you did."

Elenai noted that a muscle in N'lahr's jaw clenched. "Didn't you look for her?"

"Yes! Damnit, N'lahr, focus. The Naor sued for peace; they keep raiding and biding their time, but that's not our most important problem right now. Odds are we've got an army, our army, riding toward us with Denaven in command, and they may be in a mood to kill first and sort it out later. I might have thrown them off when I rode into the Shifting Lands, but Elenai and I can't turn off our hearthstone, so they could be right over the horizon for all I know. It really depends on how soon they found the bodies."

"Bodies?"

"Cargen, K'narr, and the other yankers who murdered Asrahn. Now. You're all caught up. What are you *doing* here?"

N'lahr looked down at his khalat and carefully hooked it up—he seemed to be deliberating. For the first time, Elenai noticed he was moving his left arm stiffly.

"I assume it's the queen and the hearthstones," he said flatly.

"Which means?" Kyrkenall demanded.

N'lahr stood to finish adjusting his robe. He then knitted his brow and simply stared into space.

After this continued for a long moment, Elenai wondered if she'd missed some telltale sign when she'd studied his magical nimbus earlier. She'd heard of powerful weavers creating images of living creatures. In the story of the "Witch of the Wastes," Derwyn had realized he was being tricked when the witch was distracted and the griffin simply stopped moving. Might N'lahr be nothing but an image controlled from afar?

She had just decided to look into the inner world to recheck when she noticed the archer actually growling in exasperation, and she was momentarily alarmed to find him addressing her while gesticulating dramatically. "He's always like this! He'll stand there working it all out and then give you a three-word answer and tell you to get moving." Kyrkenall's words lashed out with a vicious snap as he turned to N'lahr. "You miserable hastig! I thought you were dead!"

He came forward so suddenly Elenai feared he meant to tackle the other man. Instead, he hugged N'lahr tightly, the way a child hugs a returned parent. And he hung on as if he might collapse at any moment. His friend, startled, carefully patted him on the back.

"I thought you were dead," Kyrkenall repeated.

"I'm here." There was a hint of softness in that answer. N'lahr continued in a more normal voice: "We'll just have to find Kalandra and get all of this sorted out."

"Kalandra's dead." Kyrkenall broke away and cleared his throat. "She's got to be, N'lahr. I've looked for her everywhere. I'm sorry, but if she were alive she'd have returned to Darassus by now."

A momentary look of pain crossed his face before N'lahr shook his head.

Kyrkenall groaned, his customary impatience reasserting itself. "Enough about her for now, N'lahr. Say something. What's going on?"

N'lahr pursed his lips. "I'm not sure, but I can guess."

"Yes." Kyrkenall extended an open hand, then spun it in a circle, as though N'lahr should get the wheel moving.

The swordsman seemed to come to some resolution. "Healers came to me after the Second Battle of Kanesh, and they had a hearthstone. My arm wound was deep, but the weavers knitted it together. I was putting on my robe when Denaven walked in with two squires, and one of them tried to maze me. I grabbed Irion. I cut down the squire working magics, and then felt the power of the whole hearthstone bearing down. Denaven was attacking, using the healer's stone, trying to will me to sleep. I swung out and cut deep into the thing." N'lahr looked over at his sword. "A strange sharpness spread through my body, and the last I recall was Denaven screaming that I'd broken a hearthstone. And then I was here."

"Denaven." Kyrkenall spat the name like a curse. "He's commander now, by the way."

"Lovely."

"What was he after?"

"I presume he meant to silence me, at least for a crucial period. I'm sure he didn't expect for the hearthstone to break, but it appears some unforeseen magics imprisoned me. Perhaps it was easier to keep me that way once it happened."

Kyrkenall nodded. "And why would he want you out of the way?"

N'lahr looked up after rubbing one hand across his forehead. "The queen had received a Naor peace overture and I'd advised against it. Strongly. The Naor were all but beaten." He paused as if a new thought occurred. "Why isn't Aradel the commander?"

"She resigned in disgust when the queen announced the treaty. Are you saying they attacked you and faked your death because you didn't want the truce?"

"Not really. The Naor offered to trade hearthstones for our withdrawal.

A big cache of them. The queen was frantic because the Naor claimed to be able to destroy them, and threatened to do so unless we agreed."

Kyrkenall pounded his hand against the mantelpiece "So that's why she signed us over."

"Didn't anyone in the corps wonder why the Naor sent us so many hearthstones?" N'lahr asked.

"That must have been done in secret," Kyrkenall said. "The official line is that we agreed to the peace treaty 'to spare our citizens the privations of extended warfare' and 'demonstrate the civilizing influence of mercy and tolerance.' Common opinion has it the queen wasn't sure we could carry on without 'the great N'lahr.'" Kyrkenall's sideways gaze and slight crooked grin emphasized the last phrase.

N'lahr evinced no humor at the irony. "You mentioned that you were being pursued."

"We think so. It looks like some of the Altenerai are leagued with De-naven and the auxiliary and they're trying to cover up your disappearance."

"Auxiliary?"

"The queen formed them. All mages. It's like a separate corps."

"That's . . . concerning. And exactly why are you being pursued?"

"Because I avenged Asrahn. I thought finding the sword would clear things up, or at least piss them off—"

"That sounds like you."

"—but now we've found you. I guess that's what they were really wor-ried about from the beginning."

"Are they on horses, or ko'aye?" N'lahr asked.

Kyrkenall made a scoffing noise. "No one has ko'aye anymore. Except maybe Aradel."

"Why not?"

"The queen didn't honor your word to Drusa. The ko'aye were, shall we say, irritated. They didn't understand."

N'lahr scowled. "I don't imagine they did."

Elenai recalled that "Drusa" had been the name of Kyrkenall's ko'aye mount. As curious as she was for more details about the creatures, she had more pressing questions, and had been waiting for a long enough pause in the conversation to ask one. "So do you know what the hearthstones are, Alten? Commander, I mean? And why the queen wants them so much?"

N'lahr weighed his response for a moment. "I wish I knew the answers to those very questions. I sent Kalandra to find out more. I hope she's got-ten to the heart of it."

Kyrkenall's eyes widened. "Wait a moment. *You* sent her out? I thought the queen did."

"I told her to ignore the queen's instructions."

"So you know where she is?"

"I know where she was supposed to go. The fact it's been seven years has me worried. As you said, she should have been in contact with you, or Asrahn. Any of the Altenerai. How many are still alive?"

"All but Asrahn. And you." Kyrkenall smirked. "Aradel resigned, of course, and Belahn's pretty much retired to Wyndyss. Actually Aradel's been made governor of The Fragments now. Boy, did that irritate the queen. I guess that's where we'll have to go next. Aradel can give us safe haven and access to the council."

Elenai had another idea. "Even if there's a whole army after us, won't they stop once they see N'lahr's alive and well?"

Kyrkenall shook his head quickly. "First, I don't know if it really is an army. I was using—"

"Hyperbole," N'lahr supplied.

"Right. Denaven might just come with some of the Altenerai who are in on it. If they're already against N'lahr, making himself known won't matter at all."

"Why don't we just ride back to Darassus with Commander N'lahr? The more people who see us, the more uproar we'll cause, and the less likely they can act against us."

Kyrkenall looked as though he was mulling the idea over. It was N'lahr who objected.

"On the enemy's ground, when we don't know the terrain? Even presuming we survive the assassination attempts, we lack adequate information to effectively counter their treachery. We need Kalandra."

"You keep saying that." Kyrkenall sighed. "Suppose she can't be found. Suppose they found her, and killed her."

"I doubt it. She was on her guard, suspicious of the queen and her allies before I was."

"What do you think Kalandra will be able to tell us, Commander?" Elenai asked.

"Hopefully, the truth about the hearthstones. What they are, why the queen's desperate for them. How we can counter them. Everything. Beyond that, we'll profit from her advice and her skill." He paused to clear his throat. "Now. What resources do we have?"

Kyrkenall indicated himself and Elenai. "Us and our weapons. A few days' worth of dried stores. My horse. Some eight horses in the guard's barn outside, but I don't know what kind of shape they're in."

"Who can we count on?"

Elenai felt a flush of pride when Kyrkenall pointed first to her. "Elenai. I'd like to say we could trust most of the other Altenerai, but I just don't know." He shook his head. "I can't believe Decrin, Tretton, or Varama are part of some secret cabal."

"Probably not," N'lahr agreed.

"I don't think Belahn or Cerai could be involved, either. He's too homebound and she made her feelings about Denaven pretty clear. Not as clear as Aradel, of course." Kyrkenall grunted appreciatively. "She cursed Denaven to his face, right after he accepted his promotion."

"So Aradel, then. Any squires we can depend on?"

Kyrkenall shook his head. "I don't know them anymore."

"There are some fifth rankers I trust," Elenai said. "But they're in Darassus."

"So that's it?" N'lahr asked Kyrkenall.

"I'm afraid so. I haven't been around the center of things."

"You said Belahn's retired."

"Pretty much."

"Then we go to him. He can shut down Elenai's hearthstone. Then we ride for Kalandra."

"Why don't we just go straight to Kalandra?" Elenai asked.

"It's on the way, and I don't want Denaven to track us to her, which he can do as long as your hearthstone is, as you say, active. And I'd rather have Kalandra put that stone to good use for us than leave it for Denaven's purposes. Let's pack it up, along with these remnants." N'lahr indicated the broken fragments of hearthstone beside the one she'd wielded. He then looked down to the weapon in his hand; the blade that had been their goal for so long. "I don't suppose either of you have the sheath?"

"No," Kyrkenall said. "There could be one in the old barracks building. If not, the bodies out there on the plain have one or two."

N'lahr looked for a moment as if he might have more questions, then shook his head and started for the door.

"Be careful—there's a dead monster right outside. At least, I think it's dead."

N'lahr stared, as if trying to decide whether his friend was serious. "I've got a sword," he countered with a half grin, then stepped away while Kyrkenall smiled broadly.

Elenai watched him depart, still a little stunned that the legend was not only alive, but joking with them. As she stepped over to the hearthstones, she heard Kyrkenall behind her. "You'd best be careful with those hearthstone pieces. Seems like cutting the one in half made it unstable."

"I'll be careful."

"Use the cloth I was wrapping the other with."

"I'm watching through the inner world. The pieces are inactive now."

"You sure?"

"Which one of us is the mage?"

"Hah. Well, watch yourself. My supply of friends is low, despite recent events."

She stuffed the first half into her satchel and then reached for the second part. She couldn't hold back a smile of her own.

13

Secrets in the Night

Denaven reached behind him with a shaking hand to ensure the chair was where he'd thought it was before he sank nerveless into its wooden seat. He hadn't taken his eyes from the empty space where the block of crystal should have stood, before the cold stone fireplace in the main floor of the Chasm Tower.

The rounded walls remained, along with the old plank table and its mismatched chairs, bathed in red and gold from the lantern he'd set there. But the crystal with N'lahr and Irion was vanished as if it had never been.

Once Denaven had halted their search party yesterday to sense Kyrkenall's direction and learned his quarry had swung northeast, he'd been certain the little archer would end up as gralk meat or a dart cushion. He'd never imagined, even in his nightmares, Kyrkenall might triumph over both beasts, the mechanism, and the warriors.

And he would never have guessed him capable of opening the crystal prison. No one else could, and it certainly had been tried by some of the best after N'lahr got himself trapped. It defied reason that the squire, Elenai, had done it. She had minimal training in sorcery and had never before used a hearthstone.

But there was no other explanation. There were no signs of drag marks, as would certainly have been evident if Kyrkenall and Elenai had somehow managed to transport the crystal that had held N'lahr. Instead, Tretton had discovered three sets of tracks leaving the fort after only two had entered. That meant N'lahr hadn't died in the crystal, as Belahn had long since feared, and was now walking free. With *his* sword. Denaven's hands tightened into fists at the thought.

Denaven deliberately took in a series of slow breaths. There had to be a way to keep this fiasco from swallowing him whole. He had collected the wisdom of others from a very young age, inspired by his grandfather, who'd bequeathed him a well-worn book of aphorisms the old man had used to record every kind of sage advice he'd run across. But the only adage rising to the fore of his recollection was one that had never made sense: "fools never drown alone." Even as a boy he knew that fools were perfectly capable of wandering off and accomplishing something fatal only to themselves. Time and maturity had proven that true.

Now he understood his interpretation had been too literal.

To call Cargen's actions foolish was to malign fools everywhere. In killing Asrahn, Cargen had engineered such a colossal catastrophe Denaven wasn't sure he'd see the end of it. And somehow the idiocy had drawn in Kyrkenall, of all people, who managed, as ever, to stagger into Denaven's life with impeccably terrible timing, drop disaster into his lap, then wander away unharmed. There really was "no justice but that taken in hand."

Soon, very soon, the Altenerai would demand to know what Kyrkenall could possibly have wanted here. He had anticipated those questions the moment he understood Kyrkenall had changed course toward this tower, but none of the answers he'd invented would work anymore. He'd have to take this situation "in hand" to come up with something very convincing, very fast.

As he was playing with a variation of one explanation, there was a heavy footfall in the entryway, and a grunt. He imagined one of the male members of their group stepping past the expended metal trap Kyrkenall had inexplicably avoided.

"Denaven," Decrin called. "What are you in here for?"

Denaven gazed steadily at the large man, wrapped in his khalat but dimly touched by the pool of lantern light. A slimmer figure followed behind: Gyldara.

"Making choices," Denaven answered.

Decrin stepped forward, broad and dark. Gyldara came after. Her beauty was impossible to ignore, from the brilliant blue eyes, to the fine-featured face, to the golden tresses reflecting lantern light.

"You look like you've had your wits blown out of you," Decrin remarked. There was no missing a note of pleasure in his voice. It was to be expected. Decrin's skepticism of this entire enterprise lurked closely below the surface. Denaven had filtered little threads of his will past the protections of all their rings, an unprecedented skill he'd carefully developed over the last several years. But no one had proven so resistant to influence as simple-minded Decrin, who had unflagging faith in those he decided were friends.

"You have no idea," Denaven replied honestly.

Gyldara interrupted. "We just found six dead soldiers laid out in a hollow south of here."

There it was. Denaven saw an opening

"It looks like Kyrkenall's doing," Gyldara explained.

"There are sword and arrow wounds on them," Decrin admitted. "And there's another dead monster of some kind. Different than the one just outside. It was feathered with arrows, most of which are removed, and slashed with a sword."

"They were black arrows," Gyldara added pointedly.

Now he had his line of attack. Gyldara needed no persuading, so he sent energies solely through a thread invisibly connecting him to Decrin. "Kyrkenall's killed again. Surely you can't assign blame for the murders of these soldiers to anyone else, can you?"

The bigger man frowned, uncertain. "Well—why did he come here? What were these people doing here? I thought the Chasm Tower was abandoned."

Denaven was ready, now, with an answer. A least part of one. "They were on official assignment guarding something very important, and very dangerous. And now a madman has it."

"You mean Kyrkenall." Decrin lowered his voice warningly.

"Yes," Denaven said testily, "I mean Kyrkenall! I don't suppose he left a note this time, did he?"

"No. Not that we've found." Decrin's obstinate loyalty was preparing objections. "What's this secret? What was stored here? Why weren't the rest of us told about it?"

Why wouldn't he yield? Denaven resisted the impulse to draw more power from the hearthstone. It would alert the ring, and even a thick-skulled brute like Decrin might detect such an intrusion. Any changes in his thinking had to feel natural. He'd just have to keep implanting doubts. "None of that's as important as the fact Kyrkenall's killed more of our people, is it? You wanted evidence of his guilt? Well, here it is. We've got to stop him before he kills anyone else. You have to see that."

Decrin stood rock still for a long moment before Denaven saw the big man's shoulders sag a minute degree. "Yes," he admitted at last. "I suppose I do."

Denaven just barely held back a smile.

Once more he heard footfalls in the corridor. This time it was Tretton who strode forward, helmet under one arm. When he halted beside the others, he stood spear straight as always. The face beneath his trim, graying beard was solemn, yet betrayed little fatigue despite their relentless track of the fugitives, which had demanded more of him than any of the others. He was iron, that one, and Denaven privately hoped he'd never face Tretton's enmity; he would be an implacable foe.

"Report," Denaven ordered.

"They're headed east by southeast, probably on a course for The Fragments, and I estimate they have a day's lead on us."

If Kyrkenall was somehow still a day ahead it meant he had even less rest than they. That had to be wearing on him, let alone that green squire. Another advantage.

"And I poked around in the offices of those outside barracks, sir," Gyldara volunteered.

He hoped she wasn't about to tell him anything that might contradict his own planned fabrications. "What did you learn?"

"Six soldiers were posted here. I found their names and their duties. They were to keep anyone without permission from approaching the boundary markers or the tower itself, on pain of death, and were to keep the creature inside the walls steadily supplied with meals. What I can't find is why they were doing any of that."

He nodded. He'd known all about their orders because he'd handed them down, but he didn't want to draw the connection too sharply and was glad those posted hadn't been too imaginative in their paperwork. "Good. We'll need their names for the burials and to convey their honors to next of kin." He also knew that these guards had been picked for this remote duty primarily due to their lack of familial entanglements. "As for the rest, I'd like to speak to the Altenerai and Exalt Ortala. No squires. Decrin, bring them in."

The big alten nodded and left.

Denaven sat with head lowered, hand pressed to his temple, signaling that he was deep in thought and not to be disturbed. The two remaining dutiful and disciplined altens obeyed his unspoken request and departed to wait for the others. By the time Decrin returned with them and Exalt Ortala and Lasren, Denaven had the rest of his approach worked out. This would be the most daring address in his career so far, and he'd have to pitch it near perfectly. He looked up slowly, considering each of them in turn.

Gyldara was poised for action, her gold hair tightly pulled back from her forehead, eyes shining, eager as a hound straining at a leash. She wanted vengeance for her sister, and expected him to deliver some sound piece of information that would render that simply. He could do that.

Beside her stood Tretton, the model of restraint. He revealed neither fatigue nor passion for the pursuit. Though no proponent of Kyrkenall, Tretton was proving difficult to win over due to his preoccupation with justice, and the outmoded Altenerai code. More appeals to moral propriety would be needed. He'd have to add something there.

Ponderous Decrin still held himself with less than his customary assurance, his high brow wrinkled in concern. Good. Now was the time to drive the doubts home.

Then there was young Lasren, pushing hair back from his widow's peak as he strode into the light after closing the door to the outside. He seemed always to be on the cusp of smiling, as if he burned with a secret amusement; he was, Denaven had long ago decided, an intellectual nonentity. He'd happily join any purpose that would bring him fame—like taking down a renowned rogue alten. As with Gyldara, any spell work on him seemed almost superfluous. He'd make the effort on them both anyway, for safety's sake.

Solemn Ortala was one of the few who knew about N'lahr's imprisonment and the hearthstones, and she'd be the only one to note the sorcerous augmentations to his arguments this day. He actually would have preferred to have brought an entire contingent of exalts, but the queen would never have permitted so many to be away from their work on the hearthstones, and he could never have excluded the Altenerai from the hunt. Though her loyalty was certain, he'd have to be careful to advance his own agenda without offending her faith in the queen.

Denaven stood and leaned with both palms against the table. "I'd hoped to never burden another soul with what I'm about to tell you, but Kyrkenall's rampage has forced me to reveal a terrible state secret." He paused for effect, met their eyes, and continued with grim resolve. "He has deliberately released a being more dangerous than anything we've ever fought. And we're going to have to stop them before they plunge the realms into chaos."

Tretton's eyebrows rose. "What 'being'?" he asked gravely.

The five before him waited, expectant, for his reply. "A monster of our own making." Experienced orator that he was, Denaven held the pause for a moment longer than strictly necessary. "Our queen was just as distressed as the rest of us when N'lahr died. Maybe more so. She gathered the greatest weavers she had available to her, had them commune with the hearthstones, and added their power to her own in an attempt to bring him back. They failed catastrophically."

Through his light connections he enhanced their credulity. Decrin let out a muffled oath. Tretton looked outraged at the blasphemy involved with meddling in sacred matters. Gyldara's eyes widened in dismay. Lasren was rapt in fascination. Ortala's brows rose and her eyes sought his, probably in concern about his fabricated story. He returned her gaze, willing her to hold her tongue.

"The duplicate thing she brought to life wasn't truly sane. I'm told it looked like N'lahr and even sounded like him, but amounted to nothing beyond mindless rage. It cut one of the weavers down before any of the others could react. As the others tried to contain the thing, it sliced their hearthstone in two, generating a bizarre magical backlash that encased it in a huge block of crystal. There was no way to ascertain if it was dead or alive. No one, not even Belahn," and Denaven paused to let that fact sink in, "could find a way to penetrate it. In the end, the queen decided to place the stone here, under guard and away from vulnerable populated areas while some of her best weavers researched the matter."

Decrin made no effort to conceal his oath this time. He blasphemed with great volume and fecundity.

Denaven knew very well that the queen had removed N'lahr from the capital for two reasons: there had been fear his imprisonment would be discovered, and fear that more unexpected things might happen around the unstable nidus of his weird cage spurred on by the immense magical energy concentrated by the accumulation of hearthstones in Darassus. Belahn had worried that the accident which created N'lahr's prison might grow unstable and destroy him if he'd managed to survive, just as Denaven had feared it might grow unstable and release him.

He wished Belahn had been right. How that misfortune had been timed to Kyrkenall's interference Denaven still couldn't imagine. They'd had teams of weavers working to open the crystal for months, until the queen had called them back to study hearthstones, claiming it a higher priority. Why couldn't it have happened then?

"Commander, are you saying N'lahr was imprisoned here?" Lasren asked.

"Not N'lahr." Hadn't he been clear about that? He'd best reinforce the narrative, so that they wouldn't hesitate to kill the "imposter" on sight. He sent a little pulse through his connective spellthreads, one meant to enforce the weight of his words. "N'lahr is dead. We interred his corpse. This is some kind of evil perversion walking around in his shape."

"The queen did this?" Tretton's voice was icy with disdain.

Denaven nodded gravely, as if he regretted having to do so. "Only with the best of intentions, Tretton." That should help mollify Ortala.

"I don't understand how Kyrkenall found out about any of this," Decrin said.

He was still being obstinate. Denaven turned up an empty hand. "With Kyrkenall everything comes down to pure dumb luck. I suspect Cargen revealed something of significance at N'lahr's tomb. Cargen had helped me arrange the transport and guardians up here. Maybe Kyrkenall, in his own twisted way, thought he could make up for the loss of Asrahn if he brought N'lahr back to the corps. But he has to realize, by now, what he's done. I don't know how Kyrkenall is managing to control the thing, but we need to track these twin murderers of frightening skill before more people are injured or killed—or worse, before others can mistake that beast for the real N'lahr and lose faith in the institutions that guide our lives."

"Right," Tretton said. And with his nod, tension eased, even if it didn't entirely vanish. "What do you need from us?"

"We're just about done in. We need rest if we're to keep this up."

Tretton nodded once more, although he looked more energetic than he had in days. And Denaven noticed that this time Decrin nodded as well.

"While you get settled," he continued, "I'm going to risk a hearthstone consultation. I want to see if I can gain more precise information about Kyrkenall's whereabouts so we don't waste any time in reaching them."

"What do you want us to tell the squires?" Decrin asked.

"Warn them about the false N'lahr. Don't bring the queen into it. She was acting to protect her people. And this well-intentioned error shouldn't stain their faith in her."

"Yes, sir."

That simple acknowledgment was another victory. Decrin had actually replied not as an equal, but a subordinate, something that would have been unthinkable even a few hours before. Denaven was likewise pleased that he was planting greater doubt in the queen's competence even as he claimed to be doing the opposite. That might serve him well in the near future.

He allowed no sign of his satisfaction to cross his face as he nodded, solemnly. "I'll catch up with you shortly. I'm not to be disturbed." He caught Ortala's questioning look and firmly met her eyes for a brief moment. She seemed to infer from that what he'd hoped. They'd talk soon.

Once the five of them filed out he sat down in one of the chairs, pulling the hearthstone from his satchel. He thought he had handled that well. At one time he'd been uncomfortable with such outright lies, seemingly banned by their oath, but was wise enough now to recognize when they were necessary to further greater truths. Leaders must conquer perils to clear a path.

And this situation presented ample opportunity with its peril. It had been impossible to access the sword while it was trapped with N'lahr. But now it was available . . . once he got rid of N'lahr. The weapon originally crafted for Denaven, rather than that untutored farmhand, would finally rest with its intended owner. And the next time Naor even stepped a foot over the border, Denaven would lead a raid deep into their lands and wield the sword as it was fated. Mazakan's head would be his, and the queen's throne would be that much closer. He'd make sure, discreetly of course, that her insane beliefs came to light. She would be relieved of power or even brought up on charges, and he'd be a hero well positioned to step into the vacuum.

He banished the smile that crept across his face in the emptied room. It was time to speak to the very woman he ultimately plotted against.

He lifted the hearthstone in its travel pack and set it on the table. He sighed a little as he untied the pack's cover, then sat forward in the hardwood chair and pulled it free. Let other mages manipulate from afar. He preferred tactile contact.

With his mind fully focused upon the tool, there was the usual rush of energy, which set him frowning even as a tingle of pleasure set his arm hairs rising under his uniform sleeves. He tried not to stare hard into its depths.

Denaven had never particularly liked hearthstones. Their power warped those who used them. Belahn was the most obvious mess, but the queen and nearly all the weavers who'd been studying the things were twisted in some way. He ignored the temptation to consider his surroundings in a magical haze of wonder and set straight to work.

The commander sent his senses south. Normally any such projection was risky, liable to reveal one's spirit to the hungry entities that lurked in the inner world and fed upon unprotected souls. But hearthstones shielded their users to some extent, especially when they were projecting their energies to other hearthstones, as he did now.

At first he sensed nothing at the other end of the connection, and he wondered if he might be so lucky as to find the queen occupied. How simple it would be to later tell her he'd tried to contact her and she hadn't been available.

Hope passed. He felt a flare of energy, and then he regarded her image fragmented and distorted within the hearthstone.

An ivory gown draped her slim frame, and a cascade of strawberry blond hair fell in curls to her shoulder. If not quite the beauty described by minstrels, she was striking. Years before, that winsome mouth had often shaped playful expressions and her eyes had glinted with amusement. The queen's smiles were rarer now, and her green eyes seemed to stare with disquieting intensity.

"The hour is late." Leonara's voice was clear but hard, like the tolling of a funeral bell.

"Forgive me, Majesty."

"There's much to forgive. You can report success? No. I see it in your eyes." She frowned. "Where is he now?"

"Across the border in The Fragments. And he's freed N'lahr."

The queen's head drew back. "Freed him? How?" Astonishment, and a hint of alarm, rang in her voice.

"I don't know how, but the giant warped crystal is gone, and Tretton found three sets of tracks leaving the area. That can only mean Kyrkenall, the squire, and N'lahr."

"What's their destination?"

"Presumably they're seeking Aradel or Belahn. Kyrkenall will still count both as friends. I'll contact Belahn and allies in Alantris. They can delay Kyrkenall until I arrive or, if possible, finish him and the others."

"You make it all sound very simple." Something in her voice let him know her calm was poised upon a knife's edge; he sensed danger without guessing its cause. "But then you always do, don't you? It's one of your gifts."

He bowed his head as if pleased by the compliment, but did not interject.

"Tell me how it goes with the Altenerai," she continued with patently false nonchalance. "Can you depend upon them to carry out your aims?"

"Yes. They're more focused than ever, despite setbacks." He was readying to explain when she cut him off.

"Are they really?" Menace rang in the undertones of that smooth voice. "Then perhaps you can explain why the two you left in Darassus broke into the hall this evening and stole a cache of hearthstones."

Denaven knew that his eyes widened in shock and he quickly deadened his expression. Why would Varama have betrayed him? She had nothing to gain from interfering with his plans, for she lacked interest of any kind in court machinations, not to mention an understanding of the subtleties of interpersonal interaction. And surely Rylin wouldn't be so resentful at being left behind that he'd throw away all the privilege and acclaim he'd worked for?

Leonara's voice grew waspish. "As that newer alten is a nonentity, this is all Varama. You assured me she was happy with her endless experiments."

He had thought she was. Her joy involved laboring for months or even years upon strange tasks that occasionally yielded brilliant discoveries. He'd long ago decided she was a mere craftsperson, albeit one worthy of respect, like a fine blacksmith or painter.

And then he remembered her strange comment about Kyrkenall's wine bottles, and her incisive question about the hearthstones. He cursed himself for dismissing both as typical Varama oddities. Something had interested her, and if interest had transformed into fascination there was no telling where her inquiries might lead.

"What, you've no easy remedy? No smooth reassurance?" the queen jibed; then she grew fierce: "She stole the keystone!"

Sheer willpower kept him from groaning. Naturally Varama would gather up Leonara's new obsession. The queen had been blathering on about that peculiar hearthstone, which she thought crucial for her "Great Awakening," since she'd first learned of its existence; she'd rarely slept since its long-heralded discovery.

"Have the exalts been sent after the two traitors?"

"*I'm* dealing with them." She spoke with such chill finality that he involuntarily shuddered. Once, just once, he'd seen the depths of her magical strength, and it had ever after shaken him to extreme caution.

Rather than imagine the hearthstone-enhanced horrors she'd be inflicting on his subordinates, he decided to redirect her anger to focus on his own aims. "Kyrkenall must have spoken to Varama when he was in Darassus. It's the only answer. She bided her time until I was gone and everyone else was distracted. She's clever, but her powers are barely a candle to your sun. She's probably planning to meet him in The Fragments, but you'll reach them long before then. And I'll get Kyrkenall. Everything will be simpler with them gone in any case."

Leonara's manner changed. While hardly warm, she at least was no longer openly confrontational. "It's true that Varama and the other one amount to nothing in the long run. Their destruction is inconsequential. But I'm thoroughly unhappy that you've let this happen to N'lahr."

"I let nothing happen, Majesty. It is Kyrkenall—"

She cut him off. "N'lahr was our greatest weapon against the Naor. I'd thought to attempt his revival if Mazakan broke the treaty before the Great Awakening. Now you've let Kyrkenall find him."

He thought she'd long since abandoned attempts to get at N'lahr. How could she possibly expect anything good for her to come from his release? "Majesty, N'lahr never supported your efforts with the hearthstones. He never truly supported you. He was a threat to your plans, at least indirectly, the moment he became commander, and he's a worse one now. He surely knows you ordered him silenced before the peace treaty, and he's had seven years to plan revenge." Denaven had no way of knowing whether N'lahr had been conscious during his imprisonment, but it took no great leap of imagination to be certain the former commander would resent losing seven years of his life. "I mean no offense, but you can't possibly expect he'd happily serve you again after so long."

He expected an immediate reaction. A frown, or a snarl, or further accusation that this had somehow been his fault. But she simply stared at him for a long moment. Blink, he thought, looking at those immobile green eyes, so fixed they might be stones. Blink and prove you're human.

She didn't.

"N'lahr was a shield for our people," the queen said at last. "And Kyrkenall a lance with which I could attack our enemies. Thanks to you, now both of them must be eliminated. It occurs to me that you always disliked them and their removal benefits you beyond all others."

"That's not entirely—"

"You hated Kyrkenall because he stole the woman you loved. You envied N'lahr his success. And his sword. I know how much you want it."

He couldn't refute her. He'd unwillingly shared those confidences when he'd shared her bed. Damn her insistence on linking.

"Now you finally can eliminate them both, and play with his blade to your heart's content."

She deliberately omitted his legitimate claim to the famed sword N'lahr carried. She was trying to bait him. "Majesty, if I'd wanted them dead I'd have devised a better plan than this, which risks my own position."

"I'm not an idiot, Denaven. You think I'm blind to your ultimate ambition?"

He'd thought religious contemplation had blinded her to most of his actions. Apparently he'd misjudged her. How much did she guess? How much did she know?

"I see the amount of time you spend with the councilors. I know you covet a seat among them. Or at their head."

He kept his expression neutral, though he felt like sighing in relief. He'd certainly spent an immense amount of time with the councilors, though it was because he wanted to establish rapport, not because he intended to join their ranks. There'd been no king in Darassus for generations, just an unbroken line of queens, and it might be Leonara was so tradition-bound she'd never imagine he could rise to her throne even when he pulled her down from it backed by the Mage Auxiliary. Leonara might think that the exalts were her answer to the problem of Altenerai independence from the throne, but they were really his bulwark should she ever decide to harness the full power of her mastered hearthstones—and he'd worked hard to win a large portion of their loyalty.

He shook his head in honest denial. "I don't want a seat with them. I'm only trying to see your will is done. For the good of the city, and the realms."

"Is that so?" She sounded skeptical. He feared that she was ready to make a new accusation.

He retreated while deploying his best tactic, one he used only sparingly lest she grow conscious of his manipulation. "I swear that I've no interest in the council. I've merely stepped in for you so you have more time to ready the Great Awakening. I know how close it is, and want nothing to distract you."

She'd been promising the Great Awakening for at least three years. Something always delayed it, and Denaven rather expected something always would.

Finally, she took the offered hook and swam on, at great speed. Her voice gained a distant, wistful air. "Of course, Denaven. And I'm grateful for that. Sometimes I forget how much you sacrifice for me."

"For you and your sacred duty, My Queen."

"Someday soon we will have no more need of warriors. Of any kind." She was ready to waft away now into rapturous musings. "When the Goddess arrives, glories will shower from the heavens."

He nodded, as though the queen sounded perfectly rational. "I await her coming expectantly."

"As do we all. It pains me to keep this most awesome truth from the people, but they're not equipped yet to understand." She had repeated this last rationalization often, as if to convince herself.

"No, Majesty."

"Very well, Denaven. You may go. I expect," she continued, a note of remonstrance in her voice once more, "that you will report success when next we speak."

He bowed his head. "Majesty, you can depend upon me."

She bowed her head in the briefest of acknowledgments. And then her image winked out.

He sat back and breathed a sigh of relief. That had been excruciatingly unpleasant. She hadn't shown such frightening clarity in years. It was almost as though somewhere inside she remained the bright young woman who'd become so indispensable to her predecessor decades earlier. Then, Leonara had been far less narrowly focused, and far more forgiving and fond of him—and perhaps a little kinder overall.

If she was capable of pulling out of her religious haze long enough to ask such searching questions, he might have to accelerate his plans.

He brought his hands together, cracked his knuckles, and set fingers once more to the hearthstone. There was time yet for one more sending. At least he knew Belahn would be awake. Belahn was always awake.

14

Perfect Match

The remote trackways she traveled with Kyrkenall and N'lahr as they crossed into The Fragments were little more than dirt paths skirting steep slopes, usually under a tunnel of tree canopy. Intermittent vistas opened on high waterfalls plunging hundreds of feet, conjuring thunder and spray that glistened on boulder moss and the petals of wildflowers blooming in a profusion of yellow and blue and purple. Rarely cliff sides showed a mix of brown and gray shales; most everywhere was covered in a great swathe of plant life on which plentiful wildlife subsisted. Horned elk and spotted deer, as well as rabbit and smaller creatures, were often visible, and Elenai wished they could stop to bring one down. She wearied of dried rations. But then she was bone weary of nearly everything. They'd been days on the road after the recovery of N'lahr, and if anything, they'd been pressing even harder than they had since they fled Darassus.

Kyrkenall was ebullient, keeping up a running patter of reminiscences and clever commentary on the state of affairs that N'lahr encouraged with an occasional dry question or observation. When Kyrkenall proved un-knowledgeable about current events in Darassus, N'lahr turned to her, and transformed their exhausting ride into a grueling endurance challenge as she feigned a ready alertness while answering incisive inquiries about political figures and training patterns she'd hardly considered before. She felt smaller and duller for the scrutiny. This wasn't how she'd imagined in-teracting with her hero.

They settled into a welcome silence, which somehow better matched the scenery as they passed through low mountains separating narrow river val-leys. The Fragments had suffered more than any other realm during the war, and ruins dotted many places. She saw a particularly large collection of them late morning on their third day of travel through the realm, doz-ens of overgrown foundations near a crumbling stone bridge over a weed-choked rivulet. She guessed the vast surrounding meadow had once served as pasture or farmland.

Kyrkenall slowed and put his hand to the haft of the recurved black bow holstered beside his saddle. N'lahr stopped beside him and both scanned the far riverbank near the bridge.

Elenai drew to a stop behind them. "What is it?" she asked softly.

The archer whispered an answer. "Kobalin. Up ahead, there."

Elenai searched the bushes to the left of the bridge. She saw and heard nothing of interest, apart from the burble of flowing water. She realized then that she should have been hearing birdcalls and frowned at herself for being distracted. How did those two stay functioning when they were so tired?

They were used to it, she reminded herself, and probably sensing things through their rings. If she still hoped to earn a ring, she had to get used to it herself. No matter that she hadn't had more than five hours of contigu-ous sleep in days.

"Hang back," N'lahr ordered, and with a click of his tongue urged his roan gelding ahead. Kyrkenall rode with him. A disappointed Elenai found herself left shepherding their small herd of spare mounts. The extra ani-mals had enabled them to keep moving far longer than they might have, by switching between horses as they tired. Kyrkenall was the exception, for Lyria's stamina was as pronounced as his own.

Elenai watched as the pair advanced carefully. Fragrant bushes and sedges were thick around the swift-flowing stream. A little gray sapling thrust up beside a tumbled-down guardrail on the far side of the bridge and had dislodged a handful of deck stones. She saw no kobalin until N'lahr and Kyrkenall drew near the bridge. When the strange thick figure stepped out from behind the bush beside it, she thought her eyes played tricks upon her.

She'd never seen a kobalin before. Some claimed that the creatures were the monstrous offspring of the betrayer, Sartain. Others that they were descended of outcasts and criminals, misshapen by the powerful strangeness of the deeps in the Shifting Lands where they'd taken refuge. At her father's playhouse they were depicted with the most frightening shapes and outlandish colors, so Elenai had always loved assisting in the design and application of those crowd-pleasing costumes.

But this one was so profoundly ugly no one would have enjoyed it on stage. It stood no taller than Kyrkenall, with legs thick as timber barrels and torso broad as a cart. It had no real neck, just a squat, lizard-like head and two muddy eyes, large around as her clenched fist. The thing grimaced toothily, then reached up with one scaly ochre hand to tap a black horn projecting above its left eyebrow.

Elenai drew her sword, just in case, as Kyrkenall and N'lahr came to a stop. Her mount, catching the pungent scent of the kobalin, shifted nervously beneath her, and the others tossed their heads against the lead lines. She tightened her off-hand grip and frowned, wondering if poor Aron would have held himself without fidgeting.

She could just make out N'lahr's casual words to his friend. "You can take this one."

"Can it be?" the creature asked in a pleasant if startling bass. It grasped the club slung at its dirty loincloth. "Do I see Altenerai? By the deepest dark. You're Kyrkenall the Eyeless, aren't you?"

"How observant you are," Kyrkenall said. "Did the bow give it away, or was it my devastating good looks?" The creature didn't answer, so Kyrkenall tried again. "What great intellect do I have the honor of addressing?"

"I am Vorn, son of Vorag, and I have taken the heads of many who dared to pass this way without bearing gifts." A rumbling grunt of self-satisfaction punctuated this pronouncement.

"I'm sure you have, mighty seer."

"Have you come to challenge me?"

"I'm just here to cross the bridge. I can't say as I'm keen about you lopping heads, but you've found me in a forgiving mood. Why don't you take all your heads and leave—live to share your wisdom with any of your kind who will listen."

"Hah!" The kobalin danced a maniacal jig on its tree-trunk legs. "I desire greater prizes, black one! I challenge you! Turn over your stones, or die!"

"I'm afraid I need my stones, Vorn," Kyrkenall commented dryly, then turned in his saddle to N'lahr. "I don't know if he's challenging me or flirting with me." The commander responded with something Elenai couldn't catch. Then Kyrkenall returned his attention to the kobalin. "Last chance, Vorn, son of Vorag. Stand aside, or die."

The creature hooted and brandished his club.

The little archer dropped lightly from his saddle, his slim curved blade in his hand.

N'lahr watched almost lazily, hands resting upon the saddle pommel. He hadn't even drawn his sword!

The kobalin showed sharp teeth in an enormous grin. "How could one so delicate be so deadly? I say that the tales about you are lies!"

She watched in fascination. Kobalin were strange and chaotic, but reputably governed by some immutable beliefs, one being that a personal battle against a worthy foe couldn't be waged before a ritual exchange of insults. According to legend, if a kobalin felt its challenger sufficiently clever, the challenger had right of first strike without defense.

She didn't have long to wonder how Kyrkenall would counter.

"Travelers will point at twins on the grass—I'll slice off your head to lay by your ass."

Against her own better sense, the crass couplet brought a laugh to her lips. She stifled it in her sleeve as both hands were full.

"That is your poetry?" the kobalin roared. "Where is the soaring verse I've heard tell about? I say that you're a fraud!"

Kyrkenall idly twirled his sword and circled to a clear spot without taking eyes from the kobalin. "Shall I compare thee to a stinking cloud? Thou art more rancid and irrelevant. You boast of ghastly feats with manner proud; greater fame is surely due your scent."

The kobalin bellowed resentfully, "I am a worthy foe! I will meet you bravely and add your head to my collection!"

"Worthy of shrouding and worthy of jests. Count those heads while you can for you'll soon have one less!"

"That doesn't even rhyme!" The kobalin bellowed indignantly. He charged at the same time as Kyrkenall.

The kobalin swung powerfully at his chest, but Kyrkenall's advance halted just shy of the strike. He lashed out with Lothrun as the club swung past, barely parting the scales of the creature's forearm. Red blood blossomed in a line.

The kobalin advanced surprisingly fast, as a second overhand strike shook the ground where Kyrkenall had been a heartbeat earlier. The archer drove the gleaming blade of Lothrun between Vorn's shoulder and head.

The wound spurted blood, and the monster gurgled, staggered, and swung his club wildly. Elenai saw Kyrkenall's face as he dodged back. He looked not so much wary as annoyed; he cut wide a final time and sent the huge head rolling one direction while the body fell the other.

He stepped well away to wipe his sword in the grass. The kobalin kicked as it died, but Kyrkenall didn't turn back as he strode over to his horse.

It was astonishing to see it over so quickly, even being aware of just how deadly the alten was. She put away her sword and rode up to N'lahr's side with her charges.

"Are there more kobalin?"

"No."

Kyrkenall offered further explanation. "They would have come out to watch, and would be offering me part of him for a trophy. Don't forget to use your ring."

When he'd stepped to his horse, Elenai assumed he meant to mount. Instead, he removed a wineskin and uncapped it. N'lahr slid down and the two men walked to the body.

"What are you doing?" she called after.

"Now we have to drink to him," Kyrkenall answered.

"To him?" Elenai asked.

The archer shot her a dark look. "His allies weren't here to honor him, so we must. Get down, and drink."

She obeyed, even if she didn't understand, reluctantly trusting the horses to remain nearby now that the threat had passed.

Kyrkenall raised the wineskin to the sun as Elenai joined them. "Here's to Vorn, son of Vorag. He had more bluster than sense. Yet he met me bravely in battle. Let none name him coward." He pulled a drink from the skin, then passed it to her. "Now," he said, "you bear witness."

"How do you mean?"

"Just say something that indicates you agree with what I've said. Go on."

"Um. Well." She stared down at the disgusting creature, who smelled even worse at close range, especially after being cut open. "I agree that he didn't seem especially bright. He wasn't good at listening, either."

"Echo the compliment," N'lahr instructed quietly.

"Oh." Why hadn't they told her that to start with? "I have to admit he

did seem brave. You'd have to be brave to challenge Kyrkenall the Eyeless." More likely idiotic, but she knew now she was supposed to be kind.

"Now drink."

She did, and found it a cloyingly sweet berry wine with no kick. She
passed it on to the commander.

"To the undisputable bravery of Vorn," N'lahr said, and downed a drink.
He passed it back to Kyrkenall. Either the stiffness in his left arm had finally cleared up, or the swordsman had grown better at concealing it, for
the movement appeared effortless. The archer capped the winesac, and the
three walked back to their horses.

Elenai felt strangely moved, though confused.

"Is that awful wine what you used to bring to my tomb?" N'lahr asked.

"Awful?" Kyrkenall climbed into his saddle.

"Next time bring something I like."

"You didn't complain so much when you were dead."

After a brief pause, N'lahr added, "He was right, you know. That last
bit didn't properly rhyme."

"Whose side are you on?" Kyrkenall asked with mock injury. He urged
his mare forward.

Elenai gathered the lead lines and followed them both. The wind
came up almost as soon as they crossed the bridge to climb into the hills
beyond. The clouds were piling up. A storm was probably a few hours
away. Elenai finally decided that she had to have an answer. "Why did you
honor the kobalin? He wasn't famous, was he?"

Both men glanced over their shoulders at her, and she wondered if they'd
forgotten she was there. "You should honor bravery," N'lahr said, "even
in a foe."

"But we didn't drink over the dead Altenerai."

Kyrkenall all but spat his answer. "They lied, cheated, ambushed, and
murdered. The kobalin announced his presence and offered challenge. I
honored him accordingly."

That still didn't quite explain away the ceremony. "When you drank to
the dead tower guards you weren't nearly as formal as you were about Vorn."

"The kobalin are a formal people," N'lahr said.

Formal? "I don't understand, Commander. The kobalin are mad, aren't
they? I mean, what sane being would lie in wait by a bridge and challenge
all comers?"

"They drive the crazy ones from their lands," N'lahr explained. "They
have tribes and traditions, and those who can't obey get kicked out. And
sometimes the best of them journey out to prove themselves against us, or

the Naor." He paused for a moment, then added: "They aren't so bad as you think. I made overtures to some of their tribes, once, to see if they wanted to join the fight against Mazakan."

"You were going to ally with kobalin?"

"Neither the kobalin nor the Naor are stage-play villains."

She thought she'd been stunned before. "The Naor are savages!" You could excuse the kobalin a little because they weren't fully human, and because they did have a strange but fixed sense of honor. The Naor were "human," but couldn't claim to hold even to the bizarre codes of the kobalin. They sawed hearts from their living foes and piled their heads in great heaps. They treated women as chattel, and some even cut the tongues from girls' heads so they could never speak. Even their words were warped, some tribes speaking with such profound distortion they might as well be talking gibberish.

"I hope you don't underestimate them," N'lahr said.

"No, sir. I hate them, but I don't underestimate them."

He gave her a long glance from under dark brows. "Be careful with hate. It's a potent blinder."

The conversation ended with a rattle of reins as N'lahr moved ahead. Elenai simmered at the rebuke but was afraid that she'd already said too much. She knew better than to underestimate an enemy. At least, she thought she did. She remembered something Decrin had once told the squires about N'lahr; that he'd rarely wasted words, implying those he did speak were valuable. She realized that this was the longest exchange they'd had where he wasn't questioning her knowledge of current events in Darassus.

She fell quiet at the rear as they wound into the hills, turning over everything they'd said, under a downpour that didn't seem to incline her two Altenerai toward slowing. The wet march through indistinct ups and downs magnified her sense of disorientation. Comrades and heroes were enemies, and enemies deserved honor, and the queen was ignoring the laws. . . .

Madness made real.

As the day wore on, the sun returned and the hills flattened somewhat into drier grassland ringed by distant peaks. They spotted a handful of isolated homesteads built upon the slopes. A few sent streams of smoke into the sky, and she thought of cook fires and cozy hearths and wondered why she had so craved a military life. She had plenty of time to note every sore, stiff, chaffing, damp, hungry ache as she watched the presumably simple comforts slide by.

As the afternoon aged into maturity, they neared a large ruined settlement spread along the base of a valley. Crops grew wildly in the abandoned fields among weedy trees and wild plants. Here and there were burned-out support timbers and collapsed piles of masonry. What must have been streets were little more than animal trails.

Kyrkenall rode straight down the center of the path, his black eyes studying all that they passed with great care. Elenai had seen the Naor in action and steeled herself for signs of their passage. When she saw no skull mound it occurred to her that the Altenerai would have made certain all remains were buried or burned. Broken weapons, too, were absent.

All in all, it seemed an idyllic place, complete with fertile and well-watered soil. "Why didn't anyone come back here?" she asked.

"It'll be years before there are enough people to reclaim all the ruined land," Kyrkenall answered. "And even then a massacre like this leaves a stain that doesn't fade for generations. You can feel it, can't you?"

Elenai blanched. At the end of primary education, when she'd been ten, a young instructor had taken those believed of magical talent to a battle site. To prove themselves. A more experienced instructor would have known better.

Some traditions taught that spectral remnants were merely a kind of traumatic energy echo inscribed into the soil or that actual souls were trapped where they'd died terrible deaths. Whatever remained, Elenai had seen a half dozen of them staggering through the ruins of an Arappan village razed by the Naor. She had never forgotten the sight of the little girl with the missing face. It had been small recompense when the instructor realized his mistake and ushered them away with apologies and promises of sweets; he left his post soon after.

She had no intention of looking 'round the inner world now. She had enough nightmares. "I think I do feel it," she told Kyrkenall, which wasn't really a lie, because she could well imagine what she'd see if she stretched her senses any further.

They reached the end of the ruins, and the old road devolved once more into a track through wilds that had once been farmed. Here and there she saw clumps of good wheat growing amid the regular grasses, rippled now by fingers of the wind.

They rode on and up, and Kyrkenall broke his silence to tell her they were only two valleys away from the settlement where Belahn lived. Elenai could hardly wait to get out of the saddle.

As they crossed over the broad crest of a scrub-covered hill they caught sight of a trio of riders downslope from the green-brown heights of the valley's far side. The one in vanguard pointed their direction even as a column of troops climbed into view behind him.

Elenai felt her lips curling in disgust as her heart rate sped. Naor. Each wore a leather-topped helm with a nasal bar, and a heavy overshirt of banded leather. Their clothing otherwise was of different shades of blue or brown or beige, and their skin was pale and ruddy beneath shaggy beards. They bore no banners, and from this distance she couldn't see enough detail to determine whether these were one of the three clans responsible for the devastation in her own region of Arappa. It scarcely mattered; all Naor were equally bad, except those few who were a little worse. She could make out the straight tips of bows standing over their shoulders. The Naor never took the time or developed the skill to craft recurved bows.

"A whole lot of Naor," Kyrkenall announced resentfully. "A humping regiment of Naor, raiding into The Fragments. Shit. This is just what we needed."

"Do you think they've attacked Belahn's village?" Elenai asked.

"Wyndyss is still to our north. But it looks like that's where they're headed. Damn 'em to the deepest shifts!"

The commander's narrow face had grown grim. His voice was distant, nearly emotionless. "It looks like an exploratory column. They're traveling light for this far in. Only a few extra mounts. No supply wagons."

"You mean they're riding ahead for an even larger group?" Elenai asked.

"Most likely," Kyrkenall answered.

As they sat watching, one of the Naor scouts turned his horse and galloped back toward the main body of the column. Elenai felt certain he was reporting his glimpse of the Altenerai.

"What are we going to do?" Elenai asked.

N'lahr answered. "Delay them. Warn Belahn. Ready a defense."

Kyrkenall was already pulling his bow from his saddle holster. Like all horn bows, remaining strung for long periods did little harm to the weapon.

"Aren't you out of range?" Elenai asked.

"Aye, typical range for a hornbow is about five hundred yards. But Arzhun's no normal bow." He added, "Even still, this is a trick." He signaled his mount to "firm" and the dun stiffened her legs, becoming rock still. Kyrkenall rose in his stirrups, put arrow to string, breathed in and out three times, then said quietly: "'So soon it seems that they forget to ward themselves from all I know. Thus lightning falls.'"

He quoted Selana again, from her third play, *The Fall of Myralon*.

One of the distant mounted scouts stirred nervously.

"That one, I think." Kyrkenall moved, swaying gently, almost as though he had become one with the wind, then let fly.

The arrow arched out over the wide valley, high into the air. She watched in confusion. Even if Arzhun were the finest bow ever made, how could it send an arrow a distance four or more times greater than any other?

The arrow drifted wildly in the wind, yards off course, seeming to hang suspended in the sky. And then it dropped like a hawk in dive, honing in with astonishing accuracy. The scout stiffened in pain as an arrow sprouted in his leg. His horse bucked.

Elenai gaped. It had been an amazing shot, even for the greatest archer in all the realms.

Kyrkenall stood in his stirrups and shook the black bow as his ululating war whoop rang across the valley. Every one of the dozens of Naor coming up over the hill turned to look at him.

N'lahr let out a single bark of laughter and lifted his sword so that the sun shone upon it.

Elenai grinned as they retreated around a bend in the hill. "That was incredible! I can't believe you made that shot!"

"I was aiming for his head," Kyrkenall said, "but I'm glad you approve."

"Why did you do that, though? Did you want them to chase us?"

"Apart from shooting a Naor riding through our lands—which is seldom a bad idea—I let it be known I was the one doing the shooting. Now they'll be nervous to follow, because they might expect me to lie in wait and pepper anyone who comes after."

"And they might think us scouts for a larger force," N'lahr explained. "Another reason for them to delay, which will buy us time."

"*Are* we going to lie in wait and shoot them?"

Kyrkenall answered. "No, we're going to ride like the wind to Wyndyss."

N'lahr simply clicked his tongue and urged his horse into a faster pace.

They rode at a strong clip, trailed still by the spare mounts. Keen-eyed Kyrkenall brought up the rear, watching for pursuit.

N'lahr warned her to "mind the drops." In a short while Elenai knew what those enigmatic words meant. He led them into high, rocky terrain, a place where the Gods had tired of making gentle, rounded things. Far, far below lay delicate little canyons with their sparkling streams between steep outcroppings.

Neither N'lahr nor his unfamiliar mount seemed perturbed by the astonishing sheer drops that lay on the left hand, though they had to slow. Elenai had never really thought herself worried about heights, but then she'd never been quite so high before. The world below seemed a faerie land populated by miniature versions of the plants and creatures she knew.

Her new horse proved heartier than she. Like the others they'd taken from the Chasm Tower, he was a Penarda, that Kaneshi breed famed for speed, stamina, and intelligence, and he was as equable as the animals in the Altenerai stables, if not as calm before enemies. He probably hadn't been trained by Sharn, the Altenerai stable master. The chestnut moved confidently, finding sure footing no matter the narrowness of the trail. A couple of the spare mounts proved troublesome, however, balking and slowing their progress. At N'lahr's advice, she cut them free, to neigh and stamp in protest while the steadier horses moved on. Though scared to proceed, they seemed more frightened to be left and eventually followed, catching up when the trail widened.

By evening they were once more in a long lower valley, and N'lahr informed her they were nearing Wyndyss. Kyrkenall caught up, his mouth twisted in consternation.

"How many are following?"

"Oh, we're clear of the Naor. We lost them a long while back."

"Altenerai," N'lahr said flatly.

"You were supposed to let me say it."

Elenai felt her heart spurring to gallop. So at long last the Altenerai had found their trail. Or, more like, finally caught up to the trail they'd long pursued.

"When the Naor noted six in blue hot after our own line," Kyrkenall continued, "they veered off. I suppose some of our pursuers might be exalts. They've got squires, too. And a whole lot of spare horses."

"How far back?" N'lahr asked.

"Only a few hours. There's no point in trying to lose them. I'm sure the lead was Tretton."

N'lahr frowned as he shifted in his saddle.

"But we'll get to Wyndyss before them, right?" Elenai asked. "And we can get fresh horses there, and turn off this hearthstone."

"Sure," Kyrkenall said.

She wished his tone were more reassuring. "Do you think Belahn's going to believe us?"

"Kind of hard not to be convincing when we've got someone returned from the dead," Kyrkenall pointed out.

"But what will he think if the rest of the Altenerai come riding up right after we meet him? Will he listen to us quickly? Is he . . . reasonable?"

"In some ways, he's the most well-balanced of us," N'lahr said, with an intriguing hint of sentiment. "He has a wife, children, grandchildren. He's had a distinguished career in the corps, but it's not his whole life. Nevertheless, I suggest we hurry so we have time with him before the others." He touched heels to his horse's flanks and galloped deeper into the valley.

He slowed as the ground rose into rocky prominence to right and left, creating a narrow defile just beyond a well-built tower of black basalt.

"What's wrong?" Elenai asked, breathing hard. Her damp horse was puffing beneath her.

"This pass to Wyndyss used to be wider."

Elenai cast around for an explanation, given there were no visible signs of a catastrophe. "Could Belahn have altered it, with magic?"

"Looks like," Kyrkenall offered with a serious expression as he reined up next to her. The commander guided his horse straight for the tower.

Elenai eyed its blank windows in concern. There was no movement save the low wind shaking trees on the surrounding mountainsides. An owl hooted, whistling down the twilight as if to emphasize the desolation.

N'lahr dismounted before the tower and tested the weathered oaken door. It yielded to his hand. With a glance back in their direction, he headed in. Elenai listened to his footsteps scuffing the stairs, and after a time she saw him walk out onto the crenelated height three stories above. He stood there for a time before retreating.

When at last he emerged, he climbed immediately into the saddle. "Empty," he said. "Looks like it's been abandoned for months."

"Do you think the Naor have already been here?"

"No skull mounds," was the succinct answer.

Kyrkenall followed N'lahr into the defile, and she went after.

It proved scarcely wide enough for two wagons to roll side by side, and darker than N'lahr's tomb. The bowman kept shifting his gaze between the height, some thirty feet overhead, and the lighter opening. Elenai was acutely aware of their vulnerability. There was no way to see, or counter, any attack that might drop on them from above, and she felt her tension ease only when they emerged safely into the dying light of a valley beyond.

Once there she gasped in wonder.

The wide, verdant basin before them was a paradise. To their north, twin waterfalls cascaded from the mountain heights, sending spray flying. The water was diverted into streams that flowed through terraced rice paddies stacked on the steep hillsides. Reflecting pools and shade trees were sprinkled regularly among them.

A little river gathered from the irrigation effluence and flowed past the valley entrance before winding east along a well-tended orchard with trees carefully trimmed to resemble one another. The wildflower-bordered road before them crossed the river via an arched stone bridge and led through pasture and grain fields to a small walled village tucked along the sheer cliffside at the valley rear. Gabled slate roofs caught the last slanting rays above well-tended wattle and daub houses, some three stories high.

"It's beautiful," Elenai breathed.

"Yes," N'lahr agreed. But he didn't sound very happy, and he explained why a moment later. "There should be signs of life."

He was right, and she'd missed it in the charming view. The village was completely dark, and at dusk there should have been lights in a number of the cottages, and certainly smoke from the cookfires. Perhaps lanterns along the battlements or farm animals moving in the fields. She saw nothing.

Kyrkenall whistled. "This is just weird. If there are gods, they love screwing with us. Why couldn't we just have found some friendly faces, some fresh food, and some warm beds? Instead we get this."

"Boring would be nice sometimes," N'lahr agreed. "Wait here a moment." He dismounted.

"What are you doing?" Kyrkenall asked.

N'lahr paused only briefly. "Buying us time." He jogged for the cliff to the right side of the defile, then started up a narrow stair notched into the rock, almost impossible to see in the fading light. He hurried to a height of at least a hundred feet, then vanished into a dark tunnel.

"What's going on?" Elenai asked.

"No idea." Kyrkenall looked as if he were about to say something, but hesitated before speaking uncertainly. "He squired with Belahn and once mentioned helping him improve the defenses at Wyndyss. Maybe he's got something . . ." Kyrkenall's voice trailed off as a great rumble of rock and earth came from within the defile. It shook the ground beneath them. Their horses shifted nervously, pricking their ears and whinnying alarm.

Kyrkenall tensed and stared into the darkness.

"What's happening?" Elenai asked. "Is it an attack?"

"Avalanche," Kyrkenall answered, then said nothing more, all of his attention focused toward the defile.

Studying it carefully herself, Elenai made out a plume of dust, almost invisible against the dark sky and the cliff below it.

Beside her, Kyrkenall slowly relaxed. After another moment she saw why. His friend was descending the staircase unharmed. Kyrkenall called to him once he reached the ground.

"What was that?"

"A protection Belahn devised if the valley was threatened with invasion."

"And just anyone can walk up and set it off?"

"Normally it's under guard. And it takes either a team of warriors, or someone with a ring." He raised his hand, showing his sapphire.

"So did you block the whole pass?"

"Most likely. It's hard to tell, and it's never been tested."

Kyrkenall nodded. "Nice. It will take them a while to clear that out, even with a hearthstone. But that means we're locked in, doesn't it?"

N'lahr shook his head. "There's a back way out. Come on. You worry too much."

"*I* worry too much?"

N'lahr didn't answer as he climbed into his saddle, shook his reins, and started down from the pass toward the bridge.

After she fell in with him, Elenai spotted something that stopped her cold. "Commander!" She rode up to his side and pointed ahead. "That straight post there—that's like those around the Chasm Tower."

"Shit," Kyrkenall said. "Let me find the sigil." Kyrkenall reached behind to dig through his saddlebag.

The object standing a hundred paces before the bridge was the same height and width as the obelisks that had trapped the creature she and Kyrkenall had killed, and it was topped by the same sort of pyramid. They'd shown those fence posts to N'lahr as they left, which was probably why he drew Irion now.

"Are we inside or outside the enclosure?" N'lahr asked.

"I can't tell," Elenai said, "but I'll check through the inner world."

"Quickly."

Funny now how easy it was to switch between her ordinary sight and magical. The fence posts here glowed with similar energy but were spaced a bit closer than those near the Chasm Tower, centered in a wide space around the bridge. And she found the guardian creature almost immediately, or rather, its long, scaly, emaciated body. It lay a few paces to the right of the road under a large flowering bush, its magic collar wrapped about its neck. Elenai wanted to be certain of her answer, so she peered carefully all along the fenced area. "We're inside, but the guardian beast is dead," she said at last.

"How did we get so lucky?" Kyrkenall asked.

"It's very thin. It may have starved to death." Elenai indicated the direction where the remains lay.

The commander urged his mount toward it. "Are there others?"

"I don't sense any."

While Kyrkenall kept watch with his arrow nocked, N'lahr examined the desiccated beast without dismounting or relaxing his guard. Then he wordlessly returned to the road and started forward. Elenai followed, her senses stretched taut. She used the power of her borrowed ring to search, fearing that she had missed something and that some other monster might wait to pounce upon them. The loose spare mounts that paused to crop green stuff beside the road would make tempting targets for a hungry beast.

Kyrkenall brought up the rear, bow still at the ready.

But nothing appeared as N'lahr urged his horse onto the bridge deck. The arching structure was wide, well-made, and fashioned with lovely artistic touches. Even in the fading light Elenai saw that the stone sides were arranged in hexagonal patterns and that the wooden decking planks were inlaid with images of swirling leaves and nuts. Hollow hoofbeats rang out at their crossing and set her last nerve on edge.

She began to breathe properly again when they passed the second row of posts. "It's the same kind of fence and a similar beast that they used to protect the Chasm Tower. Do you think they imprisoned Belahn as well?"

N'lahr's voice had a flinty edge. "No. Keep alert."

She glanced back at Kyrkenall to see if he had any more to offer, but he was silent.

As they advanced along the well-packed dirt road, N'lahr stared intently toward the line of pear trees in the orchard. "Elenai," he said finally, "can you look again through the inner world without tiring?"

Fatigue clawed at her but was kept at bay by the hammering of her heart. "What am I looking for?"

"The trees." He held up a hand and halted, considering the distance carefully in each direction before nodding his permission to begin.

The archer must have noticed just then whatever was the problem, because she heard him curse softly, almost in wonder.

Elenai didn't see anything amiss. Around her was the steady bleat of courting frogs and the chirrup of crickets. Was there something lurking *within* the trees?

Despite her fatigue, she easily slipped into magical sight. She tore her eyes away from the glow of the hearthstones in her pack and looked beyond the simple bright structures against the darkness that was the crops.

There were no large life-forms among them. "There's nothing hiding there," she reported, a little breathless from the effort.

"They're all the same," Kyrkenall murmured. "Every single one of them."

With a start she saw he was right. Each pear tree was identical. It wasn't that they resembled one another, or that they were pruned into similar designs. Each had one thick straight trunk and four main branches rising at the same angle, and each had the same configuration of smaller branches bearing fruit

"Gods," she whispered. "Yes, they're identical." How had she missed that? "Shaped with hearthstone magics?"

N'lahr answered her. "Almost surely. Drop back. Save your energy." He sheathed his sword but didn't look any less wary.

Elenai was about to do as he commanded until she noticed something else. After the ranks of trees, from slope to road, the valley was a grain field. And every single stalk was precisely the same height. "The same thing's been done to the grains." She dropped her inner sight. Without the hearthstone, her brief magical exercises had left her short of breath, but she spoke on. "You find the perfect plant, and then you duplicate it, right? The tree that bears the most fruit, or the barley that grows the tallest."

"Likely," N'lahr agreed.

"Belahn's been practicing." Kyrkenall whistled appreciatively.

"When's the last time you visited him?" she asked.

"Years. No mage could do this kind of stuff, last I knew. Maybe Rialla."

She wondered if the same kind of duplication might be worked with animals. Surely not. That would be even more complicated, wouldn't it? And where were all the livestock, anyway? "We should be seeing animals by now, shouldn't we?"

N'lahr's answer was short. "Animals, and people."

Dusk was giving way to night. The horses and pair of men with her became dull shapes in the gloom.

A little way on, the ground grew flat and level. The fields ceased, and the grass was but ankle high up to the steep slope of the defensive wall, two good bowshots on. She suddenly realized they were on "killing ground," a clear area before a defensive line with no land features for attackers to hide behind. Elenai eyed the battlements as they advanced, searching for helmed heads or the points of arrows. None appeared, not even when they rode into the narrow corridor that pushed into the city and led to its gates. She continued to look for signs of warriors along the merlon-topped walls on either side, her neck tingling with the sense an arrow might wing toward her at any moment.

But there were no defenders. Past the open city gates and the village square just beyond it, neat, ordered rows of cottages with window boxes and fine carvings along the timber supports stretched before them. These, at least, didn't appear to be completely identical, for she saw some were wider or taller than their neighbors.

But the streets were silent, empty, and dark.

N'lahr dismounted at the first cottage and rapped loudly on the wooden door while Kyrkenall scanned the empty streets. When there was no answer, the commander opened it, hand on his hilt. Elenai waited to one side, sword out, ready to reach through the inner world and touch the power of the hearthstones in her shoulder pack.

N'lahr motioned her to wait and stepped inside. A short while later there was a glow from within that could only have come from a lantern. After several tense moments, he called to them. "Come see this." There was an odd note to the man's voice. "Bring the hearthstones."

Just beyond the door was a small dining room little different from thousands across the realms. To the left was a stone fireplace, soot stained but tidy. Beside rested a carefully ordered pyramid of firewood. On her right was a square table, and four people sat there: a man, a woman, and two young girls. N'lahr shone the lantern light directly upon them, and Elenai advanced, her breath in her throat.

The family didn't move.

Each was frozen in mid-motion: the young father with hand raised, head turning toward the door; the fair-skinned woman's plain face wide with surprise; the younger, smaller girl pointing at the other, her teeth showing in laughter.

"What's wrong with them?" Kyrkenall asked.

"Touch one," N'lahr suggested grimly. He set the lantern upon the table. Elenai tried to do as he suggested. Her hand met resistance a finger's width from the shoulder where the woman's dark hair touched the edge of her green collar.

She peered across the table to the man. His eyes were bright, and a smile touched his mouth, as if he'd just heard something funny. Despite the lack of movement, the skin of the townsfolk held a healthy glow. In repugnant contrast, their plates contained a pile of crusty mush in which small worms writhed.

"They've been put under a spell," N'lahr said. "Elenai, can you free them?"

She needed no urging, and reached out with her will to touch the stone in her pack. Now, wielding the energy of the artifact was as simple as slipping on a glove.

What she discovered was that someone had woven a protective barrier about the people, rooting a golden net through every single portion of their bodies. Their life force glowed, dully, but it didn't pulse. It had been arrested.

"I'm not sure, Commander. It's as if they've each been impaled by magical energies in a thousand places. No, ten thousand places."

"You'll not be interfering." The deep voice came from behind her, and even as she reached out with the hearthstone to explore the surge of energy rolling toward her, her hearthstone shrank in upon itself. She felt as though she were trapped in a collapsing tunnel, and struggled in the darkness to scramble free. The hearthstone had been forcefully closed!

She just managed to pull into the real world, turned, then found herself willed into place, her body unresponsive to her own commands. Her vision was tinged by blue from the quartet of sapphires glowing on four hands: her own, N'lahr's, Kyrkenall's, and that upon the ring of a gaunt, tall figure in the doorway. He resembled no Altenerai she'd ever heard about. His old brown robe draped him like a sack, as though borrowed from a much larger man. His dark eyes were hazy, his hair unkempt, his long gray-tinged beard a tangle. As he sidled toward the fireplace corner, his left arm tightened around a silvery-blue hearthstone that glowed and winked in hypnotically shifting patterns.

Kyrkenall stood still on the other side of the table, Arzhun gripped in his right hand, arrow to string, though he hadn't pulled it back. The light from the sapphires was mirrored in his ebon eyes. Was he, too, frozen?

With Irion unsheathed and leveled toward the intruder, N'lahr stood motionless beside the table. Elenai thought he, too, might be under a spell until she saw his hand tighten upon the grip of the blade. Did the sword protect him from the magic, the way Kyrkenall's bow had protected her from hearthstone sorcery? It must. Irion, from what she understood, was more powerful than Kyrkenall's weapons. Unlike the sapphires set into their rings, though, the stone in Irion wasn't glowing. It didn't seem to have been crafted with any sorcery.

"I won't allow you to interfere," the man repeated simply. "And you, woman, reach your power toward my stone and I will destroy you in an instant. Do not doubt it."

"Take no action, Elenai," N'lahr ordered quickly.

She had no way of moving, but until that command she'd thought she might fight the stranger for control of his hearthstone.

"Belahn," N'lahr said with a fair semblance of calm, "if you hurt her, you'll have to answer to me."

This was Belahn? He looked nothing like the paintings and tapestries Elenai had seen. Belahn was a bear of a man, and this fellow was little more than a bent scarecrow.

"I don't plan to hurt anyone," Belahn said.

"You've a strange way of showing it," Kyrkenall complained. He apparently wasn't as much hindered as she. Elenai was fairly sure she couldn't speak. Perhaps he was keeping still so as not to excite the mage.

"If you don't want to hurt anyone," N'lahr said, "why are you attacking?"

"Denaven warned me you were coming." Belahn's voice was resonant, expressive—much larger than his presence. "To seek vengeance."

"We came for your help. But I see you helped Denaven erect the fence that hid me. Probably you helped him trap the monster that guarded the tower where I was held."

Kyrkenall cursed softly. Apparently that was as much a surprise to him as it was to Elenai, who was disappointed she hadn't deduced it.

"That fence was just a safeguard," Belahn admitted. "Until they could find a way to free you. I want you to know that I didn't try to keep you in that stone. I just cleaned up the spell after the accident, and I wasn't even sure you were still alive. I'd have gotten you out if I could."

Elenai tapped into the inner world without looking fully away from the outer. She saw that the energies of the stone and the energies of the man were so tightly interwoven there was no distinguishing between them. Careful as she was to keep her own threads from the mage, Belahn's eyes narrowed and his voice took on a keen edge. "I warned you once, woman. This stone and I are practically one. I'm not wanting to hurt you, but I will if you interfere in any way."

"So Denaven told you to expect us?" N'lahr's voice was calm, careful. He seemed to be trying to keep Belahn's attention on himself. "Is he here?"

A sad smile crossed Belahn's lips. "No. Don't play the fool."

"I'm just trying to get caught up," N'lahr said. "You're saying that the rest of you figured out how to talk through the stones like Rialla used to do?"

Belahn's brow knitted irritably. "All initiates can communicate from afar, once fully attuned to the sacred stones of the Goddess."

"Initiates?" N'lahr repeated.

"You're stalling. Waiting for me to make a mistake. I'm not going to do that. Now, put down your weapons."

Kyrkenall snorted.

N'lahr shook his head, never shifting his eyes from Belahn or dropping the angle of his sword. Elenai marveled over how steady his hand was.

"There's no need to resist. All three of you will be fine if you do as I say."

She wondered if "fine" meant being rendered fully immobile and silent like these people in the cottage. She wished she could think of something effective she could do without fighting him for the hearthstone.

"Belahn," N'lahr said. "I don't know what you've been told. The hearth-stone 'accident' that imprisoned me occurred solely because Denaven attacked me with it. He's the reason I was in the stone. He wanted me gone. And he must have lied to get you to help him."

"How did you get out?" Belahn asked. "I tried everything."

"Elenai managed it," Kyrkenall said with a hint of derision.

The spell caster's troubled eyes searched her own before they shifted to the archer. "I can trust nothing from you, Kyrkenall."

"You think I set him free?"

"No. But I know you killed Asrahn."

Kyrkenall's answer was explosive. "The fuck I did!"

"How can you believe that, Belahn?" N'lahr broke in. "You know that Asrahn was the closest thing Kyrkenall ever had to a father."

Elenai's eyes strayed to the archer, whose mouth tightened a bit.

N'lahr continued when Belahn made no comment. "Denaven's obviously misled you. Kyrkenall didn't kill Asrahn—renegade Altenerai and Mage Auxiliary officers did. And they sought to kill Kyrkenall and Elenai, who suspected. She stands as witness. Question her."

Belahn merely frowned.

N'lahr persisted. "Were you told I was heading here for revenge? Does that sound right to you?"

"I was informed your years of confinement had driven you mad."

"Do I seem insane? Denaven trapped me for seven years, Belahn. Seven years of my life were stolen. I'm angry, but I haven't lost my mind."

Belahn's expression was pained. "I didn't know it would take so long." He looked weaker, deflated, and confused.

"Look at us Belahn. Do you honestly think we've abandoned the code? That oath has been our life. You know that. You were one of the three who named me to the ring, remember?"

"Yes, but—"

"Do you remember what you said?"

"Of course I remember! I was first witness."

"And how did you begin?"

Belahn swallowed. For a moment Elenai thought he'd stay silent, but he spoke, finally, his voice more formal. She immediately recognized the start to the pledge of the first witness. By ancient decree, a veteran had to declare a squire fit for the ring. "I know his character. I have seen his deeds . . ." Suddenly Belahn faltered, seemed to grow frustrated. "It's all just the same thing I'd say at any ring ceremony."

As if those time-honored words rendered a ring ceremony ordinary. Even in Belahn's irritation there was something in his manner that belied the insinuation.

"But you believed the words, didn't you?" N'lahr asked. "You'd not have nominated me if you hadn't. I heeded your counsel before and after that day. And that's what I came for. Not to hurt your valley. Wyndyss is a treasure, and I know why the land and people are so important to you. They became important to me, too."

Belahn said nothing to this. Nor did he move, but that lack of motion betrayed something Elenai couldn't quite determine. Doubt? Wariness? Dismay?

"Where's Melysynde?" N'lahr asked. "Have you 'protected' her, like these people?"

The shaggy weaver's bearded mouth opened and closed, but no sound emerged for a long moment. "She died. I wasn't paying enough attention."

N'lahr's tone softened. "I'm sorry, Belahn. Truly."

Kyrkenall exhaled slowly.

Elenai supposed that Melysynde was the name of Belahn's wife.

"I resolved then and there I wouldn't let that happen to anyone else," Belahn declared with conviction. "No one else on my watch is going to die. I learned a few things from your situation. But I improved it." Belahn's voice trembled, almost pleading. "Everything in Wyndyss is precious. Every flower. Every tree. Every person. But it was all decaying. People got injured. Some of them died, no matter my efforts. Never again! I've almost finished preserving the valley. Everyone here must remain safe until the Goddess comes, so they'll all be able to share in her glories."

"The Goddess?" N'lahr prompted.

Even in his disheveled state, the mage managed a semblance of respectability as he straightened a little. "The true Goddess will return soon. Not her four false servants, but the real Goddess. And when she comes, she'll reward her faithful."

"That's a new bit," Kyrkenall declared. "You think someone might have mentioned her before."

Belahn's voice took on a fervent tone. "The pretenders betrayed her and turned away from her vision. And she left the world of men. But when the altar is ready, she will return, and lead us all to unending peace and bliss."

"What sort of altar?" N'lahr asked.

"The hearthstones, of course," he continued. "They're broken remnants, so imagine when assembled . . . But then you probably can't know what they're like." His regard shifted to Elenai. "You've felt a hearthstone.

Imagine all that love, that warmth, surrounding everyone always. The Goddess will watch over and guide and protect all."

There was that word "protect" again. Did he imagine that the Goddess would do as he had done? Was he blind to the horror of his actions?

"How do you know that's what she'll do?" N'lahr asked, drawing Belahn's attention back to himself. Elenai wasn't certain what spells Belahn could bring to bear or how they could be countered, but N'lahr was clearly trying to prevent bloodshed. And it was fascinating to watch the famous general work to avoid battle.

"The queen showed me her vision. And I was all but weeping with joy at the sight of the Goddess and the touch of her benevolence. If only Queen Leonara could share this revelation with all her people, the whole nation would toil to achieve her dream."

"So the queen's acting to bring back an all-powerful goddess without telling people."

"Yes. All will be revealed in time, and then everyone will rejoice."

"You know this sounds crazy, right?" Kyrkenall asked.

Belahn frowned.

N'lahr ignored Kyrkenall's interruption and proceeded with his somehow-compelling inquiries. "Did you tell your people in Wyndyss what you'd do to protect them?"

"None of them yet know about the Goddess, or her coming. I had to act before any more could die."

N'lahr pressed in a philosophical tone. "Belahn, you've taught dozens how to use magic—not just effectively, but rightly. Isn't the first rule that you must never perform magic without permission on any but enemies?"

The older man's eyes narrowed, as if he'd caught onto a trick. "I must protect those who cannot protect themselves. I have to do what's best for them."

"The guardian monster in its barrier outside is dead," N'lahr said. "Were you aware of that?"

Belahn's expression soured. "I should have guessed you'd remain shrewd regardless of how far you fell, but that lie reveals you, N'lahr. I conjured food for the guardian only two days ago."

"It's been dead at least a week," N'lahr insisted. "And its been starving for far longer. Check."

Belahn stared at him, suddenly uncertain. He extended searching threads of magic, and his eyes widened in shock for a moment before casting about as if lost. He sounded a little frantic and spoke as if to himself. "Well, I've almost got the gap closed. I suppose it's not needed anymore."

"It needed sustenance. Just like you." N'lahr's arm still hadn't wavered. "You're dropping important details because you're carrying too many, aren't you? Have you looked in a mirror? You're wasting away, just like it did. When's the last time you ate—or bathed, for that matter?"

"That's all irrelevant."

"It doesn't smell irrelevant," Kyrkenall remarked softly.

"Your physical reality is hardly irrelevant. How can you protect your charges when your health is failing?"

"I'm fine." His voice betrayed further uncertainty, as if even he were aware he deceived himself.

"You need help," N'lahr said. "You've spent too much time in the company of that thing." He nodded at the hearthstone shining in his comrade's hand.

Belahn's grip on the glowing object tightened, as if he could embrace it even more closely. "Denaven warned me you'd be clever about trying to take it away."

"I don't want to take it away. I won't touch it. I came here for your help, but I think we can help each other."

Belahn hesitated for a long moment before continuing in a soft voice. "I'm just not sure I can trust you."

"I'll put up my sword if you disengage from the hearthstone."

"I can't do that." A panicky note crept into his voice. "I have to monitor everything."

"I know you want to trust me, Belahn. I can see it in your eyes. You want me to trust you, too, don't you?"

The answer was obvious, but Belahn had to struggle to get it out. "Yes. But I don't think you can." This last was added with quiet despair.

"I can. The first step is for you to turn off the stone."

After a long period of silence, during which Elenai scarcely breathed, the ragged mage sighed. "I suppose . . . I suppose a rest would be nice. You'll help me watch my people?"

"Of course. I swear it by my ring."

Little by little, the lines in his brow eased. He sounded very tired when he spoke again. "Very well. But only for a short time."

Belahn studied the stone in his arms. Elenai peered through the inner world to watch, but didn't dare reach out. She had no intention of startling him.

Last time she'd felt the play of energies swirl around her as the hearthstone's power cycled shut. This time she saw him manipulate the threads from a more comfortable vantage. He moved his hands almost like a child does when creating a whirlpool in a tub, moving the magical energies so that they twisted in upon themselves, diminished. The hearthstone's glow faded. Where before the hearthstone's sorcery had been like unto a raging thunderstorm, now, deactivated, it was a tiny drip.

Belahn breathed raggedly, and staggered as N'lahr sheathed his sword. Elenai discovered herself in control of her own body when she found she could rush forward to catch Belahn when he sagged. Gods but he reeked. The mage hugged the stone tight to his body, as if to protect it. He sucked in a dry, shaking breath.

"Belahn!" Kyrkenall cried. He and N'lahr were there in a heartbeat.

N'lahr took the mage's shoulders and helped ease him to the ground. "Don't die on me, Belahn," he growled.

Die? Elenai had thought the mage was merely weak. Was that noise she'd heard the infamous death rattle?

N'lahr's look was desperate as he looked over the withered alten. He shouted into his face. *"Stay with me!"*

The mage's limbs shook as his lips moved. N'lahr bent close, and then Belahn slumped in his arms.

"Damnit!" N'lahr shook him again. His voice held a pained, urgent quality that she'd never heard in him before. The commander's eyes were like points of flame as he shifted attention to her. "Can you turn the hearthstone on?"

"I don't know how," she said. "Wait. Maybe."

"Do it!"

She'd seen it done, after all. So why not? She put a hand to Belahn's stone as she knelt. In a moment she was in the inner world and staring at the artifact, so similar to the one she'd been wielding. First she sent her own magical energies at it in a counterclockwise pattern. Then she realized her stupidity and reversed the motion. The other direction, she thought. But that didn't work either.

N'lahr pressed his ear to the filthy robe draping Belahn's chest.

Kyrkenall was feeling his neck. "He's got no pulse," he reported fretfully.

Perhaps there was some kind of entry point for the energy? Elenai struggled to remember where Belahn had centered his own sorceries, then looked more closely at the stone. He'd been staring down at it, there. She felt no obvious weak point, but—

She willed all the sorcerous energy she had left and sent it in a slow spiral toward the nub where Belahn had been looking.

The magic of the hearthstone opened to her like a flower. A web of energy sparkled into existence, connecting the mage's body to the stone. "Come on, Alten," she whispered.

"Is it working?" N'lahr asked.

The mage didn't rouse.

The commander all but shouted at her. *"Can you heal him?"*

She had no practice whatsoever with healing energies. Yet she'd watched that done, too, over the years, so she examined the body more carefully, only to find it an empty vessel. The embers in the fire were still warm, but the flame itself had burned away. Distressed, she cast about the room. She wasn't sure what she'd hoped to find. A spirit to reattach?

"I'm sorry," she said at last. "He's not here anymore."

Kyrkenall startled her by kicking a metal pail across the room and cursing loudly.

The commander just stared at the dirty, emaciated body beneath him. His gaze was bleak, and Elenai understood that the man's ordinary distance had nothing to do with lack of feeling. He kept himself remote lest he be seared once more by some loss that had already scarred him badly. Seeing the pain writ so starkly on his face she had the sense that N'lahr had been alone for a very, very long time. The imprisonment of such a man was an entirely different kind of betrayal than she'd ever conceived.

His voice was a whisper now. "Shut it down."

"Yes, sir." She didn't want to, and that frightened her. This stone was different from hers, and she wanted to examine it. Somehow it seemed ripe with possibilities and potential, as if ideas lay within just waiting to be un-wrapped.

Yet she fought the temptation, frightened now that she might end up like the dead man below her. If she continued to wield these stones, would she be so tied to the things that stepping away would kill her?

In moments, Belahn's hearthstone was as dulled as her own.

Heart slamming in her chest, she forced herself to rise.

N'lahr handed the hearthstone up to her, and to keep it away she set it on the mantel, paying it no heed but utterly aware it remained at the corner of her vision, as if she were smitten and pretending not to notice the man she fancied at the table beside her.

The swordsman straightened Belahn's limbs. Kyrkenall bent to help him.

She wasn't sure what to say. "I'm sorry about your friend."

"I'm sorry you saw him like that," N'lahr said quietly. "I knew the hearthstones were alluring, but I never thought Belahn would drown in one."

Elenai spoke softly. "Didn't you say Kalandra was studying them? Do you think she'll be all right?" Clearly that idea hadn't occurred to Kyrkenall yet, for his expression blanked.

N'lahr's eyes, though, were haunted, and she realized he'd already been wondering the same thing. "I hope so." He stood.

Kyrkenall looked to the door as if he wanted to fly out of it. "You think she's off somewhere playing god in the deeps?"

"No. Not her," N'lahr said.

"Not Belahn either, though, right? The kindest of us? The most normal? The one who turned his entire village into a knickknack shelf?"

"I don't know what's happened to her," N'lahr said. "And it's pointless to worry at the moment." He changed the subject and his tone as he shifted attention to her. "Elenai. Can you undo his spell on the villagers?"

She should have guessed he'd ask that. An ordinary spell would have been expected to fade when its caster died, but this one hadn't. The nearby people were still motionless. "It looks really complicated. I can try, but I think it will take a while."

"We don't have a while," Kyrkenall said.

"Try," N'lahr said simply. He considered the dead man beneath him. "We'll see to Belahn."

The two of them searched through the home and found a simple patchwork blanket. To Elenai, it was the most comfortable looking thing she'd seen in days. They carried the body of their old friend, wrapped in that blanket, out the door while she struggled in vain to find a way to alter the spell enveloping the happy, frozen family.

"We should leave a note," Kyrkenall said on their return, "so the Altenerai can find him."

"Any progress?" N'lahr asked her.

She shook her head, noting the pained look hadn't left his eyes.

Kyrkenall groused, "This isn't the welcome we deserve. One more comrade lost. No fresh horses. No willing beds or warm women, or even the reverse."

Elenai was so very weary. She said nothing, but the commander must have guessed what she was thinking.

"I'm afraid we won't even get the comfort of a cold, dusty bed this night. We'll cover our tracks and ride for a few more hours, then rest. They'll have to waste some time picking up our trail in the morning."

Kyrkenall just sighed. "Let's find some paper. I have an idea."

15

The Forging

Denaven sat brooding on the porch of the empty house in the empty village as the sun rose. The home Ortala had found for him at least contained none of the eerie, immobile living people. He'd managed sleep in the narrow bed, but he was hardly refreshed, for instead of the resolution he'd expected he was left with more complications. Kyrkenall left them in his wake like a weaving drunkard dropping bottles.

Somehow Belahn had failed him. Somehow Elenai had killed him, for there wasn't a mark on his body. It defied reasoning that such a newcomer could defeat someone so skilled with the stones. Maybe he'd just been too weakened to combat her. He looked like he should have died weeks ago.

Finally there were the notes, stabbed into one of the gate doors courtesy of kitchen knives. The more alarming of them had been terse and direct for all the precise elegance of the hand that had written it:

> We observed a Naor troop that is likely in advance of a larger
> force. Send warning to all Allied Realms. Mobilize defenses.
> Summon mages to release the trapped here in Wyndyss.
> Belahn's body lies within his home. See to his funeral. We lacked
> time to inter him properly.
> N'lahr, Altenerai Commander

If not for Denaven's spell of influence, that one note would have shattered the fragile shield of lies he'd forged. He'd had to apply a great deal of careful pressure through the links to both Decrin and Tretton, reminding them that Kyrkenall might easily mimic the look of N'lahr's orders. Fortunately, sight of Belahn's remains had eased their building skepticism, for it certainly appeared as though Kyrkenall had been responsible for the death of another alten.

As for the second note, well, that had been signed by Kyrkenall himself: a bit of doggerel that suggested improbable events involved in Denaven's conception and ancestry. That had neither helped nor hindered his cause with the others, but the lines of verse set Denaven gritting his teeth each time he thought of them.

This morning Decrin and the squires were escorting Belahn's emaciated body to the village's cliffside crypts, Tretton and Lasren were following subtle tracks out a hidden exit, and Ortala was inspecting the statue-like citizens for some clue as to what had happened. He was left with Gyldara, on the off chance Kyrkenall and N'lahr had doubled back. You could never quite predict either of them, and when they worked together they were doubly problematic.

The younger woman was restlessly looking over her gear. Moments ago she'd left off sharpening a sword that needed no honing, and was now sitting on the porch edge inspecting her arrow points.

He could see her crisp profile as she stared into the distance. The lines of her face were exquisitely arranged: high cheekbones, full lips, slim-nostriled nose. It was a shame she was said to have no interest in men. At some other time he would have been delighted to have the company of so beautiful a woman, and to see about proving those rumors wrong.

As she sorted the belongings in her pack there was something pensive and bitter to her expression. He hoped she wasn't questioning their goals, as he was quite tired.

He tried a jest. "Are you thinking of where you'll plant those arrows?" He certainly was.

She was silent for a long moment, then blurted: "I can't recall the last time I spoke to my sister."

That was what she was thinking about?

She shifted closer and looked over at him, her lovely eyes shadowed with fatigue. "I didn't really see her very often. We're both . . . I mean we *were* both . . . busy with our duties. And I can't remember if I saw her last when we shared a meal a few weeks ago, or when we stopped in a hall for a brief chat. I'd like to know which came first. Or last. It's been driving me mad."

He tried to sound interested. "Why is it important to you?"

"I'd like to know what our last words were."

"Grasping at memory is like clutching at fog. You come away with nothing but the sense you missed something. And in this case it's pointless. The important thing is that she thought well of you. She told me several times how proud she was of you."

"She did?"

She hadn't at all, but a little fabrication seemed most likely to bring this dull talk to conclusion. "I can't recall her exact words, but I mentioned you in conversation, and she told me that she'd always admired your dedication."

"I didn't know."

"Who doesn't admire it? You've proven yourself the most devoted of the newly appointed Altenerai. I think you have a real future with the corps."

There was sincere gratitude in her voice. "Thank you, sir."

"Don't thank me. You've earned it."

He thought that would close things, but she kept talking.

"I've been thinking an awful lot about Kyrkenall, too, Commander. He was a hero, once. He was best friends with the best of us all, wasn't he? Commander N'lahr, I mean."

Denaven considered pointing out that being famous or particularly skilled in one area didn't mean you were the best, then decided not to interrupt.

"Yet he went crazy. What could make someone go bad like that?"

That was easy to explain. "You take someone with a little talent and then offer them everything in the world and they get to thinking they deserve it. And maybe they take more than their fair share and they get used to that. They make excuses for themselves, and bend the rules a little, and before they know it they're less than they used to be."

At that mention of unfairness, his own feelings of resentment flared. He'd earned his ring. Unlike Kyrkenall and N'lahr, he'd followed orders, yet they'd won the accolades, and the promotions, months before him. N'lahr had taken *his* sword. Irion. And Kyrkenall had taken Rialla.

Denaven still remembered the strangely opalescent corona around the sun that day. They'd been in Alantris, only a few days after Rialla had helped forge Irion, and the night after she'd been awarded the ring. He'd come by early that morning to ask her to breakfast. And who should come sliding out of her door, boots in hand, khalat undone, but Kyrkenall.

He snarled at the memory, remembering the satisfaction of seeing the breath go out of the smaller man as he smashed him in the stomach. Kyrkenall had been outmatched by Denaven's ferocity and his combined use of spell work and physical combat. And Kyrkenall had been an alten, with him a lowly squire.

Gyldara interrupted his memory. "If Kyrkenall really did see some Naor, is it possible they put the spell on these people?"

"No. That's hearthstone work." More specifically that was Belahn's work. He'd been obsessed with finding ways to preserve, or "protect," living creatures ever since N'lahr had cut open a hearthstone and somehow frozen himself. But Denaven had convinced them that the squire had wrought the spell. He didn't want them at all inclined to think Elenai an innocent. She had to be killed along with the others.

"I just can't imagine that Elenai did this," Gyldara said. Her bright eyes were heavy with regret. "I had no idea she was so powerful. She . . . she seemed a nice young woman."

And here he thought Gyldara was firmly on his side and needed little urging. "She's probably been deluded by Kyrkenall. He can be very charming. I know. I used to think he was my friend."

He shifted the subject back to the squire and pushed a little energy through the invisible thread he'd tied to the young woman beside him. "Elenai had tremendous potential before all this. And she's using the stone of Rialla. I don't know if you've heard of her or not, but she was a great weaver, and her stone was one of the easiest to use with sorcery." Many thought that wasn't luck, but because Rialla herself had somehow altered it to her will.

"I haven't heard much about her," Gyldara admitted. "What was she like?"

"The most talented mage the corps had ever seen," he admitted, a little wistful in memory. "She was the first one to learn how hearthstones could be opened for use. No one's ever been better at it, even after all these years. She's the reason Irion is such a fantastic sword."

"How so?"

He spoke on, a little cautiously. "She was there when it was forged," he went on, "and imbued it with magic. I saw the whole thing. She had planned to give it to me."

He decided to test some version of the truth with her. He could better argue his right to the weapon, now that it would finally be available to him, if the younger corps officers understood his connection.

"I never knew that," Gyldara said. "Why did she give it to N'lahr, then?"

He was silent for a moment, thinking how best to begin.

With Rialla. So much of it started with Rialla. "She'd been experimenting with enhancing weapons, and she told me she'd like to make one for me." This was a drastic oversimplification. She'd actually manufactured Lothrun and Arzhun for Kyrkenall first. She and the little archer had developed a weirdly close relationship, though both denied it was sexual.

They'd been lying, of course, but he hadn't known it then.

No one, not even Renik, had managed to unravel the secrets of the hearthstones before Rialla. No one, not even the Mage Auxiliary that followed, had such an intuitive grasp of them. And no one ever cast so beautifully. Seeing her work in the inner world was like watching a master painter lay brush to canvas. Everything she touched became perfection. He'd decided she was someone he needed to know better, no matter how odd she was.

But he was out of time. Rialla, Kyrkenall, and N'lahr were to be awarded the sapphire for a controversial bit of heroics that happened to work in their favor. Soon she'd be consumed with responsibility and, with a brevet between them, any pretense of friendship would be even more challenging. He had to create an opening.

The ceremony was planned for that evening. They'd be sworn in before the whole of Alantris and the assembled members of the corps. Even if a Naor army hadn't been expected on the city's doorstep any day, Denaven knew that morning was likely his best chance to get her alone.

Rialla, though removed as ever, was fairly tractable. She clearly liked experimenting with the hearthstones, and he suggested that another great weapon could help in the battle to come. To his delight, she'd agreed to fashion one right away. She rose early to walk with him through the streets in search of a blacksmith.

The air in the city had been clear and chill, but there was no missing the oppressive mood. Denaven had no way of knowing that the woman at his side would be dead soon. That day he merely savored her company, smiling down at her as they walked. She was a full head shorter than he, with fine, straight dark hair that swayed with every swing of her wide hips.

They turned a corner by one of the city's impossibly beautiful flower gardens and passed through a stone arch into an open courtyard where three heavy-limbed men worked lengths of metal over molten red coals and boys pumped bellows near at hand. The craftsmen had been laboring long hours to make as many weapons as possible ahead of the invasion and they all looked tired.

A rank of finished swords hung on a rack nearby, and there were varied lengths and weights and hilts that were adorned or plain. Mostly, there were spears of different heights and thicknesses. A half-dozen serious youths sat beneath an awning, working in two assembly lines to take finished points, slide them into precut lengths of wood, then lace them in with cord and glue.

A slim teenaged girl, hair wrapped tightly in a white scarf, emerged to greet them. "How may we serve you?"

"We will be purchasing a weapon this day," Rialla answered with abstract assurance.

Denaven's eyes swept over the swords laid out on the tables even as the girl started her patter about this being the finest metalwork in the city.

"I know," Rialla said distantly. Her face was rarely home to much expression, which lent her a serene, withdrawn quality, heightened by her pale blue eyes, the color of a washed out summer sky. "May I speak to the black-smith?"

"Which one do you want? My brother, or my father? Or my uncle?"

"I want the best," Rialla said, and the girl's face clouded with perplexity. After a moment, she stepped away, and before long she returned with a thickly muscled, bearded man, shirtless but wearing a heavy leather apron. There was gray along his temples, and lines creased his face. He dabbed his sweaty forehead with a brown rag.

His voice was hoarse. "How can I help you, Squires?"

"Are you at work on any blades?" Rialla asked.

"I am."

"I wish to be involved in the crafting of a sword for my comrade."

Denaven's heart swelled to hear these words drop from her lips. This would be life changing.

"We'll do whatever we can to aid the war effort," the blacksmith said. "What do you mean by being involved, though?"

"I mean to work a spell while you work the metal. I want to make sure you're comfortable with that." Her airy, rather emotionless way of talking didn't sound especially reassuring. The blacksmith's forehead wrinkled.

"This is Squire Rialla," Denaven said quickly. "I don't know if you've heard of her or not, but she's to be inducted as an alten tonight. She's the most gifted sorceress in the entire corps."

The blacksmith's bloodshot eyes studied the strange young woman.

"You'll be in no danger," Denaven assured him.

After a long moment, the blacksmith nodded. "If it will help the corps, then I'll try."

"Good. I wish a long, straight blade," Rialla stated.

This was going quite well. Denaven preferred a straight sword and such would set his apart from that reckless Kyrkenall's.

The blacksmith—Denaven learned his name was Bralt—said that he had four blades in process, and then asked Rialla which of the half-finished swords she liked best. She pointed to one without hesitation.

Bralt bowed his head formally to her. "That's my favorite as well."

The smith set immediately to work, shoving calloused hands into thick gloves and then heating the metal over coals. Before long, he used tongs to carry it to his anvil to beat at the glowing cherry steel as red sparks flew.

"It's almost time to start," Rialla said blandly.

"Do you mind if I watch while you work?" Denaven asked. "From the inner world?"

Her eyes met his for a brief, rare moment, and the sight of that pale blue staring into his own soul left him feeling exquisitely vulnerable. She looked away. "If you wish." She didn't sound especially happy with the idea.

Denaven politely bowed his head. "I thank you," he said, deciding he would leave her be. He should simply have left his mouth shut and watched without asking.

A change came gradually to the blacksmith as he hammered the metal. His focus seemed greater, his breathing deeper.

The same transformation struck Rialla. The little woman grew fixed, rigid, and her fair eyes burned fiercely. She had grown positively stunning, and Denaven's heart thrummed at the sight of her. He hesitated no longer to watch through the inner world.

He was instantly spellbound by the flow of energies wrapped about the little mage. He'd known she carried one of the hearthstones in her shoulder pack and had likewise guessed she'd call upon it, but he'd never imagined one person could control so much at the same time. The glowing tendrils that writhed between her and the blacksmith were beyond counting. She wasn't just linked to him; astoundingly, she was linked to the sword as well, reshaping the character of the steel so that portions of the hearthstone's intricate pattern were worked into its surface.

Gods, what a weapon this would be! And for him! He could feel the future opening wide before him, knew that he would be renowned as one of the great heroes of the corps, one celebrated for generations, like Alvor, or Altenara herself.

A hand closed on his shoulder. He heard Kyrkenall's voice, hushed beside him. "What's going on?"

Denaven turned on the instant, his sense of elation falling at sight of the shorter man. Like Rialla, and Denaven himself, Kyrkenall wore the gray tabard of the Altenerai squires, and his shoulder was decorated with six brevets. Beside him, naturally, stood tall, solemn N'lahr, his attention centered upon the blacksmith.

"She's making me a sword," Denaven said.

"I was hoping she would. I talked with her about it last night."

Denaven frowned. Dammit. It had been foolish to think he'd begun to have some influence upon her. It had been Kyrkenall, of course.

The little man nodded. "We all feel bad about you being left out."

Left out. That was a wholly inadequate way to describe what had happened. He'd obeyed the orders, and they hadn't. And yet they'd received commendations, and risen in importance. Him, well, he'd gotten a kind word but also the implication that he hadn't acted because he was too cautious. Or worse. It was monumentally unfair, and he wouldn't forget. He'd find some way to repay the debt of inequity.

But he fought his anger. Only a fool grabbed the edge when the pommel was offered.

"Are you sure you two should be taxing her before the battle?" N'lahr asked.

Kyrkenall answered, "Well, I didn't expect her to get on it this quickly. But I'm sure Rialla has a good reason for such effort. Maybe she thinks it'll be key in coming days."

N'lahr nodded as if it were well understood they defer to Rialla's judgment on matters of timing.

One of the young assistants let out an exultant cry, and then another called out: "He's done!"

Denaven and Kyrkenall and N'lahr turned to watch as the blacksmith set down the hammer, took his tongs, and plunged the blade into a barrel of water. He lifted it—steam rising at the same time searing water rolled down the naked blade—gleaming almost with a light of its own. Then, in his gloved hand, he raised it to the blue vault of the sky.

Rialla lifted her own right hand, swordless, at the same moment as the smith. She and Bralt spoke as one, her alto and his baritone echoing somehow across the whole of the blacksmith's shop. All there halted their work to listen.

"Behold Irion," they said, one being with two voices, "forged for the killing of kings, for he who shall be alten and commander, slayer of Mazakan!"

Denaven grinned, his hands tightening into fists. Already he imagined himself holding that sword and lifting it on high.

The two spoke on together: "Forever and always shall their names be linked: Irion, and its bearer, N'lahr Barcahnis!"

Even as Denaven's mouth fell open at this betrayal, both the blacksmith and Rialla dropped as if sleep had struck them while standing. Kyrkenall raced to her side, shouting her name. And N'lahr turned to Denaven, confusion writ on his face. "I thought it was meant for you?"

"Apparently not," he'd answered, stunned and bitter. To this day he wondered if he could have salvaged the debacle if he'd kept his wits to say something better.

His only consolation in that horrible moment had been watching the orphaned rustic scramble to pay the new weapon's cost.

As he concluded his simplified account of the incident to Gyldara, he played the matter to his advantage, lying to reinforce his rightful ownership at the same time he strengthened the thread between them with the weight of truth: "Even though Rialla had changed her mind while she was working on it, N'lahr himself said it was meant for me."

"Then you should be carrying it now he's gone," she told him. "Especially if the Naor really are on the march."

He shook his head with weary reluctance. "Maybe I should have taken it up sooner, but that didn't seem right after his untimely death."

"You're his successor," Gyldara said. "And if Rialla had begun the sword for you, and even Commander N'lahr acknowledged it was rightfully yours, you shouldn't hesitate."

Exactly so. Except that he hadn't been able to use the sword because it was locked away in a hunk of crystal for seven years. Now, though, it was time to fulfill his destiny.

"We'll reexamine the whole matter should it prove necessary." He wasn't sure how he'd explain laying hands upon the sword they'd surely recover from N'lahr when there was a duplicate weapon in the hall, but he supposed he'd work that out when the time came.

Deciding there was nothing more to be gained from talking with Gyldara, he rose. "Excuse me. I've other matters I'd best look in on."

"Of course."

As he left her, he congratulated himself again on the lengthy experiments he'd performed against the defenses of the vaunted sapphire rings. Long years of effort had prepared him for exactly this kind of moment, when it had become necessary to shape the opinions of the Altenerai, allegedly unassailable by all but the most powerful, and obvious, sorceries.

His success was just further evidence that no problem was insurmountable if you put in the proper amount of preparation, especially if blessed with ample savvy and determination. He smiled grimly as he climbed onto the porch of another house farther down the lane. Sooner or later, his skill would overcome Kyrkenall's luck.

Inside the home, Ortala was sitting right on the bench where he'd left her, the hearthstone on the little table beside it.

The exalt's eyes were glazed, and the hearthstone shone from within.

Ostensibly the bony weaver stared at the figures seated statue-like around a cold stone hearth, though he knew that she considered the delicate magical filaments that sustained, protected, and bound them in place.

He stepped deliberately into her line of sight and willed his Altenerai ring to full power. Even to someone enmeshed in the hearthstone, the sudden flare of magical energy would draw attention. "Report," he said. "Are you any closer to freeing them?"

Ortala sat blinking against the slatted bench back before she could focus well enough to meet Denaven's eyes.

She started to rise and he shook his head. "At ease. What have you found?"

Ortala's square face was almost a comical scowl. "I'm just not sure if we can free them, Commander. It's going to take a lot of effort. For each one."

"It'll have to wait then. I need the hearthstone to check on Kyrkenall's whereabouts." He actually didn't want to have anything to do with the stone, but he couldn't afford any more disasters. After the long ride and the expenditure of effort getting into the valley, neither he nor Ortala had been eager to magically track them last night, not when there were other signs Tretton could follow.

Ortala handed it up. Denaven nodded his thanks and left her there. The frozen woman and children in the home's central room were unsettling, so he stepped for the porch, then sat down against the outer wall. He didn't like holding the hearthstone in his lap as if it were a baby, either, and thus placed it under his hand on the planks beside him before slipping into the inner world.

It unnerved him that it was growing simpler and simpler to use this hearthstone. Once he returned to Darassus, he'd hand it back into the storeroom and make sure he requisitioned a different one the next time it proved necessary. The more he acclimatized himself to one particular stone, the more likely he'd end up like Belahn or the queen or one of the others enthralled to the cursed things.

He sent his spirit forth, seeking hearthstones northwest, the direction the outlaws had been heading.

Oddly, he felt nothing. Perhaps Kyrkenall and N'lahr had made excellent time, so he reached farther, drawing closer and closer to that maelstrom of incipient chaos that was the border of The Fragments and the Shifting Lands.

Might Kyrkenall already be traveling there?

He was loathe to search the nearby Shifting Lands with a hearthstone, dangerous as it was, but he did so.

And he discovered no active hearthstones inside.

Fighting down panic, he pulled back closer. They must have changed directions after they left the village. Yet there was nothing to north, or northeast, or west, or southwest, or south . . . more and more frantic, he searched each direction, discovering no stones active anywhere within days of travel.

He pulled back, stunned, and saw that Gyldara and Tretton stood on the porch beside him, and Decrin waited on the steps below. The larger man looked more weary than Tretton, though that might have been grief. Lasren, he finally noticed, sat on the steps swigging from his winesac.

"They're gone," Denaven said, immediately hating himself for the panicked edge in his voice.

Tretton disagreed. "They can't be more than two or three hours ahead. Riding roughly northeast. They won't hit the border for a few more hours. We can catch them."

"But they're not there," Denaven said. "I can't find their hearthstone."

"I don't know what to tell you," Tretton said, dismissive. "The tracks don't lie. They're riding for the border."

The answer came to him like a sword thrust. "By the gods." Denaven held no faith whatsoever in gods and had long since struck reference to them from his vocabulary save for when he spoke to the religious. He put aside his surprise before the greater one of his revelation. "Elenai's figured out how to turn down the hearthstone."

Tretton understood his worry at last. "If even a minor storm whips up . . ." The older alten didn't bother finishing his sentence. It was just possible to follow someone through the Shifting Lands, even without tracks, by detecting little echoes of order left in the wake of travelers. That assumed that the lands would remain calm, and that was far less likely than it used to be.

Denaven climbed to his feet, pushing Gyldara's helping hand off. He could hope they'd catch them before they entered the shifts, or hope that when they entered there'd be no storm, but he wouldn't "hang hereafter on a hope." He put thunder into his voice. "Ortala!"

The exalt hurried out of the door and crowded onto the porch.

"I want you to seek the northeast border of the shifts through the inner world. And I want you to raise a storm. One so vast he won't dare to venture into it."

"Sir?" Ortala looked at him as if he were demented.

"It can be done," Denaven said, striving his best to sound reassuring. Confident. "I saw Kalandra do it." He'd do it himself, but it would badly

weaken him. He couldn't afford that, right now. "You're one of the strongest casters in the auxiliary."

"I'll try, sir," Ortala promised.

Tretton challenged him with his eyes. "If you raise a storm, they'll become nearly impossible to find."

"We're going to stop them before they enter," Denaven said. He called
to the squires. "Ready the horses! It's time to ride!"

16

---◆---

Reunion

As Elenai woke, she realized the voices intruding into her confused
dream were those of N'lahr and Kyrkenall. They spoke in low tones
on the other side of the camp. She could see the leaves in the canopy overhead, which meant dawn had come and gone and that, once again, she'd
probably only managed a few hours' sleep. And this was the last she'd get
before they crossed the shifts.

She stilled, listening in on Kyrkenall in midsentence: ". . . for a long
time."

"It's hard to adjust," N'lahr admitted. "I'm seven years out of step. I
had . . . plans. And I've yet to learn all that's been taken from me."

Several moments passed with only the dull clank of tin on tin.

Kyrkenall's next question was hesitant. "Were you awake in there?"

"No. Praise the Gods. I'd probably have been driven mad."

"Oh, yes, praise them roundly." Kyrkenall's voice was heavy with sarcasm. "In their infinite wisdom they locked you away and let everyone
think you were dead while the Naor waxed in power and our defenses
rotted away. Nice fucking job."

"Asrahn would tell you not to blaspheme."

"Sure," Kyrkenall said quietly. "I wish he would. Not that I was ever
that good at listening."

N'lahr broke the morose silence with a different line of questioning. "I've
been meaning to ask. What's been done with my savings?"

"I think they divided your effects between a couple of second cousins."

"Which ones"

"I don't know. One had a big nose. The other was kind of cute. I didn't talk to anyone. Wait. You had money?"

"Not much, but it was a start."

"What were you saving for?"

There was a pause while Elenai wondered if she should rise and let them know she could hear, but it was oddly pleasant to listen to them talking. Besides, sleep still clung to her. It wouldn't take much to lose herself to the darkness again.

"Well. I thought I'd get some property. For when I retire."

"You? Retire?" Kyrkenall laughed. "Did you honestly think you'd ever leave the corps?"

"I thought I might, when the war was over. If I lived."

"That's always the hurdle, isn't it. Wait—the war was practically won. Did you plan to retire straight after?"

N'lahr actually sounded a little defensive. "I'd been thinking about it. Don't tell me you never thought about what you'd do when the war was over?"

"I planned on having a lot more baths, and a lot more sex."

N'lahr chuckled. "And here I was thinking you'd changed."

"You think I've changed?"

"A little."

"How?"

Elenai smiled to herself as N'lahr subtly needled his friend.

"I thought you'd grown a little more careful with age. It might have been wishful thinking, though."

"I'm practically the soul of caution now. I learned it through abstention, righteous contemplation, and devoted prayer."

N'lahr snorted.

One of them stirred the fire before Kyrkenall spoke, serious once more. "Something's been bothering me."

"Do tell."

"I just can't believe Denaven and his lot brought Belahn in on their side."

"It probably wasn't easy. I'd guess Denaven worked on him a while."

"That snake's always working on someone. Maybe he's more like a spider, except they're a lot easier to kill."

"I underestimated him," N'lahr admitted. "I thought him ambitious, but not treacherous."

Kyrkenall said something softly.

"You were right," the commander responded. His tone changed as he shifted subjects. "Your squire's handling herself well."

Elenai stilled even further, for a moment forgetting even to breathe.

"She's not my squire."

"Then whose squire is she?"

"She's more just along for the ride. You don't see her spending her spare time polishing up my sword or saddling my horse, do you?"

Is that what he expected her to be doing? She supposed she really hadn't been acting the part of a real squire. But hadn't he told her to stop being deferential to him?

"She sleeps more than we do," Kyrkenall went on. "You think old Temahr would have let us sleep longer than him?"

Both men laughed.

"Are you saying we should send her on pointless elk hunts in the rain?" N'lahr asked good-humoredly.

"She's holding her own. With us. That's pretty good. And she's picked up on the hearthstone a lot faster than I'd ever have guessed. She's also pulled me right out of it a few times."

N'lahr agreed. "It sounds like she's shown some real ingenuity."

She couldn't help smiling at that.

"Asrahn trained her," Kyrkenall said, and silence fell. Even from here she sensed their mood had become somber, then his voice grew so soft Elenai strained to hear him. "Do you really think we'll find her?"

He had to mean Kalandra.

N'lahr's answer was simple. "Yes."

"And do you think she'll be as messed up as Belahn?"

"No." N'lahr's voice was heavy. "But I'm worried about her, too. And beyond that, we *need* Kalandra. We needed Belahn."

Some rustling and clinking carried on for a few moments and then it became quiet awhile.

Kyrkenall broke the silence. "Mazakan doesn't know he's going to get you. And Irion."

"I don't have the faintest idea how I'm going to get near enough to fulfill this damned prophecy."

"You'll think of something."

"Right now we've other things to worry about. Speaking of which, it's time to rouse your squire."

"I think she's *our* squire."

"Whatever she is, it's time to wake her."

"Great. Time to ride again. If I find out that they've stopped chasing us, I'm going to be pretty irritated."

From the sound of rustling clothes and footfalls she imagined him rising and striding her way. She closed her eyes, hating the deception she played but hating more the thought of revealing that she'd eavesdropped.

Thus she shammed a stir as he drew close.

"Time to wake," he urged, and Elenai sat up on her bedroll, blinking in the pale sunlight. Despite being fairly alert, she ached terribly in her shoulders and thighs. And there was dried dirt all over the back of her hand, stiff as a second skin. Dawn might already have arrived, but the sky was darkening and the wind rising.

"How long did I sleep?"

"Six hours."

It didn't seem that much. "And how long did you sleep?"

"About three hours."

"You should have let me take some of the watch." Elenai was feeling especially self-conscious after he'd jokingly referenced her sleeping in.

"You're our only mage," he explained. "We've got to keep you fresh. Well, fresh-ish." He didn't look at all disappointed with her.

Nearby trees shivered in the wind as the sky darkened further.

Kyrkenall noticed it with a frown. "We may be in for a rough crossing."

She took a close look at him for the first time that morning. He needed a shave and the dark circles under his black eyes gave him a hollowed-out look.

"Grab your gear and some griddle cakes. N'lahr's saddling the horses."

She nodded and took a deep breath, centering herself. It was time for morning prayers. Before she could move, a confused jumble of images washed over her—a blur of galloping horses and arrow flights. Men and women in khalats rode hard toward them, weapons bared. She saw a dozen different versions of the same moment playing before her at the same time. Sometimes Gyldara led, sometimes Tretton. Sometimes a sober-faced Decrin was shouting for the others. But always they drove on, and their swords were raised to strike.

Death was coming. Fast. Unless they fled now, in one direction. "Northeast."

"What?" Kyrkenall asked, half turned.

"We should ride northeast!" she practically shouted while rising. "And fast."

"Easy there. No magery—"

"The Altenerai are coming," she said through gritted teeth. "We need to go. Now! Northeast."

Kyrkenall froze for two heartbeats, staring at her as if suddenly remembering something. Then he raced off to N'lahr while she snatched up her bedroll.

The first time she'd glimpsed the future she'd thought it was related to her connection with the hearthstone. This time it had come while the hearthstone was off. There was no doubting this vision's veracity, though—it was clearer and stronger than last time. Such was the certainty of the images, she had little time to trouble herself with their origin or what it might mean for her.

When Kyrkenall returned with N'lahr, the commander had questions. "How do you know they're nearly here and why do you suggest that direction?" She hadn't noticed last night, but he looked drained, and drawn. Probably he hadn't had a proper rest since before the Battle of Kanesh, seven years ago.

Elenai struggled to find words, so Kyrkenall answered. "She's done this once before, and it saved my life. Same look in her eyes. If she's wrong, what does it hurt? We were going to go north anyway. Now we just veer a little."

N'lahr's eyes were piercing. She opened her mouth to say more, to try to make him understand, but it wasn't necessary.

"Right," he said. "Northeast."

They mounted up and started off, advancing across the forested hilltop that had sheltered them for half a night. The low-slung branches they pushed through and dodged swayed wildly in the stiff winds. They diverted past a rocky outcrop shaped like an anvil until they looked down on a deep grassy valley with gently sloping sides that wound back the way they'd come and stretched on to the northeast as if laid out for them.

It was filled with an immense herd of animals. Gusts brought them the pungent scent of the massive wild oxen known in Kanesh as "eshlack." Each stood half again the height of a full-grown horse and were crowned by a pair of long, downward pointing horns. Thousands of the shaggy gray beasts grazed fitfully, heads up and down watching the weather. Here and there smaller, younger eshlack chased each other through the grasses as if excited by the bluster. Sentinel beasts, near the edge of the herd, stamped and shook their manes, dark eyes peering keenly at the blue-coated trio through wind-whipped shaggy strands of fur.

"That's a whole lot of dangerous meat," Kyrkenall remarked loudly before they started down the grassy slope, parallel to but maintaining a respectful distance from the herd.

"Eshlack live in Kanesh," Elenai called up to him. "Not The Fragments."

Kyrkenall half shouted his reply to be heard over the wind and cattle. "They could have wandered over through the Shifting Lands during a calm spell."

Elenai's horse snorted at the scent of the eshlack they neared. She would have preferred riding her chestnut, but he trailed on the lead line, along with the other spares. Kyrkenall, as usual, rode Lyria.

They kept to the upper slope, downwind of the wary cattle. Elenai couldn't help looking both at them and behind. Despite her own cautions, it was Kyrkenall who first spotted their pursuit.

The archer called warning: "Behind us!"

Elenai glanced over her shoulder, and her breath caught. Mounted troops had topped the forested line they'd come from two miles back. A half-dozen figures sat saddle.

They were too far away for Elenai to recognize all of them, though she picked out two. Tretton was in the lead; there was no missing the dark face and short gray beard that hid the chin strap of his helmet. The sturdy figure on the larger horse a few yards back could only be Decrin. The sun gleamed off the round buckler on his arm, emphasizing his identity as the bearer of the Shining Shield.

She would have liked N'lahr to suggest a more brilliant plan. Instead, he yelled, "Loose the spares!"

He meant the mounts. As she released the lines, Elenai sighed at thought of the chestnut lost to her, lamenting she'd never bothered to name him.

They kicked their animals into a hard gallop, setting the nearer oxen to bellowing alarm. Hundreds more raised their horned heads and snorted indignation at the intrusion of riders.

Surely, the border wasn't too far off. If the Shifting Lands were shifting, they might be able to lose their pursuers in the chaos. They'd be much less trackable there now that the hearthstone was inactive. She grimaced that it had become worse to be caught by Altenerai than a shift storm.

Even as she thought it, the sky ahead thickened with black clouds, and flashes of lightning played sharply from earth to heaven. A storm to hide them! The agitation of the gigantic cattle grew. More stirred and bellowed as she and N'lahr and Kyrkenall rode on the slope above them.

Thunder rolled. And from ahead Kyrkenall shouted a warning. "Naor!"

Before she could even worry about where the Naor had come from or what they were doing, a flight of arrows sped from a rise of boulders ahead. N'lahr diverted downslope toward the herd and she rode with him. The flight went wide, but the half-dozen archers hidden among the rocks were already launching another sally.

No matter that he rode a running horse along an uneven hillside on a windy day, Kyrkenall was returning fire. As Elenai searched the distance ahead to learn the strength of their foes, she saw one archer sprawl backward across dark boulders, a black-feathered arrow standing out from his face.

They had chanced upon a small Naor troop, for some reason taking its ease on the slope of the valley beside the eshlack. A red-cloaked officer goaded a handful of bowmen to fire even as another ten rushed to climb onto their restive mounts. So far the Naor shots were inaccurate despite the narrowing range, likely because Kyrkenall's arrows sent them scurrying for cover. Or it might be that the Naor thought them the advance attack of the larger force of Altenerai behind.

Elenai leaned away from an oncoming arrow. It passed within an arm's length of her head.

The sky darkened further and clouds tumbled over one another. A startling sheet of lightning lit the entire horizon, and a blast of thunder shook the air. There was answering thunder from below when the eshlack began running along the floor of the valley toward its southern exit, as if they were one mighty beast with ten thousand legs. They apparently didn't care for the flurry of nearby human activities, nor the light show in the sky.

The Naor only managed to throw out five horse warriors in an interception line. N'lahr, riding point, plowed straight into them. With a single slash he cut through a leveled spear and into a horse's neck, dropping one opponent in a flurry of kicking hooves. His backhand strike slashed through sword arm, scale armor, and the chest of a second foe. Kyrkenall sent a shaft at short range straight through another warrior's heart. In an instant they were through with only a few errant arrows reaching out for them.

She didn't have time to feel relief, for the stampeding cattle were spreading out as they ran past. One lowered horns and charged her.

Elenai reached into the inner world to access magics, seeing, once more, the possible outcomes strung before her like beads. She acted upon the information without deliberation, veering closer to the herd. The beast, struck by an arrow either from the pursuing Altenerai or Naor, swung left, goring the air where Elenai would have been.

Was she glimpsing futures because she'd spent so much time using hearthstones? How far forward could she see? The visions seemed restricted mostly to immediate moments.

Her horse squealed nervously to be so near the mass of gray animals galloping the opposite direction on either side, and she carefully swung him back into line after her companions. She'd lost some ground and urged him to a faster pace. From behind came a shout. Elenai risked a glance, saw that Tretton's horse was down near the boulders and four Naor were running for him. Her heart was in her throat. Much as she feared capture, she didn't want the alten killed.

Kyrkenall had seen. He spun in his saddle and launched two arrows, one after the other. They struck through one attacker's knee and another's chest. Both dropped. A mass of dust raised by the eshlack interposed itself before she saw the resolution to the older alten's situation.

When Elenai next checked behind, a single blue-coated pursuer followed at a mad pace, golden hair streaming after. Gyldara. She was gaining, and reached for more arrows to put to her bow despite the distance between them.

She was damnably good. Her missile snapped past Elenai and struck Lyria's side, where it stuck out at an angle. Elenai gasped, then realized the arrow had embedded itself along the edge of Kyrkenall's saddle. He tore out the shaft, fitted it to his own bow, twisted to fire.

Gyldara and her horse went down in a jumble. Somehow the alten threw herself free and came up in a crouch with her bow, fitted another arrow to it.

Elenai was impressed despite herself. She tensed at the thought of an arrow soaring at them on the wings of deadly skill, then saw Gyldara stare at her bow. Her fall had broken its tip, and the string hung slack. The woman flung it aside in anger.

They galloped on, and soon Gyldara, too, was lost behind with the Naor and the rest of the Altenerai. The stream of eshlack dwindled to a few stragglers, the dust their swifter relatives raised blowing in fits with them. Soon all that remained was the storm-eaten sky. The entire horizon was a swirling wall of gray and black, shot through with flashes of blue-and-yellow lightning. Its breadth and power were terrifying. N'lahr paused just a few dozen feet shy of it.

For once, even he looked nervous.

"Denaven's got to be doing this," Kyrkenall spat.

N'lahr nodded and looked to Elenai. "Can you get us through?"

She reached out to the storm through the inner world, her Altenerai ring flashing blue. It was like laying hand to a great, quivering muscle. "It's stronger than the last one," she said dubiously.

"But you're stronger, too, right?" Kyrkenall prompted. His ring was already alight, as was N'lahr's.

"I'll have to use the hearthstone." She wished the thought didn't thrill her so much. Partly because she feared it, she looked at N'lahr.

He met her eyes. "Are you up to this, Elenai?"

"We don't have much choice, do we?" She reached into the hearthstone, trying not to savor too much the rush of power and pleasure that permeated her to the core. She shuddered involuntarily.

"Ready?" N'lahr asked.

She nodded, then, when she saw him fighting his mount forward, she reached forth with threads of intent and calmed their horses.

N'lahr led them into the storm.

At first she fought only to keep the winds away. Then, after the first few hundred yards, the landscape shook, and melted. Grass, rock, trees—all that lay ahead swirled away into tiny black motes. Heart slamming, she reached out and, with the hearthstone, firmed the ground beneath them. Apart from the narrow band of naked dirt, they soon existed in a nothingness buffeted by angry winds. Darkness stretched away in every direction. The horses rolled nervous eyes, and she sent soothing energy to them again, wondering how often she'd have to do that.

"Can you keep us moving?" N'lahr called to her. His voice was strangely muted, no matter that she'd gentled the nearest air currents, as if sound wasn't working normally.

She stared at him in disbelief. "Can't we just stay here until the storm blows through?" That's what Kyrkenall had told her Altenerai usually did during a storm, protected by the power of the sacred rings, which reinforced their own reality amidst one that constantly changed.

N'lahr shook his head. "If this is Denaven's doing, he won't let this end."

He might, she thought, when he tires. But how long could he hold it? And suppose he came after them. What if he came near enough to fight her for control of the hearthstone? How close would he have to be for that?

"When we needed to carry on," Kyrkenall said, "Kalandra used to shape matter ahead of us to form roads."

Elenai wanted to tell them that she wasn't the peerless Kalandra. It was hard enough to ward off the intense energies trying to invade their little zone of order. But then maybe it wasn't impossible. She'd just have to strengthen the environment ahead a bit.

She looked out farther and found the void alive with glowing, whirling motes of energy, each sparkling with potential. Why not? She started small, astonished at how simple it was to coax those bits close with threads of desire, to sculpt them into forms similar to the gray soil under hoof, to firm them into place. In moments she'd extended their narrow point of land a few feet forward.

"Good," N'lahr called. And he urged his mount ahead with a click of his tongue.

Elenai choked back a cry of amazement and coalesced more soil before N'lahr, setting threads to calm each of the mounts again a moment after.

"Keep it coming," Kyrkenall said with a grin, and he followed in the wake of his friend.

Didn't they realize she was just experimenting?

There wasn't time to explain. She threw more of the mixture together as her horse walked after the others of its own accord, then repeated the actions again and again. After fifty feet she was feeling a little stretched and risked letting go of her attention upon the material behind. It slipped away like mounded sand into the waves. Too late she realized it might be easier to shift the soil over which they'd traveled so that it would lift again ahead of them.

The winds rose, tore at their hair, set the horses sidestepping close to the right edge. Once more she eased their fright, then elected to stay tethered to them by threads of will so it would be easier to send soothing commands.

"Can you keep the ground coming faster?" Kyrkenall asked. "I think the storm's getting worse." He stared at the void beyond her shoulder, his ring shining like a beacon.

She wanted to tell him she was weaving energies as quickly as she could, but she didn't have excess mental strength to reply. And so she winged the soil they'd crossed beneath the ground holding them and fitted it ahead. Over and again she repeated the process. There was one close call when the lead horse's hooves almost stepped into nothingness, but she somehow accelerated the process she used, too frightened to actually be pleased with herself.

The Altenerai must have thought her more capable than she was, because N'lahr increased the pace. She'd thought Kyrkenall the more reckless, but the swordsman pushed into a canter as the winds howled, and then a gallop.

Gritting her teeth, she kept up the preposterous demands, maintaining the horses and flinging then firming the dirt and anticipating the worst of the wind gusts with counter ones of her own. All the while they rode through the vast darkness, like heroes in a tapestry woven by some drug-addled madwoman. She'd heard tales of Altenerai travels through the storms, but never such a one as this.

She was just about to congratulate herself for managing so well when she sensed presences riding the empty currents of nothingness.

Something followed them.

17

Faces in the Storm

Her first thought was that Denaven and the Altenerai had caught up, but it soon became clear they were pursued by nothing human. When viewed through the inner world, men and women were complex outlines filled with threadlike energies of varied color. The things behind, she saw, were a seething maelstrom of hunger. Almost anticolor. As she watched, they closed upon their fragile strip of road, and the nearest resolved into the glowing outline of a mountain-sized man, a bearded Naor. It was a chalk sketch come to life. On either side of his form she saw only the star-shot void.

Impossibly the outline strode forward, as if it walked on ground invisible to her, and it stretched hands toward her conjured road.

Kyrkenall looked over his shoulder at their pursuer, his mouth gaping and his ring shining brightly, but he didn't draw his weapons. What could he do against such a creature? She reached deep within the hearthstone's limitless energies, shaped a vast length of road before N'lahr, then turned the whole of her attention on the closing monster.

She formed the drifting energies around to send them hurtling at the thing's face.

Rather than throwing up its ghostly arms to ward against the attack, the Naor-shaped entity reached out with impossibly huge hands, welcoming it. Even as that one fell behind, others drifted from the darkness to either side.

From then on, their journey was nightmare. Before, she'd been worried that she'd lose control and they'd fall into nothingness forever. Now she was terrified that they'd be consumed by the titanic entities. One by one the things emerged from the black, stark outlines of the men and women who'd died in combat against them: The kobalin Kyrkenall had slain, its horn glowing like starlight. The woman Elenai had stabbed through the neck. The soldiers at the tower, some of them afire with not quite blue flames that had consumed their bodies. All stumbled after, clutching at their road like hungry children reaching for fresh-baked breads on the window-sill. Elenai swept more and more energy toward them.

She hadn't the time to wonder what they were. She had no illusions about what would happen if the things got hold of her and her friends, for she saw the matter she sent disappearing entirely the moment the spirits mimed consuming it.

They followed in ones, twos, sometimes as many as three or four at once, and each time she distracted them others crowded forward, until finally she wept from the stress.

But she did not give up.

While blasting at a disturbingly Belahn-shaped specter, her senses bumped into a new object. Something solid lurked out there ahead in the void. A fragment, or a smaller splinter? Whatever it might be, she threw the road toward it, realizing as they fled closer that the landform was large.

Better, the storm at last was dying in strength, and the darkness trickled away until they rode through a wasteland of red rock under an orange sky. It was still the Shifting Lands, but had a semblance of normal reality. She laughed in relief until she saw that the things drifted after. Were they going to pursue them even onto solid ground?

They did. Without her directing energy their way, they tore into the fragile matter that was the sky and soil, ripping holes through which she could see that starless void. She tried resuming the weird feeding, but the matter around her was increasingly difficult to move.

The character of the land changed as they passed over it. Grass sprouted, the land rose into gentle hillocks, and they emerged onto a rolling plain. The chaotic entities finally seemed unable to proceed and were left, howling, behind.

N'lahr eased their laboring mounts to a trot. The lungs of Elenai's poor gray heaved like a bellows.

"Elenai," N'lahr said from just ahead, "let go the stone."

Kyrkenall appraised her with a sympathetic look. "Last time she let go of the hearthstone after working that kind of magic, it drained her."

She resented that. "I think I know how to handle it better, now."

"We have to chance it," N'lahr said. "Denaven can sense the stone so long as you have it active. We don't want him able to follow."

Cautious of what might happen if she relinquished hold too quickly, Elenai siphoned off some of the energy as she closed it. A wave of dizziness washed over her and she sagged as everything went black.

She didn't feel herself roll off the animal and hit the ground, but she felt someone shaking her and looked blearily up into Kyrkenall's strange eyes. Behind him the sky was the same washed-out blue it had been prior to her collapse.

"You all right?" Kyrkenall asked.

She nodded weakly, flushing because she'd made a fool of herself. She'd thought she could handle the situation better this time. "How long have I been out?"

"Only until I could reach you. You hit kind of hard." He touched her scalp above her ear as she sat up. "Any pain there?"

"I can't tell. I ache all over."

He laughed at that, as though she'd planned a joke, then helped her to her feet. She was angry with herself, and with him for laughing, so his smile surprised her.

"That was well done. Top-rank spell work. A few days ago, I'd never have believed you could do something like that."

"Neither would I," she admitted.

N'lahr guided his horse up on her right. "I don't think Kalandra herself could have done better."

She felt a smile rise, and turned away to take in the rolling hills, tall grasses, and occasional scrubby trees. A constant wind blew from the left, rippling through the plants so that they showed green, now white. It looked almost normal, save for the strands of shifting chartreuse bands fluttering in the sky, as if the Gods dragged festive banners through the heavens. It reminded her of the auroras that sometimes shimmered in the skies of home. Except those occurred at night.

"What were those . . . things in the storm? Were those . . ." She hesitated. "Demons? Spirits?"

She waved off Kyrkenall's proffered winesac as he answered her question with one of his own. "What did you see?"

"Giants. Phantom giants. One was a bearded Naor. Another was that kobalin you killed. Every one of them was reaching for us." She fumbled with the watersac on her belt.

"I'd bet we each saw different things," he said. "The wild energy in the Shifting Lands is perceived by intent, or the memory of intent."

"So I imagined them?"

N'lahr shook his head as he climbed down from his horse. "No."

Kyrkenall finished a swig of wine and capped it off. "Remember how I told you there's stuff in the shifts that feeds on magical force? That's what those were, drawn by your work through the storm. And there were a lot of them. But they don't look like anything we'd understand. So their image is shaped by us. By our fears, mostly."

"So you saw something different?"

"Yes."

"What did you see?"

Kyrkenall hesitated a moment, then spoke without his usual easy confidence. "Long, delicate hands, pale and dead. Trying to drag us down."

N'lahr didn't say anything at all, even when Elenai stared at him. "What about you?" It still felt odd addressing him without rank, even though she'd inferred that he felt the same way Kyrkenall did about formal titles.

"I'd rather not say."

"Cabbages," Kyrkenall quipped.

The absurdity of the image brought a laugh to Elenai's throat. She quickly stifled it.

"He hates green cabbages. They were rolling at us from the horizon."

"No," N'lahr said, adding after a moment, "But I do dislike cabbage."

"So," Elenai ventured. "Where are we? Have we crossed into Kanesh by now?" She supposed it was possible they were in some odd corner of Arappa.

N'lahr shook his head and sank to the soil, elbows against his knees. His head didn't quite rest against his forearms, but he looked as though he wanted it to.

"We're in the deeps," Kyrkenall said. "You've heard the expression 'sideways,' haven't you? Kalandra thought it might actually mean we're under the other realms. Whatever it is, exactly, we're pretty much off the map."

Hot as she was from the physical exertion, she still felt chilled as blood drained from her face. Only the most practiced of weaver guides went "sideways," and returned to report their experiences.

Kyrkenall misunderstood her expression for one of confusion. "Think of the shifts more like ocean inlets than a level surface."

She knew. If you were experimental or careless or the Gods were in a capricious mood, the space between the realms might not be a simple obstacle in the middle of a straight-line journey. Some philosophers thought that the Shifting Lands lay beneath and around all the realms.

"So when you've been saying 'deep in the shifts' you didn't mean far away, you meant below."

"Yes," N'lahr said. She would have preferred a more detailed answer, but N'lahr seemed pensive. "We should be safe from Denaven and the search party," he said slowly.

"How far to Kalandra?" Kyrkenall asked.

"A day or two, at best. I'm told this is the only large fragment on the way, about an hour to ride across. There's supposed to be some splinters in about eight hours."

"I've searched some of the deeps for her," Kyrkenall said. "But I've never found this place."

"Don't feel bad. She's well hidden." N'lahr stood stiffly. "I'd prefer to keep going."

Kyrkenall interupted. "N'lahr, we're dead on our feet. If we don't rest we're going to trip up somewhere." He sank to the dusty ground with his back to a short, scaly, mud-colored tree.

"I know." He looked unhappy, but resigned. "We'll camp here. It's not particularly safe, but we won't encounter better until we reach Kalandra. I'll take first watch." He looked ghastly tired, but she wasn't in a position to argue.

Elenai slipped quickly into a dreamless rest without bothering to lay out her bedroll. She wasn't sure how long she'd slept, but it didn't feel like enough. The sky was still the same, but that might just have been the way of things on this fragment. She felt moderately less bleary, and N'lahr actually looked more alert and more determined. He hurried them into the saddle after the briefest of meals.

They plodded on, and on again, and the steady "land" eventually gave way to one that rolled as they rode it, as though ocean waves were hidden beneath its surface. The sky changed from blue to shifting green to shifting black, and once, gibbering rose-shaped things shimmered upon a nearby hill and gave chase for several miles, untroubled by Kyrkenall's dwindling arrows, which passed right through them.

But by and by they arrived at one of the promised splinters, a tiny, desolate strip of blasted barrens, and there Elenai shared the last of her water with her exhausted horse, and fed it the last of the oats. Most of their supplies had been lost when they left the spare horses behind. She had half a watersac of Wyndyss wine and a handful of jerky, but nothing else.

After came another, calmer march. No winds blew. A violet sea drew nearer upon their left, lapping lonely shores where stubby black grasses sprouted near fruiting palms. N'lahr warned them well away, saying that the grass was poison. "Kalandra lost her horse here the first time out."

"So she's been here twice?"

"Yes. But she couldn't stay long, the first time. There were pressing concerns in Kanesh."

Elenai wasn't certain how he was navigating, but he seemed heartened to find a landmark he recognized. They later stopped briefly in a strange locale with pulsing cinnamon rocks, but N'lahr didn't comment on those.

After a long stony waste, the character of the land transformed again by fits and starts until they approached a huge peach-colored lake ringed by blue sand. A light misting of moisture fell around them, and far ahead, across dunes of increasingly lighter blue, was a cliff with a flattened top, crowned with greenery and flashes of purple and yellow, presumably wildflowers. It towered at least two hundred feet over the surrounding terrain. N'lahr rode unerringly for it for over a mile, and it soon grew apparent that was his likely destination.

"Is that it?" Kyrkenall asked.

"Yes."

The archer looked sidelong at his friend. "You're just full of information, aren't you?"

"Yes."

Elenai studied the strange landform more carefully as they neared, and estimated it at several miles wide.

The cliff wall was sheer, formed all of rough gray-and-white stone, completely out of place surrounded by the endless stretch of sand, as if dropped there. She'd seen so many odd things in the last week that its peculiarity seemed almost mundane. Of more immediate concern was how to reach the top. She hoped they wouldn't have to scale hand over hand. Maybe there'd be a slope for the horses, hidden off to one side or around its back. It wasn't that she couldn't climb, just that she hardly welcomed the thought of expending any extra effort right now.

Casually N'lahr grabbed the one javelin remaining alongside his saddle.

Kyrkenall saw that. "Anything in particular we're on watch for?"

"Aren't you always on guard?" N'lahr chided.

"You're in rare form today, N'lahr. Simply hilarious."

"You must be worn out. I'm really not that funny."

"I can believe that."

They'd closed within a hundred paces, and Elenai saw Kyrkenall, like herself, scanning the heights.

Only the grass moved above, in the wind, and soon sight of the crown was blocked by their approach angle.

Fifty paces out, something appeared at the very base of the cliff. A dark, fur-cloaked figure seemed to slide right out of the stone.

Kyrkenall cursed and raised his bow, knocking an arrow.

The thing raised a thick black arm, as if in greeting. A kobalin lord? What was it doing here, in Kalandra's place of safety?

Its voice was deep. "Ho, N'lahr! Have you come at last to die?"

18

Those Left Behind

N'lahr's horse snorted in displeasure. He mastered the animal with rein and leg but didn't raise his javelin. The roan's ears shifted nervously between rider and the kobalin crunching across the sand toward them.

Elenai reached for her hilt, and Kyrkenall sighted on the beast, addressing N'lahr from the side of his mouth. "Looks like this one's yours."

The creature's savage grin remained fixed as it hefted a huge hammer. What did this mean for Kalandra? Could she have been killed by that kobalin? Was that why no one had heard from her since before N'lahr's disappearance?

She thought to see the swordsman return the thing's challenge with one of his own. He nodded to Kyrkenall, slid down from his horse, put up the javelin, but then didn't draw his blade as he strode toward the beast. It towered a head higher than N'lahr and was half again as wide. The thing wasn't wearing a cloak; rather it was covered in black fur from head to toe. A plain brown kilt was fastened at its waist. Its heavy jaw was outthrust and two large eyes blazed redly at them, like fiery coals among ebon ash.

"Well?" the creature roared when they were a few paces apart. "Is it time?"

N'lahr raised his hand. "Kill me later, Ortok. I'm in the middle of something."

Ortok sighed heavily.

Kyrkenall gaped. "You *know* him?"

"Yes." N'lahr answered without turning.

The archer relaxed tension on his bow. He called incredulously to his friend, "And you're not worried that there's a kobalin here in your secret stronghold?"

"He's supposed to be here. Long story." N'lahr looked up into the kobalin's large, flat face. "Ortok, how's Kalandra?"

"I don't know."

Clearly the commander hadn't expected that answer. "You don't know? Why not?"

"She's not really here."

Kyrkenall had lowered his bow, though he had yet to replace it, or restore his arrow to its quiver. "What in the sucking abyss does that mean?"

The kobalin turned glowing eyes toward him. "I am Ortok," he said in his growling baritone. "And you are Kyrkenall. But you have not introduced yourself. It is proper to do so before speaking."

Elenai didn't catch what the archer mumbled, though from his tone she guessed it wasn't an especially refined comment.

"Ortok," N'lahr said, "where's Kalandra?"

"She's partly here, but mostly gone."

Elenai couldn't suppress a horrid thought—a bloody, amputated limb under glass in the kobalin's lair. Surely that wasn't what he meant.

"You mean she's dead?" Kyrkenall demanded.

The kobalin drew back the corners of his mouth to show upward-pointing fangs as he regarded the archer. His voice was sonorous, like a rumble drum. "I really must insist on introduction. But no, she's not dead. At least not as known to me. She left part of her spirit, but it's much duller than she is."

"What the fuck is he talking about, N'lahr?"

"I have no idea. Ortok, slayer of Nemrose, this is Kyrkenall Serevan, also known as Kyrkenall the Eyeless, bearer of the sacred ring."

"Ah!" The kobalin showed two sets of long matched fangs in a fearsome smile an inch or two wider than humanly feasible. "I thought it might be you," he continued, as if he hadn't stated as much mere moments ago. "It is a pleasure to meet you! If I were not already sworn to kill N'lahr, I should like to challenge you."

"So you're the one who offed Nemrose, huh?" Kyrkenall sounded impressed. "Nice. I hated that hastig."

"Who's Nemrose?" Elenai asked.

"A Naor king," Kyrkenall explained. "One of Mazakan's chief leaders. Razed a bunch of villages in The Fragments."

Ortok smote his chest with one closed fist. "He was a brave and mighty foe, but not an honorable one. He attacked me with all his guard!"

"And Ortok killed him anyway," N'lahr said.

Ortok beamed at him. "It pleases me still you heard of that day."

N'lahr indicated Elenai with a jab of his hand. "And this is Elenai Dartaan, of Vedessus, also known as Elenai Oddsbreaker."

Kyrkenall chuckled. "I like that."

Elenai had never been known as "Oddsbreaker." She stared at the commander, a little confused, and caught him nodding at her with a slight grin. She blushed. He'd given her a heroic sobriquet!

"Of you I have not heard," Ortok said. "But I look forward to learning of your deeds. I have been here some while. I imagine there are bold stories that have not come to me."

"Later," N'lahr said. "I want to see what you're talking about with Kalandra. I'm having a hard time picturing what you mean. Are you saying Kalandra's not here?"

"That is right. She left, but part of her spirit stayed. It is strange to me. You can talk with her, but she mostly says the same thing."

"How did she leave her spirit?" Kyrkenall asked skeptically.

"Magic."

Kyrkenall sighed. "Thanks. I'd never have guessed that."

"You should have," Ortok said. "She is good with magics."

Kobalin, apparently, were strangers to sarcasm.

"Where's the real Kalandra?" N'lahr asked.

"Out looking for something."

"What?"

The kobalin gave a huge shrug. "She didn't say."

"How long has she been gone?" Kyrkenall interrupted.

"A long while."

Kyrkenall's frustration was evident from his tone. "Days? Weeks? Months? Years?"

Ortok grunted. "Some of those. You can ask her. She will know."

Kyrkenall looked as though he was ready to knife the kobalin. His discomfiture might have been more amusing if Elenai weren't equally confused and frustrated. Had they come all this way for nothing?

"Why don't you take us to her . . . spirit," N'lahr suggested.

"She said you'd ask that. Follow me." Ortok turned and exposed his huge, ridged, and hairy back to them as he plodded into the darkness of what turned out to be a narrow passage twisting into a shadowy portion of the rock. After the opening it was just feasible to ride side by side. N'lahr walked with Ortok, leading his horse, who snorted with displeasure and folded his ears back. Elenai knew how the animal felt. She rode beside Kyrkenall several paces back. The rough cliff wall rose steeply on either hand. Beneath, the bluish sands gave way to rich earth in which bright green grass alternated with clumps of small violet flowers.

Kyrkenall shook his head. "Can you believe this? There was a kobalin here the whole time and he didn't bother to warn us. Typical. Him and his answerless answers."

"You do the same thing."

Kyrkenall sounded genuinely offended. "No I don't. Name one time."

"What about when I asked you what the hearthstones were and you told me I was better off not knowing?"

"That's different. There are things I don't like talking about. But if I was taking you to some mysterious place where there was a kobalin lord I happened to be friends with, you can be damned sure I'd have mentioned it."

"I'm not sure I'd call them friends," Elenai said. "He wants to kill the commander."

"That's a mark of respect from a kobalin. And this is a deadly one, if he nailed Nemrose and his honor guard. That's like ten guys as good as third rankers, backed up by a newbie alten. As much as they love stories, kobalin are pretty terrible at telling them."

"So you can be . . . friends with kobalin?"

Kyrkenall raised one hand and tilted it back and forth. "Not so much. I mean—you can have mutual regard."

N'lahr said something that set Ortok roaring. Elenai reached for her sword as he shifted his hammer and lifted one great arm, thinking the kobalin had decided to attack.

Then Ortok clapped N'lahr on the back and laughed. N'lahr, recovering his balance, chuckled himself.

"Damn." Even Kyrkenall looked startled.

"But he still wants to kill him?" Elenai asked.

"He said it, so he means it. But you don't need to worry about that until N'lahr accepts the challenge."

"You're sure?"

"I'm sure."

"That seems a little strange."

"I think it's refreshing. With kobalin you always know where you stand."

"You mean they always want to kill you."

"I mean they'll fight you openly. Not like Denaven." Kyrkenall's mouth twisted.

More unsettling truth. Elenai shook herself mentally.

The trail wound on for a few hundred more feet before emerging into a wide oval garden space surrounded by cliff walls. Elenai stopped to take it in, marveling. There was the sound of flowing water from somewhere off to her right, where rows of exotic fruit trees blossomed amid cool mists. Bushes heavy with lush scarlet berries grew on her left. Bright insects flashed

and fluttered. Rising in the dead center of the space was a squarish blue
marble building with pillared portico and a slanted partial roof bearing
overlapping onyx shingles that glistened in the sun. And most surprising,
looking down upon the space from niches higher in the cliffside were six
great statues of smiling figures. Not four, but six . . . was the betrayer Sartain's statue up there along with the Goddess he'd killed and the others
who'd first ruled the realms?

Kyrkenall climbed down from his mare and took off her halter and
saddle following N'lahr's lead. Lyria immediately set to cropping grass and
N'lahr's animal wandered to her far side, away from Ortok. While Elenai
eased the gear off her own mount, Kyrkenall joined N'lahr. "I see the statues. The Five, and the betrayer?"

The swordsman's answer was almost laconic. "That's what Kalandra
thought."

"The Gods were supposed to have warred before the start of civiliza-
tion." Kyrkenall's wide sweeping arm indicated the whole of the place. "So
who made this?"

Only N'lahr could have sounded so matter-of-fact with his answer. "The
Gods."

Ortok set his hammer beside one fluted blue column. "Come, come."

"You might have mentioned there was a kobalin guard," Kyrkenall said.

"The less either of you knew about this place the better."

"Why's that?" Elenai asked, catching up.

"In case we were captured." He gestured ahead of him. "Now let's go
see what Ortok's trying to tell us."

Elenai didn't quite catch Kyrkenall's disgruntled comment. They followed the kobalin under the cool portico and through an arching passage-
way. It led into a square chamber that was more or less empty and mostly
open to the sky.

Ortok halted just before an emerald-studded flagstone on the far left,
facing the wall where a matching stone as large as Elenai's fist glittered from
a niche. The startlingly large and stunning gem was flawless and perfectly
cut so that all its faces were the same size. Elenai noted similar jewels of
different hues occupying niches all around the hall. What kind of place was
this?

The kobalin raised his hands and addressed the glittering jade diamond.
"Kalandra, I'm back once more. You have visitors."

There was a sound of chiming bells, and she was there upon the flagstones, shimmering, vaporous. Her slender body was wrapped by the blue
Altenerai khalat, and foaming brown hair crowned her brow. From under

the curling locks, piercing hazel eyes looked out. A sword was slung along one hip.

Elenai couldn't keep back a gasp of surprise.

Kalandra's voice was tired. "Show me your rings."

N'lahr raised his on the instant and set it glowing. A dumbstruck Kyrkenall obeyed a moment later, and Elenai followed his example.

She'd always thought the woman plain in depictions back in Darassus, rather unglamorous, but when the image of Kalandra moved and smiled it somehow conveyed a charm that still likenesses could not. She looked younger than expected but carried herself with a graceful assurance. "N'lahr, Kyrkenall, it's been a long time. Who's that with you?"

"By the gods," Kyrkenall whispered.

N'lahr answered the vision. "This is Elenai."

Kyrkenall got over his surprise. "Kalandra, is that really you?"

The transparent image shook her head. "No, old friend. Think of me as an imprint of memory. I created this device so you could speak with me while I went out searching."

"When did you leave?" N'lahr asked.

Elenai doubted that this magical image could answer that, but the reply came without hesitation.

"Five years, nine months, two weeks, and one day past."

Kyrkenall shook his head. "Are you all right?"

Her brow furrowed. "I don't understand."

That troubled Kyrkenall; N'lahr, though, pressed on.

"What did you learn?"

"Can you be more specific?"

"Let's start with this place. What did you learn about it?"

She nodded. "The six men and women we thought of as gods gathered here to begin designing the realms. Each of them fashioned places of their heart's desire and set them apart from one another so that their creations wouldn't interfere with what each was doing. This haven was jointly constructed with some of their favorite elements so that they would be comfortable when they met. Beyond that wall are sleeping and living quarters." She pointed to a blank spot to the right of one of the gems.

"How do you know this?" Kyrkenall cut in.

Eerie that the transparent figure's eyes were so piercing. This imitation Kalandra certainly acted like a real person. "Information can be extracted from the other gems stored here. Once I learned the trick, I pored over the memories that the Gods left. I spoke with two of them. The others either left no direct impressions or they were inaccessible to me."

"Who left impressions?" N'lahr asked.

"Kantahl and Sartain."

Elenai could scarce believe what she'd heard. N'lahr was clearly startled himself.

Kyrkenall swore. "The betrayer?"

Kalandra's brow furrowed once more. "I don't understand."

"She does that all the time." Ortok's low voice startled her. Elenai had almost forgotten he waited behind them. "You're getting a lot more talk out of her than I usually do. She never told me this. Why didn't you tell me any of this god talk, Kalandra?"

Once again, Kalandra looked puzzled, and Elenai saw that her expression was identical to the first two times. Even her inflection was the same. "I don't understand."

The kobalin grunted. "You see? Why doesn't she speak to me of these things? I guarded her life."

"I told her to share some of these matters only with me," N'lahr offered.

Elenai was astonished such a simulation existed. That it also retained some kind of limited judgment was astounding.

Kalandra stood waiting, her expression once more vaguely sad.

Kyrkenall shifted, his face twisted in worry. "Do you think she's still alive out there, somewhere?"

"We'll find her." The commander didn't look any less upset than Kyrkenall, despite his confident proclamation. "Kalandra, I asked you to learn about the hearthstones you'd gathered. Did you?"

Her expression clouded. "They're very dangerous, N'lahr. Tell our friends to stop using them. I once lost myself in one for almost a year."

"What are the hearthstones?"

Once again, Kalandra sounded so real it was almost as if she were there. "They are pieces of a larger whole, but I'm unable to determine the shape and purpose of their original form. Either in whole or in parts, they were used by the Gods to fashion the realms, and the effects of their work are more comprehensive and lasting than I can currently manage with my own experiments. Each of the hearthstones seems infused with different kinds of energy, and the various energies color the perceptions of those who use them, leading to somewhat divergent effects."

The figure paused briefly. She spoke with such easy confidence, her words well-chosen and her manner authoritative, that Elenai now understood a little why both N'lahr and Kyrkenall held her in such high regard.

Kalandra's image continued: "They tend to subtly alter the reality around them, even when inactive, and present greater danger in altering those most susceptible to their influence, those open to the inner world. Some hearth-stones appear to display affinity for others, as if they wish to be merged, and once joined the character of the larger piece changes. In short they are powerful objects that modify, or perhaps even transform, what's around them in ways that cannot be fully predicted. I suspect that removing all of them to Darassus may have a continual and unpredictable warping effect upon the realm itself."

N'lahr thrust one leg forward. "Kalandra, Belahn thought that the hearthstones were some kind of altar to a greater god. What do you think of that?

"I don't understand."

N'lahr tried again. "Could the hearthstones be part of a shattered altar to a god?"

"I don't understand."

"Why can't she?" Kyrkenall asked.

Elenai thought she knew the answer. "She can react to us but she can't draw new conclusions. She can only comment about what she knew or felt when she left this impression."

Kyrkenall sighed. "Damnit, Kalandra."

The image looked right at him. "What's wrong Kyrkenall? You seem sad."

"What's wrong is that you're not really here! I've looked everywhere for you and had almost given up. Then N'lahr got my hopes up, and Be-lahn got me worried. We finally found you but you're gone, and there's nothing here but this . . . thing that sounds like you."

"I don't understand."

Kyrkenall's next question was plaintive. "Why aren't you here?"

That set the image in motion again. She gestured to the surrounding walls. "When Commander Renik described a strange garden he'd found in the deeps, I'd thought this was the one, but the more I considered the matter the less his description truly matched this place. He said there were four statues. He couldn't have miscounted, even if that one to the south is hard to spot in the afternoon, nor failed to note the inclusion of Sartain. So I decided that there must be another place, built after the betrayer warred with the others."

"You went looking for that place?" N'lahr asked.

"Yes."

"Did you have any idea where it was?"

"Somewhere beyond Ekhem."

Kyrkenall groaned. "That seals it. She's not coming back."

"Not necessarily," N'lahr objected.

Kyrkenall shook his head. "Don't you see, if she went looking for that other place, she would have crossed one of the realms and heard you were dead. She couldn't have traveled in the deeps the entire time. It wouldn't have been safe, or practical. And once she'd heard about what happened she would have come looking for me or Asrahn, someone. She's vanished, like Commander Renik."

Ortok grinned. "Ah! Renik. The deadliest of all Altenerai! My people say he was an even greater swordsman than you, N'lahr!"

"He was," N'lahr agreed without hesitation.

"And a greater mage than Kalandra," Ortok went on.

This time Kyrkenall answered. "He was."

"What happened to him? I always wanted to battle him."

"The queen kept ordering him deeper and deeper into the shifts," Kyrkenall answered morosely. "And one day he didn't come back."

N'lahr explained further. "He was trying to find a way back to the place Kalandra's talking about."

"Wait," Kyrkenall said, "are you saying the commander knew about all of this?"

"He didn't know about this place. He'd already disappeared by the first time Kalandra got here. He'd been investigating the origin of hearthstones. He told Kalandra what concerned him, and eventually she told me."

"Why didn't you say anything to me?"

"Kalandra asked me not to. She wanted to understand the danger before sharing it with anyone else. Besides, we had a lot of other problems needing attention."

Kyrkenall threw up his hands. "What a great idea that was! You two wait to tell anyone then both of you end up dead! Denaven takes over and starts lifting simpletons to the ring and shuffling the mages into the auxilary! And no one knows enough to stop him!"

"I couldn't anticipate that." N'lahr looked a little hurt by the accusation.

Ortok stepped closer to Elenai. She supposed the slightly lower volume of his booming voice was meant to be subdued. "Are they going to fight?"

"No." At least Elenai didn't think so. Ortok looked disappointed.

Kyrkenall's voice rose. "You didn't plan. All these secrets, N'lahr, and you didn't plan for what would happen to everyone else if you were gone! And neither did you, Kalandra!" He pointed angrily at the transparent image.

"I don't understand."

He gnashed his teeth and his clenched fists shook. "Damnit, I loved you!"

Kalandra's expression softened. "And I have always loved you."

Kyrkenall groaned as if in physical pain.

As Kalandra's double smiled, her affection was so clear, so intensely personal, that Elenai suddenly felt as though she were intruding upon a private moment. The memory of the enchantress continued with great fondness: "You're so fierce, but so vulnerable. So tender, so dangerous." She laughed a little. "Oh, you're a glorious mess, Kyrkenall, but I love you."

Kyrkenall stared at her image in stunned silence and shot a brief anguished look to N'lahr and Elenai. "I can't . . . I can't take this," he muttered, turning on his heel and hurrying from the room. He disappeared into the hallway. They heard the sound of his retreating footsteps echoing on the stone.

For so long the archer had been talking about the greatness of Kalandra that Elenai had assumed admiration of a senior colleague, but with sudden clarity she understood a greater attachment had always been noticeable, if she'd paid attention. She was surprised to feel both sympathy and a pinprick of jealousy.

She turned to N'lahr to gauge his reaction and saw his eyes alive with shared pain as they followed his friend's departure. He watched him for a long while, his expression somber.

After several tense moments, Elenai cleared her throat. She was vaguely aware of Ortok behind her, who remained at a discreet distance. "What are we going to do now, Commander? Are we going to look for her?"

N'lahr shook his head. "No. We have to go to Arappa."

"Why?"

He met her eyes steadily. "Because the Naor are invading it."

"What?" The question was choked from her. Surely she'd heard wrong. Arappa?

N'lahr spoke grimly on. "That's why they were herding eshlack through the north border of The Fragments. They're supplying an army. They can't get that herd past the mountains to Alantris or to any other southern city. And the closest realm to the north border of The Fragments is Arappa."

"Eshlack are delicious," Ortok averred.

Elenai ignored him as she shook her head in denial. "How could they move an army or a herd without detection?"

"We don't know that they weren't detected. If our forces and borders are as weak as you've told me, detection won't matter."

Elenai knew blood was draining from her face. Unbidden, a rush of memories washed over. Her little sister waving to her from the city walls as Elenai journeyed forth for the great games. Her father standing in the dim recesses of the theater, taking a planer to a beam where a stage back-drop would be hung. She thought of the detailed clay carvings projecting from house eaves, and the great statue of Vedessa in the central square, where she'd first met N'lahr. She remembered the pounding from siege engines echoing through the empty streets as she and others huddled in sturdy corners, the random death from above from boulders or debris, and the pang of hunger.

"Why didn't you say something sooner?" she asked. Her voice sounded stripped of all weight, as though she were a child.

"By the time I put it together we were fleeing Denaven's band and near enough to Kalandra."

She licked her lips and fought against her rising panic. But N'lahr was the remedy, wasn't he? "If Mazakan's on the move, you can finally finish him off. That would break them."

N'lahr smiled slightly and rubbed his face. "It's true that Mazakan's most likely leading them, and if he were removed it might throw them into chaos. No other Naor, ever, has been able to unite more than a couple of tribes for a few years. But unless I have an army to counterbalance his I'll be hard-pressed to get close, no matter how fine my sword."

She was stunned he looked so resigned. Where was the battlefield ge-nius she'd heard so much about? Couldn't he cook up something clever? "Mazakan always fights at the front, right? You can use that."

He arched an eyebrow at her suggestion.

"Or maybe if he learns you're back he'll flee." She realized she was sounding desperate.

"Mazakan's set on our extermination. You have to know your enemy better than that to defeat him."

"What do you mean?" She was getting angry.

"I mean Mazakan's personal qualities don't include cowardice." He paused, seeming to wait for her to speak or to acknowledge understand-ing, and at her confused stare explained. "He's ruthless, but impartial. He promotes by ability rather than giving any tribe precedence. He's fearless, and tough, and his word is his bond—to his allies, at least. He shares plun-der equitably and punishes lawbreakers, even if they've supported him. And he's been able to communicate a vision."

There was nothing so special about that. "So you're saying he's a good leader," she scoffed.

"Maybe it sounds obvious to you. But you're not blinded by generations of tribal affiliations and blood feuds. Other Naor haven't seen past those things. If Mazakan was killed seven years ago, his generals would have torn into each other over whatever they could get of his empire. Now, we can only hope they haven't learned from his example."

Her voice sounded small even to herself. "So what do we do?"

"We'll ride to Arappa."

It was exactly what he'd told her minutes ago, and she looked to him for a more reassuring answer.

Apparently he didn't have one. "We'll aid them as we can. First, I have more questions for Kalandra's likeness." He looked to the silent kobalin behind her. "Have Ortok show you where the food is. Eat. Rest. You'll need to be in better shape for all that lies ahead."

She nodded her understanding and he turned away. Even Ortok was quiet as they walked off, leaving N'lahr alone in the hall with the ghostly image of his old friend.

19

—⁓—

Time Alone

Ortok extended one huge furred arm to point at a thick, leafy bush heavy with red-and-gold fruit that resembled raspberries. "Those are the sweetest of all."

The first berry was so ripe it dropped to the grass the moment she touched it. She bent, grasped its soft flesh between fingertips, and lifted it to her lips.

A cool, sweet flavor burst over her tongue, and she smiled in pleasure despite herself. It was the most delicious thing she'd eaten in weeks.

Ortok's wide smile displayed a long row of sharp teeth. "Ah! You are pleased. You see?"

"They're wonderful," she admitted.

"Gather as many as you want. They grow back swiftly."

It said much for the strangeness of her circumstances that the least peculiar part of them was picking berries with a kobalin lord. She sucked in a breath, willing herself to steady. She should be in Vedessus, helping with the defenses. Had she the strength and means, she would have headed back already. Yet she needed food, and exhaustion still weighed her down. Like N'lahr said, she'd have to be in better shape for a long ride and the fight at its end.

She found she'd been staring at the berries she cradled rather than eating them. Elenai shook her head to clear it, and smiled encouragingly to the kobalin waiting beside her. He was eager that she enjoy herself.

"Is this what you live on, Ortok?"

"Yes. These and the nuts. There are other plants, too." Ortok suggested the distant cliff wall with an encompassing arm sweep. "The bugs are not nice to eat. There are no animals, and sometimes I miss the taste of flesh, and the sensation of blood running through my teeth, but I am pledged to guard."

"Why?" Elenai lifted a small handful of berries to her lips and began to chew, savoring each bite.

"I do not know. I have always preferred meat. Yet the berries are good."

She swallowed. Kobalin, it seemed, were difficult to talk with. "I mean, why are you here guarding?"

"Eh, N'lahr didn't tell you?" Ortok touched a branch with delicate care, then shook it with vigor. Red-and-gold berries rained to the ground, and the kobalin immediately dropped to the grasses on all fours. He spoke as he rooted around and popped them into his mouth. "N'lahr asked me to serve Kalandra, and I owe him my life. Then she asked me to guard this place. Here, shake that branch." He pointed and cupped two clawed hands. His palms were padded, like the paws of a dog.

Elenai chose the limb he indicated and set it swaying back and forth. Dozens of berries dropped into his grasp. Ortok quickly shoved them into his mouth and devoured them with lip-smacking pleasure.

She watched for a moment, smiling inwardly. What a contrast to the torments and troubles beyond this sheltered zone. Her heart ached, and she found herself angry at Kalandra for putting them all through this, for diverting them, for failing to be where she was needed, for hurting Kyrkenall. What more was N'lahr finding out from her image? Would anything she said help? For that matter, was there anything that Elenai could say to Kyrkenall that would help?

She tried speaking to the kobalin in the manner he seemed to prefer: direct, and slightly formal. "How did you come to be indebted to N'lahr?"

"Ah!" Ortok's chin thrust out and his eyes gleamed. He licked red berry juice from the pad of his right hand, then climbed to his feet and smote his chest. "I, Ortok, will tell you. It happened on a day when N'lahr had gone hunting Naor."

Elenai knew very well that N'lahr didn't "hunt" Naor, so the statement puzzled her. Had the commander been on patrol?

Ortok continued. "He came upon a number who were hunting me! It was a brave battle with much slashing and crushing. He and I, we fought the Naor as one! The blood flowed. He was mighty." Ortok lifted his hands together as though he wielded an axe. "Back to back we faced them until all were food for worms!" He laughed, that black-furred face with its dark nose bright with delight. "I wanted to challenge him then and there, but I owed him my life. Some day, when N'lahr declares my debt repaid, we will duel, he and I."

She couldn't help staring. He was just as mad as the other kobalin. "Do you think you'll win?"

"Only the Gods can say," Ortok admitted. "But it will be a glorious death for one of us, and a mighty memory for the other."

"Why don't you both just live, and be friends?"

He stared at her, then laughed. "You Altenerai are so strange."

She had nothing to say to that, so she ate another handful of berries. Ortok's mention of Gods had her reflecting again that Kalandra's memory had said something about "the people they'd thought were gods." She'd seemed to imply the Gods weren't gods but ordinary men and women, except that made no sense. If they were just mortals, where had they come from? Wouldn't someone have to have created them? She shook her head, unwilling to accept the information as truth without further verification.

Now wasn't the time for such musings, in any case. She could imagine what Alten Asrahn would have said if he were with her. Focus on the task at hand. The Gods and their origins were all very interesting, but their nature didn't have much impact upon her present. More important was what she and the others did next. Mazakan had sent a Naor army against Arappa. They could be at the gates of Vedessus right now. They had to be stopped.

She had trusted N'lahr's assurances that they needed to seek Kalandra, whereupon all would be well. But Kalandra was long since vanished, and the memory she'd left in her place merely left them with more questions. It might be fine for N'lahr to dig for information about lost Kalandra and the hearthstones, but that didn't help them with the pressing matter of the Naor invading her homeland to rape and murder. They needed to plan how to stop them. If they could.

She needed to talk to the others. N'lahr was still busy, so that left Kyrkenall. Though the interior of this refuge was a mile in diameter, at best, it was uneven and studded with little groves of plants and trees. Somewhere the archer was hiding among them, unless he'd left. Surely he wouldn't have done that.

Ortok broke into her musings. "Speak to me, Elenai Oddsbreaker. Walk with me. I shall take you to the most delicious of the nuts."

She smiled at mention of the nickname N'lahr had awarded her.

The kobalin started forward on broad feet. She'd noted before that his tread barely rippled the grass, and she marveled again at how fluid the movements of so ungainly a creature were.

She fell in step with him and they passed where the horses grazed. Kyrkenall's mount looked up at her and cocked her ears, curious. The little archer had to be somewhere close.

"How did you win the ring?" Ortok asked, his voice rich and low. "Surely it is a brave story."

It occurred to her that the kobalin might only have been treating her equitably because he assumed she was Altenerai. She'd heard once that kobalin lords considered squires unworthy of notice. If she admitted her true status, would she immediately face hostility? She watched the play of muscle beneath Ortok's fur as his huge arms swung. She'd be hard-pressed to stop him if he grew aggressive.

"It's best if N'lahr or Kyrkenall told that story," she answered.

"Ho! Aren't you proud of it?"

She did her best to speak the truth without revealing her true circumstance. "I was only recently given the ring," she said. "I helped defend Kyrkenall from an ambush."

"Were there many foes?" he asked eagerly.

"There were four, but two were mages." Elenai warmed to the topic. "Kyrkenall was trapped by a spell, and the woman and her friend were ready to kill him."

"And then you leapt upon them?" Ortok suggested.

She didn't want to explain about the hearthstone battle, so she merely nodded affirmation. "Something like that."

Ortok's next question was lost to her, because she'd grown conscious of a scraping noise. Something was hacking at wood in the copse of birch ahead of them.

Elenai tensed. "Is there anyone else here?"

"Only the four of us."

"Are there any other ways in?"

"There is only the one. But there is no need for worry. Kalandra's voice alerts me when more come. That sound is only Kyrkenall. He is making arrows."

That made perfect sense, once her tired eyes had followed the furred, pointing finger and resolved the hunched shape in the midst of white trunks into the familiar outline of Kyrkenall. By unspoken agreement they diverted toward him. Hopefully he'd had enough time to himself.

The archer was pruning a pile of slim branches. His eerie black eyes flicked up to them as he brought his long, sharp knife down along the bark of a slender limb to pare off a nub.

"Ortok," Elenai said, "can you go collect some of those nuts? I want to talk to Kyrkenall alone for a few moments. We can share some wine when you get back."

"That would be most fine. It is long since I tasted something new. I will return." Ortok strode away.

Kyrkenall turned the limb, working deftly to strip the bark. "Where's N'lahr?"

"He's still talking to the image of Kalandra. He thinks that the Naor are marching on Arappa. And probably Vedessus."

"Most like."

She blinked in astonishment. "You knew? Neither of you said anything?"

"I guess we thought it was obvious." He paused for only a moment, his gaze faintly contemptuous, then looked back down at his work.

She ignored his unexpectedly rude manner. "Why didn't we divert then and there?"

"N'lahr was leading, not me. He said we were close to her."

Why was he being evasive? "You wanted to go find Kalandra anyway, didn't you?"

"Three Altenerai are better than two. Especially these three."

For the briefest moment, her weary brain thought he complimented her. Then she realized he referred to himself, N'lahr, and Kalandra. She was increasingly irritated at the sound of that woman's name.

Kyrkenall continued: "But it turns out she's not really here. So I'm going to find her."

Was he losing his mind? "How?"

"Her spirit thing said she was heading for the shifts near Ekhem. It's the best lead I've had in years. I'll start there."

"All by yourself?"

"I might as well be by myself." He indicated the distant building with an angry jab. "It's not as if he shares anything anyway, is it?"

"That's why you're angry?" Not that Naor were invading? Not that they'd risked everything to seek a woman who'd long since left?

"I'm not angry. I'm happy."

"You don't look happy."

He paused in his work and glanced up at her. "To be clear, I'm angry with N'lahr. But I'm happy to have an idea where Kalandra is."

"Do you really think she's still there?"

"I guess I'll find out, won't I?"

"You can't survive the storms in the deeps without a weaver. Not even your ring can protect against the worst of them."

"Then come with me."

She shook her head. He shrugged, then returned to working his knife along the stick. "I'll manage on my own. I always have."

"Like you managed at N'lahr's tomb? Like you would have managed at the Chasm Tower?" She spoke on, emboldened by his blindness to his own fallibility. Why couldn't he see? "You can't go alone!"

Ever so slowly, he looked up and met her eyes. "She may be alive. Maybe she's like Belahn, caught up in hearthstone magics. Maybe she's imprisoned. Maybe she's lost. Every moment could count, couldn't it?"

"That's right. Every moment could count. We have to put the people we're sworn to protect before ourselves and our friends in uniform. You know that." She saw Kyrkenall's jaw tighten, and decided on a different angle of attack. "I'm sorry that she wasn't here. Especially given—" Elenai's hand fluttered uselessly as her words failed her. "Especially because I didn't realize how close you two were."

His mouth turned further down at that. He rotated his half-trimmed branch.

"But if Kalandra's alive, she's managed to stay that way all this time without us. And if she isn't, it doesn't matter. Our duty to the realms comes first. She'd understand that. We have to get to Vedessus."

He looked up. "Saving Vedessus doesn't have anything to do with the fact your family lives there, does it? I don't hear you worrying about Arappa's outlying villages."

The truth of that point stung a little.

"You do realize that by the time we get to Vedessus the Altenerai chasing us will have told every Arappan they find that the three of us are criminals or traitors or murderers or whatever it is they think we are, thanks to Denaven."

She hadn't actually thought about that. Her mouth was suddenly dry.

What would her family and friends say to those falsehoods? Would they believe them? Even if they didn't—and she couldn't possibly imagine that her father and sister would be convinced she was a traitor—they'd be distraught with worry.

He laughed without humor. "We'd be fighting our own people *and* the Naor."

She steeled herself. "We'll have to convince them. We have to convince the rest of the Altenerai anyway. That doesn't change anything. None of this will be easy."

Ortok arrived with a large woven basket heaped with little black-topped nuts. "If you wish to share the wine now, I have food." He lifted the basket in proof.

Kyrkenall stared daggers at the big kobalin.

Elenai pulled the winesac from her belt and passed it over. "There's not much, but it's yours."

Ortok made a pleased noise as he grasped it. He smiled at her. "I have not had wine in a long span of nights."

"Fine," Kyrkenall barked. "Go drink it somewhere else."

"If that is what you both wish."

Elenai didn't really wish that. With Kyrkenall in such a difficult mood she would have preferred Ortok's bluntly honest company. Still, right now she needed to talk to Kyrkenall privately. "We'll share food later. Have as much of the wine as you like."

Ortok showed that immense display of teeth as he smiled even wider. "I thank you for this gift, Elenai Oddsbreaker." He walked away, warbling a strange melody in time with his stride.

Kyrkenall shook his head, then his eyes sought hers. The interruption seemed to have gentled him. "There's no winning this one, Squire. Sometimes you have to admit defeat."

She wanted to shout him down, but her counterarguments felt too weak. How could she win him over when she had no idea how they could win in Arappa?

"If you want to do something useful," he said in a more kindly tone, "some of the Altenerai weavers have a trick. They learned it from Rialla. And I figured, with the hearthstones, you might manage it."

She could muster only mild curiosity, for she struggled still for a means to change his mind. And to reassure herself that he was wrong. Besides, Kalandra's warning against the hearthstones gave her pause. "What's the trick?"

"You know how long it takes to cure arrows. Well, a skilled mage can accelerate the process. Dry them out. Straighten them. Harden them. All that."

She nodded. Manipulating something like a branch would be very different from shaping structure in the Shifting Lands, but she supposed the process was similar. Maybe she could even try it without the hearthstone. "I'd need some rest first."

"Well sure, but we can't take too much time."

"And I can't extend a whole lot of energy because we have a long ride to Arappa."

His voice rose in exasperation. "We're not going to Arappa!"

"Yes. We are," came a calm, familiar voice. N'lahr rounded the copse of trees. Elenai had forgotten just how exhausted he looked.

Kyrkenall set his work aside and climbed to his feet. "So! Friend to kobalin! Come to favor us with more mysterious half-truths?"

N'lahr halted a few paces off. He nodded to Elenai, but faced Kyrkenall. "What Kalandra said must have been hard for you."

"The hard part was learning just how little you both trusted me. Why didn't you tell me you were worried about the hearthstones—"

"I did."

"—and that you were sending Kalandra out to find more about them? You told Ortok. A kobalin. But not me! Who else did you tell?"

"No one."

Kyrkenall's voice was sure and sharp as a well-honed knife, and soft as a thrust from behind. "She was here when I first started looking. If you'd told me, I could have found her! Do you understand? It's your fault she's alone."

N'lahr's eyes shut, and it was perfectly obvious to Elenai that he'd long since understood that.

Ortok returned and stood watching quietly for a moment, then pointed to the commander. "Why are his eyes closed?"

Kyrkenall answered. "He's thinking about how much he's screwed up."

When the commander opened his eyes and spoke it was with weary patience. "She left only a few hours after the battle, remember? You were drinking deep with the survivors. There was no chance to talk about something like this. And then late that evening I 'died of my wounds.' I didn't plan to exclude you. It was poor timing. And what you said earlier was right. I didn't anticipate what might come if I were suddenly taken out. Any more than you do."

Kyrkenall scowled and averted his eyes

"You do not seem dead," Ortok observed quizzically.

Kyrkenall indicated the kobalin with a jab of his hand. "You might have at least mentioned you'd made friends with a kobalin lord. Why'd you send him instead of me?"

"With the war resolved, Kalandra was determined to get answers. Immediately. You know how she was. You were in your cups. But Ortok was free, and he owed me a debt of honor. I thought you might ride after. But I never got to tell you."

Elenai found herself reflecting how different things might have been if Kalandra had been just a little more patient. Maybe that would have made everything better. Or maybe Kyrkenall would have gotten lost with her, and N'lahr would still be trapped.

Kyrkenall let out a long, quavering breath. "Did her ghost have anything else to say?"

"It's not a ghost," N'lahr answered his friend. "Kalandra believes the hearthstones are innately tied to the stability of the various realms, fragments, and splinters. She suggests the storms have strengthened and the borders weakened because they've been removed to Darassus."

Kyrkenall swore. "Figures. So do we have to put them back, now?"

"Probably. If I had time to think of more questions, I suspect her image might share further conclusions. But we have to concentrate on the situation in Arappa. If we survive that, we can go after Kalandra." His mouth was tight. "I want to find her, too," he said slowly. "But we can't. She'd understand why."

Kyrkenall frowned again. "Don't you think the rest of the Altenerai are going to manage things? Tretton and Decrin know how to handle a siege. They have to have figured out what's going on with the Naor."

"I think that they'll act as best as they can. But Mazakan's had years to develop a way around our walls. We have to surprise him."

"With what?" Kyrkenall said. "All three of us? We might surprise him, but we won't impress him."

"I have a plan." N'lahr looked over to her. "It will require an expenditure of effort on Elenai's part. At least as great as that she used during that storm she faced."

She answered without hesitation. "Whatever it takes." Even if using the hearthstones would alter her irrevocably.

"I thought you'd say that."

"Is there to be fighting?" Ortok asked.

"We'll be fighting a lot of Naor," N'lahr told him. "But you'll have to follow behind. Once we get through the worst of the shifts it'll be hard for you to keep up. We're on horseback," he added.

The kobalin grunted and handed Elenai her empty winesac. "I can run. I want to kill Naor."

Kyrkenall rolled his eyes. "As much as I love a good scrape, I'm a little worried my friend here has lost his mind, because there are more than enough for all of us." He spread his hands. "We can't fight an army without one of our own."

N'lahr smiled thinly. "I'm going to get us one."

20

---~---

First Flight

The first attacks struck the night they fled Darassus. They allowed the squires to bed down for a few short hours before the dawn, and when it came time to rouse them they found six would never move again. In their sleep they'd been transformed into rigid, distorted, almost crystalline lumps of flesh.

They lost five more the night after they dared a howling storm in the Shifting Lands to get through to The Fragments, when they mistakenly thought they were far enough away to be safe. One of them was a fifth ranker Varama had been mentoring.

The assaults continued as they advanced into the wilds of The Fragments. For two nights Varama used the power of one of the hearthstones to weave a protective energy barrier about them, but on the second they were woken by the sentries to hear of three more casualties. The barrier had been breached.

As yet there was no sign of physical pursuit. Apparently there was no need.

"Why would there be. She can attack us whenever she wants all by herself," Sansyra said. Varama had invited the last remaining fifth ranker into their meeting. Rylin had always sensed that the young woman disliked him, although her dour tone that night likely had more to do with their situation than any lingering resentment.

Varama normally maintained a calm, pragmatic demeanor; even she, though, seemed drained and glum. She had called this middle-of-the-night meeting, yet so far she sat quietly. If Rylin didn't know her better, he'd have described her manner as despondent.

He let out an exasperated sigh. "Why is she targeting the squires instead of us?"

Varama answered. "Hasn't she been talking with you?"

"No." That was startling. "How do you mean?"

"She speaks to me, in dreams. She tells me that she'll slay more if I don't relinquish the larger, round hearthstone she called a 'keystone.' At first I thought she didn't act against us because she hoped to turn us to her bidding. But I think it's because she can't move against us while we wear the rings."

"Even with so many hearthstones at her command?" Sansyra asked.

"Perhaps not at such distance. But regrettably I have little sense of her powers. I'm stunned she can act at such range, much less find us so easily with all the hearthstones shut down. It may be that she's so sensitive to them now she can detect them regardless, or she may be honing in on the keystone specifically." Varama's gaze shifted briefly to the pack at her side and he could almost sense her frustration that she'd had so little time to examine the thing. She'd yet to understand why it was so important to the queen. Especially as it seemed to house significantly less power than any of the other hearthstones in their possession.

Her voice was strained. "I brought the squires along for protection, lest they be used as her pawns, or be slain in a fruitless attempt to stop us. But out of the seventy-three that rode out with us fourteen have perished." She delivered her words with an edge of steel. "These young people are a finite and precious resource. They are carefully prepared, both before and after entering the corps, to serve their fellow citizens even to the end of their own existence. And Leonara has murdered them indifferently." Her hands shook with anger as she finished.

"You're not to blame, Alten," Sansyra said. "All of your choices—"

Varama cut her off. "I miscalculated. I couldn't know the extent of our queen's current power, but I was well enough acquainted with her ruthlessness to factor in this kind of response."

Rylin dearly wished there were something more for him to do. He hated this helplessness more than anything else they were experiencing. "We're going to have to separate," he suggested.

"Yes." Varama nodded once, apparently satisfied he'd come to the conclusion she'd hoped. "Sansyra, I'm placing you in charge of the squires.

You're to divide the remainder into five squads and lead them to Alantris at a spacing of maximum visual distance. Use lanterns to signal. If you keep a good pace you should be there by evening."

"Yes, Alten." Rylin saw her dark shape nod. "Do you think that she may be able to attack us while we're awake?"

"I think it a possibility we should entertain. But she hasn't done so thus far, and placing the squires farther from Rylin and me and the hearthstones should improve your odds. Here's a note detailing our findings. Share the contents with the five squad leaders and have them report only to Aradel. Destroy the writing and deny if others press."

Sansyra nodded her understanding and quickly roused the squires. After their departure, Rylin volunteered to let the exhausted Varama grab a little more rest. She hadn't slept since the second attack. She returned to the fireside, kicked off her boots, lay down in her blanket, and was out almost instantly. Rylin smiled a little at the ease of it.

She had adjusted much faster than he to life on the road. He hadn't realized how soft he'd gotten. He missed warm sheets, well-cooked food, and regular sex. Not to mention heretofore unappreciated comforts like a lack of imminent threat of death, or an absence of seeing those under your command attacked when you had no recourse.

He had to admit he wasn't used to worry. And he naively hadn't realized how much uncertainty would accompany adventure. It hadn't been like this in the war when he'd been told where to go and had only to dull the doubt of his next encounter in the echoed bravado of his comrades. He recalled now that Asrahn used to say "body training is the easy part" of becoming a soldier. Rylin had associated that with encouragement to pay attention to the more dull bookwork that made up a fair portion of each squire's day, but it seemed clearer now that Asrahn was referencing emotional discipline.

He set about ordering his thoughts. Sending the squires ahead would seem to give them the best chance for survival, and the redundant plan for communicating with Aradel, former alten and current governor of The Fragments, would virtually ensure the truth would reach her. If Varama was right—and she almost always was—Kyrkenall and Elenai had already met Aradel and had started a campaign to convince the other four governors to act decisively about the queen's conspiracy. He and Varama would serve as additional witnesses, a less-than-glorious role but contributory to the cause.

That, though, assumed that all had gone well with Kyrkenall and Elenai. Denaven and his search party might have found them, and Rylin had few illusions as to their fate if that were the case.

Not for the first time, his thoughts turned to Lasren. While he dismissed the idea that his friend had been part of the conspiracy, Lasren might well believe whatever Denaven told him, without question. He hoped he wouldn't commit some grievous error before learning the truth.

And he hoped he wouldn't end up facing his friend in battle. If they were to come to blows, one of them would end up dead, and Rylin wasn't entirely sure it would be Lasren. What he lacked in sorcery, his larger friend could make up for in superior reach.

Rylin shook his head. Surely it wouldn't come to that. He was starting to overthink everything. He'd have to decide on the demands of the moment. And right now, he and Varama needed a breakfast prepared.

Eventually he sensed a predawn still in the air, an impending sense of excitement, as if the land knew the sun would shortly come. He took the porridge off the fire, scooped a hot helping, cleaned up what little wasn't packed up, then woke Varama. As she got up, he headed off to get the lay of the land by new light.

It felt good to move. Their camp lay only a few hundred paces downhill from a rocky outcrop that had commanded a fine view yesterday evening and would probably be brilliant this morning. He climbed up to it and stepped right to the edge. With that first red sliver of the sun warming the sky on his right, he could pick out sparkles reflecting in the swift-flowing stream running through the valley floor hundreds of feet below. He lingered, watching the color conjured from varied grasses and the tree-skirted hills rising one above the other, deciding this was one of the most splendid vistas he'd ever seen. He relished the sights even as he searched for signs of unlikely pursuers.

"You're a little close to the rim, aren't you?"

Rylin hadn't heard Varama's approach. She gripped a sturdy young tree several paces away and smoothed back a stray strand from her high blue forehead.

She was forever noticing things he hadn't, so Rylin took a long look at the rock he stood upon jutting into the abyss. It seemed securely rooted to the cliff side. "I'm fine."

"Yes, I think you've probably seen all you need to see," Varama said. And that, too, wasn't especially normal, because she didn't make a habit of useless talk.

"I think you're afraid of heights," he said slowly. He couldn't help the grin rising on his face.

"Not exactly."

"No? So this doesn't make you nervous?" Rylin raised his right leg and extended it over the edge.

"You look foolish."

"Really?" He hopped back and forth from leg to leg. "Don't tell me you don't like dancing?"

"You're not the least bit funny."

Seeing her expression, he had a hard time leaving off, but stepped toward her anyway. "That's the most I've smiled in days. It's nice to see you have some weakness, after all."

"I *am* overly patient with idiots," Varama said brusquely. "Now come along."

Rylin turned for a last look from his vantage point. And froze. To the northeast a large column of black smoke climbed toward the heavens. It might have been a wildfire, except that there hadn't been any lightning last night. And it was far too large to be a cookfire.

He felt an ominous foreboding. "That cloud looks an awful lot like one from the war."

"When the Naor were burning villages," Varama confirmed behind him. "They're here."

He stared, and his hands tightened into fists. Could they be this unlucky?

"Our squires." Varama said nothing more.

"The smoke's well east of here," Rylin said, hoping that meant Sansyra and the others hadn't blundered into a huge Naor force.

Varama caught his attention a second time. "Look. Directly ahead."

How had he missed that? There, suspended on currents of air, was an enormous bird.

No. Not a bird. A ko'aye. He hadn't seen one of the famed creatures since his early squire days, when they were dangerous and capable war allies. Long tapering wedges backlit by the dawn glare kept the creature afloat, stretching more than twelve times the length of its narrow, flexible body. A slender, oval head was thrust forward, clearly focused upon them as it glided closer.

"There's no rider," Varama said.

The ko'aye hadn't really understood the peace agreement forged with the Naor after N'lahr's death, especially why the Altenerai couldn't help them drive the Naor from their hunting grounds. They'd vowed never again to ally with Altenerai, and some had reputedly sworn vengeance against them, which is why seeing one wasn't entirely reassuring. Rylin's hand drifted to his hilt as the thing closed on their position.

"It's Lelanc," Varama decided. "Aradel's. Get away from the edge."

"I'm not going to fall." He stared, not for the first time wondering how Aradel had maintained her bond with her war mount when no one else had.

"She needs room to land, so get back." Varama sounded faintly annoyed, as she always did when she had to repeat herself.

Rylin stepped quickly aside, for the wyrm was even now closing on the cliff's edge. He noted that the graceful flier was wearing an odd-shaped saddle.

Lelanc latched her front claws to the outcrop Rylin had recently quitted and beat her wings madly as her lower half swung under the rock and impacted the supporting earth with a ground-shaking thud. The stirred air rushed past Rylin as he backstepped toward Varama to cede more space. The wind rider pulled herself up, still flapping as back talons audibly scratched stone. Once the majority of her weight was above the edge, she folded her wings and lowered her swanny neck, so her head hung only a few feet before the two Altenerai.

A ko'aye was both vaguely birdlike and lizard-like, with toothed beak and feathers, but Lelanc's strange wide eyes struck him as preternaturally lucid and sharp, their ruddy orange color so bright it practically glowed. She was mostly a warm russet color with white and darker brown markings, but her underside was a creamy ivory. The tapering tail, and its wickedly barbed end, dangled out of sight beneath the precipice.

Lelanc dipped her crested head respectfully and spoke in a voice marked with clicks and whistles, as the sounds were shaped deep in her throat. The effect was oddly musical. "With pleasure I come again into your company, high-browed crafter." Her unwinking eyes met their own with disquieting intensity.

Varama answered with an incline of her head. "With pleasure I greet you, catcher of winds. How fare your nest mates?"

Lelanc opened her beaked mouth to let out a mournful trilling noise. "All ride the red winds." She arched her neck a little but kept her head on level with Varama's. "And have you a mate now, and hatchlings?"

"No."

"I sorrow for you, then."

Varama extended a hand toward Rylin. "This is Alten Rylin. He would be your friend."

Lelanc's head tilted, and those glowing eyes fixed upon him. "That is a fine thought," she said after a time. "Who does not have need of friends? But it is hard to know among you humans. Your scents do not show me the truth of your words."

"If you recall, Lelanc, I always spoke truth to you," Varama said. "He would be a true friend."

Lelanc bowed her head with great solemnity. "I will believe you."

Rylin found Varama's introduction strangely touching. "It's an honor to meet you, Lelanc." He presented himself with a courtly bow.

Lelanc responded with a regal nod.

"We're looking for Aradel," Varama said, as though visiting a neighborhood rather than fleeing to an uncertain sanctuary.

"I guessed this when Rylin signaled from the cliff side."

"Signaled?" Rylin repeated, and then the matter was clear to him. His little cliffside jig.

"Yes. I diverted. I was surprised to hear no whistle."

"Mine is at our camp. We weren't expecting to see you today," Varama said. "How is Aradel?"

"She is on the ground, looking for Naor. I seek them from the air."

Varama sounded resigned. "How many Naor? How close?"

"There are many numbers. As near as that smoke." She indicated the ugly black column with a turn of her head. "Aradel stopped to talk with fleeing friends and sent me aloft to seek enemies. I should not tarry."

Rylin let out a little sigh of relief. That burning was miles off their intended route. Probably the squires were all right, for now.

"We need to speak with Aradel," Varama said.

"Then come with me." The creature nodded to the battered sorrel seat strapped to her back.

Varama shook her head quickly.

"I'll go," Rylin volunteered.

Lelanc thrust her head at him. "You, whom I have just met, wish to sit upon my back?"

Rylin understood immediately that he'd committed a breach of courtesy. "I apologize for my effrontery," he said quickly.

Lelanc considered him with unwinking eyes and then stretched her head closer to Varama. Two small arched nostrils above her beak flared, and then she withdrew her head. "I think you must travel the horse trail, Varama. I recall that you fear leaving ground. Look for Aradel in the valley north. Take the higher opening, for the Naor are nearer the lower. Rylin, have you ridden the air before?"

"Never." His heart sped at the thought, and he wasn't sure if it was unease or excitement or both.

"If you wish to trust me, then I suppose I will trust you. Do you have weapons?"

Rylin assumed she meant some that might be effective from the air, as his sword was plainly at his side. "In the camp. I'll get them."

"Hurry."

By the time he returned, Lelanc had clambered up and around to stand on solid ground looking out over the valley, head snaking to east then west.

While she scanned the sky, Rylin and Varama attached his bow sheath and quiver to the saddle. He strapped their only two javelins sideways across his back, then Lelanc again called that they must hurry.

"I'll do as Lelanc suggested," Varama said to Rylin, speaking quickly, "and be along as soon as I can manage. Tell Aradel what we've learned."

"All of it?" Rylin wondered if he needed to explain, but Varama's sharp-eyed gaze let him know she understood the implications of his simple question.

"Every last detail."

He nodded.

"The talking must cease and we must fly," an impatient Lelanc insisted.

"I'll help him with the saddle." Varama motioned Rylin forward.

As Rylin climbed into place, he found the wind rider too wide to straddle, necessitating that his legs be slung with knees bent to either side of the saddle itself. Only his booted feet touched the wind rider's short body feathers.

He was surprised when Varama slid two arms about his waist, though he quickly realized she was belting him in place. She touched a buckle slightly off-center. "Pull here if you need release immediately."

He couldn't possibly imagine why he'd want to unstrap himself from Lelanc while in the air, but he held off asking about that. "If you hate heights, how do you know so much about how this saddle works?"

"I designed them." A hint of a smile turned up Varama's lips.

"What are we going to do about the Naor?" He meant to ask a more nuanced question, but he felt Lelanc stir beneath him and sensed they were out of time.

Varama answered swiftly. "Drive them back."

Was that a joke? He'd meant her to be more specific, and had wondered how the Naor raid would affect the rest of their problems.

Lelanc unfolded her wings and sent a gust blooming again. Her long neck turned sideways so she could observe him. "You are ready now?"

"I am." He resisted the impulse to click his tongue, as he'd have done with his horse.

"Grip the front of the saddle if you need. Varama, fare you well." Lelanc leaned out over the cliff edge and Rylin's heart hammered as he felt her gather her weight into her back legs. Then, without any further notice, she flung herself into the air.

Rylin grabbed for a handhold, but found none as he was jerked back by the sudden drop. His heart slammed with terror, as if desperate to communicate to him that he was shortly to die. He might have screamed, except that he didn't seem to have any air in his lungs.

For a few stomach-lurching moments they plummeted toward the greenery waving along the valley floor, then the wind caught Lelanc's wings and she leveled out.

Rylin closed hands around the pommel at last, clenching it with whitened fingers. Lelanc beat her wings to gain more altitude, and Rylin felt his body lurching up and down against the saddle in a way very different from riding a horse. It felt almost as though he were kneeling in a boat on rough waters.

As Lelanc tilted her wings and rose into a glide, the wind eased, only stirring his hair. He looked out upon the distant valley below. His heart still thumped frantic alarm, but he laughed in a mix of relief and delight, then let out a whoop and raised one hand in an exultant salute as they soared on. The view was somehow far better than that from the outcrop. Spines of tree-steepled mountains swept far east and west, green and brown and lovely, ornamented by shining strands of silvery-blue creeks and rivers, mirroring the perfect cerulean sky.

Yet marring an otherwise glorious experience, he could now see several dark pillars rising skyward, marking what was probably horrific destruction below. Only one had been visible before, but now clearly there were five columns of smoke, fading in strength as they stretched into the distant east. Rylin thought to direct Lelanc over to the nearest, but noted suddenly there were no reins, nor any clear method of communication over the rush of wind. He didn't dare kick at the ko'aye beneath him. Apparently he was not to be in control of their route.

Rylin had fought the Naor as a squire, upon the plains of Kanesh. It was there, too, that he'd first seen the fierce aerial hunters. Most had served as scouts, only a handful ever welcoming mounted companionship. But it had never occurred to him to inquire about how the rare couples coordinated in the air.

He wondered again what had kept Lelanc and Aradel together after the war. He'd met the famous alten briefly in Kanesh, long years before, but could hardly say to have known her well enough to guess the reason her bond with the wind rider remained so strong. The short, no-nonsense woman had been N'lahr's second-in-command and handpicked successor, just as N'lahr had been Renik's. Traditionally, the previous commander's opinion counted for much, but after N'lahr's death the queen had overridden his express wishes, and those of the Altenerai, and chosen her own, after which Aradel had resigned. At the time, Rylin had been a little disappointed with her, thinking it was poor form on her part. Now he understood that she must have guessed how things would rot under Denaven's stewardship.

Aradel had been instrumental in many of the victories late in the war. Kyrkenall might have been N'lahr's shadow, Kalandra and Asrahn his chief counselors, but Aradel had been his right hand, the alten he most trusted to lead large forces in his absence, sometimes on the back of Lelanc. While other Altenerai were perfectly capable—and Enada was justly famed as a daring cavalry officer—Aradel was the only one who could duplicate anything like N'lahr's famed battlefield improvisations.

They passed through a cleft in the pine-covered mountains and Lelanc slowed and dropped altitude. There was no missing the distant, snaking line of Naor troops moving west in two columns. Rylin's eyes narrowed. This was an especially large force, probably numbering in the high hundreds, at least. Ranged out well in advance was a contingent of horse troops, some of whom neared a rocky, scrub-covered hill where a band of mailed warriors from The Fragments had set up a defensive post. Hidden as they were by the foliage, he couldn't get an exact count, but they didn't seem terribly numerous. Nearly two dozen Naor had dismounted to charge the hill. Dozens more lay twisted and still at its base.

Lelanc trilled a warning call and banked lower. "I have been gone too long!" she cried. Her voice carried more clearly back to him than he'd have guessed.

Rylin pulled a javelin. Had his preparations put Aradel and others in jeopardy? He couldn't have left without grabbing weapons, so there was no point in regret, and certainly no time.

He could just make out bands of unarmed men and women peering out from the forest highland up from the lower rise where the defenders had taken position. Carts and animals had been abandoned near the hill. That explained the strange choice of battle sites. Aradel was protecting refugees.

"My sister is attacked!" Lelanc shouted.

Sister? There were no other ko'aye, so Lelanc had to mean Aradel, almost surely the woman he saw shouting orders to the defenders from the front. Why wasn't she wearing her khalat?

Because Aradel had resigned from the corps, of course. He shook his head at himself and prepared to do what he could to thin out the enemies on their approach.

Lelanc dropped suddenly, presumably anticipating a landing somehow on the defender's ridge. Rylin's stomach somersaulted. He gripped tight to the saddle, alarmed by the amount of pressure against the belt. He prayed it was secure.

A little lightheaded, Rylin nonetheless sent his javelin hurtling through an enemy shoulder. He took out another before Lelanc's shadow scattered their horses. His javelin supply exhausted, Rylin whipped up his bow and sought more targets.

Javelin fire and archery were trickier than he supposed from the back of a ko'aye. Lelanc was a steadier platform than a horse, but provided a more narrow field of fire owing to the vast spread of her wings. Still, he killed three before the horsemen swung too far away to right and left.

The Naor wouldn't abandon the attack, but there'd be a delay before they regrouped to assault the slope. A quick look confirmed the defenders had finished off one wave and were feathering another ten to fifteen Naor as they struggled for the top.

"Can you get us down?" Rylin shouted.

"There's no room to get to ground." Though there was no condemnation in Lelanc's voice, he felt the fool. Of course there wasn't. The rough, scrub-covered earth was littered with Naor dead and weapons, and otherwise filled by the defenders and the living enemy. Even supposing Lelanc could settle, she'd be exposed and unlikely to be able to get airborne once more.

"I'll drop!" Rylin called up. And to think he'd been wondering why a quick saddle release would be necessary. He'd practiced spell-assisted jumps as an upper ranker, but he'd never imagined he'd try one from a moving platform higher than a roof.

Rylin barely had time to reflect that this wasn't one of his better ideas. He grabbed bow and arrows, and called up his sorcerous energies as Lelanc drew closer and closer to the hill, a good thirty feet below.

"You will be hurt," Lelanc replied with a backward look.

"Can you get lower? Or slow down? A little?"

"I will turn. It will be dangerous."

He didn't know if she meant for him or for her. He could make out the clang of weaponry, the shouts and cries as the next wave of fighting had joined while he searched for a clear spot. The wind rider banked, and her words were lost in her warning vocalization.

Rylin ignored every instinct of self-preservation, pulled at the release mechanism, and pushed off the saddle. He just missed the downsweep of Lelanc's wing as the ground closed fast, but his magical sight was active and he aligned the threads of his will with the vagrant wind currents, which he sent to correct his angle of descent.

The gust hit him from below, knocking his legs askew, and he adjusted and frantically sent another blast, choking with dust and the scent of sweat, pine, and blood. It slowed him mere handspans from the ground, so that when he struck, it was as though he'd only dropped from six or seven feet onto the uneven slope. Still the jolt lost him hold of both bow and quiver as he threw out his hands for balance.

There was no time to seek them, for one of the nearby Naor had already turned to attack. Rylin drew his sword in a flash of steel and lopped clean through the man's arm before he could block. The bearded attacker screamed and fell to join dead or dying Naor scattered leaf-like before him.

The largest number of bodies lay uphill clustered about a short, dark woman he knew for Aradel. There was no missing her for a warrior of stunning skill. She caught a blow on her shield at the same moment she skewered another opponent, then maneuvered the dying man into the first as she parried a third.

An attacker shouted from the rear, swinging wildly. Rylin's khalat absorbed a blow, but the man's strength knocked him forward. He pivoted and parried a spear thrust before sending threads of fear coursing toward the three closest Naor. One actually turned to stumble downhill; the other stood gaping.

He cut into an enemy shoulder, then butted him in the face with his sword hilt. At Aradel's shout, defenders pierced the surprised Naor with arrows, and they dropped, all but silent in their death throes.

That was the end of the current assault, but before Rylin clambered over the bodies to join the beckoning friendly soldiers, he scanned the battlefield.

Lelanc swept after a trio of fleeing Naor. That was promising, except that another group of horsemen was only a few minutes away from reaching the hill, some three dozen strong. It wasn't going to be easy, but if they could hold that group off, they might have time to get away, because the column of Naor foot soldiers he'd seen from Lelanc's saddle was at least an hour out. It would all depend on how swiftly the refugees could move. His eyes raked up the slope beyond the rocky defense and saw at least ten faces peering down at him from the trees, some of them very young. His heart fell. This was no place for children.

He bent over a dead Naor to retrieve his bow when he realized that the defenders were still beckoning and shouting intently. "Alten! Help! The governor's been injured!"

He hurried past the panting, frantic-looking Alantran soldiers in dark ring mail. It was only when he stepped around a young pine bole that he saw Aradel down, holding her left thigh while two ripped open her leggings to apply a tourniquet. He stepped over a bearded Naor corpse staring sightlessly at the commotion, passed his bow to a bright-eyed woman warrior, and bent beside the governor.

She was older than he'd remembered, and her flat brown face was hardly glamorous, streaked as it was with blood and sweat. Strong white teeth were bared in pain. Her helmet lay beside her and her damp hair was flattened to her scalp.

Rylin wasn't a healer, but he could tell when someone was bleeding out. That tourniquet wasn't going to be enough to save her.

The woman saw her fate in his look. It startled her only for a moment. Then she was once more composed. "Should have worn the khalat." Her voice was a husky growl. "Rylin, isn't it?"

"Yes. Let me see if there's anything I can do. You, get her some wine." He said this to the warrior woman he'd handed his bow but didn't look at her, for he was already opening his sight to the inner world.

When he tapped into his magical strength he felt lightheaded. He was near his limit. He saw the overlay of patterns and the countless ruptured threads of Aradel's life leaking energy away. Gods! How did healers do it? How could you even tell what thread went where?

He froze long enough to be worried that he waited too long, then fought off panic and decided he'd best do something for Aradel's life energy paled with every heartbeat. There were just so many threads. He started touching them together and strengthening them. Each expenditure of energy linked one, probably the wrong one. With the fifth connection he felt he was trying to bail out a sinking boat with a spoon.

Aradel's hand gripped his arm, and he heard his name hissed. She was urging him to stop, to listen. "Don't waste it," she said. "There are more on the way."

Waste it? She meant his magical energies. He dropped out of the inner world.

Aradel's eyes were fever bright as they bored into his. Her voice, quavering, yet had strength. "Naor are invading The Fragments and Arappa both," she said.

Could the news be any worse? "Both realms? Raiders, or armies?"

"Armies. Thousands strong. Mazakan himself is attacking Arappa. He's riding for the city of Vedessus."

He felt blood draining from his face. Mazakan, king of the Naor, warrior supreme. Fated only to die by the hand of N'lahr the Grim, wielding Irion, both lost for seven years.

Aradel winced, then resumed in a softer voice. "Once they have The Fragments and Arappa a third army's coming for Erymyr. Caught a scout and made him talk. They're—"

The young woman, oblivious to Aradel's words, pushed in at his shoulder and drowned her out. "Can't you save her?" she pleaded.

He could only shake his head. Right now he was trying to honor the dying woman's final wish, which was to be heard. And the last words of a brilliant veteran were more precious than jewels.

Aradel's eyes narrowed in irritation, and she gritted her teeth. Her grip was unnaturally tight, and he had the sense the moment she released him she would be gone. She locked eyes with him. "Third army is coming," she whispered. "For death blow against the Allied Realms. Some kind of secret weapon. You've got to get queen and Denaven to hear." Her voice grew softer. "Evacuate settlements to Alantris. High ground east of Alantris. Lure Naor into ambush . . ." She blinked, slowly, and he felt her hand slackening. But then it tightened and her paling eyes wheeled. Her voice was a croak. "Promise me you'll save Alantris!"

When dying, she was more afraid for The Fragments and its capital than herself. That sense of dedication brought a lump to his throat, and his reply was hoarse with contained emotion. "I promise."

That seemed to appease her. Her fingers slipped from his arm.

"Where's Kyrkenall?" he asked quickly.

Confusion washed across Aradel's face. As her arm hit the ground he saw that her lips still moved.

Rylin leaned down as the young woman beside him wailed in sorrow.

By putting his ear to her lips he could just hear Aradel's last words. They had nothing to do with Kyrkenall. "Thank Lelanc. Shield my people. Hail Altenerai."

Her eyes relaxed and stared only into the great mystery.

The woman beside him wept inconsolably, and tears tracked the bloodsmeared faces of the two who'd given up trying to bandage their governor.

Numb, Rylin climbed to his feet. With N'lahr gone, Aradel had been their best chance. And now she, too, was dead, expired beside him because he'd never studied the healing arts. A living legend had perished practically in his arms and he hadn't been able to do a thing.

A fractured corps, a traitorous queen, a second Naor war.

And Kyrkenall, apparently, hadn't met with Aradel at all. Did that mean he and Elenai were dead?

What should he do?

He looked down at the small, dark woman in the old armor and realized he'd been luckier than her, at least. And probably less deserving of it. Would he be thinking of duty in his final moments? He glanced up at the pale faces of farmfolk and fighters, alike in expressions of desolation no matter the differing shapes. He felt his jaw quivering. He noticed that she still wore the sacred sapphire. Aradel might have resigned, and never again donned her hard-won khalat, but she hadn't laid the ring aside. Once Altenerai, always Altenerai. He put his hand to his heart in salute, then turned to see the Naor approaching in two separate groups, front and left, almost close enough for him to make out individual faces.

This was no time to mourn. Somehow he had to lead six tired, wounded, and demoralized defenders against almost thirty Naor horsemen.

21

The Rider on the Black Horse

Rylin grabbed his sword from beside Aradel's body. No point in wiping it now. There'd be more blood on it shortly.

The blade shook in his hand until he tightened his grip. Between his earlier spell use and his fruitless efforts to save the governor he was mostly spent. A quick glance over the troops didn't give him a great deal of confidence. They looked bereft, staring dumbly at Aradel's body or out at the Naor riding on their position. Up slope, among the trees, he heard wailing from the civilians. If he had a few moments he might be able to organize them into a makeshift spear wall, for surely they had knives they could tie to tree limbs.

But he didn't have enough moments. He ordered the dull defenders to range themselves and got a quick count of their arrows. They had eleven.

"Hold your fire 'til my command," he said. "Each shot has to count!"

Either eager or foolhardy, one enemy rider pressed hard toward the hill,

two horselengths ahead of his companions. He threw himself from the
saddle and started up the slope without a backward glance.

Rylin snapped a command. "You, woman, aim for his throat. The rest
of you continue to hold."

She might still have been sniffling, but the young woman dropped the
lead warrior halfway up. Six more came after, but nine arrows brought
them down. A dark-eyed youth nocked his final shaft in readiness for the
next wave of shouting, painted enemies.

Rylin spied his own quiver lying just beyond the rise. Lucky, except that
four Naor were halfway up the hill toward it already.

"Hold your line," he called, and vaulted a sheltering boulder to advance
across the field of Naor bodies.

He met the first two attackers as they reached his former landing area,
knocking one tentative swipe aside before driving his blade through a
bearded face. He backstepped a mad thrust from a snarling redhead, kicked
his knee from the side, then hacked deep through his abdomen. As that one
dropped, screaming, Rylin reached for the quiver's strap with his left hand
and nearly got himself impaled on a well-cast spear. He snatched it up from
where it stood vibrating in the earth, reversed it, and pitched it at the Naor
who'd thrown it.

The warrior's hands wrapped the haft as it tore through his leather cuirass, and his eyes met Rylin's in surprise before he collapsed, blood drib-
bling from his mouth.

Rylin grabbed the strap and took in the field. Lelanc had swooped in
again to scatter some of the horsemen, but they were regrouping. As best
as Rylin could judge, they had only a short while before a wave of ten hit,
and then a further fifteen or so weren't far behind. Still, they wouldn't reach
the hill at the same time, which made matters a little less impossible.

The defenders eyed him with respect as he rejoined them. That was
something—they no longer looked as though they were on the verge of
crumbling.

The young woman had seemed a fine archer, so he handed her his arrows. He had a paltry dozen. A man with a bandaged arm passed Rylin a
watersac and he took it, but he addressed the woman. "Take the leaders
down as soon as they hit the hill. You." He pointed to a muscular man beside the one with the wound. "Gather the closest spears while bandage-
arm here watches."

The man nodded once and leapt over, keeping low as he searched among
the dead and dying enemies. His friend kept a tense running commentary
on the approaching Naor.

Rylin nodded to the remaining defenders, then took a quick swig. Stale water was rarely so refreshing as when downed during combat.

Soon the respite was over. The spear-gatherer nearly got skewered when one of the foremost riders hurled his weapon. It clattered off a boulder an arm's length from where he was bent. Poles in hand, the warrior quickly clambered to join his friends, snagging even the late-coming weapon on his way.

"These Naor look different," the woman soldier remarked. Her voice had lost its former tremble.

She was right. The incoming lot had white feathers in their helms, and their armored shirts were a mix of leather and bronze plate. Rylin wasn't as seasoned as the previous generation of Altenerai, who knew each Naor tribe by sight, but grasping at an old memory of something Asrahn had said, he thought it likely these warriors were from Almaza, one of the most hospitable and populated of Naor realms, and the second Mazakan had "unified." They were supposed to be a cut above the regular soldiers. Damn.

"It's only three to one," Rylin told his people, "and we have a hill, and a crack archer."

"And an alten," the young woman returned, then asked, impulsively: "What's your name?"

He half smiled. Everyone recognized the old guard by sight, even if they'd never seen one in person, but he was still unknown, no matter three years with the ring. She must have been distracted when Aradel had greeted him. "What's yours?"

The question seemed to surprise her. "Denalia." She nocked her arrow, and let fly as the first three started up the hill.

She took down two, but more followed in their wake. Screaming enthusiastically in the front was a warrior with a scarred bronze face and large round shield held high. Denalia scored a hit against his shoulder, but it stuck in the armor and bobbed like a strange flag as he kept on.

Rylin told her to continue shooting at the more distant ones to slow the advance, and commanded the others to reserve one spear but loose the rest as they wished.

Then he leapt into the fight.

The Naor leader thrust a barbed spear at his chest. Rylin sidestepped and knocked the polearm out of line with a sword blow. The attacker swung his shield into Rylin's off arm. Ignoring the stinging pain, Rylin threw himself forward and drove his blade through the gap under the warrior's left arm.

The leader cried out, then shouted again as bandage-arm thrust a spear deep into the Naor's back. Rylin backstepped as blood spattered in his direction and the enemy warrior tumbled.

Then the rest of the Naor ran up, and his whole life was reduced to instincts developed over the course of years of practice bouts. In the heat of battle there was no time to debate which sort of parry to use or when to strike, there was only action honed by experience, as one bearded, deadly adversary after another lunged at him. Here one was jabbing with a spear, there another coming in from the side with a sword. He felled both with deft footwork and lightning strikes, then maneuvered another to trip over one of the corpses. This lot was tougher, and fought on even with gory wounds. Twice they got past Rylin, only to be stopped by a trio of defenders with spears, and once Denalia shot one flanking him at point-blank range.

Finally, though, he stood panting, aching from where his khalat had fended off several blows that would leave him bruised. He thought to see ten or more Naor on the heels of these when he looked out.

Only then did he observe that his weary band had reinforcement, of a sort.

Another alten had arrived at the base of their hill, astride a coal-black horse. A heavy cloak trailed behind the rider, obscuring parts of a khalat, and a helm concealed the person's features. Rylin could just make out a sapphire glittering on the sword-wielding hand that deftly eviscerated one of three remaining Almaza riders. The rest of their looming enemies hadn't vanished, exactly. One lay in the grasses separate from his head; another, dead or mortally wounded, was being dragged away by his horse. Several more had been cast off from frightened horses and lay twitching among the grasses, with no mark upon them. There was no mistaking the signs. This alten was a weaver.

In the haze of battle, it took longer than Rylin would like to guess the alten's identity. Given that the newcomer employed magic, unless this was Kalandra returned from beyond, it could only be one of three people: Denaven, who almost surely wouldn't ride alone to their assistance; Belahn, who would be broader through the shoulders; or Cerai, that famously independent alten who'd gone her own way ever since Denaven's appointment as commander. Rylin had met her on only a couple of occasions, and hadn't seen her since he'd been awarded his ring.

She-who-was-probably-Cerai downed her final opponent with an exact and deadly swipe.

In moments, the sapphire-bearing rider had reached the summit, her horse somehow, incredibly, picking its way up the slope through the scree and corpses. Rylin marveled over the animal, a creature of midnight and nightmares. It stood eerily still, like a gameboard piece, as the alten swung down from the saddle and took off her helmet, cloak unfurling behind her.

He hadn't remembered Cerai was so striking.

There was no one single feature of the woman that captivated him, though he liked the high arch of her eyebrows, the fine straight nose with an upturned tip, the long-lashed, azure eyes, the mane of lusterous black hair. Though fifteen or more years his senior, the lines about her eyes and cheeks were less detraction than refinement to her allure. Rylin's lust was tempered with the appreciation one might feel at sight of a natural wonder, like a perfect sunset over wave-kissed cliffs.

She paused in front of him and raised her hand. He shifted his sword to his left and saluted her in return, still panting from his exertions

"Hail, Alten." Her voice was warm and a little husky. "Rylin, isn't it?"

That was exactly what Aradel had said. "Alten Cerai. Yes, I'm Rylin."

"Any others with you?"

He assumed she meant Altenerai. "Varama is on her way. Aradel was commanding when I got here, but . . ."

Cerai's lips tightened; she asked where Aradel was, then pushed brusquely through to the body before kneeling next to it, hand to the fallen woman's chest. Rylin glanced at the faces of the rest of the soldiers, and found renewed grief. He didn't need to open his eyes to the inner world to guess Cerai was examining her old comrade for any lingering signs of life. And he wondered: skilled as Cerai was, might she be able to pull Aradel back from the final realm? Might there still be a faint spark to set blazing once more?

Apparently not, for after a long while Cerai looked stonily down, her own hand pressed across her heart. She stood slowly, continuing to regard her fallen comrade.

From somewhere behind came the whoosh of enormous wings. Rylin turned to see Lelanc descending close to their hill, her clawed back feet angled lower so that they would first strike the earth. She touched lightly to the clear ground at the bottom of the rise and carried on at an ungainly run that brought her bounding up, over, or around debris, with surprising speed.

He felt heartsick as the ko'aye folded her wings and searched the gathered humans with her huge luminous eyes, heedless that her left rear leg pressed a Naor corpse more deeply into the soil. "Aradel?" she asked directly of Rylin, ignoring the weeping soldiers around him.

Rylin answered softly. "I'm sorry, Lelanc. She's dead."

A short outraged cry slipped from the ko'aye's beaked mouth, and her head thrust forward, followed closely by the rest of her feathered body, which scattered the startled mourners.

As Lelanc peered down upon the still form of her longtime companion, Rylin turned to Cerai quietly. "Can you get the defenders organized? There's some refugees higher up slope."

"I'll get them moving," Cerai asserted, picking up on his hint; after a last look down at Aradel, she stepped away. The snap in her voice brooked no opposition as she addressed the soldiers. "Time to go! The Naor aren't that far behind. Hop to it."

Only Denalia lingered, wiping tears from her eyes. "We need to transport the body," she said.

"Of course. Lelanc needs a moment, though."

Denalia nodded absently before stepping away.

Rylin waited beside Lelanc, watching the creature. He saw the feathered neck rising and perceived a mournful trill growing slowly into a resonant growl before exploding into a startling, ear-rending shriek of pain, as though a sword had been driven into a sheet of metal and then dragged through it blade first. All the humans turned to them in alarm while Rylin resisted the insane urge to draw his weapon. The ko'aye fixed him with a fierce expression that made him feel like a rodent under the gaze of a stooping hawk.

"I will slay many Naor for this," the creature vowed.

He wasn't sure what to say but figured he should calm her before she flew off and got herself killed. "Some of Aradel's last words were of you," he said carefully. "She wanted to thank you."

"Thank me?"

"She said to thank you. I think she meant for your friendship."

Lelanc clicked her beak.

"I want to avenge her, too," Rylin said.

"Then come with me."

For a moment, his spirit rose to have earned the trust of so fierce and magnificent a beast. But then, seeing the dozens of men, women, and children clambering down from the higher forested slope behind them, watching them drag cautious horses after them by their lead lines as the soldiers called them to hurry, he knew where his true duty lay. They had to be escorted to safety. He turned back to Lelanc. "I have to guard these people first. Come with us. There are too many Naor to fight alone."

"You would have me wait? To delay?"

How to reason with her? "First we care for the living. If we don't they may die. Then we will see to the honored dead."

"The dead are meat," Lelanc objected. "They do not need to be seen."

"You're right," he agreed, much as he disliked the way the ko'aye expressed her sentiment. "Only the living cry for vengeance. But don't risk your life alone. Fight at our side. We'll slay many more that way."

Lelanc's head cocked. "I hear wisdom in your words. But my heart cries! It needs the blood of enemies!"

"Give us time."

Lelanc's head bobbed and her nostrils flared. She spoke very slowly, as if vocalizing each word was a silent struggle. "My sister shared words with you, which is not smoke. You share the ring, so you are something like blood. And Varama said you would be my friend, and she has never lied." Lelanc seemed to be reasoning aloud. She raised her head above his own. "I will hear the call of your wisdom and not the red beat of my heart. What would you have me do?"

"Help watch for us. See how close the Naor are. And if you would, bear word to Varama."

"I will do these things. But if the enemies come close to your people, you will fly with me?"

"I'd like that very much." He bowed his head to her.

Lelanc looked a final time at her fallen friend, then backed away and turned to pick her way awkwardly down the slope, using her half-opened wings for balance, before leaping and beating her way into the air. Rylin noted that Cerai's strange horse didn't shy no matter that Lelanc's left wing came within a handspan of its head.

To the left of where the ko'aye gained the sky, Denalia was organizing refugees into a column. Cerai stood nearby and worked the air with one hand, the way some weavers did as they manipulated tendrils of will. He was too tired to watch in the inner world, and her intentions were clear in any case, for the dozen or so riderless Naor mounts that had been ambling uncertainly came trotting up in a line.

Gathering all of them at once was an impressive feat, something he himself couldn't have managed. And yet Cerai didn't seem remotely tired.

Rylin whistled for bandage-arm and his friend, and when he got their attention he helped them ready Aradel's body for transport on one of the carts. While they finished wrapping her in some worn camp blankets, Denalia filled him in on how they'd gotten here. Her soft brown eyes were red-rimmed, but her voice was even.

Before dawn, she told him, Aradel had flown out with a small cavalry troop to learn why one of her signal towers had stopped reporting. They'd found an exhausted group of fleeing villagers, and while Aradel conferred with them she'd sent Lelanc aloft to reconnoiter. The Naor had discovered them soon after Lelanc was out of sight. Aradel hadn't encountered any of Varama's squires.

"You know the rest," Denalia said, then added, "it was an honor to fight beside you, Alten."

"Likewise."

"You were incredible." Though weary, she spoke with youthful sincerity. How young was she, exactly? Nineteen? Sixteen?

He appreciated the compliment, but he was already revisiting his actions and wondering what he might have done differently if he'd had Cerai's level of power. "I'm glad I could help."

"Help? You stopped an entire regiment of Naor. Single-handedly. You dropped straight out of the sky to our rescue!"

Well, sort of. "It wasn't a whole regiment."

"As though that makes it unworthy!" She shook her head. "We'd all be dead if you hadn't come. I'm sorry if I sounded critical when you were working on the governor. I just—I really wanted you to save her. She's my aunt," she blurted.

There was a world of difference between Denalia's peaches-and-cream complexion, just visible beneath the layer of grime, and Aradel's nut brown, but there had been frequent intermingling between denizens of the realms for generations. Rylin was less puzzled by the declaration of familial connection than he was further saddened. "I'm sorry. I wish I could have done more. I served with her, briefly, when I was a squire, and I always respected her."

"She was brilliant," Denalia agreed.

"Are you an officer?"

Denalia blushed. "Sort of. I mean, yes." She lowered her voice. "The Naor killed Officer Etrin, so that left me next in line. I've a lot to live up to."

"You're a fine shot."

He saw a pretty smile bloom under her dirt. She might clean up nicely.

Denalia seemed inclined to talk further until he reminded her they needed to get moving. She grew solemn as her companions secured their dead to a sturdy cart. Rylin was turning away when a trio of ladies stopped to thank him. They looked bone-tired and their clothes were flecked with mud, but they'd maintained their complicated head scarves. Like most women of The

Fragments, the garments hid all but a single lock of hair that lay neatly against their foreheads.

He exchanged a few hurried pleasantries as boys and girls, some staring his direction, clambered into wagons with the old ones.

Cerai finished distributing the captured horses among the allies, seeing to it that those not in wagons were mounted, then joined Rylin. "We should be able to get these people to safety, assuming we don't run into another column."

"I sent Lelanc aloft to check," he said. "And to send word to Varama."

"How close is she? Does she have many troops with her?"

"She's alone. We've got almost sixty squires of varied ranks, but they're probably halfway to Alantris by now. Assuming they didn't run into a Naor patrol. I don't suppose you've seen Kyrkenall?"

"Is he here too?"

He smiled wryly. "It doesn't seem like it. What are you doing here?"

"I've been keeping an eye on the Naor," she said. "Although I see now I should have been doing a better job." Before he could ask for further details, she asked another question of her own. "Are you wounded? Is any of that blood yours?"

He looked down at his splattered khalat, raised a hand, touched something wet on his cheek. "I'm fine. Just winded," he admitted. "I used a little too much magic."

"Then take some of mine."

Before he could object she pressed a hand to his throat. Her skin was cool but her presence was like a thunderbolt, and he tried not to stare.

Energy coursed back into him; limbs that had felt like lead returned to something approximating normal, and his breath eased. She lowered her hand and smiled at him, seemingly none the worse for wear.

"Better?"

"I am, thank you." Life just wasn't fair. Some weavers were born with greater gifts than others. He'd long heard that Cerai had more energy at call than the average weaver, and now he'd experienced it. She'd used sorcery to fell multiple opponents, control scattered horses, then had magics left to rejuvenate him.

She smiled again and stepped back. "I think we've much to discuss, but we'd best get things going. I'll take the van, you take the rear, right?"

"Right." That felt more like a suggestion from a colleague than an order from a senior alten. And it made sense, so there was no reason to debate.

Cerai continued: "We're near the Hawklan pass. From there it's a fairly easy ride to Alantris."

"That sounds fine."

In only a few moments, Cerai was once more in the saddle of her peculiar mount, leading the way, and a train of horse-pulled carts and mounted riders followed. It seemed a pitifully small number of dejected people huddled in the backs of the carts, and Rylin wondered how many of their friends and families had been left behind. How many were even now laboring for the Naor, or lay dead on their pyres?

Try as he might, those concerns were never terribly far from his mind, because he had to keep looking back, vigilant for new pursuers. He watched, too, for Lelanc, bearing word about Varama or the enemy, yet saw nobody above or between the towering pines on either hand. He followed the transport wagon for the dead, which bore Aradel, nearly a dozen soldiers, and two villagers.

The survivors were indeed fortunate he'd come along when he did, and he was fortunate Cerai had popped up out of nowhere. Much as he was grateful for her timely arrival, she was a disquieting mystery. After the war she'd been posted to the outer realms, riding her own way much as Kyrkenall had done. Varama didn't count her among their enemies, but they'd found her name all over the ledgers in the Hall of Exalts. She was the only alten still seeking hearthstones.

If that weren't enough to arouse some suspicion on his part, there was her bizarre horse. The thing had continued to stand impossibly still until Cerai had climbed into the saddle to depart. The creature's discipline surpassed any he'd ever seen. Even the finest animals would be expected to shake their head every now and then, or twitch an ear, or even surreptitiously bend to snatch a little grass. All Cerai's did was stand and breathe.

What manner of horse was it, and where had Cerai found it?

He watched uneasily for several hours, sometimes trailing at quite a distance, but he never sighted any Naor. Finally they arrived at a pretty hillside village, and one of the elders there was happy to relay that all five groups of Altenerai squires had passed through earlier in the day. Thank the Gods. Rylin was about to join Cerai in a more and more agitated conversation about the villagers' need to evacuate, but a check overhead showed him Lelanc had at last returned.

The ko'aye descended upon a meadow just beyond a wheat field, beating wings to slow her speed. Rylin rode forth to meet her. He was halfway through the field when he heard hooves pounding behind him, and he turned to discover Cerai cantering after on her strange black horse. As she reined in beside him, he noted again that her mount loomed two hands higher than his black.

They halted as Lelanc struck the ground with surprising delicacy and then raised her head to stare at them. She waited a hundred yards out, her wings only partly folded and fluttering a little as if in nervous agitation.

At the snort of Rylin's horse, he understood the reason for Lelanc's hesitance. She must know that horses were, at the least, uncomfortable around her. He climbed out of his saddle and started toward the ko'aye, Cerai walking at his side.

Once they'd drawn within ten feet, Lelanc dipped her head to them. "I greet you, ring family of my ground sister."

Rylin bowed in response. "We greet you, rider of winds." Strange, how easily formality came to him when speaking to the great feathered serpent.

Lelanc wasted no time. "Varama comes. She is not far behind. On this trail."

Excellent. "What about the Naor?"

"Those who sent the ones we killed have halted. They scurry back and forth, uncertain." With all of their mounted scouts eliminated, the contingent must be regrouping. "But a larger amount is in the valley east. Maybe two days away when walking. Maybe less. They march toward Alantris."

Good news and bad. Probably the Naor they'd encountered had been an advance column—one sent off from the host to secure the inhabited southern valleys and win plunder for its kinglet.

"Are the Naor likely to come upon Varama?" he asked.

"Not unless she slows or the enemies move faster."

Rylin turned to the woman beside him. "I'll go out to meet her." He was about to ask if Cerai would mind taking his horse to the village so he could fly with Lelanc.

"I'll go with you," Cerai said. "I think there's a lot we need to discuss."

There was, at that. A little disappointed he wouldn't be taking to the air, he nonetheless nodded acknowledgment, then spoke to Lelanc. "Cerai and I are going to double back and rendezvous with Varama. Can you keep a watch on the Naor columns until we get her safe?"

Lelanc took a moment to digest this question. "I will do this for you. But later we will kill Naor, yes?"

"Depend upon it."

"I will. Clear a way for me, Rylin. Your horses will not like when I run forward."

He and Cerai retreated. The hill villagers were hurriedly yoking horses to wagons they loaded with belongings. Cerai galloped back to speak with them while Rylin watched Lelanc take flight.

He stared until she vanished into the distance. Cerai joined him a short time later. "All the outlying villages will have to retreat to Alantris," she said.

"That's as Aradel wished. Can the city hold them all?"

She arched an eyebrow at him, and he felt as though he must have said something stupid, though he couldn't imagine what it had been.

"There's been plenty of room in Alantris," she said. "Ever since the war."

He nodded. Of course.

"Let's get moving," Cerai said, as if eager to break the awkward silence, and they started back down the trail. She addressed him casually. "I've heard some of the veterans scoffing about you newly ringed, but I should have known better, as Asrahn remained in charge of training. It seems you acquitted yourself well today."

"That's kind of you. The tales I've heard don't do you justice." He decided against mentioning that her beauty had been undersold as well. "Where did you get your horse?"

"The Shifting Lands."

That surprised him. "I didn't know there were horses in the Shifting Lands."

Her smile was self-satisfied. "Oh, there are some horselike things there, but I shaped him."

"You *shaped* your horse?" He made no effort to conceal his amazement.

"Trial and error. And practice. Something I'm sure an alten is intimately familiar with."

He nodded. While it was true he'd played with land features a time or two, out in the shifts, he'd never dared try to mold a life-form. So far as he knew, no one but stage villains ever succeeded with that kind of experimentation. That level of capability both impressed and alarmed him.

She downplayed her obvious self-satisfaction. "He's not a complete success. He has no will. I forged a living tool, no more. He's like a puppet. I have to command him to do nearly everything but the most rudimentary of tasks. Yet," she added, "he's more powerful than any other horse I've ever ridden. He rarely tires. He has no fear. He feels no pain. And, because he's formed from stuff of the Shifting Lands, he's easy to mend."

How many thousands of infinitesimal adjustments must she have made to succeed? Over what period of time? "Could you change a living horse?"

"I've been experimenting with that," she admitted. "It's a lot more challenging. But you know that. That's why our weaving is usually about changing energy states rather than altering physical conditions."

"Of course." Guiding a gust of wind was far more difficult when there were no air currents. Changing the consistency of matter was one of the most challenging, painstaking, and draining of magics. It was why the best healers were highly specialized and usually aged. It required decades to gain the knowledge and experience to work with severe injuries.

The wind picked up and shook tree limbs to either side of the track.

Interesting as all this talk was, it was time to get some answers. "I'm still unclear about what you were doing in The Fragments. You said you were monitoring the Naor?"

"Yes, since our pointless commander hasn't been heeding my warnings. They've been a little quiet, which is usually a sign they're up to something, so I went over to take a look myself." She glanced sidelong at him. "Well, as I said, I should have looked into things a little sooner. By the time I swung through I found they'd left for an entirely new war. If we had more watchers on the borders, like we did in the old days, our defenders would greet them instead of our villagers."

He wished he didn't have to be so cautious around a wearer of the sacred ring. Once, perhaps, he would have been able to trust and depend upon her without question. He frowned that it was no longer so. "Aradel told me the Naor are marching on Arappa at the same time. And Mazakan's leading them."

"Fabulous. Did she say anything else?"

"She didn't have time to say much. She bade me to get help from the queen and Denaven—"

At this Cerai snorted.

"—and to safeguard Alantris."

"Nothing else?"

"She said there's a third army on the way, probably intent on using The Fragments as a staging post before it hits Erymyr."

Cerai frowned. "Did she know how far out it was?"

"She didn't say. She did have some tactical tips. She said that there's high ground near Alantris that the Naor should be lured toward."

Cerai nodded as if she knew immediately what Aradel had meant. "Oligar Ridge. That will be tricky unless we get enough troops from Darassus to back us up."

"I didn't have a chance to get more details."

She pensively regarded the road leading down the tree-lined hill. "It was strange, wasn't it, that a woman from Kanesh could so fall in love with The Fragments? I asked her once if she missed the plains, and she said she did, sometimes. But she loved this land of little valleys even more. I suppose they'll inter her here."

Rylin thought back to the still form in the back of the cart and wished her spirit well.

"So are you and Varama scouting ahead for the Darassan army?" Cerai asked.

He'd hoped to steer clear of any discussion about their activities, leaving that for Varama, but he supposed that had been too much to wish for. "We're looking for Kyrkenall." He watched her for some sign of reaction, but she only looked puzzled.

"What happened to him?"

"Denaven thinks he killed Asrahn."

Cerai's voice registered her surprise. "Asrahn's dead?"

"I'm afraid so. He drowned in the Idris, and Denaven blamed Kyrkenall for it."

"He's hated Kyrkenall for years," Cerai said. "Does anyone else think Kyrkenall did it?"

"Some. They're hunting him with Denaven."

Cerai shook her head in dismay.

"Why does Denaven hate him?"

"Because he thinks Kyrkenall won the woman he wanted. The whole thing's childish."

"Who was the woman?"

"Rialla."

"The one who was so good with hearthstones." Everything seemed to come back to the hearthstones. "Are you still searching for them?"

Cerai favored him with a thin smile. "I didn't realize that was common knowledge."

"I've been getting more and more curious about hearthstones," he said. "So I've been asking a lot more questions."

"And not getting many answers, I'd bet."

Rylin's horse, Rurudan, perked up his ears, and Rylin scanned the trees they passed until he spotted a lynx watching from the undergrowth. It crept away.

"You'd win that bet. Anything you'd care to share with a promising young alten?" He flashed her his best smile.

She laughed lightly. "You're pouring it on a little thick, aren't you?"

"I'd like some resolution," he admitted. "Recently it feels like I'm surrounded by people keeping secrets. I didn't think the corps was going to be like that."

"It didn't used to be," Cerai acknowledged.

The sky rumbled overhead and a wispy trail of clouds veiled the sun. Cerai hesitated before speaking. "So what do you know about them?"

"Not a lot, really. Except that the Mage Auxiliary is hoarding them, that the queen and the Altenerai were at odds about spending resources to look for them, and that they're too dangerous to be used in battle. Why does the queen want them in the first place if they can't be used to defend the realms?"

Cerai brushed back a curling lock of dark hair. "If you'd spent much time in the Shifting Lands you'd know. The shifts are growing more and more unstable. Realm borders are decaying and blowing away and the *real* is shrinking. The queen and the auxiliary believe the key to saving the realms lies in mastering the hearthstones. And I think they're right."

"What are they going to do with them?"

"You can use a hearthstone to build things in the Shifting Lands. Make them more real. Maybe even rebuild the borders, but you'd need a lot of power and a whole lot of mages. You getting the idea?"

He was, and it shocked him. "So they're stockpiling the things and training sorcerers for a sort of land recovery project?"

"Yes, and they don't want to frighten the general populace, or alert our enemies to everything that might be at stake."

Something about that didn't quite ring true, no matter Cerai's sincerity. He wondered if she herself had been fooled. "Why didn't the queen simply tell the Altenerai? We're sworn to protect the realms."

"I gather that the queen told Renik. I don't know if she told N'lahr or not, but things were already pretty sour between her and the Altenerai by the time he took over. I suppose she may have told her pet, Denaven."

Rylin halted them upon a forested promontory overlooking the narrow valley through which they'd ridden earlier. The wind was rising and the sky darkening. First they scanned to the east, seeking signs of Naor and finding none, just as Lelanc had promised. They looked south, toward a gap between the hills that Varama would be crossing. Assuming that she would hold to her plan, and that nothing had happened to her.

He strove for delicacy as he broached his next question. "Don't you think it would be wiser if she told all of us?"

"You can't always agree with your commanders, Rylin. You should know that by now. But you still have to follow orders. The borders *are* weakening. The storms have trebled in the last ten years. Something will have to be done, and soon. The queen expected things to decay faster than they have, but it doesn't mean she's wrong about the basic concept."

He leaned down to pat Rurudan's neck. He was shifting nervously. Cerai's giant, coal-black mount stood motionless and stiff. He was debating telling her just what her rational-sounding queen had done to their squires when Cerai suddenly stilled.

Following her gaze, Rylin saw a lone figure emerge from the trees a few miles south. He quickly recognized Varama, distinctive in her khalat and blue-tinted skin. The wind was really active now, the sky darkening.

As he looked across the ground Varama rode through, the grasses shimmered, as if he was observing her through heat haze.

He called up his view through the inner world and lit his ring even as the ground Varama rode shifted into a swathe of glowing red powder. Was that snow? He didn't need his inner sight to see that she passed over one of the veins from the shifts that crisscrossed The Fragments to give them their name.

Just as he was turning to say something to Cerai, the older woman straightened in her saddle and raised both palms.

Out there in a suddenly bizarre landscape, reality fell away beneath Varama, ring blazing, leaving a pulsing purple void, except for the strip of crimson snow beneath her, a bridge of matter. Rylin looked again to Cerai, frozen in concentration, and knew it was her doing. Damn, but she was impressive. No matter how much he trained he could never approach that level of power.

He stared at her sitting statue still, confident, wind blowing across her perfectly sculpted features. With his magical sight he saw her entire body limned with glowing energies, greater than he'd seen in any other living being. She was terrifyingly beautiful both within and without. A bright magical nimbus glowed not only about her horse, but radiated from the pack on her saddle. He understood that Cerai carried not one but two hearthstones, and that she had tapped their power. He was still watching when she relinquished her hold upon them and relaxed in her saddle.

It was all he could do to tear his eyes away to see that his friend had made her way through the red snow field and onto safe land.

Cerai wiped her brow and then smiled knowingly at Rylin, as if to say that she was not only aware that she'd done well, but that she looked great doing it and appreciated him noticing.

Rylin relinquished his hold on the inner world. "That was astounding."

"You could manage it if you've practiced with a hearthstone," she assured him.

"I don't have your stamina."

"You might, if you use a hearthstone long enough."

"Stamina can change?"

"Hearthstones alter your magical prowess. I thought you knew that. They can hone your gifts. So long as you're careful about it." She laughed lightly. "I see you haven't been told that, either."

"Mostly I've heard they're dangerously seductive."

"Aren't all good things?" At his look, she smiled slyly, then guided her animal away from their lookout point and down toward Varama.

Damn, he thought. She's flirting with me. He liked that, too.

Rylin urged his own horse after, even though the animal snorted unhappily about riding closer to the weird chaotic area. The vein of shifting land had altered now to a deep blue, and a great river flowed behind Varama, crackling with scarlet lightning.

"Hail, Altenerai," Varama said to them, raising her sapphire. Her expression was strangely neutral.

"Hail," he and Cerai answered as one.

"It's been a long time, Varama," Cerai said.

"Yes," Varama agreed. "You're far more beautiful than I remember."

It wasn't spoken as a compliment, but an observation. Cerai smiled. "Thank you."

"What have you done to yourself?" Varama asked.

What did that mean? He looked back and forth between them.

"I've merely made some adjustments," Cerai answered. For the first time Rylin detected a note of annoyance. "No word of thanks?"

"Thank you," Varama said. "Your intervention was timely."

"There it is." Cerai sounded faintly amused. "You haven't changed at all. Rylin's caught me up on your adventures. It sounds as though we have a lot to discuss."

"I gather that we do."

"It looks as if we've arrived in The Fragments just in time for war."

22

Ring Wearers

With Ortok standing watch, the three of them managed an unbroken stretch of sleep. It wasn't enough to be fully restorative, yet when they moved out it was with renewed energy and purpose. The mysteries and troubles that plagued them had been set aside. N'lahr had a plan and the people of Arappa needed them. That was all the focus they required.

They pushed their pace as they ventured across the shifts, speaking little. Even Kyrkenall was mostly silent, though it was not because he brooded over his argument with N'lahr. As far as Elenai could tell, that had passed like a summer rainstorm. Instead, each seemed grimly centered on the immediate future, and the challenges it brought.

Ortok was as quiet as the rest of them, although he had to keep pace at an unflagging jog. His steady breathing was usually audible over other sounds and soon became a strangely reassuring constant that even the horses stopped alerting to with their ears.

Just after a series of rises topped by a smattering of those unpleasant scaly trees, they approached the shores of a great void, very much like the one they'd passed through during the storm. A faded yellow sun burned in an umber sky to the right but darkness cut a ragged and abrupt line across the land and firmament beyond. Elenai watched it warily as they drew closer, fearful that she'd glimpse matter-eating entities within. She worried, too, that she might be called upon to build another land bridge, but so far the empty zone with its uninterrupted twinkling points of light seemed not to intrude upon their intended line of travel.

Even with the distracting starry void looming on their left, she was pleased to recognize the rolling hills and general shape of the splinter where they'd rested the "day" before. She was starting to sense the land better, as Kyrkenall had tried to show her.

They picked their way through the hills for several hours, the void never very far away. It was only a few yards to their left when darkness suddenly washed over them.

N'lahr shouted to get down even as Elenai warmed the hearthstone to life, which alerted her to the ebon spellthreads penetrating their conscious-nesses. This was no natural phenomenon—an enemy hearthstone was powering the blinding spell.

Though her eyes registered no light while she slid to the ground, she sensed all the living beings around her: Kyrkenall, N'lahr, Ortok, the horses. On the nearby hill were twenty or so more. She heard Ortok grunt, felt his life force ebb a modest degree. He'd been struck. Their attackers must have bows.

She discarded the notion of trying to clip off all the tiny threads of the darkness and instead called forth a desperate, disruptive wash of golden energy.

The darkness broke like black shards as more arrows arced in. Elenai rolled aside. One narrowly missed a kneeling Kyrkenall, letting fly with shafts of his own now that he had targets. On the hill above Elenai felt the life force weakening from one of the archers, who screamed as she fell. A squire, she saw, in traditional gray-liveried armor. Kyrkenall's arrow dropped another dead; she saw his life force leave him in an explosive gust in the same moment she recognized him as Velnik, a friendly, freckled third ranker.

Blue-coated Altenerai charged down the hill, huge Decrin in the lead with the Shining Shield on his arm. At his side was tall, spare, gray-bearded Tretton, and after came broad-shouldered Lasren, Denaven on his heels with two competent-looking fourth rankers. She saw Gyldara pause at the height of the hill, throwing axe raised like an avenging goddess, but Kyrke-nall stepped aside as the spinning missle hurtled down at him.

Denaven shouted. "Lasren, take the kobalin with the squires. Decrin, Kyrkenall's yours."

"He's mine!" Gyldara screamed, and raced to catch up.

Elenai sent a thread at the restive horses to urge them clear of attack and was deciding what more to do when a stream of energy slammed through her defenses and sent her reeling. An intruder latched on to her hearthstone and used its own power against her. It wasn't Denaven, she noted through a disorienting haze of torment; some new and powerful mage was boring in.

The instinctual choice was to throw all remaining energy to self-defense, but even as she felt a new attack build, a wiser idea occurred to her. She slipped from her hastily thrown protective energies, effectively climbing through the layers that bound her to the hearthstone. The stranger battered her as she worked free, and Elenai gasped at the lancing pain and nauseat-ing vertigo.

As both were linked to the same stone, a small part of each consciousness was bared to the other. Elenai sensed her opponent's smug confidence that she faced an inferior foe, and she glimpsed her name as well. Ortala didn't seem concerned with the novice's retreat until only a few tendrils connected Elenai to the stone. Sudden insight set the woman struggling to free herself from the thicket of magery.

But it was too late. Elenai drank in a modicum of energy before she released a final thread, then cycled the hearthstone closed.

Ortala's panic as she fought to break clear of the clinging and unyielding matrices stabbed at Elenai. But there simply wasn't enough time for the woman to escape the entanglements before the stone snapped shut upon the strands that tied her spirit to her distant body. The connective spiritual tissue, once severed, blew away like a cobweb on the winds. Upslope, Ortala's body fell limply.

Elenai felt little remorse for this death, for she was certain Ortala had planned some similar fate for her. She had little time to reflect upon it in any case. Winded by the invisible conflict, Elenai gasped in air and took stock of her surroundings.

Nearest at hand, Ortok had borne several cuts and was fending off sword attacks from two squires while Lasren struggled to stand, shaking his head blearily. As she watched, one of the squires went down with a hammer blow to his shoulder, mouth working silently in pain.

On her right-hand side, Kyrkenall fended off attack from two Altenerai. Gyldara must have flung her second ax, for she was trading blows with her blade, striving to maneuver Kyrkenall toward Decrin's heavier length of steel.

Gyldara shouted in frustration. "Stop toying with us and fight!"

"I'll have you know," Kyrkenall objected, "that 'not killing' you . . . isn't as easy as I make it look." His breathing was heavy but a rakish grin lit his face. "Maybe you should try it."

Clearly both her altens were hampered by their efforts to avoid mortal blows. N'lahr was in more dire straits, engaged in swirling combat with Tretton and Denaven near the void's edge. As Elenai watched, the swordsman dodged a lethal overhand strike from Tretton, then barely sidestepped a powerful back swipe from the older swordsman's offhand knife. Denaven, advancing cautiously from the right, attempted a lunge, but N'lahr caught the blade with his own, sliding it aside as he jumped in close to knock Denaven over a precisely placed leg. Presumably unable to employ mental magic against someone bearing Irion, Denaven blasted N'lahr with swept-up bits of grit and dirt as the swordsmage fell to his backside.

Tretton, moving on N'lahr's rear, caught nearly as much of the debris as the intended target. The graybeard stepped back, sputtering. Rather than pressing an attack, N'lahr spoke to him. "We should be fighting the Naor, not each other!"

Tretton wiped his face with his arm, looking as discomfited as if his dog had discovered speech. "I wish I didn't have to do this." He sounded more like he was thinking aloud than addressing N'lahr. He resumed his attack with grim ferocity.

N'lahr parried the blow and slid away from a sweep with the man's long knife. He then beat away a wicked flanking slash from Denaven, riposting with deadly force.

Irion sliced through even the Altenerai armor, leaving a gash along Denaven's arm. The traitorous commander just managed to avoid the point and retreated. Was he afraid to resume attack, or was he readying new magics? Or both?

Elenai shook herself to action. She'd have to even the odds. Narrowing her eyes, she called up the inner world. Each knee-high blade of grass was a complex tapestry of form. Like Denaven and Tretton and N'lahr. Like everything, save for the solid light of an active hearthstone borne in the pack hung at Denaven's waist.

Without further consideration, she confidently set her own hearthstone blazing back to life. She passed through the tattered remnants of Ortala's consciousness, eerily brushing against her last moments of fear, then sent a shining filament of will at Denaven. Elenai drew her sword and advanced even as she commanded "sleep," as M'lahna had done.

She saw him start, then turn away from the engrossed fighters. He sneered and took a step toward her. "You're a talented amateur, now, aren't you."

With stunning speed, his own will leapt out and touched her. She thought she'd known pain from Ortala. Now she was afire with blinding agony and she barely managed to lift her sword to intercept his overhand swing.

She gritted her teeth and reflected the same attack toward its originator.

That seemed to surprise Denaven. His own assault halted for a span of a single heartbeat. Then he bore in again. This time she willed his attacking threads to split asunder as she parried another sword stroke. She still felt pain but at least she could see clearly. Undaunted, Denaven pressed in again, and once more. As they warred she heard N'lahr again, though she didn't catch his words.

"—just a monster in a friendly shape." Tretton growled back. Each utterance was punctuated by clangs or thuds.

"Your attention's wandering, Squire," Denaven spat, and lunged.

Elenai parried, but it was a close thing, and she backed even as he resumed his magical press, scowling. His attack tore through her defenses like a hammer through a pane of glass. She realized she'd sunk to her knees when they contacted the ground and her vision spun with pulsing points of light. Denaven might have finished her then if he'd closed.

Instead, the commander pivoted to direct a magical assault against N'lahr with a veritable blizzard of threads. He willed his own hearthstone to disrupt the ground. Soil undulated like ocean waves. Elenai was impressed despite herself.

He might have meant the attack only for N'lahr, but it vaulted Tretton toward N'lahr's outstretched weapon and both toward the edge into nothingness. The two went down in a tangle, and the next moment that Elenai could sort out had N'lahr driving a bloodied Irion deep into the ground with his off hand while the other maintained a hold on the older man's collar as most of Tretton dangled over the drop into the pitiless void. Kyrkenall bellowed alarm.

And Denaven strode forward to kill N'lahr. Kyrkenall, desperate to free himself, struck with blinding precision right through an opening in Decrin's guard, over his shield and apparently through his armor, for the huge alten sank to his knees. Gyldara rushed in with an enraged onslaught and held Kyrkenall in an earnest dance of destruction.

No one else could help. Ortok remained locked in combat with Lasren and the final squire. It was up to her. Elenai was still seeing spots, but she got her feet under her.

She lashed Denaven with a blast of pain. His spine stiffened and he faltered a few steps shy of his blade's reach.

N'lahr took the respite to release Irion and grasp Tretton with both hands, to haul him to safety.

Elenai raced forward. "Face me!"

Denaven half turned so he included her as a target, then sliced out to keep her at bay.

She dropped under the cut, rolled near to the edge and N'lahr, and rose between him and Denaven. On sudden inspiration she left her own sword in the grass, and pulled Irion instead.

Denaven's visage vibrated with shock and anger, and somehow she knew it was about the blade she now held.

With a choked roar he thrust at her with his own weapon, battering her at the same moment with threads from his hearthstone. She felt the intents rise one after the other, shooting toward her like lead-weighted rope.

She lifted threads from her hearthstone to obstruct them, but was so busy upon them she barely blocked another thrust, and then ducked a swipe that would have taken her head.

"No helm? You're not good enough"—he swung again, and she sidestepped—"to be so careless!"

He was right. She retreated from the edge, drawing Denaven farther from N'lahr and wishing she could send a wave of earth as he had done. She wasn't sure she could, so she sent the thought of one toward him, complete with the image of him fighting for balance.

And she saw him hesitate, the fraction of an instant. In that tiny respite she glimpsed that near invisible line of branching possibility that only she seemed to perceive. Her off hand grasped it, though there was nothing physical to hold, and she followed it forward. A thousand minutely different futures blossomed like flowers in a hedge maze.

He slashed at her, then seemed startled he missed. She and Denaven whirled into a manic duel. On and on he came, and now she blocked him almost before he struck. He cursed at her. His blows came, the spells fell, but each time he struck she was to the side of where he aimed, countering each sorcery with a new blaze of energy. She sensed his frustration rise when her satisfaction rose.

"What are you doing?"

He wasted words, and Asrahn would have told him so. All of Elenai's attention was centered on the pinpoint moment that lay just ahead of the now. Denaven ceased his forward momentum and reached deeper within his hearthstone. She supposed he pulled more energy, but the result was too far forward to know.

He drove hard at her, screaming some meaningless insult, but she danced to one side and suddenly she had the perfect opening. In the next moment Denaven's hand was arcing away from his body, still grasping his sword.

He screeched and grabbed at the horrible wound with his other hand. Through the inner world Elenai saw life roaring away from the injury like water streaming from a pipe.

He screamed again, and she felt him drawing on the hearthstone, knew his desperation, knew another opening when she had one, and jammed Irion's point through his neck. She felt it catch in his spinal column. The moment she pulled it free he dropped, gracelessly, and slammed face-first into the ground.

She turned, breathing heavily, still sighted in the inner world, paying no more heed to Denaven's corpse than she might have regarded a rock, then shut down his hearthstone before scanning the battlefield.

Ortok and Lasren still traded blows. The other squire was down. Near at hand N'lahr crouched at Tretton's side, and the two conversed in low tones. Through her inner sight it was clear that Tretton's life force was diminished, but that he was in no grave danger. She would not have been able to tell it by the man's pose, but she saw pulsing lines of red all about his right upper arm that she knew signified pain. Gyldara was retreating before Kyrkenall as the archer attacked with mad abandon.

Elenai shouted: "Kyrkenall, stop!"

But either he didn't hear, or he could no longer control himself, for he pressed on. Gyldara proved even a finer blade than Elenai would have guessed, somehow anticipating or avoiding every mad flurry, but her energy flagged and she was clearly on the defense.

"Stop!"

Gyldara saw Elenai's rush and wrenched to the left, trying to keep her from flanking. Kyrkenall seized the opening, struck, and deftly knocked the woman's sword, spinning and shining, to the ground; he drew back for the death blow, grinning terribly.

His blade met Elenai's with a weird greenish spark, and his eyes shifted to hers in frustrated rage.

"She was misled!" Elenai avowed

"I don't care!" he cried.

Gyldara snarled in fury at the same time. "He killed my sister!"

Elenai pushed back on Kyrkenall's sword, looking not at him but Gyldara, who clearly waited for an opening to renew the attack. Elenai struck at her, not with blade, but mind.

The alten fought as her ring lit, her head swaying right and left as though she might hold back the mental assault with physical action. Yet Elenai bore down with the full power of the hearthstone and forced a mental link. The woman's sapphire slowed but could not contain the attack.

The golden-haired alten choked back a curse as she saw what Elenai remembered. That moment, ages but merely weeks ago, when Elenai had stood before the tomb with Kyrkenall as a similar-looking woman circled with a hearthstone and talked to them of Asrahn's death. M'lahna, Gyldara's sister.

Elenai pushed the memories forward, one after the other in quick succession. M'lahna's words, M'lahna's death, Cargen's denials and his memory of the tower, the long, long ride through the Shifting Lands, the recovery of N'lahr, the discovery of Belahn, the perilous flight into chaos. She gave her all of it, then traced it back to herself, lying in the mud while M'lahna spoke with the motionless Kyrkenall.

Gyldara shook. Had she been party to it all? Was this some kind of trick or had she simply been blinded by vengeance and deceived by Denaven? Seeing the woman's stricken expression, Elenai thought she knew, and dropped the link.

Kyrkenall stepped back, Lothrun lowered but teeth gritted, very much like a wolf waiting for his moment. He breathed heavily without much noise.

Gyldara's eyes glistened with tears. Her voice was low, trembling. "Is it true?"

"Is what true?" Kyrkenall rasped.

"That my sister murdered Asrahn. That she tried to kill you both." Gyldara searched Elenai's eyes, as if for confirmation. She must have found it there. Her voice dropped to a whisper. "Gods. What have I done?"

"What have I done?" Kyrkenall repeated. And his gaze swung to his right, where Decrin lay. N'lahr was there now, kneeling by the man as his life force faded, and Tretton looked on, haggard, right arm stiffly at his side. It was scarlet with pain.

Kyrkenall moved toward them almost mechanically.

Elenai tore her eyes from Gyldara and looked over to where Ortok now loomed, shoulders heaving from exertion, beside Lasren. The young alten was struggling to his feet, eyeing the kobalin with distrust and fear. She couldn't know if N'lahr had shouted something or if Ortok and the alten had come to terms on their own. And somehow she felt it difficult to care, for the music of the hearthstone was so alluring. Now that the combat was over and she was no longer focused each moment upon life and death, she heard its siren call, and wanted to hear nothing else. At some level she knew that she was hypnotized by its sweet sound, but that didn't matter. She wanted to lose herself within it, leave this scene of devastation, as though she were sinking into a warm tub of water.

A question from Gyldara pulled her back. "And that's really Commander N'lahr?"

"Yes." Wasn't it obvious? Why was she asking such irritating questions? Why was any of this, here, in the regular world, of interest in any way?

"Are you all right?" Gyldara asked in a tiny voice. And then something in Elenai's look must have warned her that she wasn't, for the other woman reached out to grasp one arm, and then the other, staring into her eyes. Elenai felt herself rigid in Gyldara's hands, unable to breathe. "Squire?"

For reasons she didn't fully understand, that human contact was the release she needed. She relinquished her hold on the hearthstone, or gave it permission to release her, and cycled it closed. Her body was her own once more. It was as if she'd stepped out of a role she'd adopted for the stage, a demanding one, for she had to shake her head to clear her thoughts. To Gyldara's questioning look, she nodded her thanks. The alten released her and then the two, wordless, joined the knot about Decrin.

Kyrkenall and N'lahr sat on either side of him. The prone alten still had his shield strapped across his left arm. His khalat had been unhooked and N'lahr pulled back from examining the wound, an ugly vertical opening driven right through the center of his chest. He reeked of blood, and he'd lost a lot of it, because his broad square face was pale. Even without her inner sight, Elenai could see he was dying.

Kyrkenall, head bowed, gripped Decrin's right hand tightly in his own.

Decrin's face was ghastly as he smiled. There was blood on his lips, and his voice cracked as he rolled his head to better see Kyrkenall. "Varama never doubted you. I should have believed her. She was always the smartest."

Kyrkenall seemed to grow conscious of Elenai and Gyldara, though he ignored the other woman and fixed Elenai with a stricken stare. "Can't you do something? Stop the blood?"

She started to say she might try, but then admitted to herself she had no healing skills. She barely had proficiency in field dressings, let alone their magical counterparts. And this wound was beyond any she'd seen trained healers struggle with. She shook her head no.

Decrin grinned up at Kyrkenall. "You were too good," he said with a wan smile. "I didn't know my guard gaped that wide."

"It only takes a little opening," Kyrkenall said in a small voice.

"Why did you stay away, Kyrkenall?" Decrin asked. His voice was so quiet, the question so raw and honest that the big man sounded like a little child. "I missed you."

"I'm sorry," Kyrkenall said. Tears coursed unashamedly down his cheeks.

"I would have helped, if you'd come to me," he said. "You could have trusted me."

"Would that I had," Kyrkenall said, choking.

"I don't know how he convinced us. Every time I was suspicious, he showed me I was wrong. What was it all about, anyway?" Decrin asked. "I'd like to know that, before I die."

N'lahr answered him. "Denaven and the queen traded my 'death' for hearthstones from Mazakan. They trapped me with magic, although that might have been an accident."

"There's a lot we don't know," Elenai added.

"Hearthstones," Tretton observed bitterly.

"What does she even want them for?" Decrin asked.

"Belahn thought it was all about some lost goddess," N'lahr replied. "But the hearthstones had driven him half mad, so we don't really know."

Elenai had once heard Decrin roar orders on the practice field, and his voice was a ghost of that strength, though he tried to raise it. "Gods damn it! What a time to die." He gritted his teeth and shook his head, weakly. "The Naor invading, N'lahr back, that shit-sore Denaven dead." He looked between his friends. "Hey, you'll visit my vault, won't you, sometimes?"

"I will," Kyrkenall vowed. His eyes had filled with tears.

N'lahr nodded once.

"Every year," Tretton promised solemnly.

"Leave some bottles there," Decrin muttered toward Kyrkenall. "But don't put me in. Burn me up. Somewhere with clean wood. I want my soul launched pure and proper, right?"

"Right," Tretton answered. Ekhem's traditions would no doubt be upheld.

Gyldara stepped closer, wiping tears from her face.

Elenai had never known Decrin well. By the time she'd reached third rank, the alten was rarely to be found in Darassus. Yet he was a legend, as famous for his booming laugh as his prowess on the battlefield, and his loss was a blow not just to the corps but to the realms themselves. Gyldara had squired with him, which explained the depth of her grief, but Elenai found herself weeping as well.

"Gyldara," Decrin said, brightening as if he'd only now noticed her. "It's him. It's really N'lahr."

"I know," Gyldara whispered.

"Should have known the truth when Kyrkenall shot Tretton's Naor." Decrin's voice was failing.

"We all should have," Gyldara said.

But Decrin of the Shining Shield couldn't hear her anymore.

Kyrkenall let out a soul-searing cry of anguish. He stood, searching them all, as if he hoped to find an enemy. But there was none.

"I killed my brother!" Kyrkenall raged. He shouted at N'lahr, "I slew Decrin Henahdra!" He slashed through several nearby branches before launching Lothrun spinning from his hands into the distant grass. His hands went to his hair and pushed it wildly back. His eyes were mad as he broke into verse, facing Gyldara: "Even with the lies laid bare, I faced you, and longed to see your blood upon my sword. I lusted for revenge, all reason lost." He looked as if he invited attack, and she recoiled. Then he turned, sharply, and his words grew almost incoherent as sorrow garbled his speech. "Wind back time's march, you useless, pointless Gods. Surely you have cursed me; I curse you all!" He sank to his knees, head low, and his shoulders shook with grief, framed by the endless void.

Elenai feared he'd cast himself into the abyss, but N'lahr approached, alone. "All battles are fought in darkness," he said softly. "And blood stains all who still move. Only right action can redeem the necessities of survival." He put a hand to his friend's shoulder and helped him rise. They embraced briefly before the commander pointed and Kyrkenall left to retrieve his sword.

N'lahr looked over to her at last, and nodded once, gravely. "You did well."

She bowed her head in acknowledgment, appreciating the compliment and wondering why she did not blush, as she would have done only a few days before. Perhaps it was her fatigue. "Thank you, sir."

"I should like my sword back."

She'd actually forgotten she still held it, and looked down to see it gripped tightly in her hand. "Yes, of course."

She passed it over, glumly, and he considered Irion for a moment before he bent to wipe Denaven's blood on the grass.

Elenai grew conscious that Lasren had limped forward, Ortok a cautious five paces to his right. The kobalin's furry torso was crossed with blood, but she couldn't tell if he himself was in much pain. He licked the fur of his left forearm like an injured dog.

"Two of the squires are still alive, sir," Lasren announced meekly. "One of them's hurt pretty bad."

"Are any of you healers?" N'lahr asked.

Gyldara and Lasren both shook their heads no. "We've trained to dress battle injuries, though."

"She's better at it than me," Lasren admitted.

"See what you can do for them," N'lahr replied to Gyldara's questioning look. "I'll be along momentarily."

"Yes, Commander." She turned and walked off. Lasren stared wonderingly at N'lahr for a moment, then limped after.

N'lahr looked briefly after Kyrkenall's direction, then over to Ortok. "How are you?"

"The pain is not bad. I will live." He indicated Decrin with a bob of his head. "Is that one really Kyrkenall's brother?"

"All who join the corps are brothers and sisters," N'lahr explained.

"I'm sorry I killed one, then. But they were trying to kill me."

"You did what you had to do, Ortok. No apology is necessary. I thank you for your help. I'll take a look at your wounds in a moment." N'lahr shifted his attention to Tretton. "Shouldn't you be bleeding? You haven't had time to bandage yourself."

The old soldier spoke with the faintest suggestion of amusement. "You youngsters always think you're the only ones with enchantments. I know how to keep the blood in my body."

"Is your arm broken?" Elenai asked.

"Something's been damaged," Tretton said dismissively. "I can't move it very well. Perhaps you can explain, N'lahr, why's there a kobalin with you?"

"Long story," N'lahr said tiredly.

Elenai, thinking of Kyrkenall, pulled out a quote from Selena. "'Some whom we thought our friends were enemies. And some whom we thought enemies are friends.'"

She expected Tretton to question further, but he merely nodded, sagely.

"How did you track us?" Elenai asked. "I had the hearthstone off."

"Denaven knew the general direction you'd been heading. And I followed the signs. Getting us here exhausted everyone. While we recovered, Denaven hatched plans for an ambush and quickly put them to action when he detected your approach. He was clever, you know."

"More's the pity," N'lahr said.

The final toll could have been worse, but given the state of the corps and the challenges before them, the deaths here were a blow that could ill be afforded. In addition to Denaven and Ortala, they'd lost Decrin and two squires. A third was suffering from agonizing pain where Ortok had struck him in the shoulder, and Yeva, who Elenai had helped tutor in sword drills, had narrowly escaped death from one of Kyrkenall's arrows, for it had struck the meat of her throat but miraculously avoided both windpipe and major vessels.

Tretton's arm had been pierced and suffered some sort of nerve damage. The best hope for both him and the most severely wounded squire was a talented healer. Any of those, though, were days away.

Ortok's wounds were mostly superficial but required a lot of tending. He hadn't approved of that, and had liked N'lahr's sewing even less, though he'd submitted to treatment and bandaging in the end.

Lasren's thigh was bruised and swollen thanks to a glancing blow he'd taken from Ortok's hammer. He could barely walk, but insisted that he would ride with the rest of them as N'lahr explained what must be done. The commander had shared his plan, the steps they had to take to enact it, and the speed at which they had to travel, and Tretton reluctantly agreed that he would follow behind with the wounded. There was no horse that would seat Ortok, so he, too, would have to catch up later as N'lahr intended to make up time with an even harder ride.

"We can't stay for funerals," N'lahr said soberly. He glanced to Kyrkenall, but the little archer stood drained and vacant-eyed beside him, and did not react.

"We'll bear the others to hallowed ground but we'll consign Decrin to the flames," Tretton said, "once we reach a land with good timber."

N'lahr nodded. "We'll drink to him, should we meet again on this side of the line."

By that, Elenai knew he meant the line separating life from death.

N'lahr's gaze roved over to Ortok, then to Gyldara. How much the bright-eyed woman had changed, since the last time Elenai had seen her. Her sister's death and the long chase and the unveiling of the lies had left her gaunt and shadowed with grief and shame. Gone, too, was Lasren's insouciance. A pall hung over him, as though he felt chastened. Kyrkenall looked the worst of all, as though burdened by all the world's wrongs.

Only Tretton appeared much as Elenai had always seen him, save that the arm slung across his chest in an off-white bandage was held immobile.

"Before we go, there's one last thing that must be done," N'lahr said. "I hold that Elenai has reached our circle." Without pausing for breath, he began the formal recitation of the ceremony of the ring. "I know her character, I have seen her deeds, and bear witness to their virtue. She shall shield the defenseless. Who stands in accord with me?"

At these words, these ancient ritual words, Elenai felt a start despite fatigue. She looked in surprise at N'lahr, wondering why he should do this now. What had it been, exactly, that brought her to this? She'd always imagined the day she'd won the ring would be filled with glory, and that she would stand exultant after accomplishing some impossible deed.

Today she only felt numb, and that wasn't how she'd dreamed it, not at all. In any case, how could she ever have envisioned that a man she'd thought dead would nominate her, or that it would occur on the field of battle after she'd slain an Altenerai commander?

Kyrkenall spoke next. His words might have been rote, but he delivered them with such conviction that they seemed spontaneous and entirely natural. "I stand with you," he said, and his eyes flickered to weary life as he turned to N'lahr. "I have seen her skill with sword, and spell, and bear witness to their excellence. She shall defeat our enemies. Who stands with us?"

Gyldara spoke last, her voice remote and almost ghostlike. "I stand with you. I have seen her reason fairly and bear witness to her wisdom. She shall mete justice to high, and to low."

N'lahr met her eyes, his weary face strikingly solemn. "Elenai Dartaan, we three nominate you to our ranks. You know well the standards of the corps. You stand ready to carry mighty burdens, and to walk a narrow path trod only by the brave. Do you pledge to honor the laws of our people, the traditions of the corps, and to emulate the conduct of the best who have worn the ring before you?"

She thought of Decrin, lying still and silent under the blanket only a dozen paces off, and nodded once, formally. "I do."

"Then join us in recitation of the oath." N'lahr spoke first, but she joined in with him. The others took up the lines, quickly adapting to his rhythm.

> "When comes my numbered day, I will meet it smiling. For I'll have kept this oath.
> I shall use my arms to shield the weak.
> I shall use my lips to speak the truth, and my eyes to seek it.
> I shall use my hand to mete justice to high and to low, and I will weigh all things with heart and mind.
> Where I walk the laws will follow, for I am the sword of my people and the shepherd of their lands.
> When I fall, I will rise through my brothers and my sisters, for I am eternal."

Tears, unwanted, stood in her eyes. She had thought she'd be elated when she won the ring. Why was she crying? She wiped them away with the back of her hand.

"Hail, Alten Elenai." N'lahr put his palm to his heart in salute and set his sapphire ring blazing.

Kyrkenall, Gyldara, Lasren, and Tretton already had hands to chest, and set their own rings burning. Their voices rose as one. "Hail, Alten Elenai!"

"Long may you wear the ring," Kyrkenall said.

"I . . ." She fumbled with speech only for a moment, then bowed her head, wishing eloquence might come to her. But sometimes the simplest words were best. "I thank you."

"I've had Lasren ready Ortala's khalat for you," N'lahr said. "You'll find it a better fit. We'll remove the exalt piping later. Don it, and mount up. We've far to ride."

23

Wind Rider

The bed was soft, the sheets warm and smooth. Rylin opened his eyes in the morning sun and stretched his arms and legs, luxuriating.

He had awakened in a rectangular stone room they'd given him in the citadel, and the air within was cool and fresh. Light from the curtainless window streamed through slats and threw lines over the covers that hid his legs. He was naked apart from his undergarments. His Altenerai khalat and pants lay folded on the small dressing table with the rest of his clothes, where his sheathed sword and knife leaned.

Once they'd reached Alantris, night had fallen and Varama had told him to rest and recuperate. He'd rather have stayed to talk with her, but he couldn't get her alone. She and Cerai were deep in consultation with the Alantran Council about the realm's defenses and sundry other matters, and he felt unnecessary. And besides, he'd been exhausted after all the exercise, both physical and magical.

Rylin climbed out of bed, drew on fresh undergarments, pants, and socks and boots. He groaned as he pulled on his undershirt. The healers of Alantris had spent a little time with him, or he'd have been feeling more than twinges after his combat yesterday. Still, there were bruises blossoming across his chest from where his armor had blunted Naor blows.

He threw on his overshirt and buttoned it closed, then stepped to the window.

The clean breeze chilled him as he gazed out from high in a stone tower of the citadel. His eyes were drawn first to the far distance, well beyond the wall of black stone that surrounded the outer city, the first and highest of three concentric defensive rings. Four, he supposed, if you counted the wall surrounding the citadel itself.

To the east, the sky was thick with dark clouds that were no storm. They hung in the clear sky, tethered to the earth by roiling pillars of smoke. A stream of refugees flooded toward the city's eastern gate, many afoot, but a few on horses or guiding wagons overloaded with men, women, and children.

The Naor had brought the red flame of war to this realm, and the citizens of The Fragments were retreating to their oft-tested but never-defeated capital. Rylin's hands tightened on the sill. Where was the excitement he'd always expected when he craved action? Did he no longer thrill to it because he felt the toll on others more keenly? Or was he just getting older?

He gazed down on the refugees threading through the streets and considered the city itself. Green and orderly farm fields and orchards heavy with blossoms took up much of the space between the outer wall and the first inner barrier. The complex system of canals that nourished them twinkled blue and white in the morning sun. The old aqueducts slanting between the walls were heavy with flowering greenery.

The next rings, too, had occasional fields, but were mostly given over to buildings arranged in orderly rows. They rarely rose higher than two stories, and they were fashioned chiefly from wood, with green shingled roofs, a marked difference from Darassus. Fountains burbled and flowering gardens bloomed upon every well-ordered block, and among them were man-sized statues rather than the immense monuments he was used to seeing every day in Erymyr's capital. Men, women, and the children who dashed around them were garbed in loose smocks and strapped sandals. The women and older girls additionally wore colorful scarves that hid all but that one lock of hair. Rylin recalled that the different scarf colors signified status or occupation or possibly both.

In Darassus, a change in altitude was an excuse for winding roads, but the founders of Alantris had laid straight lines everywhere, even up the steep incline to the city's second level, and on toward the citadel, hills and vales be damned.

The citadel he'd slept in loomed over both the city and the hill it crowned, in the dead center of Alantris. As he looked to right and left to take in its slender black beauty once more he admired the graceful central keep from which multiple towers soared, linked to one another by slim bridges. It was even more lovely than the songs devoted to it. Though built of the same dark stone that walled the city, it was neither somber nor ponderous, but a work of art, its arches and balconies looking somehow delicate even though the structure was solid and dangerous to enemies. Like a wasp.

His fingers finished with the shirt, and he tucked it into his trousers. How long had he slept? And where could he find breakfast? He was reaching for his khalat when he saw a familiar figure in the sky. Lelanc, riderless, was flying for the citadel.

His stomach grumbled, but Rylin ignored it and stepped to the bowl to wash his face. He wanted to see how the ko'aye was faring.

Someone rapped on his door.

"Come." Rylin shook droplets from his hands and turned.

He expected Varama, but the woman who stood with hand on door latch was a stranger. She had a pert nose and long lashes over soft brown eyes. Her hair was wound up in her decorative blue scarf, but she had lovely cheekbones and a trim figure revealed by the hug of her robe and the belt that girdled her small waist.

"Alten!" She brightened. "I thought you could be close to waking, but I was afraid you might still be asleep."

"I'm awake," he said with a tentative smile. "Who are you?"

"It's me." When that didn't provoke any obvious sign of recognition, her expression fell. "Denalia." She sounded hurt.

"Oh—I'm sorry. I didn't recognize you without your gear." He'd been right, she did clean up nicely, though, he had to admit, she was still no Cerai. But then Cerai had been magically altered, from what Varama said. He still wasn't sure how he felt about that. "You're a beautiful sight in the morning."

She smiled prettily at the compliment. "You're very kind. Are you hungry? Thirsty?"

He was famished. "Both. But I need to see Lelanc first."

She stepped closer, peering at his face from one angle, then the other.

She raised her right hand and placed the first two fingers along his neck.

"What are you doing?" he asked, slightly startled.

"I'm feeling your heart rate."

Denalia smelled of wildflowers and, faintly, of honey, and her proximity stirred him.

"The beating's still rapid," she said. "I'm not sure you should be out of bed. Alten Cerai told me you stretched yourself further than you should have."

Nonsense. "If my heart speeds, it's for sight of you."

She actually blushed. No woman in Darassus would have done that. As Denalia looked at him through her lashes, he realized her shyness was genuine.

"Where's Varama?"

"Somewhere on the walls, I think. With Alten Cerai."

"Any word on the Naor numbers?"

"Not yet. But Lelanc has been scouting, so there should be more information soon. She's not very good at counting troops but we'll estimate the numbers from how long it takes them to pass through the Pine Bole Narrows. It's already clear there's a lot of them heading our way. They must be idiots, because no army can take Alantris. We've fruit trees within the city. We've deep wells, and storehouses crammed with grain."

"The Naor are stubborn and determined," he reminded her.

"And foolish."

He had an inkling that she was overlooking something. He stepped away to buckle his sword belt. He caught his reflection in a bronze mirror and ran his hands through his hair; shaving would have to wait.

"Are you going straight out to find Lelanc? I'm not sure she's back yet."

"I just saw her fly in."

"You won't have a meal at least?"

At the mention of food his stomach tightened to remind him he was empty. "I'll grab something on the way out."

"Oh."

As he saw her crestfallen expression, he understood finally that the young woman fancied him. He wondered how he hadn't noticed right off.

He gave her his best smile. "I'm sorry, Denalia. I'd love to spend more time with you. But duty calls. I've overslept as it is. The other Altenerai have given me too much latitude." Cerai had patently worked more magics than he, and he was a little embarrassed that she might think he required a longer recovery. He was even more ashamed because he knew she was right.

He assuaged her disappointment by asking a favor. "Can you show me how to get there? I don't know my way through the citadel very well."

She brightened. "Of course."

They fell in step as they left the room.

"How did Aradel manage to stay friends with a ko'aye, anyway?" he asked. "I thought they were all mad at us."

"They had a deep bond," Denalia said, as if that were all the explanation needed. And perhaps it was.

He asked her about her homeland, particularly what they usually served to break morning fast. Her description of smoked mountain trout, cool apple juice, mixed greens with apricot slices, and fresh poached eggs set his stomach to grumbling such that she laughed at him.

He thanked her as he left her on the near side of a bridge stretching to the tower she'd identified as Lelanc's, then headed across and up a steep flight of wooden stairs, encountering a soldier in the green livery of the Arappan signal corps on the way down. He was accompanied by a weathered man with spear-straight posture. This fellow wore neither sword nor armor but his manner was unmistakably soldierly.

He stopped at the sight of Rylin and snapped off a salute. "Hail, Alten."

His voice was as gruff as his exterior. "I'm Captain Toln, head of the defense forces."

"Of course." Rylin returned the salute. He remembered the name among notable veterans of the last war, but couldn't recall any specifics.

"Do you have a moment?" Toln asked.

"A moment," he said. "I'm heading to speak with Lelanc."

"It's her I want to talk about." At a look from the signalman, Toln nodded to him. "Go on. I'll be along in a moment."

"Yes, sir." The signalman hurried downstairs.

Toln motioned Rylin to one side of the dark-paneled landing.

His gaze was level and direct. "I'm told you rode with Lelanc yesterday."

"Briefly."

"And that you fought from her back."

"I did."

That seemed to make some kind of decision for Toln, for he nodded once, sharply. "She's never let anyone but the governor do that."

He felt a flush of pride that Lelanc had already asked him to ride with her again.

"Would you be interested in going aloft right now and scouting with her?"

"I'd be honored to fly with her. But Officer Denalia tells me that Lelanc's already been scouting. Why do you need a rider to go with her?" Rylin didn't want to disappear on Lelanc until he'd had a chance to check in with Varama.

"Lelanc has excellent eyes, but she doesn't always get the right information because she's no good at gauging large numbers, and she can't decide what might be in the baggage trains. I'm looking for a count of siege engines, that sort of thing. I need military eyes."

"I see."

Either the mild joke didn't register with Toln or he chose to ignore it, for he simply watched Rylin expectantly.

"I'll ask her," Rylin said.

"I'd be grateful. Then report to me on your return."

"Of course." Though he'd preferred to break his fast and finally speak in private with Varama, it seemed he was locked in. "I'll be back with details as soon as I can."

"Thank you, Alten," Toln said gravely. He hesitated, then added: "We heard what you did, dropping in to fight off the Naor, and risking your own life for the governor. The council and I are grateful."

Rylin returned the old soldier's slow head bow. "Thank you," he answered. He didn't deserve much praise. "I wish I could have saved her."

"You can't save everyone, lad," Toln said with weary authority. "Be careful out there." He saluted, and Rylin returned the gesture before starting up the stairs.

Almost certainly Toln had trained at the Altenerai academy, and he wondered idly if he'd gotten out at third rank and worked his way up through service, or if he'd come out as an officer around fourth or fifth rank.

After two more flights of stairs he emerged on the square tower battlement to find Lelanc with head sunk into a large water vat. Green banners fluttered on flagpoles, and a pair of green-garbed men from the signal corps waited near a large swivel-mounted brass plate that was highly polished. They studied the south, where Rylin saw distant flashes, and the taller of the men scribbled with white chalk on a black slate.

While one signalman deftly maneuvered the mirror to cast a response, the chalker looked up as Rylin stopped beside him.

"What's the message?" Rylin asked.

"Bad news, Alten. The Naor vanguard's only a few hours from the last refugees, and their signal tower's going to have to be evacuated."

Rylin nodded. "Any idea on numbers yet?"

"They're moving in three columns, with five or six thousand in the closest."

Rylin restrained himself from showing any visible reaction to those huge numbers. He merely nodded and started to move past before the signalman stopped him.

"Alten, we heard what you did for the governor and her niece."

He wished that people would stop complimenting him about that. He hadn't managed to rescue the person who'd probably mattered most. "Just doing my job."

The second signalman stepped away from the bronze plate and saluted him. "You ready to take the fight to the Naor, Alten?"

"I'm always ready for that." Rylin spotted a waterskin at the man's waist, then his eyes drifted to a small cache of jars on a little table beside the mirror. Of course. The signalmen might be up here for hours waiting on communication. They probably kept a supply of food on hand. "I wonder if I might prevail on your hospitality."

The first one noted the direction of his look. "Of course, Alten. We'd be honored. I'd best get this to the captain." He started for the stairs.

The tall one, a broad fellow with a mustache, shook his head at Rylin. "You don't want our fare. It's nothing but some cured meat and raisins and nuts, things we can snack on a bit. And some watered wine. We can have something better brought up—"

"That's good enough for me." Rylin meant to say that he hadn't eaten breakfast yet, but at the way the signalman lit up at the idea of sharing food, he didn't elaborate. The fellow was positively delighted to be passing over the pale wine and the dried food, and watched as Rylin brought up a handful of raisins and nuts.

The explosion of flavor once he crunched down was a tremendous pleasure, and he closed his eyes as he chewed. The simple mix was immensely satisfying, an unfortunate reminder of just how famished he really was. A lot of spell work could do that to a person. It was all he could do to keep from wolfing the contents.

Much as he wanted to stay and gorge himself, he kept to a few mouthfuls and a couple of drinks to wash it down, for he saw Lelanc staring at him. He thanked the signalman again, made his farewells, and joined the ko'aye.

Lelanc took him in with those great amber eyes as he walked up, then bobbed her head as he stopped. "I greet you, Rylin."

Rylin bowed formally. "I greet you, Lelanc. How are you feeling today?"

The creature regarded him with unblinking eyes. "I ache for my sister."

He thought about saying the corps and the people of Arappa would miss Aradel, too, but something about Lelanc's dejectedly hanging head brought him up short. "Until yesterday I didn't realize how close the two of you were."

"My nest mates ride the red wind, and her mate and her blood sisters had passed into the fire. We joked that we were war mates."

"I have sisters and a brother," he said, wondering why he did so even as he continued. "We're not as close as we ought to be. I should probably see them more often."

"Yes," Lelanc said. "Because one day you will be able to look upon them only with the eye of your mind."

Rylin cleared his throat. "What did you see while you were flying today?"

"Two long lines of Naor, but a third comes from farther off. Behind them were many who walked, or who drove wagons. Also there were herds of grass-eating animals behind."

"What was on those wagons?"

"Many food things."

"Were there any signs of siege engines?" Rylin asked. "Ladders, catapults, battering rams?"

"I do not know what is battering rams. Ladders there were. I saw no fling machines."

"Were there any strange vehicles carried on wheels?"

"Nothing aside from wagons."

Rylin now understood what Toln had meant about the ko'aye's lack of understanding. He supposed this was as good a time as any to broach a delicate subject. "Would you mind if I tagged along on the next flight?"

Lelanc's narrow head lowered and pointed more directly at him. "Do you wish to ride with me?"

"If you would have me."

Lelanc blinked once, slowly. "I have already said I would. Is it time to fight Naor?"

"It may be. First I want to see their numbers."

"It is good to count the teeth of your enemy before you bring out your claws." Lelanc extended her head toward him and her voice grew softer. "Rylin, I am told that they will take the meat of my ground sister and burn it, so her spirit will fly free. What do you think of that?"

He attempted to puzzle out the creature's meaning.

She explained further. "Do you believe this is when the spirit goes?"

"Ah. Not all of us believe the same thing. It depends upon where we're from. People of The Fragments burn their dead. So do those in Ekhem. We from Erymyr inter them."

"I have heard this. Both are strange, I think. Ko'aye spirit goes when the heart stops and the light dies, and then there is nothing but meat. Why burn the meat you will not eat, or let it rot in the stone house?"

"It's the way things are done," he answered.

"But does this help the spirit of ground walkers?"

"I think funerals are more about the living than the dead." It was what his own brother had told him at their father's wake. "It's a ceremony for saying good-bye, so that those who loved the dead can remember together."

Lelanc's head rose. "This has more sense," she said. Then: "I think I like it. I had not wanted to watch the meat burn, but I think now I will see it."

The creature bobbed her head once as if in silent agreement with her decision, then regarded Rylin again. "Are you ready to fly?"

"I need weapons. Spears and arrows, I mean. And what about your saddle?"

"It is kept there." Lelanc pointed with her snout to a rack of spears, a cache of arrows, and an unstrung bow over by the signalman, as well as a large wooden chest.

The signalman helped him remove the bulky saddle from the chest and

lift it over the ko'aye. He and Rylin fastened it around Lelanc, who confirmed where certain straps were supposed to go, and notified them when
one was too loose. Very soon, he was once more buckled in, and owing to
anticipation, his hunger pangs had mostly vanished.

Rylin pretended ease rather than betraying a hammering mix of excitement and fear. He scarcely had time to return the signalman's salute before
the feathered reptile was advancing on the battlement. Lelanc paused to
rest front feet on the stones, and glanced back at Rylin.

"Now we go." As Lelanc faced forward once more, she unfolded her
great russet wings with a snap of feathers, then pushed off back legs and
hurtled out beyond the tower.

This time he knew to grasp the horn, though it was hard to hold to it at
the sudden jerk of their descent. Rylin's stomach lurched, and he praised
all the Gods for the strap that kept him from flying out of the saddle. Lelanc
dropped fifty feet, caught a current, then banked right.

After the ungainly exit, the astonishing rise was a pleasure. With the
smallest of adjustments Lelanc changed their direction and soon they had
soared far out over the countryside. To right and left Rylin saw countless
winding valleys. The view was invigorating, despite the cold air that chilled
his hands and face.

It eventually proved worrying as well. Not because of the height, to
which he became accustomed, but because there were so many Naor. Beyond a short column of horse troops there were two more long ones on
foot, and more driving supply wagons. And behind them were blackened
villages that sent smoke curling into the sky all along the great Yevlin River
that threaded through and gave name to the realm's central valley.

He urged Lelanc to fly closer over the supply train, but spotted no siege
engines among the men and horses. There were only small wagons, likely
carrying tools and weapons. It made no sense. From the size of their force,
the Naor were planning a long campaign, and they were marching on Alantris, the central city of the realm. How were they planning to overcome the
city walls?

He had to find answers. He leaned forward in his saddle and shouted
up. "Lelanc, do you feel like hunting some Naor?"

The creature let out a fierce, triumphant shriek and turned her head sideways. Her voice drifted back to him. "The Naor hunt my people, and
carry their skulls on poles. It pleased me to hunt them even before they slew
my sister."

"Let's swing out in advance of the easternmost column. I spotted some
long-range scouts. I want to capture one alive."

"Very well." Lelanc beat her wings and sent them onward.

From hundreds of feet in the air, the burned-out villages left a stain that haunted the loveliness in the view. Yet pain and loss and sorrow seemed much more remote from this vantage point. Rylin wondered if that's how the Gods felt about such things.

Soon they were ahead of the main force, and before long Lelanc bore down on the five scouts he'd seen, swinging in from the west so her shadow lay behind them. Rylin feathered the lead rider in the shoulder, then shot another as the man turned to see why his friend shouted.

By then, the scouts were spreading out across the face of a hill, lifting their spears.

The last thing Rylin wanted was to get Lelanc injured, so he reached through the inner world and sent tendrils of alarm at the minds of the horses. Two of them bucked and went wild before any of the Naor could launch weapons.

Lelanc circled for another pass. Rylin called to the wind rider: "Get me close to the ground and I'll leap clear."

"As you wish."

Lelanc dropped but didn't slow her speed. Rylin conjured up energy already waning, undid the waist strap, and threw himself overside.

This time he gauged the wind better so the gust slowed him at the perfect moment. He struck the ground first with his palms to help absorb the shock of impact, then rolled into a crouch, drew his sword, and stood.

One of the Naor riders trotted forward, spear ready.

Lelanc's shadow set his beast shying, though, and Rylin closed quickly to drive his blade into the man's side. The scout cried out and dropped from his saddle as his panicked horse galloped off.

Two dehorsed Naor charged from the waist-high grass. Rylin laughed as they advanced, hoping he sounded as mad as Kyrkenall. He'd always wanted to try that.

The Naor roared battle cries in return. So much for intimidating them. The one he'd struck in the shoulder trotted forward on his mount, smiling fiercely as he lifted his spear.

Rylin paused, readying another slide into the inner world, then saw Lelanc glide in behind the Naor horseman and swat him with an extended tail. The warrior shouted in surprise as he was lifted from the saddle and smashed face-first into the ground. The attack startled his horse as well. It leapt over its stunned passenger. Lelanc banked then dropped like a great hawk, both claws aimed for the prone warrior.

The last two Naor closed on Rylin.

He ducked the first swing at his head, and thrust, but the redhead's bronze cuirass absorbed the blow. The second enemy simultaneously lashed at his side, and he felt his wind leave him even though the khalat kept the blow from his skin. That was going to leave a deeper bruise.

Rylin drove his sword up through the second man's chin and kicked the dying man toward the last warrior.

The remaining Naor jumped clear, shouted, and slashed wildly. Rylin parried once, twice, backstepped, then hit the man with a blast of untethered pain.

That stopped him in his tracks, leaving him open enough for Rylin to smack the sword from the Naor's shaking fingers. He kicked the fellow's legs out from under him and then put sword to the warrior's throat.

His opponent, an older Naor with gray in his yellow beard, frowned up at him. "You unmanned me with your spell, boy lover."

"Boy lover?" Rylin repeated.

"That's right," he drawled. "You rump-loving fairy boys always cheat."

Rylin didn't know what to make of that. "Are those supposed to be insults?"

The Naor just glared.

"I mean, I love a shapely ass as much as anyone. Maybe more."

"Man ass."

What was wrong with him? Why did it matter to the Naor who he found attractive? And what sort of degenerate would think of sexual contact with children, even as an insult? "I think I just caught the world's dumbest Naor," he said aloud.

The warrior glowered. "Who are you?"

Rylin's name was so poorly known it wouldn't matter. Although . . . if he let the man live his own reputation might grow. While that was an attractive thought, he was seized by a strange whim. "I'm N'lahr the Grim, risen from the dead."

The effect upon the Naor was far greater than Rylin might have hoped, for his eyes bulged. Rylin had never thought so bold-faced a lie would be taken seriously.

"I didn't know you could use magic!" he said, openmouthed.

"How do you think I brought myself back?"

The whitening of the Naor's weathered face was almost comical.

Rylin stared as menacingly as he could manage, and thought again of the promise Cerai had held out, that hearthstones could boost magical stamina. One encounter and he was nearly out of power. No matter. He would use what little he had to get some answers.

"How are you planning to get through the walls of Alantris?" he asked. The man's mind flooded with images and Rylin began to sift them.

24

A Fresher Look

High windows were thrown open in the meeting room so that dust motes danced in the wan gold light of morning. Birds called merrily, uncaring that the Naor would soon attack the walls they perched on.

Rylin finished summarizing his scouting foray and paused to bring wine to his dry throat, his gaze roving over the assembled listeners. He wished he'd taken time to shave. Varama, silent and unreadable as ever, sat on his left. On his right was Alten Cerai, her long black hair a lustrous complement to her sophisticated charm.

Across from him was the city guard officer, Toln, flinty blue eyes bright. He hadn't bothered to remove his leather and ringmail cuirass, but his helm sat beside his chair. The acting governor, Feolia, elevated from the five-member city council, sat at the head, her round face pale and haggard, head wrapped in an embroidered silver scarf. The other councilors ranged solemnly to either side.

Feolia looked perplexed. With good reason. The numbers he'd reported were impossibly vast; half the population of Alantris itself. Toln shifted uncomfortably. The Altenerai showed little reaction.

"You're sure the Naor are fielding that many?" Toln asked. "I don't mean to doubt you, lad. I just hope you're wrong."

Rylin swallowed the weak wine. He'd never been partial to vintages from The Fragments. As he sat the goblet down, he repeated the most alarming of his observations. "Yes. There are close to fifteen thousand warriors and three thousand support troops moving toward Alantris. They'll be here within a couple of hours." He didn't add that he'd some experience counting in the field from the last war. "There's another strange thing. I didn't see any equipment for siege warfare. No towers or catapults of any kind.

The scout I questioned had heard gossip that his kinsmen command ko'aye, but I saw none, and Lelanc tells me her kind would never ally with those who hunted them."

"She's right," Cerai asserted.

"It's a strange rumor, though, don't you think?" Rylin asked. "The scout hadn't seen the ko'aye, but he'd heard they were going to be used to open the city."

Varama seized upon a different concern. "The last time the Naor came for Alantris they had a good long look at the walls. They know how hard it is to get in. They're planning something new."

"Maybe they expect to build siege engines when they get here," one of the councilors suggested. Her voice was surprisingly mild.

Varama shook her head. "There's too little time for a siege before our reinforcements arrive and they know it. The Allied Realms will have troops here in less than five days at this point."

Rylin silently agreed. Word was sent to the border by signal tower, and horsed messengers would have surely galloped the length of Erymyr by now. The Kaneshi cavalry, always ready for action, would slaughter any Naor caught outside of fortifications. So they must think they could get behind walls, presumably the walls of Alantris, before then.

"Surely," Cerai acknowledged. "But remember that reinforcements will have to choose between us and Arappa since the Naor are apparently attacking both cities. Any reinforcements will be stretched thin."

Rylin thought that Feolia paled further, if that was possible, at this news.

"We can hold out," Toln asserted, patting the table. "There's no way the Naor can breach all three rings of walls. Even one is a stretch in the time they have. We've arrows and spears sharpened and ready for them. We've a year's worth of grain. The wells run deep. When the reinforcements turn up we'll have Kaneshi cavalry. The Naor never had much that could counter them."

Denalia had said almost exactly the same thing.

"That may be true," Feolia agreed. "But they'll lay waste to everything. Fields. Homes. Temples. They'll kill and cook any animals they lay hands on. They'll kill anyone brave enough to make a stand, and some of our scouts or signal corps along with them."

Toln acknowledged that with a grim nod. "I know their methods."

Another of the councilors, a ruddy middle-aged man, spoke up. "Isn't it possible that this is just a very large raid and that it wasn't planned very well?"

Rylin recognized a note of impatience in Varama's answer, probably because she had to repeat herself: "An operation this large took an immense amount of preparation. They wouldn't just trust to chance. They're planning something unusual."

Feolia fixed Rylin with a hard stare. "Didn't Governor Aradel have some suggestion for a battle plan?"

"She did," Rylin answered. He hated to dash the new governor's hopes even further. He'd talked over what Aradel had said with Varama and Cerai on the ride toward Alantris yesterday. "But we have to have larger numbers to carry it off. We can lure the bulk of their force to the killing ground but can't ambush them successfully with only a few hundred soldiers of our own."

"Aradel might have managed something," Cerai admitted reluctantly. "But we unfortunately don't know what she had in mind."

The acting governor sighed quietly, visibly marshaled herself, then leaned forward. "Well? What do you advise?"

Varama spoke first. "The defenses are in good condition. Aradel has well prepared the city for another attack. But it's almost certain the Naor have had scouts in here disguised as merchants or travelers. You must assume they've gotten a good look at nearly everything important."

Judging from Feolia's expression, she hadn't considered that possibility.

Varama continued. "Even an inept spy could find out about the grain silos, and the fields in the city, and they already knew about the deep wells. Yet they've come anyway."

Varama looked as though she meant to say more, but Cerai interrupted smoothly. "We have to concentrate on making adjustments the Naor won't know about. There have to be weaker places in the walls, blind spots, things like that. We can fortify them. Magically if necessary."

Rylin saw Toln nodding at this suggestion.

"Varama and I can spearhead those efforts. We need any extra spell casters you have on staff. Do you have hearthstones, Governor?"

Feolia looked blankly at her, then licked her lips. Rylin doubted she knew what a hearthstone was until a thoughtful look came into her eyes. Of course. It had been Alantris, after all, where the things had last been deployed against the Naor, and when the enemy's proximity to them had proved so dangerous. Probably some councilors knew exactly what hearthstones were. "We turned all of ours over to the crown. I thought they were too dangerous to use in battle."

Cerai nodded. "They are. But we'll use the ones we have with us before the Naor arrive. If we gather the city's most powerful mages we can definitely reinforce any vulnerable spots. We might even adjust the terrain a little, the way Rialla did."

"Bolstering our defenses is first priority," Varama agreed. "I've designed a new catapult that will be of better use against aerial attacks, if the rumors of enemy ko'aye are true." She looked over at Toln. "I'll need your best carpenters and bowyers."

"Of course," the officer replied. "Whatever you need."

"I've also been working on some other experiments that should prove useful. I'll need to put my squires in charge of additional workmen."

"Their knowledge is welcome," Feolia said.

Varama had already enlisted Sansyra and some of her other favorite squires to deploy the city's existing ballistae and catapults, for they'd learned a lot under her tutelage.

Varama turned to Rylin. "What we lack is comprehensive intelligence. We're going to need an officer, preferably someone high in their chain of command."

She didn't ask much, he thought, but he nodded, as though it would be a simple thing to slip deeply behind enemy lines, infiltrate their camp, interrogate the right kind of officer, and return. He hoped his nonchalance sounded suitably Altenerai-like. "I'll have better luck grabbing one at night."

"Of course."

They'd probably erect their camps surrounding the city, well outside bow or catapult range. He'd have to fly out on Lelanc, and it occurred to him he could use one of Varama's semblance stones, but a lot would be left to opportunity and instinct.

There was a rap on the door and it opened before the acting governor realized it was up to her to grant permission to enter. Denalia stepped through and bowed her head respectfully toward the table.

She had very nice legs, Rylin decided, and they were hard to miss in that armored skirt, which struck just above her knees. Presumably she'd be donning boots and shin greaves for the battle, but skillfully tied sandals showcased her slim ankles and toned calves nicely. The rest of her more feminine assets were disguised by a leather cuirass, though there was no missing the clean, youthful lines of her face and her high cheekbones. He suddenly wanted to know, very much, what her hair looked like beneath that dark red head wrap. He would never have thought a scarf alluring until it kept him from seeing what he desired.

"Your pardon, my Governor," she said, bowing her head.

"Of course," Feolia replied. "Has something happened?"

Denalia presented a stained piece of parchment. "The Naor have sent a message." She gulped and steeled herself. "It was driven through a dead squire they had tied to a nag."

"What squire?" Varama asked. Once, Rylin might have thought her un-fazed by the information. Now he recognized by the intensity of her gaze that she was as troubled as he.

"I don't know his name, Alten," Denalia said. "He's a fifth ranker."

Rylin knew a pang at the thought of any brave soldier treated so shab-bily. It was hard to imagine a good reason for the squire to have been wan-dering by himself unless he were a messenger from Erymyr or Arappa. Or Denaven. At that thought, Rylin's hands involuntarily tightened against the table's edge.

"Can we see the note?" Feolia asked.

Denalia walked solemnly forward to present the rough scrap.

The acting governor scanned the writing there, then passed it to Varama, who stared for a moment before reading aloud. "Open your gates before sunfall and we will let your women live. Otherwise all sit the pyres when we break your walls."

"Who signed it?" Cerai asked.

"Some Naor general I've never heard of." Varama handed the missive to her matter-of-factly.

"They sound pretty sure about breaking the walls," Toln said. "If you're going to work any magic you'd best get on it. You think they have some mages of their own?"

"I doubt they've anyone approaching our skill," Cerai said confidently. "And they can't have expected Varama to turn up with most of the squire corps, some of whom are mages."

That was an excellent point. Probably no one among the city's usual spell casters approached Cerai's ability; hopefully no one among the Naor did, either.

Varama looked across the table to Toln. "Summon your best. Cerai and I will start work immediately."

"Very good, Alten."

Varama's eyes flicked to Rylin, and her voice was low. "Examine the body. Closely. Ignore nothing. I'll need a report."

He started to reassure her he would, then realized that she stressed the first because she expected, or hoped, to find something and couldn't be there.

Rylin had wished a private word with her after the meeting, particu-larly about their search for Kyrkenall and how to deal with the conspiracy. He'd yet to speak with her alone since he'd flown with Lelanc yesterday morning. It didn't look as though he'd have the chance now. Fair enough. He supposed that an invasion took precedence over everything else. "Acknowledged."

"We'd best convene again after Aradel's funeral," Varama suggested to Feolia. It was scheduled to be held that evening.

"Certainly," the acting governor said.

At unspoken agreement, they all stood. Cerai and Varama left with Toln, who followed the governor. Rylin turned to the young woman warrior. "Denalia, can you show me the way to the body?"

Her eyes flashed warning. "It's not very pleasant."

"I have my orders."

Denalia's head scarf bobbed as she nodded. He watched her turn and enjoyed the view.

They followed the rest down a long flight of wooden stairs. Denalia looked back at him. "It's truly barbaric, Alten."

"I'm sure it is." He tried to shift his mind from the mystery of her hair to the unpleasant task that lay before him.

At the main floor they left the others and turned down a wide hallway. Denalia spoke over the smack of her strap sandals on the granite floor.

"I've never seen anything like it. I'm sure you Altenerai are used to this sort of thing."

"This is all new to me, I'm afraid."

When they arrived at a two-story brick barracks across from the stables, Rylin spotted a small pile of bloodstained squire gear beside its doorway and his heart dropped. How was he supposed to examine anything if others were already rifling through it all? Stepping inside, he discovered the squires had laid the body on a table. They were dipping into buckets with cloths to wash him clean.

"Stop." Rylin's voice was harsher than he intended.

They looked up, their faces stricken with grief, then struggled to come to attention.

"At ease. Varama wants the body and all of his belongings examined carefully," he explained as he came forward.

The squires stepped aside for him. Each wore the gray tabards typical of their position.

"It's Danik, sir," said one with a sob, a wide-hipped blond third ranker.

"Well, damn," Rylin said quietly. Danik was Lasren's preferred squire, the one he usually took on patrol runs. He'd taken him along on the search for Kyrkenall. Did that mean that Lasren was somewhere nearby? And might Lasren himself be dead?

Rylin decided that unlikely. If Lasren were dead, the Naor would have sent his body rather than a squire's, the better to strike fear into the hearts of the people of Alantris.

Possibly the squire had been sent toward Alantris to deliver a message, although for all Rylin knew the Naor might have found him on the way to some other destination.

Sighing sadly, Rylin stepped forward to consider Danik. He almost didn't recognize the fifth ranker. His chest was a horror of blood and torn skin. His face was bruised and bloody, the chin twisted out of line. His eyes were open and staring, locked somehow in rage and pain both.

"Do you think they tore his heart out while he was still alive, Alten?" the squire asked, her eyes intent upon him. "Or did they just make it look that way?"

A fair question. He hated to think Danik had suffered. How to tell? Of course. "Are his wrists chafed? His ankles?"

The squires stepped forward at his question and looked. Rylin gratefully tore his eyes away from the poor man's face.

Danik's legs and ankles were free of any bruises or lesions. One of his hands had skinned knuckles, but there were no marks on his wrists.

The female squire came to the same conclusion. "It doesn't look like it, sir."

"Then they did this after his death. Danik didn't die easy, but he didn't die on their altars." He was startled to hear his voice crack a little. "He was a good man."

Rylin forced himself to look at the body again. Though he had no experience "closely examining" dead people, he'd seen enough battle casualties to be aware of some general principles. "He can't have been dead very long. He's not stiff yet." Danik's condition suggested that he'd been killed somewhere close, so he most likely was sent to Alantris specifically. Had it been to tell them reinforcements were on the way, or to request assistance in Denaven's search for Elenai and Kyrkenall? Or could Danik have been contacting them about something else altogether?

Rylin grasped the dead man's shoulder, thinking of how he'd sometimes patted him there when he'd shot well.

He rolled the body onto its side so he could look at his back, noting that the head lolled oddly, even for someone loose with death. Danik had taken a nasty gash to the back of his neck, right near the base of the skull. Rylin pushed hair aside to look at the injury. "I think a spear blow here's what killed him." Gently, he returned the body to its back.

Denalia had watched silently from afar until she addressed Rylin in a soft voice. "If he had a message, do you think he could have hidden it on his clothes?"

"No." Rylin shook his head. "It would have been verbal."

"And do you think it was about reinforcements?"

"It's hard to know." Rylin mulled over what else he could learn from the body. What, he wondered, would Varama do?

Rylin couldn't be sure of that, but he guessed that she'd somehow pull more information out of the scene than he'd managed.

He wished Varama's own squires were on hand rather than these lower rankers. Both Sansyra and Lemahl were more used to her methods of thought than he was. But they would likely be busy with the city's defenses until the Naor attacked.

He stared uselessly at the body, doing his best to ignore the way the squires watched him. It was as if they expected him to say or do something amazing, and he had nothing to give.

Finally, resigned that there didn't seem to be much more he could learn from the corpse, he told the squires they could return to preparing it for burial, and bent to examine the dead man's clothing. Information there proved elusive as well. There were certainly no hidden pockets in his tunic, and his storage pouches were gone. The armor was savaged and bloody and splattered with mud. Dirt caked his riding boots.

"Have you found anything?" Denalia asked.

Rylin set aside the second boot and shook his head no.

"What were you looking for?"

"I'd have known it if I found it." He offered a weak smile. No one could accuse him of failing to be thorough. "I'd like to wash up."

"Of course." She appraised his appearance with a quick glance, and he was suddenly aware of his beard stubble and the dust and dirt clinging to his own clothing. He'd washed face and hands after he'd returned from his scouting trip, but he felt grimy. "Can you show me to the baths?"

"Certainly."

"Lead on." He gestured for her to precede him.

Aradel's niece guided him to the governor's own baths on the ground floor of the citadel, stating she expected he might want some privacy, then ensured there was a supply of soaps, oils, and towels before shooing servants away and opening the door into a tiled room with steaming, recessed pools.

"That one on the left is the warmest." Denalia raised one arm so that it brushed against his own. She looked at him through long lashes. "Do you need any help?"

Yes, he thought, gods yes, that would be lovely, but for some reason, he only smiled. "I think I can manage."

Hearing a footfall, he turned to discover Varama had advanced into the area behind them and was now stepping closer, having scuffed her heel on a tile.

"Now that the bathing arrangements are settled," she announced, "I hope I might have a moment with the alten myself."

Denalia reddened. "Of course, Alten. He . . . I . . . Yes, here he is." And Denalia darted quickly away without even a backward glance.

Amused, Rylin noted with approval the way she swayed even when she hurried.

"It's nice to see that you've retained your priorities," Varama told him.

"I didn't expect to see you so soon. I need to wash up."

"That can wait a moment." She closed the door, leaving them alone in the baths.

He supposed it could, although perhaps she'd forgotten he'd been handling a corpse.

"How did the examination go?"

He offered empty palms, wishing he had more to tell her. "He'd been killed from behind, by a spear thrust, and slain before they mutilated him. He clearly went down fighting."

"Do you have any idea from which way he'd come?"

Rylin shook his head.

"I think we should link."

He nodded once, and sighed inwardly. He didn't relish the inevitable criticism for failing to do or think something.

"Order your thoughts," she said. He wondered at the sharp tone to her voice. She was almost snapping at him. "Think about what you saw."

"I'm ready."

He willed his ring not to defend him as her mind touched his own. It was simpler to share his thoughts than it had been the previous time, for there was but one incident, rather than a whole series of them, and he'd been so consumed with both regret for what had happened to the squire and mild disgust to be inspecting him, that those emotions pushed most stray thoughts aside.

She drew back after only a few moments, and blinked at him. "Your conclusions are accurate, if a little elementary."

"You mean they're wrong?"

"I didn't say that. But there was more to be gained by what you saw."

"What did I miss?"

"A dozen details about his personal habits, but more important for our purposes: the wear on the inseam of his breeches, compared to the better condition of other parts of the garment, indicates a great deal of hard riding, and the dirt on upper sole seams was the chalky soil of the mountainous uplands to the northeast, not the richer loam of the valleys in the southern Fragments."

Damn. He could only stare, dumbly. How had she known what dirt to expect from different parts of the realm?

There was no missing the disappointment in her eyes, and he fought against rising resentment. He shouldn't resent her, he knew, but his own inadequacy. If he'd been paying attention, he might well have noted the color of the earth of various places. His eyes worked as well as the next person's, after all, and so did his memory. How was it that Varama seemed always to be aware? Could he really learn the trick himself?

"So they're to the north of us, then."

"Yes. Apparently Kyrkenall and the squire have thus far evaded Denaven's party, hence the great deal of time and toil in the saddle, but they almost surely dispatched Danik to Alantris from the northern Fragments because they've found Kyrkenall and need some additional support. It's possible something is wrong with Wyndyss as they could hardly fail to seek Belahn's aid first. It's also possible that the Naor have encroached up there, but Denaven's group would have traveled to Alantris directly if they'd learned the extent of the Naor invasion, rather than sending a lone squire. And if that were the case they could hardly have departed for the longer journey to Arappa without sending one or two Altenerai here."

Rylin nodded. Her deductions were as logical as ever. "So what are we going to do with that information?"

"Unfortunately, there's nothing we can do about it, now. If all goes well with your expedition this evening, you can try flying north and looking for signs of Kyrkenall via Denaven's encampment. The latter will be more obvious than the former, I'm sure."

Finding Denaven's camp would be nearly impossible in the forested mountains and dales to the north, and spotting a wily pair of fugitives under those circumstances even worse. But he supposed he'd "eat that bread when it was baked," as Denaven himself might say. Surviving his mission tonight into the heart of the enemy's camp should be his main concern at the moment.

He half expected her to suggest even more outlandish assignments for him when she added. "Tell me what you plan after you freshen up. Food, I suppose?"

"A little something," he admitted. "I haven't eaten properly yet. But I mean to walk the walls," he added quickly.

"Yes. Walk the walls. Note where the best archers should be posted and where the fire brigades should be stationed. Learn the number of soldiers at each gate, and the names of the commanders."

"If you like," he said. That sounded a bit much.

"It's not what I like, it's what's needed, Rylin. I need," she said as she stepped closer to him, "to depend upon you. I need to know that you're not distracted, and that you're fully engaged. Not watching women's legs or thinking about their breasts or dreaming of cool wine or whatever else."

"Right, I understand."

"Do you? When the pieces are in motion you always find focus. But I want you to be thinking about the pieces all the time. Do you understand?"

"You think I'm not being observant enough."

"Yes. Observe more. There's much more going on here than an invasion."

"What do you mean?"

She looked over her shoulder as if to verify that the door was closed. He then saw her ring flare and she glanced all around, presumably sensing for others somehow hidden and close enough to hear. Satisfied at last, she addressed him softly. "I've finally examined the keystone and it's very different from other hearthstones."

"How?"

"When you link to it, instead of finding a subtly subversive source of power, you're looking on stunningly realistic portrayals of the realms. I don't mean of landscapes from a window, I mean painted from on high as if you're on the highest cliff imaginable."

"Like very detailed maps?"

"Precisely."

"What would the point of that be?"

"I hope the answer will be more obvious after further study."

It was probably useless to ask her to speculate, so he decided to ask after a more immediate concern, her caution earlier in relaying this information. "But why does it worry you?"

"I'm worried because I think it's why Cerai came."

How did she come to that conclusion? "If that's all she wants, she could have overpowered us a while ago."

"It's not all she wants. She also wants to know our plans."

"But she's helping to defend Alantris."

"She's stuck here, now," Varama pointed out, "even if she doesn't want to defend it."

He had to remind himself that Varama was usually right, even as he continued to doubt. "So do you think she's in league with Denaven and the queen?"

Varama's frown deepened. "I don't know. I don't understand her anymore. Her power's grown, Rylin. And she's put an awful lot of effort into changing herself. And she fashioned that animal. That's . . ."

"Astonishing?"

"I was going to say horrifying. It has to have taken an inordinate amount of time, not to mention a frightening level of power. It means she's been working on honing those skills rather than defending the realms or even finding hearthstones."

"Maybe she's been trying to improve herself for the good of the realms."

Varama smiled drolly. "Yes, I'm sure that's why she made herself more beautiful."

"She hates Denaven," Rylin pointed out.

"I've no doubt of it. It doesn't mean she's not working with the queen."

Another thought had occurred to him. "I notice there've been no attacks from the queen since we arrived in Alantris. Could that be because she knows Cerai's here?"

"Possibly. Or it might be that she can no longer sense whom to attack because I'm keeping the keystone as far away from other people as I can. Or she may be biding her time so we can defend Alantris."

"What do we do? Trust Cerai, or not? And what about Kyrkenall? How do we help him?"

Varama frowned. "I'm overwhelming you, aren't I?" Her eyes bored into his. "First priority is defending the city. Don't be complacent. The Naor are planning something to breach these walls."

"Fine. But we'll stop them. And then what?"

"You're assuming it will be easy. Don't do that."

"I'm not assuming that. I'm just trying to piece out what to do about the whole reason we fled Darassus—Kyrkenall."

"Kyrkenall's not the reason we fled. We fled because we had evidence of a grand conspiracy that he was framed by."

He just managed not to sigh. She'd known what he meant.

"Kyrkenall's going to have to be on his own for now. His logical choice was to run for Aradel, but he clearly made a decision based upon circumstances I hadn't accounted for. We'll just have to pray that he chose wisely.

As to Cerai: she's already asked me about you and your capability, and whether I thought you would take offense to studying with her for a while."

Rylin jumped to the point. "You want me to spy on her."

"I want you to learn the city and its defenses better than you know your own face. But play upon Cerai's interest and see if you can learn anything whenever you're together."

"I can do that."

"I must stress that you're not dealing with a lovestruck young woman or a former flame. You must be extraordinarily careful. She's quite clever."

"I understand."

"I'm glad you do. I'd like to think you see just how dangerous she could be as an opponent. She would crush you in any sorcerous contest, Rylin."

After seeing Cerai in action he understood that all too well.

"That's nothing against you. I couldn't stand against her myself in a direct battle."

"Believe me, thanks to recent events I'm well aware of just how weak I really am," he admitted. "Compared to Cerai, I'm nothing. And you keep thinking that I can rise to your abilities, but you're ten times smarter than I am."

"We each have different gifts, Rylin. I don't expect you to suddenly develop interest or ability in the intellectual challenges that engage me, anymore than I expect you to contest with Cerai's sorcerous powers. That hardly means that you don't have prowess. Look at me. I could never have held my own against Kalandra or Commander Renik, and I couldn't outfight some of the Altenerai. But I have a niche."

"You're saying I have to find a speciality?"

"I'm saying you need to be cognizant of both your strengths and weaknesses. Be present in every moment, *and* always look ahead. Your combination of skills is impressive. You're capable of great insight, cleverness, initiative, and social grace, which distinguishes you from Kyrkenall, though you share some of his other characteristics."

Her candor made him a little uncomfortable. And how could he be looking ahead if he was being present in the moment?

"You look confused."

He offered only open palms and a weak smile.

"Your charm is another strength. As well as a somewhat tarnished sense of honor." She turned from him. "I think the coming days will be a greater test than any you've yet known. I'm going back to the walls. I expect I'll see you there. We'll speak again this evening."

He did little more than wash hands and face again, so lost in his thoughts that he hardly noted what he did. Could Varama be right about Cerai?

Knowing what he knew about the peculiar, brilliant alten, he wondered if she could be wrong. He wanted her to be. He instinctively liked Cerai. She was smart and accomplished. And quite nice to look at.

He'd have to trust his own judgment. And this time, he'd try to be alert, like Varama, to the subtle cues most people missed.

25

~

The Walls of Alantris

As Rylin left the baths, he was concerned he might encounter Denalia waiting outside, but there was no sign of her. He decided he was glad of that, because he wasn't sure what he should say when he met her again.

He spent a few moments combing down his mount before the stable boy saddled Rurudan, then rode through the city to inspect the massive reinforced gates in the imposing outer wall, and to meet the men and women who defended them.

By the second gatehouse, his mind was stuffed with information. Fortunately, long study under Asrahn had taught him tricks for memorizing details. And his eyes, free from all but thin wisps of distraction, assessed everything he found.

Alantris had three large gates and two smaller in the outer walls, which stood twenty feet high, solid, and were wide enough for four men to run abreast. The armories at the gatehouses and the guard towers that rose between them were well stocked. Morale was high, for the soldiers seemed certain the Naor were stupidly here to repeat mistakes from the previous assault. Rylin wasn't so sure, especially given Varama's certainty that they planned something unique, but he kept his worries to himself.

He meant only to introduce himself to officers, but discovered that somehow everyone already knew about him. He was used to the automatic respect he received wearing the blue khalat and ring of office, but he'd seldom been recognized as an individual outside the palace and barracks of Darassus. People brightened at mention of his name, and repeated distorted accounts of how he'd saved the refugees and defenders on the hill. There was even a further detail now; that he turned aside better fare to eat the meals of the common soldiers. He supposed that was because he'd grabbed some rations with the signalmen, but wondered how that could possibly have spread through the ranks so quickly.

This, he thought, must be what it's like for Kyrkenall and the truly famous Altenerai. Except that they deserved acclaim.

As morning wore on toward afternoon, he watched from the outer walls as the Naor turned up at last. Though their numbers were staggering they seemed in no hurry. They arrived at an almost leisurely pace throughout the afternoon, gathering around little cookfires as though they were here for a neighborly spring idle. They erected long rows of brown tents and raised banners topped with little bleached ivory objects Rylin knew for ko'aye skulls. They remained more than a half mile from the city they circled, and Rylin imagined what it would be like to walk among them late tonight, in disguise.

The defenders on the wall were tense but confident, hiding their nervousness with high-spirited jests and occasional provocatively rude gestures toward the invaders.

Rylin studied the Naor as he imagined Varama would, wondering at their seeming complacency. Maybe they assumed their numbers were so vast that no army could threaten them. They might be right. Even the Kaneshi cavalry at full strength would incur heavy losses routing this many. Strangely, though, none of the troops seemed to be engaged in the construction of engines, or even ladders. Those who weren't resting were simply tending weapons, and eating.

They were waiting for something, presumably their wall breakers, but Rylin couldn't imagine how ko'aye could breach these walls for the ground troops, even if the Naor somehow managed to hold sway over creatures that would much rather die than serve them.

Eventually concluding there was nothing more he could learn from this distance, late in the afternoon he made his way to a sally gate in the third and equally thick ring of walls. Just past it the ground rose steeply to meet the high cliff of the citadel. And there he found a trio of Alantran weavers in close consideration of the slick black stone that formed the citadel's wall, partly natural and partly shaped by generations that had gone before. A crack ran from the base, widening into a fist-sized hole at head level before spidering into surrounding stones.

Cerai stood among them with one palm pressed to the wall, eyes closed, serene and beautiful.

He couldn't help but admire her effortless skill. At her thought, defects in the stone were wiped away with the ease of a child rubbing out sketches in the dirt. The crack at the base slowly mended itself as though it had never been.

She then turned her attention to the hole above, which filled with dark matter that soon blended into the surrounding material.

One man among the Alantrans clapped his wrinkled hands with pronounced enthusiasm, as though Cerai had just performed a stage trick.

She turned with a smile, nodded her thanks to the trio, who praised her further, then acknowledged Rylin.

"Impressive work," he said.

"Thank you."

"How go the defenses?"

"Well bolstered now. I think I've done about all I can. I'm heading to the citadel. Do you want to join me?"

How astonishingly easy it had been to win the opportunity to observe her more carefully. "With pleasure."

Cerai beckoned for the graybeard, who stepped forward with a blue satchel. "My hearthstones," she explained. "Give me a moment." She turned to thank the mages with her, then faced Rylin. "Let's go."

Cerai climbed onto a stallion, a piebald rather than her curious magical animal, and the two rode into the streets. She seemed only a little tired.

"So have you really been working magic all day?" Rylin asked.

"Yes."

"And you're not exhausted?"

"I've been tapping into the hearthstones. Their energies aren't entirely free, but they certainly help. And the mages were boosting me a bit."

"I'm glad to know that they're good for something."

"You thought that I had them follow me around to applaud?" she asked with a smile.

"I didn't say that."

He liked her laugh in response, throaty and confident and unrestrained.

"What are you thinking about, Rylin?"

Did she know? Surely his ring, set to alert status, would warn him even if she were probing his mind, wouldn't it? "Earlier you said that using a hearthstone can build magical endurance."

"I find it does. If you'd like, we can experiment tomorrow morning. I'd suggest this evening, but Aradel's funeral is liable to run late."

Yes. A sorrowful reminder of all that was truly at stake.

They switched to single file to ride past a knot of children, intent upon their game of tag until they stopped to stare in awe at the Altenerai who passed. Rylin offered a friendly wave and the children raised hands in greeting.

When he and Cerai were side by side once more, she continued as if there'd been no pause. "We'll have our hands full during the siege, I'm sure, but perhaps we can work in a little practice before they start in earnest. When it's over, maybe I can tear you away from Varama and you can travel with me for a while."

"I'd be honored," he said, piqued by a little guilt. Much as Varama had assigned him to learn about Cerai, he found that he wished to do so, leaving him feeling as though he deceived both women at once.

They passed a line of soldiers carrying spears, and returned their salutes.

"I have a lot of improvements to make," Rylin admitted.

They neared the walls of the towering citadel, three-spear-lengths high, its bronze doors open onto a dusty courtyard. She didn't respond to him until she swung down from her horse. Her gaze was direct and intent. "Look, if you think you have room for improvement, then improve. N'lahr never gave up drills. Even the day after a battle. If he could move, he woke up early and practiced. And people talk about Temahr and his binges, but those were the exception, not the rule. Every day he was sober he'd exercise. You don't just have to own your skill, you have to love it."

He climbed down from his mount. She certainly sounded like an ordinary alten, not one scheming for some hidden agenda. How exactly should he try to pry more information from her? He just wasn't sure. And that probably meant he shouldn't try. Not now. Not if he wanted to be careful.

"I'm going to hit the baths," she said. "I'll see you at the ceremony this evening."

He nodded and pressed his hand to his chest in salute.

"Hail," she said, then turned on her heel.

He shook his head at himself rather than watching her walk, then shooed the stableboys away and cared for his own animal. As he brushed his horse down, he heard the hands whispering about the act in reverent tones, as though tending for his horse was somehow heroic.

He realized that nearly anything he did could be seen in a new light, now, because he'd performed one act that the populace had heard about.

All that talk of training put him in mind of the fact it had been days since he'd run any exercises, so after a light supper he retired to a small courtyard where he thought he'd be unobserved. A half-dozen windows looked down onto it, but all appeared vacant, so he was without companionship apart from the sculpture of a woman on a plinth. It was only when Rylin drew close to it that he realized the statue wore a khalat.

And he didn't recognize her. She was high-browed, sad-eyed. He supposed he should know all the Altenerai, but he hadn't spent that much time in the Hall of Remembrance. And then he saw the name inscribed below. Of course. Rialla had died saving the city the last time the Naor tried to destroy it.

He came to attention and brought his open hand to his heart in salute. It began as a lighthearted gesture, but as he lowered his arm crisply, it had lost all humor.

"I understand you were a large part of the reason this place held last time."

He looked at the young face, the compressed lips, as he continued talking. "If I must fall, I hope I'll make as much of a difference as you did." And be better remembered, he thought, but that seemed selfish. "I'll strive to live up to your example," he finished.

He stepped away from her. Probably these grounds had been flowerbeds at some point. Now the courtyard was nothing but flat green grass. Rylin drew his blade.

First he'd apply himself to that leap, turn, and strike, a variation on a movement from the twelfth sword form. He'd used it twice in the last days, and both times his landing stance had been too narrow.

Rylin worked through it and then the other higher forms, thinking of a variety of weaknesses he'd been aware of for a long time, and wondering how he got into the habit of declaring himself good enough. Was he still a boy, not a man? Was that what he and Lasren were? Children who won a prize, using it like a flashing symbol to grab at other things they craved?

That wasn't fair, though, was it? He'd worked long and hard to earn the ring. Had there been anything wrong with enjoying the privileges that came with the position?

On the face of it, no. Except that he'd been enjoying them without truly understanding the sacrifices that preceded them. Or maybe without really understanding that he wasn't as ready for those sacrifices as he'd thought.

After a quarter hour, he paused as a horn call sounded, then resumed as he realized it was only for the squires, being called to the citadel to eat, dress, and prepare for the funeral. A quarter hour after that, the sun was sinking, stretching the shadows of the citadel towers so that all of the courtyard was left in darkness. Soon the sun would set. The Naor had called for the city to surrender before then. Had that been merely an idle bluff?

He frowned to himself. Best tidy up. He was making his way to the washroom when horn calls rang from above. He ran up to the third floor, where he could look out over the citadel walls to the Naor hordes.

No longer did they take their ease. Their fires blazed high, and many lifted torches. Others cavorted about the campfires, and their war cries resounded through the evening air. Off somewhere to his right, somebody shouted that they were burning prisoners, and he searched among the countless little fires until he spotted one directly across from the central gate. There, a long row of spikes had been planted, and fire ate at a line of fifty figures bound to them as torch-holding Naor pranced and pointed to the city.

Though flame wreathed the victims, some still moved.

Rylin's hands clenched involuntarily, and almost without thought he started up the stairs toward the roof. It was time for action. He wasn't entirely sure what he planned yet, but he was no longer dreading his scouting mission. He'd kill as many Naor as he could lay hands on while he was at it.

When he reached the roof, Lelanc was gone, but the tall, mustached signalman immediately pointed him west. Shading his eyes against the sinking red ball of the sun, he saw Lelanc flapping her wings with great energy. Highlighted as she was by the sun, it took him a moment to realize something flew behind her. Another ko'aye?

From the west walls, far below and across the city, a different horn call sounded. Not of alert, but of attack

And as his eyes adjusted he suddenly understood. Lelanc streamed in over the outer wall, and on her tail came a creature borne on wings that seemed a mile long. The pursuer dwarfed her, as the citadel's height over-topped a garden fountain.

"What is that thing?" Rylin asked.

No one answered. Only the signalman was there, staring out, and he probably had no more idea than Rylin.

This was one of the ko'aye that Naor scout had told him about.

From far below, down on the distant battlements, great stones whirled into the air from two towers, but the beast beat the air and soared above the missiles as it came on for the wall. Behind and below the monster was the vast crescent horde of Naor clansman, silhouetted starkly. They raised spears that winked back the light so fiercely it seemed each was crusted in flaming gold.

Lelanc soared on and up, outpacing the thing. The pursuer seemed to have lost interest in her anyway, for it bore on toward the enormous outer wall, opened massive scaled black jaws, and roared, a twisting rumble that Rylin felt deep in his chest, like a roll of thunder.

The effect didn't stop with him. He watched, openmouthed as the wall directly in line of the beast crumbled. The height of the western wall just fell away, like leavings brushed from a plate. The soldiers posted upon it dropped to death amid the rubble. The wall still stood, but two-thirds of it had been sheared away from a span ten spears long.

Rylin felt his stomach twist. No wonder the Naor needed no siege craft. Their monstrous wyrms spewed magical destruction.

Two more catapult stones launched as the thing came on, beating great wings, but the crews hadn't sighted right, or the monster wyrm changed angle, for the missiles flew wide even as it roared a second time.

Its blast struck into the first of the inner walls, which tumbled into the rank of homes behind it. The people screamed louder as the land rocked and a dozen dwellings collapsed.

Lelanc flew on and up for the citadel. Rylin wasted no time. He raced for the weapons rack and grabbed all the javelins he could carry, aided by the signalman. The ko'aye swooped in and landed awkwardly.

"You're hurt?" Rylin asked.

"No. Hurry!" Lelanc flapped her wings in agitation.

He vaulted into the saddle and quickly secured weapons. "What is that thing?"

"Something we have to kill," Lelanc shrilled.

He liked her spirit. "Have you seen one before? Does it have weaknesses?"

"I've never seen one before now. It stinks of magic."

The signalman helped him buckle and then stepped back. "Can you stop it?" he asked.

"I mean to try. Go, Lelanc!"

The ko'aye lumbered for the edge, climbed the battlement, and flung herself over the side. They dropped down and away from the tower, curving out from the citadel as they built speed. He ignored his lurching stomach and stared at the Naor running for the breach in the outer walls.

"Keep us above that wyrm."

"Yes."

No longer sun blinded, Rylin had a better look at the beast. It resembled Lelanc only in that it was winged. More reptile than bird, the beast's black length stretched on for hundreds of feet. Barbs stuck up from its spine and skull and scorpion-like from its tail. Three riders sat it: one in front along a thick neck, and two more along its back ridge, both armed with bows. One of those helmed, bearded riders even now drew a bead upon Lelanc, who threw herself higher in the wind. His arrow missed by a wide margin.

The monster wyrm flew straight and slow for the final city wall and the walled citadel on its steep hill beyond, carried by the ponderous flap of its wings. "One more of those roars and I bet towers start tumbling," Rylin called up to Lelanc.

"Their arrow men watch us," she warned him.

"Draw their fire from above. The moment they loose, drop in close." Rylin hefted a javelin. He tried not to think about the Naor rushing the walls. If he and Lelane could bring this thing down, he thought the Alantrans could still hold them back. That outer wall hadn't fully fallen yet. And they had the power of the greatest weaver of the Altenerai. Cerai was probably riding even now to repair that gap.

Lelanc climbed high, and Rylin clung tight with one hand, his boots jammed tight into the stirrups.

There was the briefest hesitation, a moment when they seemed to float, weightless, and then they were dropping almost vertically. His heart raced like a rabbit's.

The Naor archers mounted on the beast winged arrows toward them, and Lelanc veered. Apparently she hadn't quite understood the instructions. Rylin pushed aside the thought of an arrow hitting her. If Lelanc lost control from such a height, they'd be nothing but cobblestone paste.

She leveled out above and parallel to the great blue-black monster, only a couple of spear throws from the citadel. One of the bowmen set another arrow to his string and sighted on them.

Too slow. Rylin caught him through the shoulder and he fell, screaming, arms flailing. Apparently the Naor didn't use saddle straps.

Rylin threw a second javelin, then cursed, for he saw it would be deflected by the top of the rider's flared black helmet. This was the time to risk a little magic. He coaxed the wind to swing it wide, then pushed the point the other way.

It altered in its course and took the man at the base of his skull. There was an explosion of blood, and at the same moment the man slumped the wyrm dropped like a marionette cut from its strings. It smashed through the granary at the foot of the citadel's hill, sliding on through three homes as if they were nothing but kindling. A cascade of hoarded seeds swept out like a golden wave and engulfed its tail. Rylin prayed no one had been inside those houses.

From below, a surge of cheers roared through the city, no matter the destruction.

"Damn," Rylin said. "Why couldn't the wyrm pull up on its own?"

Lelanc beat her wings to climb for the tower. "We stopped it. But they struck me."

"How badly?"

"It hurts to fly. But I can."

"Land at the citadel," he commanded. Surely there were healers there. He twisted in his saddle to look behind. The Naor were charging the low spot, but the Alantran defenders were taking a heavy toll with great flights of arrows, bolstered by catapults. The invaders dropped by the dozens, one catapult stone ploughing through a score of figures as he watched.

With a little luck, they might just hold.

They closed on the platform atop the high tower. There was no sign of the signalman as Rylin unclipped and hopped down, and for some reason his ring had lit. Maybe that was because of exposure to the beast's magic. He was less worried about that than he was of Lelanc's wound.

"Hurry," the ko'aye shouted. By now he recognized her wing fluttering as nerves.

He spotted the dark feathers of an arrow protruding from the under-side of Lelanc's right wing in the meaty leading edge. He put hand to it gently. Fully a foot of wood stood out from where it disappeared into her white feathers, so he didn't imagine it was a particularly deep wound. "Hang on," he said. "I'm going to test it a bit—"

"Rylin!"

At first he thought that Lelanc objected to the idea.

"More come!" Lelanc let out a shrill caw of alert.

At the same moment Rylin heard a second warning horn from the dis-tant wall.

He felt the blood drain from his face as he stared once more toward the sun.

Five more monster ko'aye flew from the west. Damn! The first must just have been testing their defenses. But he and Lelanc had learned its secret. They might just be able to take the things down. It would be tricky, but they could do it. With a little luck. Well, probably a lot of luck.

He pulled the arrow from her wing quickly. It bled a little but she evinced no pain. "We must fly with weapons!" Lelanc cried. "Remount!"

Rylin was readying to do just that when he froze in place. His ring still burned brightly, but his body didn't respond. He was puzzled until he understood he was under a sorcerous attack.

He might not have had physical control, but he retained consciousness, and that enabled him to slip his sight into the inner world. He discovered a veil lay across the battlement, hiding its true form. The signalman lay there beside his mirror in an awkward heap. Life energy leaked from his weakening frame, shifting in color from gold to gray. A slumped figure in a blue khalat lay nearby, and with a start Rylin recognized that wiry hair as Varama's, whose own life energy was dulled.

And creeping up on Rylin's right was Cerai, seven magnificent hearthstones, the keystone, and multiple shards shining in her pack, each one tightly sewn to her own life force.

Rylin reached out for that same hearthstone energy, but Cerai easily batted his effort aside. Her mystical attack emptied him. He tripped backward and fell to one knee. It was only then he truly understood that she was the source of the veil. It must have been her presence that set off his ring, if he'd only bothered to pay attention.

Cerai climbed into the saddle as Lelanc sat statue stiff, subdued by sorcerous threads of command.

Rylin fought the wave pounding at him to surrender, to lay still. Somehow he found the strength to pull his sword.

"I'm sorry about this," Cerai told him. "I truly am. But I don't have time for this nonsense. Up, beast!"

Lelanc beat her wings. Rylin lurched to his feet and stumbled after, grabbing a javelin. He was winding back to throw it when Cerai's assault flattened him once more. He dropped, dizzily, as she soared north upon Lelanc. He might have called to her that they could stop the Naor if she simply turned back, but he wasn't certain if he'd spoken or merely wished to, and soon it all faded to dream.

26

Battles in the Dark

She drove them to their death. Elenai had been proud that she'd mastered the hearthstone to such an extent that she'd been able to bring N'lahr's plan to fruition. But she hadn't given serious thought that she led these strong and vital creatures to their destruction until it began to happen.

No part of it had been easy, from the manipulation of the eshlack matriarch to the shepherding of the vast herd through the Shifting Lands—
the Gods be praised that there had been no storms—to the endless push
toward the distant city and the Naor army. The last three days were a blur
of short sleep and infrequent meals and cravings for things she had never
known, like the taste of succulent grass and the sun's warmth on a broad
furred back. They had traveled past hills and canyons and smoking villages
that told of the Naor's passage and pillage for supplies.

She'd barely noticed when Kyrkenall helped her down from Lyria, his
loyal mount. Vaguely, she was aware that she stood beside N'lahr near the
height of a bluff where Gyldara had slain two Naor watchmen. Almost the
whole of her consciousness lay like a web across the senses of the herd,
seeing what they saw and smelling the deep rich vegetation that they craved.
Twice during the journey she had allowed the herd to stop to eat and rest
a little, but she could spare them nothing more, and drove them on, through
their leaders, and through the occasional sharp blasts of fear she sent wave-
like through their ranks.

Already she knew that dozens were dead or dying, and they had yet to
meet the Naor horde. A few had broken legs or necks in careless falls.
Mothers left mewling calves in the wake of the rushing herd, and aged or
injured eshlack that might have lived long months under different circumstances fell behind to fend off predators alone. The insistent push she gave
to the minds of their leaders brooked no delay, and the mass of the herd
moved as if fleeing death rather than chasing it down.

This, she thought, is what it's like to lead an army, to send forth troops
to die. These might not be people, but they were her soldiers, and the casualties mounted because of her choices. Many more were to come, and it
troubled her that these particular soldiers had not asked to join the fight,
would not benefit from it, and that she sent them anyway.

N'lahr's voice was close in her ear. "Time to direct them into the
Naor."

Diverting her attention for a brief moment to look through her own
eyes, she perceived the campfires of a vast army that lay outside the plateau where her walled home city stood less than three miles away, and she
breathed a nervous sigh of relief. They'd made it in time. Vedessus was still
intact. She could see the latticework of its famed windmills rising above
the walls, their blades turning in the ever-present wind. Above them the
heavens were festooned with waving emerald and magenta auroras. Though
strange to any who had not grown up beneath them, to her they were a
reminder of times past, and early days when she had lain on the roof beside

her young mother, who'd told stories about the ghostly banners left in the skies by the warring Gods.

Yet her mind boggled at the size of the enemy horde before them. How many were they? Could her herd, immense though it was, truly wreak the damage N'lahr predicted?

Still tenuously linked to the moving matriarch, Elenai scanned her surroundings more critically. The Naor had posted their now-dead sentinels on this bluff because of the fine view across the wide old river valley to the distant city. Its northern face was a sheer drop of more than thirty feet, and its western and eastern sides were nearly as steep. Apparently N'lahr had led her up the gentle southern slope, at the base of which she noted their horses picketed, puffing hard, and cropping at low grasses just beyond a thin line of scrubby trees. Kyrkenall and N'lahr were at each elbow. Gyldara studied the distance from the edge. Lasren, more pained and exhausted than he'd admit, had removed the boot from his bandaged leg and sat massaging it on the ground nearby.

"There's something you've probably been looking for," Kyrkenall said quietly to N'lahr, pointing. Elenai was too busy fighting for control of the eshlack to study where her companions looked, for the animals struggled to run anywhere but toward the Naor camp.

Through the matriarch's eyes she saw canyon walls fall behind on either side, felt mighty legs driving her into the open, saw the signs of the two-legs and their vast dwellings where the sharp and hurting things were kept. She battled the eshlack's wish to keep well clear of their gathering.

Run, she told the matriarch, knowing as she did that she drove the animal to certain death. Awash with disgust for her betrayal, Elenai nonetheless pushed the message forward. *Death pursues you. Run. Straight into the two-legs. Guide the herd.* With all her will she bore down, and the great beast charged forward to stamp the two-legs.

Elenai brushed the minds of the nearest eshlack with that same anger just as an alarm bugle sounded in the camp ahead. The closest would follow, but those behind might start to veer. She lay her commands upon individuals in the hordes behind, and then the masses beyond them. *Kill,* she ordered, *kill the two-legs before they kill you! Bring them pain before they cause it!*

She ordered and they obeyed, rank upon rank, sweeping the Naor tents and dragging them after and stamping the men that fled to mush. Here and there a few soldiers swung up spears and formed in lines but the eshlack drove on and in, crushing through the Naor and running on even though mortally wounded.

Kyrkenall let out a whoop and struck the air with his fist before grabbing her shoulder and squeezing. "I like how you drove that one group straight for Mazakan's tents." Kyrkenall laughed.

"Mazakan's here?" she asked.

"I thought you knew."

She shook her head.

"There was no missing it," Kyrkenall protested. "The seven triangular flags flying over the big tent?"

She shook her head.

"Whether you aimed for it or not," N'lahr said, "it worked. Nicely done."

"Thank you."

They watched the chaos unfold for long minutes. By the light of the aurora, dissipating clouds of dust raised by the eshlack stampede were tinged blue and green. Any of the animals still running fled west, following the river. Tents were smashed and broken all along the valley floor, and everywhere were dark lumps. If she hadn't been looking with the inner world imposed over her sight, she wouldn't have understood them for dead Naor and horses. Larger mounds were fallen eshlack.

Vedessus was safe, but she felt a little sick.

Enemy horsemen had turned their backs to the city. Some were in full gallop, scattered wildly, but a larger mass departed in orderly ranks. All seemed on course toward their bluff, or maybe the canyon beside it, which would lead them out of the river valley.

As Elenai tried to guess at their numbers, a presence brushed against her and brightened greedily at the proximity of an active hearthstone. It had to be a Naor weaver. Tendrils of interest from that distant mage feathered about her. She shuddered as the probing presence brushed her, and she sent a blast of pain at him before she turned off her stone. That encouraged a speedy withdrawal. Only when she looked away from the inner world did she discover N'lahr waiting intently beside her.

"They know we're here, don't they," he said.

She nodded. "One of them just tried to use my hearthstone."

"They probably detected it once the attack began. We're lucky the enemy was too busy waking up and dodging eshlack to make a concerted counterattack against you."

"That wasn't luck," Kyrkenall declared. "They were outplanned. I figure we have ten minutes before they draw close. They might just ride past."

"They might," N'lahr conceded. He didn't sound optimistic.

"Our horses are too flagged to get us out of here in any case."

N'lahr agreed with a head bob. "We need to change the odds again,

Elenai. If you've any energy left for sorcery, steepen the approach to the south side of our bluff."

He called out other orders as Elenai touched her hearthstone. The moment she did, though, she felt that mage grasping for it again. Whoever it was had both power and ambition. She didn't have the time to wrestle for its control. She drew in as much energy as she dared and shut it down. If nothing else, her actions had at least lessened her own fatigue.

She looked out upon the galloping Naor. Among that larger contingent one carried a banner topped by a narrow fanged skull—a ko'aye skull, she knew from tapestries. And the seven triangular flags beneath identified it as Mazakan's standard. He was coming.

Elenai turned to N'lahr and found him bent along the top of the slope, utilizing what she recognized as Denaven's blade to pry up a skull-sized boulder. He'd suggested that they all pack extra swords, and she now understood that he'd foreseen this moment. He sent the rock rolling, then moved onto another before it came to a stop halfway down the slope.

"The Naor in that big group are carrying Mazakan's standard," she reported. "He must still be alive."

"Yes," N'lahr replied as he worked up a slightly larger rock. "I'm not surprised."

"I wasn't able to change the terrain." She was reluctant to admit she wasn't entirely certain how to do that on real ground, in any case. "Their mage is waiting to fight me for control the moment I activate the hearthstone."

"We'll make do." N'lahr sounded remarkably calm. She'd expected he might be disappointed. "Help me with this, will you? Any spots to spoil the footing of the Naor or their mounts might save our lives."

She understood on the instant—he was working to roughen the terrain. The others began imitating N'lahr in choosing medium-sized rocks to pry up. Their removal would create holes and loosen the soil on the sloped surface, slowing enemy ascent.

As she labored, oddly grateful to stretch aching muscles, Elenai imagined how the Naor might assault their position.

Their bluff looked down upon the rest of the plain from a height of thirty or thirty-five feet. Composed mostly of crumbly sandstone ornamented with only the occasional clump of grass, it was level from its edge to about twenty feet back in a rough rectangle sloping gently down to the canyon floor south. Similar rougher or taller bluffs on either hand marked the edge of Vedessus' valley, but N'lahr had chosen their ground well. The sheer drops along the north, east, and west of their escarpment made assaults from those sides unlikely, so the Naor would come up from only one side, the easier south.

Just beyond the sparse screen of trees and bushes near the bottom of the slope, Kyrkenall was hurriedly cutting the horses free of their pickets; at a slap on her rump, Lyria led the others at a tired trot into the easterly darkness. If the Naor assaulted the hill they'd probably dismount first, owing both to the difficulty of getting through the copse and of maneuvering mounts on the narrow height. The space was restricted enough it would limit the number of enemies that could come forward at once. A smart commander would send them up with spears, probably fifteen at a time.

"Do you think that they'll have archers with them?" she asked N'lahr. The Naor used archers, but owing to their general preference for larger, less refined bows, few carried them on horseback.

N'lahr continued to work at prying a larger boulder. "If they do, they'll be in small numbers. They'll station them to either side of the bluff and try to shoot up at us, although they'll be hard-pressed to see us, so they may try volleys."

Naturally he'd already thought it out.

He was unusually loquacious, for he went on: "They may attempt javelin volleys, but given the height of our post that's even less likely to help them. Before long they'll want to close with us." He succeeded at last and sat down Denaven's sword to turn over the rock, which partly rolled and partly slid a few feet down the hill. It left a large, saddle-shaped depression. N'lahr clapped dirt from his hands. "I'll manage the rest of this. See if you can aid Lasren. He'll need to be in better shape for the fight."

Elenai wasn't sure what she could manage, especially not if the Naor mage was watching for them, but she obediently looked through the inner world, and immediately she noted the relative levels of strength of their glowing energy matrices. N'lahr, still working the terrain, appeared in the best shape, though his lines were thin. Lasren's energies were tapped and graying, and Gyldara and Kyrkenall, both working farther downslope, were only a little better. Well, she could restore herself somewhat by drawing from the hearthstone. Why not try it with the others? To imagine was to do. When she activated the hearthstone this time there was no sign of her watcher, so she quickly sent threads of strength toward all four of her comrades and their weakened energy matrices glowed, shifting toward golden.

Kyrkenall straightened shoulders, then grinned up at her. "Was that you?"

She smiled.

"Hah! Nicely done."

"It's the best I can manage. I'm no healer."

"I'll take it."

Lasren and Gyldara waved and called their own thanks.

She nodded, then closed down the stone and surveyed the opposition. Small groups of Naor riders slid past their position into the canyon below. They, at least, weren't going to attack. Others were only a few hundred yards behind, and after them were the hundreds in good order led by Maza-kan's bannerman. Maybe they'd just follow the others into escape. She could hope.

"I'm afraid I don't have quite enough arrows," Kyrkenall said dryly. "But I'm tempted to start picking some of them off."

"Wait," N'lahr replied. "If they have archers, take them out when they start to range themselves. If possible, save some arrows for their charge up the hill."

"Right." Kyrkenall studied the slope. "I'd like to arrange a nice group-ing of bodies they'll have to climb over."

N'lahr nodded. "Of course."

Elenai was struck by their astonishing matter-of-factness.

Lasren limped up, sword sheathed. "I wish I had a good spear," he opined. "I'm not nearly as agile as I'd like to be for a sword fight."

"Use Decrin's shield," N'lahr suggested. "Gyldara brought it up."

"Yes, sir."

She glanced over to Kyrkenall planting arrows, then looked back to N'lahr and saw his jaw tense as dozens of horsemen around the banner-man stopped near the gentle south approach to their bluff. Dozens grew into hundreds. Elenai saw that some, riding double, were dropping from saddles and, at shouted command, arranging themselves in lines encircling their bluff.

A score to the east were readying longbows, and someone was shout-ing to let fly on his command.

"Pick your targets fast," N'lahr told Kyrkenall, and motioned everyone else back from the edge.

The archer nocked an arrow to Arzhun. "You know, this thin volley's going to be easy to see coming. I bet we can duck it in this light and en-courage another."

"Why risk it?" N'lahr asked.

"So I can use their arrows."

N'lahr nodded appreciatively. "Stand ready, everyone. Over here," N'lahr indicated. "Farther from the edge. And look to the skies."

Kyrkenall was the last to quit the verge, and a moment later a harsh Naor voice shouted to fire.

Elenai tensed, blade before her, ready to try slicing arrows from the air. She actually heard them whizzing as they arced up and over the side of the bluff, though it was more challenging to spot them against the unevenly lit sky than she would have liked. She knew a stab of fear and swirled her sword directly overhead, worried that one would come in at a slant and strike her neck.

But the Naor were challenged by their inability to see their targets. Most of the arrows passed over the Altenerai and struck the soil behind. Gyldara was the only one of them who had to step out of the way. Three landed near their feet, and two clanged off Decrin's shield. "I wasn't even trying to block them," Lasren asserted.

Kyrkenall stepped to the edge and made a rude gesture.

"Fire!" the Naor voice cried a second time.

N'lahr motioned to everyone. "Back farther now."

Elenai almost stepped on a perfectly fine arrowshaft from the first attack in her haste to comply.

The instincts of the seasoned Altenerai had been right. This time the arrows fell a little closer to the edge. The Naor were "walking" their attack forward from where they'd shot the first time. Four of the missiles came in blazing redly, trailing smoke. One of those aflame soared close to Elenai and she managed to slice it aside. The others fell harmlessly, except for one Kyrkenall snatched from the air.

It was still smoking as he pressed it up to his bow and dashed to the edge. There was only a brief delay before he fired, and from below came a garbled scream even as Kyrkenall launched a slew of his own arrows, from the line he'd set in the dirt. More outcry followed. Only a few shafts streamed up in response. Apparently most of the archers were too busy running or dying to launch new attacks of their own.

Kyrkenall drew back with a grim smile. "That's most of them." He looked to Lasren. "They'll try javelins next. Try to give them a target and catch them on your shield."

Lasren nodded once and accepted the assignment without flinching, limping boldly to the edge so he was in clear sight. All the Altenerai had been taught how to endure javelin or spear fire. When given time to ready, all but the most incompetent could avoid them, lest they came out of the sun or utter darkness.

"What are you waiting for?" Kyrkenall asked the rest of them. "Help me gather the Naor arrows."

Though it seemed at first they had almost three dozen, only twenty or so proved fully serviceable. Kyrkenall set quickly to repairing the fletching on three more, using his supplies, while the javelin fire began. He screamed once, as if in pain, to encourage the Naor to launch more.

Lasren caught five on his shield during three separate volleys, and Gyldara gathered another seven that fell nearby, returning a few with deadly effect.

After that the Naor ceased their distance attacks. The sound of riders fleeing into the canyon to the west grew louder. During the brief lull, N'lahr's attention shifted, like Kyrkenall's, to the line of scrub at the bottom of the slope. Elenai could hear the clop of horse hooves and the rustle of twigs as the Naor pushed through.

"Looks like they're going to try a horse charge," Kyrkenall said.

"Doesn't seem very wise," Gyldara offered.

"Well, they're Naor." Kyrkenall nocked one of the light feathered arrows preferred by their enemies. "This will make clogging the slope a little easier."

"Any moment now," N'lahr said. "Lasren, keep an eye on the rear in case they try more javelins, or some madman tries to climb."

"Yes, sir."

"Gyldara, hold your axes until the real assault starts."

"The real assault, sir?"

Elenai understood her confusion.

N'lahr patiently explained. "They won't send their best troops first. Kyrkenall will be able to take most of these."

"Yes, sir."

At her acknowledgment, the first horsemen appeared on the slope and kicked their mounts forward. Eight in all, they wore dark helms topped with horsehair. They tried to hold their line steady, but the ground was too uneven and soon they were advancing with little gaps.

Kyrkenall was merciless. He winged arrows into the oncoming mass, starting with the riders on either end. He fired again, and again, sometimes pausing deliberately until he had his targets just where he wished before he dropped a horse through the eye or sent it screaming to career into a neighbor with a knee shot. All the carnage bunched the rest of them toward the middle as they struggled to escape his attacks, but that was right where Kyrkenall wanted them, dead center of the slope, in a line ending a few feet shy of the summit.

Those few Kyrkenall didn't slay N'lahr moved out to finish off with astonishing economy of motion before performing a few mercy killings of the animals. He retreated just as a line of ground troops emerged from the brush and ran screaming up.

"A nice grouping," N'lahr said to Kyrkenall as he regained the height.

"Thanks."

"How are you on ammunition?"

"Enough for a little more mayhem." Kyrkenall let fly with the first arrow as a line of fifteen Naor ran at their position. More poured up behind the first, and Elenai struggled for calm. Kyrkenall and N'lahr seemed nonchalant, but soon the archer was going to run out of arrows, and there were a lot of Naor out there.

Their bluff shook as more hoofbeats slammed the earth to the west. Another group was bypassing them to escape the battlefield.

Finally Kyrkenall announced he was done, and N'lahr and Gyldara capped his attack with a few well cast javelins. One moment there was a group of charging warriors. The next there was a mass of dead and dying bearded men. The rank smell of death was borne up the wind toward them even as Kyrkenall laughed unexpectedly. He slid his bow home into its holder between his shoulders, then drew Lothrun in a flash of blue steel.

The bodies were strewn thickly upon the hillside. More Naor footmen advanced with spears, a dozen in front with four well-ordered lines behind.

Less than twelve paces out they had to divide around the bodies.

Kyrkenall looked at N'lahr and grinned. He glanced to Elenai, a mad gleam in his eye. "Come! If this be our numbered day, let us send these numbers before us to their end!"

N'lahr nodded grimly.

Five Altenerai against almost fifty Naor. And providing they survived, more would surely follow. But there was no time to worry about the future. Elenai could only focus upon getting through the present.

The helmed warriors at the forefront hurled javelins as they charged. N'lahr sidestepped, graceful as a dancer, and cut one inbound toward Gyldara from the air with his magnificent sword. Kyrkenall simply ignored them all and none came close. Luck, Elenai wondered, or would he have moved if one had?

Those who came after parted before the knots of corpses Kyrkenall had arranged so well, struggling up through the bodies in two groups. Elenai and Gyldara waited to one side, Kyrkenall and N'lahr the other. Lasren, shield on his arm, Naor javelin in hand, guarded their rear.

All then was madness as the enemy warriors rushed, some stumbling over the uneven ground. There were the screams of the dying and the scent of entrails, the war cries of Naor, the laughter of Kyrkenall and, from time to time, his macabre poetry, spoken as if in a trance. It was eerie and strange and seemed unconscious, like the way Gyldara exhaled audibly with every blow or block.

So fast did everything move that Elenai had but fleeting impressions. N'lahr, impossibly deadly with that sword that sliced equally well through flesh, bone, or steel. It seemed only necessary to touch someone to send them plunging with a torrent of blood. He swung clear of countless axe blows and spear shafts, always silent, always sure, and soon the bodies around were an impediment to reach him. She'd thought Kyrkenall the most amazing swordsman she'd ever seen, but N'lahr, with Irion, was almost deific.

Not that the swift archer was less deadly than usual. He was more active than N'lahr, taunting the Naor and shouting at them to taste his steel. Lothrun's gleam was hidden by gore, and Kyrkenall himself was a blur of motion.

Gyldara fought with a mix of Kyrkenall's eagerness and N'lahr's pin-point precision, preferring straight thrusts to Kyrkenall's wide slashes. She dealt death with either hand, driving in now with her sword, then with a deft, deadly blow to head or neck with her offhand light axe.

Elenai herself was one with her blade, and one with the moment of possibilities. Blocking, thrusting at a leering face, once dashing forward to parry when Gyldara exposed her back, once cutting down a spear thrown at Kyrkenall.

Lasren was mostly out of Elenai's visual range, but he ran forward to shield his comrades when three daring Naor strove to flank them, and he bought space later with well-timed spear jabs. His teeth were gritted in a mask of pain and determination.

Quite suddenly the attacks halted, and Elenai marveled, her sword low, her breathing heavy. The dead were mounded before them. It actually looked like more than fifty.

"By the gods," Lasren panted beside her, "we're doing it."

Kyrkenall raised his bloodied blade to the dark: *"Five they were who stood as one against the Naor tide, a blood-red wave of vicious men who came and bled and died."*

"Nicely done. Relax a moment. Conserve your strength." N'lahr unlimbered his waterskin, sipped, then passed it over to Gyldara.

"What are they waiting for?" Elenai asked. She glanced overside to their left where more than a hundred Naor still sat saddle. Lasren had retreated to watch them again.

"Now's when they send their best," N'lahr answered. He wiped his sword. Despite his advice, he didn't look particularly relaxed.

Gyldara passed the water to Elenai, who drank eagerly despite the acrid flavor, conscious not to drain it dry. Kyrkenall handed his nearly empty wineskin off to Lasren, who toasted him with it before taking a deep drink. The archer had been nursing that sweet liquid for weeks.

"Good stuff," Lasren said. The big man didn't sound the least bit sarcastic.

"He's got taste," Kyrkenall remarked to N'lahr, who broke into a smile. Lasren looked uncertain until Kyrkenall stretched up to clap him on the shoulder.

The respite ended the moment additional Naor emerged from the screen of trees, led by the bannerman. These were the largest warriors yet, bearing well-made swords and matching shields, armored in heavy shivering chain and leather. Three feathers stood out from each of their helms. Behind them were a line of seven men in resplendent and varied armor, but they remained just this side of the copse of trees; they parted deferentially for a single mounted figure who rode up past the bannerman and the nearer warriors on the largest, blackest horse Elenai had ever seen.

He was a tall, broad figure in a flat helm topped with a jawless, silvered skull inset with large faceted rubies. They shone faintly under the shifting aurora.

"Here he is," Kyrkenall said. "Mazakan's lost too much honor now. He'll have to prove himself to his underlings."

This, then, was Mazakan? Elenai stared. It was difficult to imagine that a person actually existed behind the legend.

The newcomer dropped heavily from his horse and strode forward. He stood a head higher even than the honor guard around him, a veritable giant among Naor, who were never small. Part of his chest and shoulder armor was fashioned from blue khalats. At least two Altenerai, Elenai recalled, had personally fallen to him, among them Temahr, one of the finest swordsmen of the previous generation.

She had no good view of Mazakan's face until he stopped among the dead, only three spear lengths out. He had a square, thick head with a dense beard shot with gray, two bright eyes glittering with malice, and a scarred nose that had been broken multiple times and twisted leftward.

As Mazakan's honor guard ranged neatly to either side, she spotted another figure just behind, armored but narrow-shouldered and round, picking his own way through the dead behind Mazakan. And she knew, with certainty, that this was a sorcerer. Not just owing to his carriage, but by a palpable aura about him. She tensed. "They've a weaver," she whispered to her companions.

The Naor halted their advance and Mazakan showed blocky teeth in something that might have been a grin, if there'd been any humor in it. He was clearly taller even than N'lahr.

"It *is* N'lahr." Mazakan's voice was surprisingly warm and vital. "I don't believe in ghosts. So I know that you've been cowering somewhere. Was this eshlack trick your doing?"

"It was *our* doing," N'lahr answered. For some reason, his ring lit.

Mazakan's voice rose and he indicated the surrounding territory with a sweeping gesture. "This is but a brief setback. You fey are weak, and divided. Ready to fall before a greater power. Even as we speak, another of your cities is being plundered. More will follow."

"You must think your men are pretty stupid if you're going to sell this as a 'setback,'" Kyrkenall cut in. "Your army is smashed, Mazakan. And N'lahr's going to take your head."

The Naor king grinned at him. "Brave noises won't save you, nagging wasp. The truth here is plain to see. N'lahr, the coward who hid from me for seven years, has nothing left but you, a cripple"—at this he indicated Lasren with a negligent wave—"and," he said spitefully, "two women."

The honor guard laughed roughly, as if this were high theater.

N'lahr's answer was cool. "We are Altenerai. We strike as one." The others set their sapphires aglow and Elenai hurried to do the same.

Mazakan answered after a brief pause. "Soon you'll strike at none. Come, N'lahr. Let us put an end to talk of this prophecy." So saying, he unlimbered a massive sword and turned to the man on his right. "Have the others!"

At those words, a rain of javelins arced up from the warriors. Lasren deflected two with a deft sweep of Decrin's shield. Kyrkenall simply stepped aside. Gyldara and Elenai cut at those near them, managing to avert most of the force that impacted their armored coats. None had been aimed for N'lahr, who waited for Mazakan.

The king bellowed and rushed him. His honor guard came after.

As N'lahr leapt back from a savage swipe from a sword nearly as tall as himself, the king laughed and advanced against him. Kyrkenall rolled clear of a deadly slash from one of the guardsmen.

Elenai latched once more into the complex web of probabilities and found her way among the shining strands. She just missed getting her head crushed by a two-handed overhead axe blow. In moments she'd driven her sword through a Naor shoulder and then backed away as Lasren stepped in to shield a thrust from a growling attacker. An axe sailed over him and embedded itself in a warrior's forehead, then Gyldara was in the thick of the action, fighting two warriors at once as Lasren limped to one side, struggling to fend off his own assailant. Elenai was stepping up to join him when the weaver struck at last.

She'd faced sleep and panic and pain and even seen Denaven warping the environment, but she'd never before felt the urge to bow in submission. Her ring shining, she tore the impulse apart with her own threads as his attack slipped away. She would have retaliated except that she saw Lasren too hard beset to assist Gyldara, retreating before two stout warriors. These men were good.

Elenai flanked one, kicked his knee from the side, then smashed his face with her pommel. She sent a tendril of panic winging at the mage and felt his surprise in the brief moment they touched consciousness.

Thereafter was madness and blood and momentum. Dark shapes leapt at her, and she blocked or ducked, or drove her sword into quivering meat. Some of it was armored. For every Naor that fell another was there to take his place. Three and four times she herself was struck, in shoulder, chest, thigh, and arm, and the fourth blow might have finished her, for it dropped her to her knees, but Lasren was suddenly over her, his shield ringing as he blocked a savage blade swipe. He moaned in dismay as another blow struck his spear into splintered pieces.

Elenai stabbed viciously at her opponent's thighs and then she was up and swinging at faces, her throat dry, her muscles aching, her breath a ragged gasp in her throat. It seemed impossible years ago that she'd been hesitant to kill.

The mage's spell hit her again, and if it weren't for her ring the authority in his blast would have reduced her to shaking. He insisted upon worshipful obedience, and even with the sapphire to shield her, his call was compelling. He turned his effect upon Lasren, who dropped to one knee, and just managed to lift the shield against an oncoming blow. Elenai gritted her teeth, dug for magical energy of her own, and found she had nothing left to give. Nothing more to send. She was suddenly conscious of her ribs and their frailty as her heart slammed them. If the mage cared to press his advantage, she was done.

But he didn't. Magically, as though clouds had parted, the attack ceased. A snarling Gyldara drove her sword into a final Naor and sent him to the ground in a welter of blood. The last of the honor guard was down.

Elenai discovered Kyrkenall tensely observing N'lahr dueling Mazakan.

Lasren sat on his knees, head bowed as if in prayer, absolutely drenched in blood that probably wasn't his. Gyldara leaned heavily beside him.

The nearest Naor was the bannerman, some twelve feet back, still clutching his skull-topped pole with its fluttering triangular flags. The sorcerer waited nearby, dark eyes and broad nose surrounded by reddish facial hair. The more distant line of chieftains stood impassively beneath their feathered helms. Watching.

N'lahr and Mazakan both were weary. The swordsman favored his right arm and appeared to be limping. And Mazakan weaved, bleeding from a dozen cuts to arms and legs as he drunkenly planted feet.

"They can take us," Gyldara said to no one in particular. "Why don't they call up the other warriors and lead an attack?"

Kyrkenall answered softly without taking his eyes from the battle. "Mazakan led them to the city, and lost. Mazakan sent men to our bluff, and they died." He paused as N'lahr narrowly dodged a strike that would have caved in his chest. He then nodded to the distant clansmen. "Mazakan now has to win this himself. And you can bet some of those back there don't want him to do that."

So that was why the mage wasn't pressing and none of those waiting men would rush forward. Elenai searched the figures at the slope's end for some clue to identity among the bearded faces. So busy was she that she never saw the opening N'lahr had exploited, only the jet of blood as Irion whipped past Mazakan's weapon and plunged through the cloth and metal that warded the king's collarbone.

Mazakan stepped back, lifted his huge length of steel as if he meant to bring it sweeping in from the right, then toppled to the side.

His impact upon the earth was substantial; Elenai felt it through her boots.

Kyrkenall looked over to the chiefs, who shifted uneasily, but N'lahr stood staring down at the unmoving man. He planted a foot on the body and pointed his sword at the remaining Naor. Somehow his arm still was steady.

Kyrkenall whooped approvingly and called to the watchers. "Now even the skies wear our colors, fools! Come forth, introduce yourself to our blades!" As if on cue, the aurora flared blue the moment he spoke.

He's going to get us all killed, Elenai thought. Another attack and they were through. Especially one backed by that mage. She smiled grimly. Kyrkenall was making it clear they'd take more Naor with them when they fell. Everything depended upon their reaction to this theater.

As the chieftains stared, the mage looked over his shoulder at them, as if for orders.

A piercing horn call climbed through the night air, high and clear, and Elenai could hardly believe she hadn't imagined it.

But of course. It was the Vedessi horse guard. The mounted troops of Vedessus had left the city.

She had heard that horn call on and off the whole of her life, especially during the war. And why should she not hear it? If they'd attacked before, the Vedessi cavalry would have been devoured by the numbers of Naor, but now the Naor were in flight, and easy game.

The horn blared again.

"Is that getting closer?" Gyldara asked.

"It is." So dry was her throat that her voice cracked as she answered.

"Kanesh?" Gyldara said hopefully.

"Vedessus." Nothing so grand as the famed riders of Kanesh, but fine enough. That horn call had decided things. The bannerman and the mage were hurrying away and the Naor noblemen were already turning in retreat.

"Quitters!" Kyrkenall shouted. "Come back here and die with your king!"

But now they were all leaving, as fast as they could go, and the horsemen waiting to the east of the bluff were skirting its edge at full gallop to reach the canyon.

Elenai sagged, one hand steadying herself against someone she realized was Gyldara. With help she managed to stagger up with the others to watch a tight mass of cavalry armed with lances slam into the retreating Naor flanks.

It was a bloody mess punctuated by the terrified screams of men and horses. Elenai was partly glad for the valley shadows, which obscured what was more slaughter than battle.

Lasren let out a choked gasp. Elenai turned, thinking he was more wounded than she'd first supposed. He struggled to stand on his good leg, backing as if in fright, and she saw his shaking hand point toward the mass of Naor dead upon the slope. He at last managed to speak as Elenai saw what had unsettled him.

"The blood's rising into a monster!"

Tendrils of blood swirled up from the pile of corpses on their slope to feed into the growing figure not of some monstrous being, but a man. He was a moving sculpture of liquid blood, so that as he opened his mouth to show teeth in a smile, they were red. His eyes, fashioned all of the same material, seemed as pupilless as Kyrkenall's.

The Altenerai formed a half circle around him, hands to weapons. The chest of the image took on more and more detail until it was clear he wore leather armor, and that beneath it lay a sleeved tunic. His hair was shorn short, apart from a curling braid stretched back across the top of his head.

Elenai debated the activation of the hearthstone. Exhausted as she was, if she had to manage any spell work, the hearthstone was her only hope. Yet she held off, thinking that whoever wrought this spell might draw from the hearthstone's energy, possibly more easily than her.

The man had formed fully at last, a living being of dripping blood. "I congratulate you, N'lahr." His words were clear, no matter the Naor accent and a disquieting further distortion, for he sounded as though he spoke while his mouth was half full with liquid. "You have defeated my grandfather. I thank you for that. He'd become an impediment."

"Who are you?" N'lahr asked.

"I am Chargan, conqueror of Alantris."

Elenai struggled to show no reaction to this news. Surely the man was lying about Alantris, wasn't he?

Chargan's mouth curled. "You fey vermin have had your last victory. Your days of stealing our children and harassing our people are finished."

Elenai's brows lowered in puzzlement. She wasn't aware that the realms had ever "harassed Naor," much less stolen children. Unless the former was some twisted version of their adoption of Naor children stranded when their armies fled.

He spoke on with profound bitterness. "Your cheap tricks can't hold us back, and you can't hide behind your walls. We're stronger than you. We're fiercer than you. We're better than you. We're going to root you out and consign your soulless corpses to the unending fire."

Kyrkenall countered with a savage grin. "Bold words from someone whose army was just obliterated."

"You destroyed my grandfather's army, not mine. Alantris and its lands belong to me. Darassus is next."

"You boast well," N'lahr said.

Chargan replied with profound self-confidence, and conviction that was strangely alarming. "Not boasts, but truth. I've nothing to fear from you, N'lahr. Or your sword. You fulfilled your prophecy. It's my time, now. If you're wise, you'll make peace, and I'll let you slink off to the useless wilds of Ekhem. We won't need it for a few more years."

N'lahr answered with stern surety. "There will be no peace so long as the Naor occupy our land."

"Our lands." Chargan's lips twisted in barely restrained anger. "You've hoarded our stolen homelands for too long, leaving my people to the scraps, like dogs. Now you'll feel our bite. Prepare for extermination."

These had never been Naor lands. What was the man raving about?

The horrible blackish crimson simulacrum raised his right fist and then the blood released its hold upon his image and sank once more across the bodies and into the thirsty earth beneath them. Elenai wiped a single drop from her lip, sputtering a little that it should touch her. She strove to ignore the sick pull of dread. Surely the mage exaggerated his prowess. And surely the Naor could be no match for the Altenerai, could they?

"Have you heard of him before?" N'lahr asked Kyrkenall.

As he shook his head in the negative, the commander looked in turn to the rest of them. Like Gyldara and Lasren, the man's name was unknown to Elenai.

"Do you really think he conquered Alantris?" she asked.

"I know that he'll be trouble in the future. And I know we've won a great victory this night. Right now, that's all we need."

"That was blood sorcery," Elenai said, her lip involuntarily curling in disgust. The dark practice was not only difficult to control, it was incredibly inefficient. She recoiled from the thought of just how much blood the Naor must have spilt to power Chargan's spell to reach them here. And whose blood it must have been.

"I wonder if they still sell those fried cakes in the Vedessan square—the ones with the flowers on top," Kyrkenall said, ignoring her as Vedessi cavalrymen picked their way up the slope through Naor dead.

"What are we going to do about the queen?" Elenai asked. "And whatever she's planning?"

Kyrkenall grinned thinly from the patch of ground he now reclined upon. "After we stop the Naor, we'll stop the exalts, dethrone the queen, and find Kalandra."

"That sounds simple." Elenai joined him on the rocky dirt.

"It won't be," N'lahr said. "But those are battles for another day. We have to care for ourselves, first. Just as you must wipe your sword of blood and polish its edge between battles."

"And drink wine," Kyrkenall added. "That spoils your analogy, I know, but I want some wine. And some cakes. And a really long hot soak. None of that would help my sword much."

As the sober Vedessi cavalry leader dismounted and removed his helm, N'lahr stepped forward, and the man addressed him in reverent tones.

She would have listened in, but Gyldara came over and clapped her shoulder with a tired smile. "Your first battle as Altenerai. You did well." She sat down at her side.

"We all did."

"The ring doesn't feel quite like you expected, does it?" Gyldara asked.

She looked down at the ring and wiped a smear of blood from it.

Gyldara continued. "I felt like I had to grow into mine. But I'd say yours already fits you." She hesitated briefly before saying: "I never thanked you."

For a moment, Elenai wondered what the other woman meant, for all through the battle they'd each saved the other more times than she could recall. But she must be referring to Elenai interceding in Gyldara's fight with Kyrkenall. "You would have done the same for me."

"Would I? I judged before I had the facts. At some level I knew Denaven was wrong and ignored my instinct. You really did look with both mind and heart and acted with wisdom. You gave greater meaning to those words than I understood, and I mean to remember that."

She met the woman's eyes and realized that their shared experience had forged a powerful bond. She'd heard combat could do that among soldiers, and she'd thought she understood it until experiencing the real thing. She now realized how shallow her comprehension had truly been. Throughout the harrowing ordeal, their trust and reliance upon one another had been absolute. Each of them had risked their lives for one another, moving like connected pieces of a greater whole. And because they had worked so effectively together, they had endured. This woman had guarded her back, and she knew with certainty she would do so going forward. Almost surely this same faith lay behind the deep connection between Kyrkenall and N'lahr.

Perhaps it was impossible to state the complexity of her feelings in any succinct way, or perhaps exhaustion had rendered her too weary for sophisticated expression. Instead, she simply offered her arm. Unhesitatingly, Gyldara took it, and they clasped one another below the elbow, acknowledging one another with a firm nod.

"If you two are done," Lasren said. "Can you help me up? It looks like they brought some extra horses. And I'm eager to get to the city and have my wounds looked at. Or maybe just fall asleep on something with a mattress and pillows."

"Stop complaining," Gyldara grumbled good-naturedly, and stood, then bent to assist the heavier alten. He was on his feet a moment later, and leaned against Gyldara's shoulder as she maneuvered him toward the horses.

Elenai rose and turned to stare at the city under the flickering heavens. She looked forward to seeing her family and idly wondered what they'd think to see her as a full-fledged alten. Somehow, though, that wasn't as important to her as she would once have expected.

She thought instead about the glory of being clean, and having cooked food, and lying in soft sheets, and maybe another long sleep. And she wondered, too, how they were going to stop the Naor and the queen and the Mage Auxiliary. . . .

Later, she promised herself. Later.

She stared down at her ring, then, on a whim, willed it to sapphire radiance.

Epilogue

Rylin hadn't remembered drinking, but his head pounded fitfully. When he opened his eyes he found the sky dark above him.

His thoughts tumbled suddenly into order as he sat up. Horn calls rent the air, along with shouts of men, the tinny clack of swords, the screams of dying, the roar of the great wyrms.

The wyrms.

"Lelanc," he said weakly. "Where's Lelanc?"

No one answered him.

Rylin forced himself up on unsteady feet. He couldn't help noting the ruined wall in the southwest quadrant, or the pair of winged beasts sailing over the city, one of which was even now letting go with a great rumbling roar that sent a gatehouse tumbling. Naor foot soldiers swarmed through a gap in the third wall against a thin line of defenders.

Alantris was doomed.

It was then he saw the bodies, and remembered. He felt his breath constrict as he hurried on shaking legs. The eyes of the poor signalman stared sightlessly at the stars.

Varama lay facedown. He threw himself on his knees beside her.

There wasn't a pool of blood or any obvious wound in her back, but she wasn't moving.

He grabbed her shoulder and shook and shouted her name.

She didn't stir.

He turned her over, panic growing, for she was limp in his hands and her head lolled. He fumbled to undo the stiff collar, then thrust fingers against her throat, knew with rising despair that the coolness of her skin must mean she was dead.

But a steady pulse thrummed there. Relief washed through him even as the tower shook. Something rattled the ground nearby, accompanied by dozens of frightened screams. Many of them were cut off in mid yell.

"Varama!" He shook her arms.

She groaned, almost imperceptibly, then looked at him through slitted eyes.

He slipped into the inner world. If Varama still carried her hearthstone maybe he could use it to help . . . but no. There was no gleam of the things about her, even deactivated, which jibed with his memory. Cerai had been using a stack of the artifacts, linked together. Varama must have been pursuing her.

His eyes fell to Varama's waist, and the winesac there. Of course. Her fortifying juices. That could help. He pulled the winesac free and undid the opener before gently lifting her head and pressing the rim to her lips, careful not to spill any of the precious liquid. She swallowed.

After a moment, she blinked, and with shaking hand pushed the container toward him. Her meaning was clear.

He took two swallows, felt a ghost of his own powers restored. With them came a greater measure of clarity.

While it would be enormously satisfying to die in a blaze of glory and take a whole legion of Naor along with him, it would be ultimately futile even if he killed their leader. He couldn't attempt that without abandoning Varama, and that he refused to do. He'd be damned before he relinquished the most brilliant of the Altenerai, helpless, to the Naor.

He looked down into her eyes, hazy with fatigue. She was obviously struggling to remain conscious.

Besides, it was no longer solely about the Naor. Cerai must be made to pay for her heinous betrayal. He and Lelanc could well have stopped the massive wyrms before they brought down all the walls, especially if his defense had been reinforced by a mage of Cerai's capability. Rather than honoring her oath of office and acting as shield to her people, she had stolen Lelanc and abandoned the Alantrans. Hundreds now dead would still be breathing, and tens of thousands would not be fated for slavery, or agonizing death upon Naor altars.

And prior to her cowardly departure, Cerai had slain a loyal signalman and blasted Varama senseless. He looked down at his friend, who'd closed her eyes once more. It looked as though her recovery would require time, a commodity in short supply.

He rose with her, baring his teeth at thought of the impossible odds before them. Varama moaned and just managed to get her feet under her, leaning heavily against him.

Somehow he had to get his ailing friend out of the citadel, safely through the Naor horde, and out of the city.

Somehow he had to locate Lelanc, and free her from captivity, provided she still lived.

And then, then he would find the traitor Cerai, even if it meant tracking her into the farthest reaches of the shifts. She might be privy to a hundred secret sorceries, but he would find a way to bring her to justice. Preferably on the edge of his sword.

Acknowledgments

This work would not have been possible without the assistance of numerous fine people, among them Justin Landon, Wayne Gralian, and Darian Jones, who gave vital initial feedback; Jennifer Donovan for behind-the-scenes support; and Edwin Chapman for his experienced eye. John O'Neill and Ian Tregillis provided lengthy and crucial input through several drafts, and Bob Mecoy and Peter Wolverton patiently steered me through dangerous shoals too many times to count. An extra-special thanks goes to my muse, Shannon, who helped untie plot knots, saw the forest for the trees, found the right word or phrase when I was lost in those woods, and sometimes knew Varama better than I did myself.